THE CHILDREN'S GOLDEN LIBRARY
16

The Children's Golden Library

16

The Three Musketeers
Alexandre Dumas .

First published 1844

Published © 2003 MDS BOOKS/ MEDIASAT for this edition
Original Design © Mediasat Group
Cover Ilustration Copyright © Juan Lobatón Scott

ISBN   84-9789-070-1
Dep. legal B-37 924-2003

Printed and bound in Spain
by Printer Industria Gráfica, Barcelona

Not to be sold separately from the Daily Mail.

www.mediasatgroup.com

ALEXANDRE
DUMAS
The Three Musketeers

THE CHILDREN'S GOLDEN LIBRARY

CHAPTER 1

The Three Presents of M. D'Artagnan The Elder

On the first Monday of the month of April, 1625, the bourg of Meung, in which the author of the *Romance of the Rose* was born, appeared to be in as perfect a state of revolution as if the Huguenots had just made a second Rochelle of it. Many citizens, seeing the women flying towards the High Street, leaving their children crying at the open doors, hastened to don the cuirass, and, supporting their somewhat uncertain courage with a musket or a partizan, directed their steps towards the hostelry of the Franc Meunier, before which was gathered, increasing every minute, a compact group, vociferous and full of curiosity.

In those times panics were common, and few days passed without some city or other enregistering in its archives an event of this kind. There were nobles, who made war against one another; there was the king, who made war against the cardinal; there was Spain, who made war against the king. Then in addition to these concealed or public, secret or patent wars, there were robbers, mendicants, Huguenots, wolves, and scoundrels, who made war upon everybody. The citizens always took up arms against thieves, wolves, or scoundrels, often against nobles or Huguenots, sometimes against the king, but never against the cardinal or Spain. It resulted, therefore, from this habit, that on the said first Monday of the month of April, 1625, the citizens, on hearing the clamour, and seeing neither the red and yellow standard nor the livery of the Duc de Richelieu, rushed toward the hostelry of the Franc-Meunier.

On reaching there the cause of this hubbub was apparent to all.

A young man—we can sketch his portrait at a dash: imagine Don Quixote at eighteen; Don Quixote without his corselet, without his coat of mail, without his cuisses; Don Quixote clothed in a woollen doublet, the blue colour of which had faded into a nameless shade between lees of wine and a heavenly azure; face long and brown; high cheekbones, indicating craftiness; the maxillary muscles enormously developed, an infallible sign by which a Gascon may always be detected, even without his cap—and our young man wore a cap ornamented with a kind of feather; his eye open and intelligent; his nose hooked, but finely chiselled. Too big for a youth, too small for a grown man, an experienced eye might have taken him for a farmer's son upon a journey, had it not been for the long sword, which, dangling from a leathern baldric, hit against its owner's calves as he walked, and against his steed's rough side when he was on horseback.

For our young man had a steed, which was the observed of all observers. It was a Béarn pony, from twelve to fourteen years old, with yellow coat, not a hair in his tail, but not without wind—galls on his Pegs, which, though going with his head lower than his knees, rendering a martingale quite unnecessary, contrived, nevertheless, to perform his eight leagues a day.

And this feeling was the more painful to young D'Artagnan—for so was the Don Quixote of this second Rosinante named—because he was conscious himself of the ridiculous appearance he made on such a steed, good horseman as he was. He had sighed deeply, therefore, when accepting the gift of the pony from M. d'Artagnan the elder. He was not ignorant that such a beast was worth at least twenty pounds; and the words which accompanied the gift were above all price.

"My son," said the old Gascon nobleman, in that pure Béarn *patois* of which Henry IV was never able to rid himself— "my son, this horse was born in your father's house about thirteen years ago, and has remained in it ever since, which ought to make you love it. Never sell it—allow it to die tranquilly and honourably of old age; and if you make a campaign with it, take as much care of it as you would of an old servant. At court, provided you ever have the honour—to go there," continued M. d'Artagnan the elder, "an honour to which, remember, your ancient nobility gives you the right, sustain worthily your name of *gentleman,* which has been worthy borne by your ancestors for more than five hundred years, both for your own sake and for those who belong to you. By the latter I mean your relatives and friends.

Endure nothing from any one except the cardinal and the king. It is by his courage, you understand, by his courage alone, that a gentleman makes his way to-day. I have but one more word to add, and that is to propose an example to you—not mine, for I myself have never appeared at court, and have only taken part in religious wars as a volunteer; I speak of M. de Tréville, who was formerly my neighbour, and who lead the honour to be, as a child, the playfellow of our king Louis XIII, whom God preserve! Sometimes their play degenerated into battles, and in these battles the king was not always the stronger. The blows which he received from hire caused him to entertain great esteem and friendship for M. de Tréville. Afterwards, M. de Tréville fought with others: during his first journey to Paris, five times; from the death of the late king to the majority of the young one, without reckoning wars and sieges, seven times; and from that majority up to the present day, a hundred times perhaps! So that in spite of edicts, ordinances, and decrees, behold him captain of the musketeers—that is to say, leader of a legion of Caesars, whom the king holds in great esteem, and whom the cardinal dreads—he who dreads little, as every one knows. Moreover, M. de Tréville gains ten thousand crowns a year; he is, therefore, a very great noble. He began as you begin; go to him with this letter, and make him your model, in order that you may do as he has done."

The same day the young man set forward on his journey, provided with the three paternal gifts, which consisted, as we have said, of fifteen crowns, the horse, and the letter for M. de Tréville, the counsels, as may be supposed, being thrown into the bargain.

As he was alighting from his horse at the gate of the Franc-Meunier, without any one—host, waiter, or hostler—coming to hold his stirrup or take his horse, D'Artagnan spied, through an open window on the ground floor, a man of fine figure and lofty bearing, but of rather grim countenance, talking with two persons who appeared to listen to him most respectfully. D'Artagnan fancied, as was natural for him to do, that he himself must be the object of their conversation, and listened. D'Artagnan was only in part mistaken: he himself was not the subject of remark, but his horse was.

Nevertheless, D'Artagnan was desirous of examining the appearance of this impertinent personage who was laughing at him. He fixed his haughty eye upon the stranger, and perceived a man of from forty to forty-five years of age, with black and piercing eyes, a pale complexion, a strongly-marked nose, and a black and well-shaped moustache. He was dressed in a doublet and hose of violet colour, with aiguillettes of the same, without any other ornaments than the customary slashes through which the shirt appeared. This doublet and hose, though new, looked creased, as garments do which have been long packed in a travelling-bag. D'Artagnan noticed all this with the rapidity of a most minute observer, and doubtless from an instinctive feeling that this unknown was destined to have a great influence over his future life.

Now, as at the moment in which D'Artagnan fixed his eyes upon the man in the violet doublet the man made one of his most knowing and profound remarks respecting the Béarnese pony, his two auditors burst out laughing, and he himself, though contrary to his custom, suffered a pale smile (if I may be allowed to use such an expression) to stray over his countenance. This time there could be no doubt: D'Artagnan was really insulted. Full, then, of his conviction, he pulled his cap down over his eyes, and endeavouring to copy some of the court airs he had picked up in Gascony among young travelling nobles, he advanced, with one hand on the hilt of his sword and the other resting on his hip.

"I say, sir—you, sir, who are hiding yourself behind that shutter— yes, you, sir, tell me what you are laughing at, and we will laugh together!"

The man withdrew his eyes slowly from the nag to his rider, as if he required some time to ascertain whether it could be to him that such strange reproaches were addressed; then, when he could no longer entertain any doubt of the matter, his eyebrows bent slightly, and after quite a long pause, with an accent of irony and insolence impossible to be described, he replied to D'Artagnan,

"I was not speaking to you, sir!"

"But I am speaking to you!" replied the young man, exasperated by this mixture of insolence and good manners, of politeness and scorn.

The unknown looked at him for a moment longer with his faint smile, and retiring from the window, came out of the hostelry with a slow step, and placed himself before the horse within two paces of D'Artagnan.

"This horse is decidedly, or rather has been in his youth, a buttercup," resumed the unknown, continuing the remarks he had begun, and addressing himself to his auditors at the window, without seeming in any way to notice the exasperation of D'Artagnan, who, however, remained stiffly standing between them. "It is a colour very well known in botany, but till the present time very rare among horses."

He had scarcely finished when D'Artagnan made such a furious lunge at him that if he had not sprung nimbly backward it is probable that he would have jested for the last time. The unknown then, perceiving that the matter was going beyond a joke, drew his sword, saluted his adversary, and gravely placed himself on guard. But at the same moment his two auditors, accompanied by the host, fell upon D'Artagnan with sucks, shovels, and tongs. This caused so rapid and complete a diversion to the attack that D'Artagnan's adversary, while the latter was turning round to face this shower of blows, sheathed his sword with the same precision as before, and from an actor, which lie had nearly been, became a spectator of the fight, a *rôle* in which he acquitted himself with his usual impassibility, muttering, nevertheless,

"A plague upon these Gascons! Put him on his yellow horse again and let him begone!"

"Not before I have killed you, poltroon!" cried D'Artagnan, showing the best front possible, and never falling back one step before his three assailants, who continued to shower their blows upon him.

"Another gasconade!" murmured the gentleman. "By my honour, these Gascons are incorrigible! Keep up the dance, then, since he will have it so. When he is tired, he will say that he has enough of it."

But the unknown did not yet know the headstrong personage he had to deal with; D'Artagnan was not the man ever to cry for quarter. The fight was therefore prolonged for some seconds; but at length D'Artagnan, worn out, let fall his sword, which was struck from his hand by the blow of a stick and broken in two pieces. Another blow full upon his forehead at the same moment brought him to the ground, covered with blood and almost fainting.

It was at this period that people came flocking to the scene of action from all sides. The host, fearful of consequences, with the help of his servants carried the wounded man into the kitchen, where some trifling attention was bestowed upon him.

As to the gentleman, he resumed his place at the window, and surveyed all that crowd with a certain air of impatience, evidently much annoyed by their persistence in retraining there.

"Well, how is it with this madman?" exclaimed he, turning round as the opening door announced the entrance of the host, who came to inquire whether he was hurt.

"Your excellency is safe and sound?" asked the host.

"Oh yes! perfectly safe and sound, my good host; and I now wish to know what has become of our young man."

"He is better," said the host; "he fainted quite away."

"Indeed!" said the gentleman.

"But before he fainted he collected all his strength to challenge you, and to defy you while challenging you."

"Why, this fellow must be the devil in person!" cried the unknown.

"Oh no, your Excellency," replied the host, with a grin of contempt, "he is not the devil; for during his fainting we rummaged his valise, and found nothing but a clean shirt and twelve crowns, which, however, did not prevent his saying, as he was fainting, that if such a thing had happened in Paris you should have instantly repented of it, while here you will only repent of it later on."

"Then," said the unknown coldly, "he must be some prince of the blood in disguise."

"I have told you this, good sir," resumed the host, "in order that you may be on your guard."

"Did he name no one in his passion?"

"Yes. He struck his pocket and said, 'We shall see what M. de Tréville will think of this insult offered to his *protégé.*'"

"M. de Tréville?" said the unknown, becoming attentive. "He struck his pocket while pronouncing the name of M. de Tréville? Now, my dear host, while your young man was unconscious you did not fail, —I am quite sure, to ascertain what that pocket contained. What was there in it?"

"A letter addressed to M. de Tréville, captain of the musketeers."

"Indeed!"

"Just as I have the honour to tell your Excellency."

The host, who was not endowed with great perspicacity, did not notice at all the expression which his words called up in the countenance of the unknown. The latter arose from the window, upon the sill of which he had been leaning his elbow, and knitted his brows like a man suddenly disturbed.

"The devil!" muttered he between his teeth. "Can Tréville have set this Gascon upon me? He is very young but a sword-thrust is a sword-thrust, whatever be the age of him who gives it, and a youth is less to be suspected than an older man. A weak obstacle is sometimes sufficient to ove rthrow a great design."

And the unknown fell into a reverie which lasted some minutes.

"Host," said he, "could you not contrive to get rid of this frantic boy for me? In conscience, I cannot kill him; and yet," added he, with a coldly menacing expression — "and yet he annoys me. Where is he?"

"In my wife's chamber, where they are dressing his wounds, on the first floor."

"His things and his bag are with him? Has he taken off his doublet?"

"On the contrary, everything is down in the kitchen. But if he annoys you, this crazy young fool—"

"To be sure he does. He causes a disturbance in your hostelry, which respectable people cannot put up with. Go, make out my bill, and call my servant."

"What, sir! do you mean to leave us already?"

"You knew I was going, as I ordered you to get my horse saddled. Have they not obeyed?"

"Yes, sir; and as your Excellency may have observed, lour horse is in the great gateway, ready saddled for your departure."

"That is well. Do as I have directed you, then."

"What the devil!" said the host to himself. "Can he be afraid of this boy?" But an imperious glance from the unknown stopped him short; he bowed humbly and retired.

"Milady must see nothing of this fellow," continued the stranger. "She will soon pass by; she is already late. I had better get on horseback, and go and meet her. I should like, however, to know what this letter addressed to Tréville contains."

And the unknown, muttering to himself, directed his steps towards the kitchen.

In the meantime the host, who entertained no doubt that it was the presence of the young man which was driving the unknown from his hostelry, had gone up to his wife's chamber, and found D'Artagnan entirely returned to consciousness. Giving him to understand that the police could deal with him pretty severely for having son lit a quarrel with a great lord (for in the opinion of the host the unknown could be nothing less than a great lord), he insisted that, notwithstanding his weakness, he should get up and depart as quickly as possible. D'Artagnan, half-stupefied, without his doublet, and with his head all swathed with bandages, arose then, and urged on by the host, began to descend the stairs; but on arriving at the kitchen the first thing he saw was his antagonist, who stood quietly talking beside the step of a heavy carriage drawn by two large Norman horses.

His interlocutor, whose head appeared through the carriage window, was a woman of from twenty to two-and-twenty years of age. We have already observed with what rapidity D'Artagnan took in every feature of a face. He perceived then, at a glance, that this woman was young and beautiful; and her style of beauty struck him the more forcibly on account of its being totally different from that of the southern countries in which D'Artagnan had hitherto resided. She was pale and fair, with long curls fading in profusion over her shoulders; had large languishing blue eyes, rosy lips, and hands of alabaster. She was talking with great animation with the unknown.

"His eminence, then, orders me—" said the lady.

"To return instantly to England, and to inform him immediately should the duke leave London."

"And my other instructions?" asked the fair traveller.

"They are contained in this box, which you will not open until you are on the other side of the Channel."

"Very well; and you, what are you going to do?"

"I—oh! I shall return to Paris."

"What! without chastising this insolent boy?" asked the lady.

The unknown was about to reply, but at the moment he opened his mouth D'Artagnan, who had heard all, rushed forward through the open door.

"This insolent boy chastises others," cried he; "and I sincerely hope that he whom he means to chastise will not escape him as he did before."

"Will not escape him?" replied the unknown, knitting his brow.

"No; before a woman you would not dare to fly, I presume?"

"Remember," cried milady, seeing the unknown lay his hand on his sword— "remember that the least delay may ruin everything."

"True," cried the gentleman. "Begone, then, your way, and I will go mine." And bowing to the lady, he sprang into his saddle, her coachman at the same time applying his whip vigorously to his horses. The two interlocutors thus separated, taking opposite directions, at full gallop.

"Base coward! false nobleman!" cried D'Artagnan, springing forward. But his wound had rendered him too weak to support such an exertion.

"He is a coward indeed," grumbled the host, drawing near to D'Artagnan, and endeavouring by this little flattery to make up matters with the young man, as the heron of the fable did with the snail he had despised the evening before.

"Yes, a base coward," murmured D'Artagnan; "but she—she was very beautiful."

"What she?" demanded the host.

"Milady," faltered D'Artagnan, and fainted the second time.

On the following morning, at five o'clock, D'Artagnan arose, and descending to the kitchen without help, asked, among other ingredients the list of which has not come down to us, for some oil, some wine, and some rosemary, and with his mother's recipe in his hand, composed a balsam with which he anointed his numerous wounds, replacing his bandages himself, and positively refusing the assistance of any doctor. Thanks, no doubt, to the efficacy of the gypsy's balsam, and perhaps, also, thanks to the absence of any doctor, D'Artagnan walked about that same evening, and was almost cured by the morrow.

But when the time of settlement came, D'Artagnan found nothing in his pocket but his little worn velvet purse with the eleven crowns it contained; as to the letter addressed to M. de Tréville, it had disappeared.

"My letter of recommendation!" cried D'Artagnan; "my letter of recommendation! or, by God's blood, I will spit you all like so many ortolans!"

"Does the letter contain anything valuable?" demanded the host, after a few minutes of useless investigation.

"Zounds! I think it does, indeed," cried the Gascon, who reckoned upon this letter for making his way at court; "it contained my fortune!"

A ray of light all at once broke upon the mind of the host, who vas uttering maledictions upon finding nothing.

"That letter is not lost!" cried he.

"What!" said D'Artagnan.

"No; it has been stolen from you."

"Stolen! by whom?"

"By the gentleman who was here yesterday. He came down into the kitchen, where your doublet was. He remained there some time alone. I would lay a wager he has stolen it."

"Do you think so?" answered D'Artagnan.

"I tell you I am sure of it," continued the host. "When I informed him that your lordship was the *protégé* of M. de Tréville, and that you even had a letter for that illustrious nobleman, he appeared to be very much disturbed, and asked me where that letter was, and immediately came down into the kitchen, where he knew your doublet was."

"Then he is the thief," replied D'Artagnan. "I will complain to M. de Tréville, and M. de Tréville will complain to the king." He then drew two crowns majestically from his purse, gave them to the host, who accompanied him, cap in hand, to the gate, remounted his yellow horse, which bore him without any further accident to the gate of St. Antoine at Paris, where his owner sold him for three crowns, which was a very good price, considering that D'Artagnan had ridden him hard on the last stretch.

So D'Artagnan entered Paris on foot, carrying his little packet under his arm, and wandered around till he found an apartment to be let on terms suited to the scantiness of his means. This chamber was a sort of garret, situated in the Rue des Fossoyeurs, near the Luxembourg.

Then he went to the Quai de la Ferraille, to have a new blade put to his sword, and came back to the Louvre, and inquired of the first musketeer he met the situation of the hotel of M. de Tréville, which proved to be in the Rue du Vieux-Colombier, in the immediate vicinity of the chamber hired by D'Artagnan, a circumstance which appeared to him to be a happy augury for the outcome of his journey.

After which, satisfied with the way in which he had conducted himself at Meung, without remorse for the past, confident in the present, and full of hope for the future, he retired to bed, and slept the sleep of the brave.

This sleep, rustic as it was, brought him to nine o'clock in the morning, at which hour he rose in order to repair to the residence of the famous M. de Tréville, the third personage in the kingdom, according to the estimation of his father.

Chapter 2

The Antechamber Of M. De Tréville

M. de Troisville, as his family was still called in Gascony, or M. de Tréville, as he had ended by styling himself in Paris, had really commenced life as D'Artagnan now did—that is to say, without a sou in his pocket, but with a fund of courage, shrewdness, and intelligence which makes the poorest Gascon gentleman often derive more in his imagination from the paternal inheritance than the richest nobleman of Perigord or Berry receives in reality.

He was the friend of the king, who honoured highly, as every one knows, the memory of his father, Henry IV. Louis XIII made De Tréville the captain of his musketeers, who were to Louis XIII, in devotedness, or rather in fanaticism, what his Ordinaries had been to Henry III, and his Scotch Guard to Louis XI.

On his part, and in this respect, the cardinal was not behindhand with the king. When he saw the formidable and chosen body by which Louis XIII surrounded himself, this second, or rather this first, king of France became desirous that he too should have his guard, He had his must: a leers, then, as Louis XIII had his; and these two powerful rivals vied with each other in procuring the most celebrated swordsmen, not only from all the provinces of France, but also from all foreign stares.

Loose, tipsy, gashed, the king's musketeers, or rather M. de Tréville's, spread themselves about in the saloons, in the public walks, and the public sports, shouting, twirling their moustaches, clanking their swords, and taking great pleasure in bustling against the guards of the cardinal whenever they could fall in with them; then drawing their swords in the open streets, with a thousand jests; sometimes killed, but sure in that case to be both wept and avenged; often killing others, but then certain of not rotting in prison, M. de Tréville being there to claim them. And so M. de Tréville was praised in all keys by these men, who absolutely adored him, and who, ruffians as they were, trembled before him like scholars before their master, obedient to his least word, and ready to sacrifice themselves to wipe out the least insult.

The court of his hotel, situated in the Rue du Vieux-Colombier, resembled a camp as early as six o'clock in the morning in summer and eight o'clock in winter. From fifty to sixty musketeers, who appeared to relieve each other there, in order always to present an imposing number, paraded constantly about, armed to the teeth and ready for anything. On one of those immense staircases, upon whose space modern civilization would build a whole house, ascended and descended the solicitors of Paris, who were in search of favours of any kind—gentlemen from the provinces anxious to be enrolled, and servants in all sorts of liveries, ringing messages from their masters to M. de Tréville. In the antechamber, upon long circular benches, reposed the elect—that is to say, those who were called. In this apartment a continued buzzing prevailed from morning till night, while M. de Tréville, in his office contiguous to this antechamber, received visits, listened to complaints, gave his orders, and, like the king in his balcony at the Louvre, had only to place himself at the window to review both men and arms.

The day on which D'Artagnan presented himself the assemblage was imposing, particularly for a provincial just arriving from his province. It is true that this provincial was a Gascon, and that, particularly at this period, the compatriots of D'Artagnan had the reputation of not being easily intimidated. When he had once passed the massive door, covered with long square-headed nails, he fell into the midst of a troop of military, who were passing each other in the court, calling out, quarrelling, and playing tricks one with another. To make way through these turbulent and conflicting waves it was necessary to be an officer, a great noble, or a pretty woman.

It was, then, in the midst of this tumult and disorder that our young man advanced with a beating heart. Holding his long rapier close to his lanky leg, and keeping one hand on the edge of his cap, he smiled with the embarrassment of a provincial who affects confidence.

Being, however, a perfect stranger in the crowd of M. de Tréville's courtiers, and this his first appearance in that place, he was at length noticed, and a person came to him and asked him his business there. At this demand D'Artagnan gave his name very modestly, laid a stress upon the title of compatriot, and begged the servant who had put the question to him to request a moment's audience of M. de Tréville—request which the other, with a patronizing air, promised to convey in time and season.

D'Artagnan, a little recovered from his first surprise, had now leisure to study costumes and countenances.

The centre of the most animated group was a musketeer of great height, of a haughty countenance, and dressed in a costume so peculiar as to attract general attention. He did not wear the uniform cloak—which, indeed, at that time of less liberty and greater independence was not obligatory—but a cerulean blue doublet, a little faded and worn, and over this a magnificent baldric worked in gold, which shone like water-ripples in the sun. A long cloak of crimson velvet fell in graceful folds from his shoulders, disclosing in front the splendid baldric, from which was suspended a gigantic rapier.

This musketeer had just come off guard, complained of having a cold, coughed from time to time affectedly. It was for this reason, he said to those around him, he had put on his cloak; and while he spoke with a lofty air and twirled his moustache, all admired his embroidered baldric, and D'Artagnan more than any one.

"What can you expect?" said the musketeer. "The fashion is coming in. It is a folly, I admit, but still it is the fashion. Besides, one must lay out one's inheritance somehow."

"Ah, Porthos!" cried one of his companions, "don't think to palm upon us that you obtained that baldric by paternal generosity: it must have been given to you by that veiled lady with whom f met you the other Sunday, near the gate Saint-Honoré."

"No, 'pon honour; by the faith of a gentleman. I bout it with my own money," answered he whom they had just designated by the name of Porthos.

The wonder was increased, though the doubt continued to exist.

"Didn't I, Aramis?" said Porthos, turning towards another musketeer.

This other musketeer formed a perfect contrast to his interrogator, who had just designated him by the name of Aramis. He was a young man, of about two or three and twenty, with an open, ingenuous countenance, dark mild eyes, and cheeks rosy and downy as an autumn peach; his delicate moustache marked a perfectly straight line upon his upper lip; he appeared to dread to lower his hands lest their veins should swell, and he pinched the tips of his ears from time to time to preserve their delicate pink transparency. Habitually he spoke little and slowly, bowed frequently, laughed without noise, showing his teeth, which were fine, and of which, as of the rest of his person, he appeared to take the greatest care. He answered the appeal of his friend by an affirmative nod of the head.

This affirmation appeared to dispel all doubts with regard to the baldric. They continued to admire it, but said no more about it; and by one of those rapid changes of thought, the conversation passed suddenly to another subject.

"M. de Tréville awaits M. d'Artagnan," interrupted a servant, throwing open the door of the office.

At this announcement, during which the door remained open, every one became mute, and amidst the general silence the young man crossed the antechamber at one end, and entered the apartment of the captain of the musketeers.

Chapter 3

The Audience

M. de Tréville was at this moment in a very ill-humour, nevertheless he politely saluted the young man, who bowed to the very ground, and he smiled on receiving his compliment, the Béarnese accent of which recalled to him at the same tune his youth and his country, a double remembrance which makes a man smile at all ages. But stepping almost immediately towards the antechamber, and making a sign to D'Artagnan with his hand, as if to ask his permission to finish with others before he began with him, he called three times, with a louder voice at each time, so that he went through all the tones between the imperative accent and the angry accent.

"Athos! Porthos! Aramis!"

The two musketeers with whom we have already made acquaintance, and who answered to the last two of these three names, immediately quitted the group of which they formed a part, and advanced towards the office, the door of which closed after them as soon as they had entered. Their bearing, though not entirely composed, was full of a dignified and submissive indifference, which excited the admiration of D'Artagnan, who beheld in these two men demigods, and in their leader an Olympian Jupiter, armed with all his thunders.

When the two musketeers had entered, when the door was closed behind them, when the buzzing murmur of the antechamber, to which the summons which had just been made had doubtless furnished fresh aliment, had recommenced, when M. de Tréville had three or four times paced in silence, and with a frowning brow, the whole length of his office, passing each time before Porthos and Aramis, who were as upright and silent as if on parade, he stopped all at once full in front of them, and looking at them angrily from head to foot,

"Do you know what the king said to me," cried he, "and that no longer ago than yesterday evening—do you know, gentlemen?"

"No," replied the two musketeers, after a moment's silence; "no, sir, we do not."

"But I hope that you will do us the honour to tell us," added Aramis, in his politest tone and with the most graceful bow.

"He told me that he should henceforth recruit his musketeers from among the guards of the cardinal."

"The guards of the cardinal! And why so?" asked Porthos warmly.

"Because he plainly perceives that his piquette[1] stands in need of being enlivened by a mixture of good wine:

The two musketeers coloured up to the eyes. D'Artagnan did not know where he was, and would have liked to be a hundred feet underground.

"Yes, yes," continued M. de Tréville, growing warmer as he spoke, "and his Majesty was right, for, upon my honour, it is true that the musketeers make but a miserable figure at court. The cardinal related yesterday, while playing with the king, with an air of condolence not very pleasing to me, that the day before yesterday those damned musketeers, those dare-devils—he dwelt upon those words with an ironical tone still more displeasing to me—those cleavers, added he, glancing at me with his tiger-cat's aye, had been out late in the Rue Férou, in a tavern, and that a patrol of his guards (I thought he was going to laugh in my face) had been forced to arrest the rioters. Zounds! you must know something about it! Arrest musketeers! You were among them—you were! Don't deny it; you were recognized,

1. A liquor squeezed out of grapes, when they have been pressed, and water poured upon them.

and the cardinal named you. But it's all my fault; yes, it's all my fault, because it is I myself who select my men. You, now, Aramis, why the devil did you ask me for a uniform when you were going to be so fine in a cassock? And you, Porthos, do you only wear such a fine golden baldric to suspend a sword of straw from it? And Athos—I don't see Athos! Where is he?"

"Sir," replied Aramis, in a sorrowful tone, "he is ill, very ill!"

"Ill—very ill, say you? And what is his malady?"

"Well, captain," said Porthos, quite beside himself, "the truth is that we were six against six. But we were not captured by fair means, and before we had time to draw our swords two of our party were dead; and Athos, grievously wounded, was very little better. For you know Athos. Well, captain, he endeavoured twice to get up, and fell again twice. And we did not surrender—no! they dragged us away by force. On the way we escaped. As for Athos, they believed him to be dead, and left him very quietly on the field of battle, not thinking it worth the while to carry him away. Now, that's the whole story. What the devil, captain, one cannot win all one's battles! The great Pompey lost that of Pharsalia; and Francis the First, who was, as I have heard say, as good as any one else, nevertheless lost the battle of Pavia."

"And I have the honour of assuring you that I killed one of them with his own sword," said Aramis, "for mine was broken at the first parry. Killed him, or poniarded him, sir, as is most agreeable to you."

"I did not know that," replied M. de Tréville in a somewhat softened tone. "The cardinal exaggerated, as I perceive."

"But pray, sir," continued Aramis, who, seeing his captain relenting, took courage to make a petition— "pray, sir, do not say that Athos is wounded. He would be in despair if that should come to the ears of the king; and as the wound is very serious, seeing that after crossing the shoulder it penetrates into the chest, it is to be feared—"

At this instant the tapestry was raised, and a noble and handsome face, but frightfully pale, appeared under the fringe.

"Athos!" cried the two musketeers.

"Athos!" repeated M. de Tréville to himself.

"You have sent for me, sir," said Athos to M. de Tréville in a feeble yet perfectly calm voice—"you have sent for me, as my comrades inform me, and I have hastened to receive your orders. I am here, sir; what do you want with me?"

And at these words the musketeer, in irreproachable costume, belted as usual, with a firm step entered the room. M. de Tréville, moved to the bottom of his heart by this proof of courage, sprang towards him.

"I was about to say to these gentlemen," added he, "that I forbid my musketeers to expose their lives needlessly; for brave men are very dear to the king, and the king knows that his musketeers are the bravest fellows on earth. Your hand, Athos!"

And without waiting until the newcomer should himself respond to this proof of affection, M. de Tréville seized his right hand, and pressed it with all his might, without perceiving that Athos, whatever might be his self-command, allowed a slight murmur of pain to escape him, and, if possible, grew paler than he was before.

The door had remained open, so strong was the excitement produced by the arrival of Athos, whose wound, though kept as secret as possible, was known to all. A loud murmur of satisfaction hailed the last words of the captain, and two or three persons, carried away by the enthusiasm of the moment, appeared through the openings of the tapestry. Doubtless M. de Tréville was about to reprehend severely this infringement on the rules of etiquette, when he suddenly felt the hand of Athos contract within his, and upon turning his eyes towards him, perceived he was about to faint. At the same instant Athos, who had rallied all his energies to contend against pain, at length overcome by it, fell upon the floor as if he was dead.

Immediately M. de Tréville opened the door and pointed the way to Porthos and Aramis, who carried off their comrade in their arms.

When all had gone out and the door was closed, M. de Tréville, on turning round, found himself alone with the young man. The stirring event which had just taken place had in some degree broken the thread of his ideas. He inquired what was the desire of his persevering visitor. D'Artagnan then repeated his name, and in an instant, recalling his memory of the past and the present, M. de Tréville was in possession of the situation.

"Pardon me," said he, smiling—"pardon me, my dear compatriot, but I had entirely forgotten you. But what help is there for it? A captain is nothing but a father of a family, charged with even a greater responsibility than the father of an ordinary family. Soldiers are big children; but as I maintain that the orders of the king, and more particularly the orders of the cardinal, should be executed—"

D'Artagnan could not restrain a smile. By this smile M. de Tréville judged that he had not to deal with a fool, and changing the subject, came straight to the point.

"I loved your father very much," said he. "What can I do for the son? Tell me quickly—my time is not my own."

"Sir," said D'Artagnan, "on leaving Tarbes and coming hither, it was my intention to request of you, in remembrance of the friendship which you have not forgotten, the uniform of a musketeer. But after all that I have seen during the last two hours, I have become aware of the value of such a favour, and tremble lest I should not merit it."

"Well, young man," replied M. de Tréville, "it is, in fact, a favour, but it may not be so far beyond your hopes as you believe, or rather as you appear to believe. Yet his Majesty's decision is always necessary, and I inform you with regret that no one becomes a musketeer without the preliminary ordeal of several campaigns, certain brilliant actions, or a service of two years in some regiment less favoured than ours."

D'Artagnan bowed without replying, feeling his desire to don the musketeer's uniform vastly increased by the difficulties which he had learned must precede the attainment of it.

"But," continued M. de Tréville, fixing upon his compatriot a look so piercing that it might be said he wished to read the thoughts of his heart—"but on account of my old companion, your father, as I have said, I will do something for you, young man. I will write a letter to-day to the director of the Royal Academy, and to-morrow he will admit you without any expense to yourself. Do not refuse this little service. Our best—born and richest gentlemen sometimes solicit it without being able to obtain it. You will learn riding, swordsmanship in all its branches, and dancing. You will make some desirable acquaintances, and from time to time you can call upon me, just to tell me how you are getting on, and to say whether I can be of any service to you."

D'Artagnan, stranger as he was to all the manners of a court, could not but perceive a little coldness in this reception.

"Alas, sir," said he, "I can but perceive how sadly I miss the letter of introduction which my father have me to present to you."

"I certainly am surprised," replied M. de Tréville, "that you should undertake so long a journey without that necessary viaticum, the only resource of us poor Béarnese "I had one, sir, and, thank God, such as I could wish," cried D'Artagnan, "but it was perfidiously stolen from me."

He then related the adventure at Meung, described the unknown gentleman with the greatest minuteness, and all with a warmth and truthfulness that delighted M. de Tréville.

"This is all very strange," said the latter, after meditating a minute. "You mentioned my name, then, aloud?"

"Yes, sir; I certainly committed that imprudence. But why should I have done otherwise? A name like yours was to serve me as a buckler on my way. You can fancy whether I often hid myself behind it or no!"

Flattery was at that period very much in fashion, and M. de Tréville loved incense as well as a king, or even a cardinal. He could not then refrain from a smile of evident satisfaction; but this smile soon disappeared, and returning to the adventure at Meung,

"Tell me," continued he, "had not this gentleman a slight scar on his cheek?"

"Yes, such a one as would be made by the grazing of a ball."

"Was he not a fine—looking mart?"

"Yes."

"Of lofty stature?"

"Yes."

"Of pale complexion and brown hair?"

"Yes, yes, that is he! How is it, sir, that you are acquainted with this man? If ever I should meet him again, and I will find him, I swear, were it in hell—"

"He was waiting for a woman?" continued Tréville.

"He at least departed immediately after having conversed for a minute with the one for whom he was waiting."

"You do not know what was the subject of their conversation?"

"He gave her a box, told her that box contained her instructions, and desired her not to open it before she arrived in London."

"Was this an Englishwoman?"

"He called her Milady."

"It is he! it must be he!" murmured Tréville. "I thought he was still at Brussels!"

"O sir, if you know who and what this man is," cried D'Artagnan, "tell me who he is and whence he is. I will then release you from all your promises—even that of procuring my admission into the musketeers. For, before everything I wish to avenge myself."

"Beware, young man! " cried De Tréville. "If you see him coming on one side of the street, pass by on the other. Do not cast yourself against such a rock; he would break you like glass."

"That thought will not prevent me," replied D'Artagnan, "if ever I should happen to meet with him—"

"In the meantime, if you will take my advice, you will not seek him," said Tréville, and leaving his young compatriot in the embrasure of the window, where they had talked together, he seated himself at a table, in order to write the promised letter of recommendation. While he was doing this D'Artagnan, having no better employment, amused himself with beating a march upon the window, and with looking at the musketeers, who went away, one after another, following them with his eyes till they disappeared at the bend of the street.

M. de Tréville, after having written the letter, sealed it, and rising, approached the young man in order to give it to him. But at the very moment that D'Artagnan stretched out his band to receive it, M. de Tréville was highly astonished to see his *protégé* make a sudden spring, become crimson with passion, and rush from the room, crying, "Ah, 'sblood! he shall not escape me this time."

"Who? who?" asked M. de Tréville.

"He, my thief!" replied D'Artagnan. "Ah, the traitor!" and he disappeared.

"The devil take the madman!" murmured M. de Tréville.

Chapter 4

TheShoulder Of Athos, The Baldric Of Porthos, And The Handkerchief Of Aramis

D'Artagnan, in a state of rage, crossed the antechamber in three bounds, and was darting towards the stairs, which he reckoned upon descending four steps at a time, when, in his heedless course, he ran head foremost against a musketeer who was coming out of one of M. de Tréville's private rooms, and hitting his shoulder violently, made him utter a cry, or rather a howl.

"Excuse me," said D'Artagnan, endeavouring to resume his course—excuse me, but I am in a hurry."

Scarcely had he descended the first stair when a hand of iron seized him by the scarf and stopped him.

"You are in a hurry," said the musketeer, as pale as a sheet. "Under that pretence you run against me. You say 'Excuse me!' and you believe that that is sufficient?"

"Loose your hold, then, I beg of you, and let me go where my business calls me," replied D'Artagnan.

"Sir," said Athos, letting him go, "you are not polite; it is easy to perceive that you come from a distance."

D'Artagnan had already strode down three or four stairs when Athos's last remark stopped him short.

"Zounds, sir!" said he, "however far I may have come, it is you who can give me a lesson in good manners, I warn you."

"Perhaps! " said Athos.

"Ah! if I were not in such haste, and if I were not running after some one I" said D'Artagnan.

"Mr. Man-in-a-hurry, you can find me without running after me— Do you understand me?"

"And where, I pray you?"

"Near the Carmes-Deschaux."

"At what hour?"

"About noon."

"About noon. That will do; I will be there."

"Try not to make me wait, for at a quarter-past twelve I will cut off your ears as you run."

"Good!" cried D'Artagnan; "I will be there ten minutes before twelve."

And he set off, running as if the devil possessed him, hoping that he might yet find the unknown, whose slow pace could not bawl carried him far.

But at the street gate Porthos was talking with the soldier on guard. Between the two talkers there was just room for a man to pass. D'Artagnan thought it would suffice for him, and he sprang forward like a dart between them. But D'Artagnan had reckoned without the wind. As he was about to pass the wind blew out Porthos's long cloak, and D'Artagnan rushed straight into the middle of it. Without doubt Porthos had reasons for not abandoning this essential part of his vestments, for instead of letting go the flap, which he was holding, he pulled it towards him, so at D'Artagnan rolled himself up in the velvet by a movement of rotation explained by the resistance of the obstinate Porthos.

D'Artagnan, hearing the musketeer swear, wished to escape from under the cloak which blinded him, and endeavoured to make his say out of its folds. He was particularly anxious to avoid marring the freshness of the magnificent baldric we are acquainted with; but on timidly opening his eyes, he found himself with his nose fixed between the two shoulders of Porthos —that is to say, exactly upon the baldric.

Alas! like most of the things in this world which have nothing in their favour but appearance, the baldric was glittering with gold to tie front, but was nothing but simple buff behind. Vainglorious as he was, Porthos could not afford to have an entirely gold-worked baldric, but had at least half a one. The pretext about the cold and the necessity for the cloak were thus exposed.

"Good Lord!" cried Porthos, making strong efforts to get rid of D'Artagnan, who was wriggling about his back, "the fellow must be mad to run against people in this manner."

"Excuse me," said D'Artagnan, reappearing under the shoulder of the giant, "but I am in such haste. I was running after some one, and—"

"And do you always forget your eyes when you happen to be in a hurry?" asked Porthos.

"No," replied D'Artagnan, piqued, "no; and, thanks to my eyes, can see what other people cannot see."

Whether Porthos understood him or did not understand him, the fact is that giving way to his anger,

"Sir," said he, "I warn you that you stand a chance of getting chastised if you run against musketeers in this fashion."

"Chastised, sir?" said D'Artagnan. "The expression is strong."

"It is one that becomes a man accustomed to look his enemies its the face."

"Ah, zounds! I know full well that you do not turn your back to yours."

And the young man, delighted with his joke, went away laughing with all his might.

Porthos foamed with rage, and started to rush after D'Artagnan.

"Wait awhile, wait awhile," cried the latter; "when you haven't your cloak on."

"At one o'clock, then, behind the Luxembourg."

"Very well; at one o'clock, then," replied D'Artagnan, turning the angle of the street.

But neither in the street through which he had passed, nor in the one which his glance now eagerly scanned, could he see any one. However slowly the unknown had walked, he had gained ground, or perhaps had entered some house. D'Artagnan inquired of every one he met, went down to the ferry, came up again by the Rue de Seine and the Croix Rouge, but he could see nothing of him, absolutely nothing! This race was, however, advantageous to him in one sense, for in proportion as the perspiration broke from his fore-head his heart began to cool.

He began to reflect upon the events that had passed. D'Artagnan, walking and soliloquizing, had arrived within a few steps of the Hotel d'Aiguillon, and in front of that hotel perceived Aramis chatting gaily with three gentlemen of the king's guards. D'Artagnan approached the young men with a profound bow, accompanied by a most gracious smile. Aramis bowed his head slightly, but did not smile. All four of them immediately ceased talking.

D'Artagnan was not so dull as not to perceive that he was not wanted, but he was not sufficiently acquainted with the ways of the world to know how to withdraw with ease from the awkward position of having forced himself upon persons he scarcely knew, and haven joined in a conversation which did not concern him. He was seeping in his mind, then, for the least disagreeable means of retreat, when, he remarked that Aramis had let his handkerchief fall, and by mistake, no doubt, had placed his foot upon it, and it appeared a favourable opportunity to atone for his intrusion. He stooped, and with the most gracious air he could assume, drew the handkerchief from under the of the musketeer, in spite of the efforts the latter made to detain it, and holding it out to him, said,

"I believe, sir, that this is a handkerchief you would be sorry to lose?"

The handkerchief was, in fact, richly embroidered, and had a coronet and arias at one of its corners. Aramis blushed excessively, and snatched rather than took the handkerchief from D'Artagnan's hand.

The young men burst into a loud laugh, and as may be supposed, the affair had no other sequel. In a moment or two the conversation ceased, and the three guards and the musketeer, after having cordially shaken hands, separated, the guards going one way and Aramis another.

"Now is my time to make my peace with this gentleman," said D'Artagnan to himself, having kept at a little distance all the latter part of the conversation; and with this good feeling he drew near to Aramis, who was going away without paying any attention to him.

"Sir," said he, "you will excuse me, I hope."

"Ah!" interrupted Aramis, "allow me to call to your attention that you have not acted in this affair as a man of good breeding ought to have."

"What!" cried D'Artagnan; "you suppose—"

"I suppose, sir, that you are not a fool, and that you know very well, although coming from Gascony, that people do not tread upon pocket handkerchiefs without a reason. What the devil! Paris is not paved with cambric!"

"Sir, you do wrong in endeavouring to mortify me," said D'Artagnan, to whom his quarrelsome nature began to speak more loudly than his pacific resolutions. "I am from Gascony, it is true; and since you know it, there is no need of telling you that Gascons are not very patient, so that when they have asked pardon once, were it even for a folly, they are convinced that they have done already at least as much again as they ought to have done."

"Sir, what I say to you about the matter," said Aramis, "is not for the sake of seeking a quarrel. Thank God, I am not a bully; and being a musketeer only for a time, I only fight when I am forced to do so, and always with great repugnance. But this time the affair is serious, for here is a lady compromised by you."

"By us, you mean," cried D'Artagnan.

"Why did you so awkwardly give me the handkerchief?"

"Why did you so awkwardly let it fall?"

"I have said, sir, that the handkerchief did not fall from my pocket."

"Well, and by saying so you have lied twice, sir, for I saw it fall."

"Oh, oh I you take it up in that way, do you, Master Gascon? Well, I will teach you how to behave yourself."

"And I will send you back to your mass-book, Master Abbé. Draw, if you please, and right away."

"Not at all, if you please, my good friend—not here, at least. Do you not perceive that we are opposite the Hotel d'Aiguillon, which is full of the cardinal's creatures? How do I know that it is not his Eminence who has honoured you with the commission to bring him my head? Now I really entertain a ridiculous partiality for my head, because it seems to suit my shoulders so admirably. I have no objection to killing you, depend upon that, but quietly, in a snug, remote place, where you will not be able to boast of your death to anybody."

"I agree, sir; but do not be too confident. Take away your handkerchief. Whether it belongs to you or another, you may, perhaps, stand in need of it."

"The gentleman is a Gascon?" asked Aramis,

"Yes. The gentleman does not postpone a meeting through prudence."

"Prudence, sir, is a virtue quite useless to musketeers, I know, but indispensable to churchmen; and as I am only a musketeer provisionally, I deem it best to be prudent. At two o'clock I shall have the honour of expecting you at the hotel of M. de Tréville. There I will point out to you the best place and time."

The two young men bowed and separated, Aramis ascending the street which led to the Luxembourg, while D'Artagnan, perceiving that the appointed hour was approaching, took the road to the Carmes-Deschaux, saying to himself, "Decidedly I can't draw back; but at least, if I am killed, I shall be killed by a musketeer!"

Chapter 5

The King's Musketeers And The Cardinal's Guards

When D'Artagnan arrived in sight of the bare spot of ground which stretched out at the base of the monastery, Athos had been waiting about five minutes, and twelve o'clock was striking. He was, then, as punctual as the Samaritan woman, and the most rigorous casuist on duels could have nothing to say.

Athos, who still suffered grievously from his wound, though it had been freshly dressed by M. de Tréville's surgeon, was seated on a stone, awaiting his adversary with that placid countenance and that noble air which never forsook him. At sight of D'Artagnan he arose and politely came a few steps to meet him. The latter, on his part, saluted his adversary with hat in hand, and his feather even touching the ground.

"Sir," said Athos, "I have engaged two of my friends as seconds, but these two friends have not yet come. I am astonished at their delay, as it is not at all their custom to be behindhand. We will wait for these gentlemen, if you please; I have plenty of time, and it will be more correct. Ah I here is one of them, I think."

In fact, at the end of the Rue Vaugirard the gigantic form of Porthos bean to loom.

"What!" cried D'Artagnan, "is your first second M. Porthos?"

"Yes. Does that displease you?"

"Oh, not at all."

"And here comes the other."

D'Artagnan turned in the direction pointed to by Athos, and perceived Aramis.

"What!" cried he, with an accent of greater astonishment than before, "is your second witness M. Aramis?"

"Doubtless he is. Are you not aware that we are never seen one without the others, and that we are called in the musketeers and the guards, at court and in the city, Athos, Porthos, and Aramis, or the Three Inseparables? And yet, as you come from Dax or Pau—"

"From Tarbes," said D'Artagnan.

"It is probable you are ignorant of this circumstance," said Athos.

"'Pon my word," replied D'Artagnan, "you are well named, gentlemen; and my adventure, if it should make any noise, will prove at least that your union is not founded upon contrasts."

In the meantime Porthos had come up, waved his hand to Athos, and then turning towards D'Artagnan, stopped astonished.

Permit us to say in passing that he had changed his baldric and laid aside his cloak.

"Ah, ah!" said he, "what does this mean?"

"This is the gentleman I am going to fight with," said Athos, pointing to D'Artagnan with his hand, and saluting him with the same gesture.

"Why, it is with him I am also going to fight," said Porthos.

"But not before one o'clock," replied D'Artagnan.

"Well, and I also am going to fight with that gentleman," said Aramis, coming up in his turn.

"But not till two o'clock," said D'Artagnan, with the same calmness.

"But what are you going to fight about, Athos?" asked Aramis.

"'Pon my word, I don't very well know; he hurt my shoulder— And you, Porthos?"

"'Pon my word, I am going to fight because I am going to fight." answered Porthos, colouring deeply.

Athos, whose keen eye lost nothing, perceived a sly smile pass over the lips of the young Gascon as he replied,

"We had a short discussion upon dress."

"And you, Aramis?" asked Athos.

"Oh, ours is a theological quarrel," replied Aramis, making a sign to D'Artagnan to keep secret the cause of their dispute.

Athos saw a second smile on the lips of D'Artagnan.

"Indeed?" said Athos.

"Yes; a passage of St. Augustine, upon which we could not agree," said the Gascon.

"By Jove! this is a clever fellow," murmured Athos.

"And now you are all assembled, gentlemen," said D'Artagnan, "permit me to offer you my excuses."

At this word *excuses* a cloud passed over the brow of Athos, a haughty smile curled the lip of Porthos, and a negative sign was the reply of Aramis.

"You do not understand me, gentlemen," said D'Artagnan, throwing up his head, on which was paying at that moment a ray of sunlight, gilding its clear and bold outlines. "I ask to be excused in case I should not be able to discharge my debt to all three; for M. Athos has the right to kill me first, which must much diminish the face-value of your bill, M. Porthos, and render yours almost worthless, M. Aramis. And now, gentlemen, I repeat, excuse me, but on that account only, and—on guard!"

At these words, with the most gallant air possible, D'Artagnan drew his sword.

The blood had mounted to the head of D'Artagnan, and at that moment he would have drawn his sword against all the musketeers in the kingdom as willingly as he now did against Athos, Porthos, and Aramis.

It was a quarter past twelve. The sun was in its zenith, and the spot chosen for the theatre of tile duel was exposed to its full power.

"It is very hot," said Athos, drawing his sword in his turn, "and yet I cannot take off my doublet, for only just now I felt my wound begun to bleed again, and I should not like to annoy the gentleman with the sight of blood which he has not drawn from me himself."

"That is true, sir," replied D'Artagnan; "and whether drawn by myself or another, I assure you I shall always view with regret the blood of so brave a man. I will therefore fight in my doublet, as you do."

"Come, come, enough of such compliments," cried Porthos; "please remember we are waiting our turn."

"Speak for yourself when you are inclined to utter such incongruities," interrupted Aramis. "For my part, I think what they say is very well said, and quite worthy of two gentlemen."

"When you please, sir;" said Athos, putting himself on guard.

"I was awaiting your order," said D'Artagnan, crossing swords.

But scarcely had the two rapiers clashed on meeting when a company of the guards of his Eminence, commanded by M. de Jussac. turned the angle of the convent.

"The cardinal's guards! the cardinal's guards!" cried Aramis and Porthos at the same time. "Sheathe swords, gentlemen! sheathe swords!"

But it was too late. The two combatants had been seen in a position which left no doubt of their intentions.

"Halloo!" cried Jussac, advancing towards them, and making sign to his men to do the same—"halloo, musketeers! fighting here, then, are you? And the edicts—what has become of them?"

"You are very generous, gentlemen of the guards," said Athos with acrimony, for Jussac was one of the aggressors of the preceding day. "If we were to see you fighting, I can assure you that we would make no effort to prevent you. Leave us alone, then, and you will enjoy a little amusement without cost to yourselves."

"Gentlemen," said Jussac, "I greatly regret to declare the thing impossible. Duty before everything. Sheathe, then, if you please, and follow us."

"Sir," said Aramis, parodying Jussac, "it would afford us great pleasure to obey your polite invitation if it depended upon ourselves; but unfortunately the thing is impossible: M. de Tréville has forbidden it. Pass on your way, then; it is the best thing you can do."

This raillery exasperated Jussac.

"We will charge upon you, then," said he, "if you disobey."

"There are five of them," said Athos, half aloud, "and we are but three. We shall be beaten again, and must die on the spot; for I swear it, I will never appear before the captain again as a conquered man."

Athos, Porthos, and Aramis instantly closed in, and Jussac drew up his soldiers.

This short interval was sufficient to determine D'Artagnan. It was one of those events which decide the life of a man. It was a choice between the king and the cardinal. The choice made, it must be persisted in. To fight was to disobey the law, to risk his head, to make at once an enemy of a minister more powerful than the king himself; all this the young man perceived, and yet, to his praise be it said, he did not hesitate a second. Turning towards Athos and his friends,

"Gentlemen," said he, "allow me to correct your words, if you please. You said you were but three, but it appears to me we are four."

"But you are not one of us," said Porthos.

"That's true," replied D'Artagnan; "I do not wear the uniform, but I am with you in spirit. My heart is that of a musketeer. I feel it, sir, and that urges me on."

"Withdraw, young man," cried Jussac, who, doubtless by his gestures and the expression of his countenance, had guessed D'Artagnan's design. "You may retire; we allow you to do so. Save your skin; begone quickly."

D'Artagnan did not move.

"Well, you are a real good fellow," said Athos, pressing the young man's hand.

"Come, come, decide one way or the other," replied Jussac.

"Well," said Porthos to Aramis, "we must do something."

"You are very generous," said Athos.

But all three were thinking of the youthfulness of D'Artagnan, and dreaded his inexperience.

"We would be only three, one of whom is wounded, with the addition of a boy," resumed Athos, "and yet they will say none the less that we were four men."

"Yes, but to yield!" said Porthos.

"That's rather difficult," replied Athos.

D'Artagnan understood their hesitancy.

"Try me, gentlemen," said he, "and I swear to you by my honour that I will not go hence if we are conquered."

"What is your name, my brave fellow?" said Athos.

"D'Artagnan, sir."

"Well, then, Athos, Porthos, Aramis, and D'Artagnan, forward!" cried Athos.

"Come, gentlemen, have you made your minds up?" cried Jussac for the third time.

"It is done, gentlemen," said Athos.

"And what do you mean to do?" asked Jussac.

"We are about to have the honour of charging you," replied Aramis, lifting his hat with one hand and drawing his sword with the other.

"Oh! you resist, do you?" cried Jussac.

"'Sblood! does that astonish you?"

And the nine combatants rushed at one another with a madness which, however, did not exclude a certain amount of method.

Athos fixed upon Cahusac, a favourite of the cardinal's, Porthos had Bicarat, and Aramis found himself opposed to two adversaries. As to D'Artagnan, he sprang towards Jussac himself.

The heart of the young Gascon beat as though it would burst its fetters—not from fear, God be thanked (he had not the shade of it), but with emulation. He fought like a mad tiger, turning ten times round his adversary, and changing his ground and his guard twenty times. Jussac was, as they said then, fond of the sword, and had had much practice; nevertheless it required all his skill to defend himself against an adversary who, active and energetic, departed every instant from received rules, attacking him on all sides at once, and yet parrying like a man who had the greatest respect for his own epidermis.

This contest at length exhausted Jussac's patience. Furious at being held in check by one whom he had considered a boy, he grew angry and began to make mistakes. D'Artagnan, who, though wanting in practice, had a profound theory, redoubled his agility. Jussac, anxious to put an end to this, springing forward, aimed a terrible thrust at his adversary, but the latter parried it; and while Jussac was recovering himself, glided like a serpent beneath his blade, and passed his sword through his body. Jussac fell in a heap.

D'Artagnan then cast an anxious and rapid glance over the field of battle.

Aramis had already killed one of his adversaries, but the other was pressing him warmly. Nevertheless Aramis was in a good situation and still able to defend himself.

Bicarat and Porthos had just made counter hits. Porthos had received a thrust through his arm, and Bicarat one through his thigh. But neither of the wounds was serious, and they only fought the more earnestly for them.

Athos, wounded again by Cahusac, was steadily growing paler, but slid not give way a foot; he had only changed his sword-hand, and was fighting with his left.

According to the laws of duelling at that period, D'Artagnan was at liberty to assist the one he pleased. While he was trying to find out which of his companions needed his aid, he caught a glance from Athos. This glance was of sublime eloquence. Athos would have died rather than appeal for help; but he could look, and with that look ask assistance. D'Artagnan interpreted it. With a terrible bound he sprang to the side of Cahusac, crying,

"To me, Sir Guard, or I will slay you!"

Cahusac turned. It was time, for Athos, whose great courage alone supported him, sank upon his knee.

"'Sblood!" cried he to D'Artagnan, "do not kill him, young man, I beg of you. I have an old affair to settle with him when I am healed and sound again. Disarm him only; make sure of his sword. That's it! that's it! well done! very well done! "

This exclamation was drawn from Athos by seeing the sword of Cahusac fly twenty paces from him. D'Artagnan and Cahusac sprang forward at the same instant, the one to recover, the other to obtain, the sword; but D'Artagnan, being the more active, reached it first and placed his foot upon it.

Cahusac immediately ran to the guardsman whom Aramis had killed, seized his rapier, and returned towards D'Artagnan; but on his way he met Athos, who, during the momentary relief which D'Artagnan had procured for him, had recovered his breath, and who, for fear that D'Artagnan should kill his own personal enemy, wished to resume the fight.

D'Artagnan perceived that it would be disobliging Athos not to leave him alone; and in a few minutes Cahusac fell, with a sword-thrust through his throat.

At the same instant Aramis placed his sword-point on the breast of his fallen enemy, and compelled him to ask for mercy.

Only Porthos and Bicarat remained. Porthos was boasting merrily, asking Bicarat what o'clock it could be, and offering him his compliments upon his brother having just obtained a company in the regiment of Navarre; but joke as he might, he gained no advantage. Bicarat was one of those iron men who never fall dead.

Nevertheless it was necessary to put an end to the affair. The watch might come up and take all the combatants, wounded or not, royalists or cardinalists. Athos, Aramis, and D'Artagnan surrounded Bicarat and summoned him to surrender. Though alone against all, and with a wound in his thigh, Bicarat wished to hold out; but Jussac, who had risen upon his elbow, cried out to him to yield. Bicarat was a Gascon, as D'Artagnan was; he turned a deaf ear, and contented himself with laughing; and between two parries, finding time to point to a spot of earth with his sword,

"Here," cried he, parodying a verse of the Bible—"here will Bicarat die, the only one of those who are with him!"

"But there are four against you; leave off, I command you!"

"Ah, if you command me, that's another thing," said Bicarat; "you being my sergeant, it is my duty to obey."

And springing backward, he broke his sword across his knee to avoid the necessity of surrendering it, threw the pieces over the convent wall, and crossed his arms, whistling a cardinalist air.

Bravery is always respected, even in an enemy. The musketeers saluted Bicarat with their swords, and returned them to their sheaths. D'Artagnan did the same; then assisted by Bicarat, the only one left standing, he bore Jussac, Cahusac, and that one of Aramis's adversaries who was only wounded, under the porch of the convent. The fourth, as we have said, was dead. They then rang the bell, and carrying away four swords out of five, they took their road, intoxicated with joy, towards the hotel of M. de Tréville.

They walked arm in arm, occupying the whole width of the street, and accosting every musketeer they met, so that in the end it became a triumphal march. The heart of D'Artagnan throbbed with wild delight; he walked between Athos and Porthos, pressing them tenderly.

"If I am not yet a musketeer," said he to his new friends, as he passed through the gateway of M. de Tréville's hotel, "at least I have entered upon my apprenticeship, haven't I?"

CHAPTER 6

His Majesty King Louis XIII

This affair made a great noise. M. de Tréville scolded his musketeers in public and congratulated them in private; but as no time was to be lost in gaining the king, M. de Tréville made all haste to the Louvre. But he was too late; the king was closeted with the cardinal, and M. de Tréville was informed that the king was busy and could not receive him. In the evening M. de Tréville went to the king's card—table. The king was winning, and as his Majesty was very avaricious, he was in an excellent humour; therefore, perceiving M. de Tréville at a distance,

"Come here, captain," said he—"come here, that I may scold you. Do you know that his Eminence has just made fresh complaints against your musketeers, and with so much emotion that his Eminence is indisposed this evening? Why, these musketeers of yours are very devils—fellows to be hanged!"

"No, sire," replied Tréville, who saw at the first glance which way things would turn—"no, sire; on the contrary, they are good creatures, as meek as lambs, and have but one desire, I'll be their warranty; and this is, that their swords may never leave their scabbards but in your Majesty's service. But what are they to do? The guards of the cardinal are for ever seeking quarrels with them, and for the honour of the corps even the poor young men are obliged to defend themselves."

"Listen to M. de Tréville," said the king, "listen to him! Would not one say he was speaking of a religious community?

"La Vieuville," said he, "take my place; I must speak to M. de Tréville on an affair of importance. Ah, I had eighty louis before me; put down the same sum, so that they who have lost may have nothing to complain of—justice before everything." Then turning towards M. de Tréville, and walking with him towards the embrasure of a window,

"Well, monsieur," continued he, "you say it is his Eminence's guards who sought a quarrel with your musketeers?"

"Yes, sir, as they always do."

"And how did the thing happen? Let us see, for you know, my dear captain, a judge must hear both sides."

"Good Lord! in the most simple and natural manner possible. Three of my best soldiers, whom your Majesty knows by name, and whose devotion you have more than once appreciated, and who have, I can assure the king, his service much at heart—three of my best soldiers, I say—Athos, Porthos, and Aramis— had made a party of pleasure with a young cadet from Gascony, whom I had introduced to them the same morning. The party was to take place at St. Germain, I believe, and they had appointed to meet at the Carmes-Deschaux, when they were disturbed by De Jussac, Cahusac, Bicarat, and two other guards, who certainly did not go there in a body without some ill intention against the edicts."

"Ah, ah! you incline me to think so," said the king. "There is no doubt they went thither with the intention of fighting."

"I do not accuse them, sire; but I leave your Majesty to judge what five armed men could possibly be going to do in such a retired spot as the environs of the Convent des Carmes."

"You are right, Tréville, you are right!"

"Then, upon seeing my musketeers, they changed their minds, and forgot their private hatred for their corps feuds; for your Majesty cannot be ignorant that the musketeers, who belong to the king, and to nobody but the king, are the natural enemies of the guards, who belong to the cardinal."

"Yes, Tréville, yes," said the king in a melancholy tone; "and it is very sad, believe me, to see thus two parties in France, two heads to royalty. But all this will come to an end, Tréville, will come to an end. You say, then, that the guards sought a quarrel with the musketeers?"

"I say that it is probable that things did happen thus, but I will not swear to it, sire. You know how difficult it is to discover the truth; and unless a man be endowed with that admirable instinct which causes Louis XIII to be termed the just—"

"You are right, Tréville. But they were not alone, your musketeers; they had a youth with them?"

"Yes, sire, and one wounded man; so that three of the king's musketeers—one of whom was wounded—and a youth not only maintained their ground against five of the most terrible of his Eminence's guards, but absolutely brought four of them to the earth."

"Why, this is a victory!" cried the king, glowing with delight, "a complete victory!"

"Yes, sire; as complete as that of the Bridge of Cé."

"Four men, one of them wounded, and a youth, say you?"

"One scarcely a grown man, but who, however, behaved himself so admirably on this occasion that I will take the liberty of: recommending him to your Majesty."

"What is his name?"

"D'Artagnan, sire; he is the son of one of my oldest friends—the son of a man who served under your father of glorious memory in the civil war."

"And you say that this young man behaved himself well? Tell me how, De Tréville; you know how I delight in accounts of war and fights."

And Louis XIII twirled his moustache proudly and placed his hand upon his hip.

"Sire," resumed Tréville, "as I told you, M. d'Artagnan is little more than a boy, and as he has not the honour of being a musketeer, he was dressed as a private citizen. The guards of the cardinal, perceiving his youth, and still more that he did not belong to the corps, urged him to retire before they made the attack."

"So you may plainly see, Tréville," interrupted the king, "it was they who attacked?"

"That is true, sire; there can be no more doubt on that head. They called upon him, then, to retire, but he answered that he was a musketeer at heart, entirely devoted to your Majesty, and that he would therefore remain with the musketeers."

"Brave young man!" murmured the king.

"Well, he did remain with them; and your Majesty has in him so firm a champion that it was he who gave Jussac the terrible swordthrust which has made the cardinal so angry."

"He who wounded Jussac!" cried the king— "he, a boy! Tréville, that's impossible!"

"It is as I have the honour to relate it to your Majesty."

"Jussac, one of the first swordsmen in the kingdom?"

"Well, sire, for once he found his master."

"I should like to see this young man, Tréville —I should like to see him; and if anything can be done—well, we will make it our business to do it."

"When will your Majesty deign to receive him?"

"To-morrow at midday, Tréville."

"Shall I bring him alone?"

"No, bring me all four together; I wish to thank them all at once. Devoted men are so rare, Tréville, we must recompense devotion."

"At twelve o'clock, sire, we will be at the Louvre."

"Ah! by the back staircase, Tréville, by the back staircase. It is useless to let the cardinal know."

"Yes, sire."

"You understand, Tréville; an edict is still an edict; it is forbidden to fight, after all."

"But this encounter, sire, is quite out of the ordinary conditions of a duel. It is a brawl; and the proof is that there were five of the cardinal's guards against my three musketeers and M. d'Artagnan."

"That is true," said the king; "but never mind, Tréville; come anyway by the back staircase."

Tréville smiled. But as it was already something to have prevailed upon this child to rebel against his master, he saluted the king respectfully, and with this agreement took leave of him.

That evening the three musketeers were informed of the honour which was bestowed upon them. As they had long been acquainted with the king, they were not much excited by the circumstance; but D'Artagnan, with his Gascon imagination, saw in it his future fortune, and passed the night in golden dreams.

M. de Tréville had ordered his three musketeers and their companion to be with him at half-past six in the morning. He took them with him, without assuring them or promising them anything.

When they had reached the foot of the back stairs he desired them to wait.

Ten minutes had scarcely passed away when the door of the king's closet opened, and M. de Tréville saw the king advancing to the door.—"Ah! that's you, Tréville. Where are your musketeers? I told you to bring them with you. Why have you not done so?"

"They are below, sire; and with your permission La Chesnaye will tell them to come up."

"Yes, yes, let them come up immediately. It is nearly eight o'clock, and at nine I expect a visit. Come in, Tréville."

At that moment the three musketeers and D'Artagnan, led by La Chesnaye, the King's valet appeared at the top of the staircase.

"Come in, my braves," said the king, "come in; I have a scolding for you."

"Therefore, sire, your Majesty sees that they are come quite contrite and repentant to offer you their excuses."

"Quite contrite and repentant! Hem!" said the king, "I place no confidence in their hypocritical faces. In particular, there is one yonder with a Gascon face.—Come here, sir."

D'Artagnan, who understood that it was to him this compliment was addressed, approached, assuming a most despondent air.

"Why, you told me he was a young man! This is a boy, Tréville, a mere boy! Do you mean to say that it was he who bestowed that severe thrust upon Jussac?"

"Without reckoning," said Athos, "that if he had not rescued me from the hands of Cahusac, I should not now have the honour of making my very humble reverence to your Majesty."

"Why, this Béarnais is a very devil! *Ventre-saint-gris!* Monsieur de Tréville, as the king my father would have said. But at this sort of work many doublets must be slashed and many swords broken. But Gascons are always poor, are they not?"

"Sire, I must say that they have not yet discovered any gold mines in their mountains; though the Lord owes them this miracle in recompense for the manner in which they supported the claims of the king, your father."

"Which means that the Gascons made a king of me myself, seeing that I am my father's son, does it not, Tréville? Well, in good faith, I don't say nay to it.—La Chesnaye, go and see if, by rummaging all my pockets, you can find forty pistoles; and if you find them bring them to me.—And now let us see, young man, with your hand upon your conscience, how did all this come to pass?"

D'Artagnan related the adventure in all its details.

"This is all very well," murmured the king. "But that's quite enough, gentlemen; please to understand that's enough. You have taken your revenge and you ought to be satisfied."

"If your Majesty is," said Tréville, "we are."

"Oh yes, I am," added the king taking a handful of gold from La Chesnaye and putting it into the hand of D'Artagnan. "Here," said he, "is a proof of my satisfaction."

At this period the ideas of pride which are in fashion in our days did not prevail. A gentleman received money directly from the king's hand, and was not in the least humiliated. D'Artagnan put his forty pistoles into his pocket without any scruple; on the contrary, he thanked his Majesty most heartily.

"There," said the king, looking at a clock—"there now, as it is half past eight, you may retire; for, as I told you, I expect some one at nine. Thanks for your devotion, gentlemen. I may continue to rely upon it, may I not?"

"O sire!" cried the four companions with one voice, "we would allow ourselves to be cut to pieces in your Majesty's service!"

"Well, well, but keep whole; that will be better, and you will be more useful to me. Tréville," added the king in a low voice, as the others were retiring, "as you have no room in your musketeers, and as we have besides decided that a novitiate is necessary before entering that corps, place this young man in the company of guards commanded by your brother-in-law, M. des Essarts. Ah, zounds! I enjoy in advance the face the cardinal will make. He will be furious; but I don't care. I am doing what is right."

And the king waved his hand to Tréville, who left him and rejoined the musketeers, whom he found sharing the forty pistoles with D'Artagnan.

And the cardinal, as his Majesty had said, was really furious, so furious that for a whole week he absented himself from the king's card—table, which did not prevent the king from being as complacent to him as possible, or, whenever he met him, from asking in the kindest tone,

"Well, cardinal, how fares it with that poor Jussac of yours?"

CHAPTER 7

The Musketeers' Establishments

When D'Artagnan had left the Louvre he was advised by Athos to order a good repast at the Pomme-de-Pin, by Porthos to engage a lackey, and by Aramis to provide himself with a suitable mistress.

The repast was carried into effect that very day, and the lackey waited at table. The repast had been ordered by Athos, and the lackey furni-

shed by Porthos. This fellow was a Picard, whom the vain musketeer had picked up that very day and for this occasion on the bridge
De la Tournelle while he was spitting in the water to make rings.

Athos, on his part, had a valet whom he had trained in his service in a very peculiar fashion, and who was named Grimaud. He was
very taciturn, this worthy signor. Be it understood we are speaking
of Athos. During the five or six years that he had lived in perfect intimacy with his companions Porthos and Aramis, they could remember having often seen him smile, but had never heard him laugh.

His words were brief and expressive, conveying all that was
meant, and no more—no embellishments, no embroidery, no ara-
besques. His conversation was matter of fact, without any orna-
mentation.

Although Athos was scarcely thirty years old, and possessed of
great physical and mental beauty, no one knew that he had ever had
a mistress. He never spoke of women. His reserve, his roughness, and
his silence made almost an old man of him; he had then, in order
not to interfere with his habits, accustomed Grimaud to obey him
upon a simple gesture, or at the mere movement of his lips. He never
spoke to him but upon the most extraordinary occasions.

Porthos's character, as we have seen, was exactly opposite to that
of Athos. He not only talked much, but he talked loudly, little caring, we must do him the justice to say, whether anybody listened to
him or not. An old proverb says, "Like master, like man." Let us pass
then from the valet of Athos to the valet of Porthos, from Grimaud
to Mousqueton.

Mousqueton was a Norman, whose pacific name of Boniface his
master had changed into the infinitely more sonorous one of Mousqueton. He had entered Porthos's service upon condition that he
should only be clothed and lodged, but in a handsome manner; he
claimed but two hours a day for himself to consecrate to an employment which would provide for his other wants. Porthos agreed to tine
bargain; this arrangement suited him wonderfully well.

As for Aramis, whose character we believe we have sufficiently
explained—a character, moreover, which, like that of his companions, we shall be able to follow in its development—his lackey was

called Bazin. Thanks to the hopes which his master entertained of some day entering into orders, he was always clothed in black, as became the servant of a churchman. He was a Berrichon of from thirty—five to forty years of age, mild, peaceable, sleek, employing the leisure his master left him in the perusal of pious works, providing for the two, to be sure, a frugal but excellent dinner. In addition, he was dumb, blind, and deaf, and of unimpeachable fidelity.

The life of the four young men had become common to each and all. D'Artagnan, who had no settled habits of his own, since he had just dropped from his province into the midst of a word quite new to him, assumed immediately the habits of his friends.

They rose about eight o'clock in the winter, about six in summer, and went to get the countersign and see how things were at M. de Tréville's. D'Artagnan, although he was not a musketeer, performed the duty of one with touching punctuality. He was always mounting guard, because he always kept that one of his friends company who mounted his. He was well known at the hotel of the musketeers, where every one considered him a good comrade. M. de Tréville, who had appreciated his worth at the first glance, and who bore him a real affection, never ceased recommending him to the king.

On their side, the three musketeers were much attached to their young comrade. The friendship which united these four men, and the need they felt for meeting three or four times a day, whether for duels, business, or pleasure, caused them to be continually running after one another like shadows; and you constantly met the inseparables looking one for the other, from the Luxembourg to the Place Saint-Sulpice, or from the Rue du Vieux-Colombier to the Luxembourg.

In the meanwhile the promises of M. de Tréville were accomplishing. One fine morning the king commanded the Chevalier des Essarts to admit D'Artagnan as a cadet in his company of guards. D'Artagnan, with a sigh, donned this uniform, which he would have exchanged for that of a musketeer at the price of ten years of his existence. But M. de Tréville promised this favour after a novitiate of two years—a novitiate which might, besides, be abridged if an opportunity should present itself for D'Artagnan to render the king any signal service, or to distinguish himself by some brilliant action. Upon this promise D'Artagnan withdrew, and the next day began service.

Then it became the turn of Athos, Porthos, and Aramis to mount guard with D'Artagnan when he was on duty. By admitting D'Artagnan, the company of the Chevalier des Essarts thus received four men instead of one.

Chapter 8

A Court Intrigue

Meanwhile the forty pistoles of King Louis XIII, like all other things in this world, after having had a beginning had had an end, and after this end our four companions began to be somewhat embarrassed. At first Athos supported the association for a time with his own means. Porthos succeeded him, and thanks to one of those disappearances to which people were accustomed, he was able to provide for the wants of all for a fortnight more. At last it became Aramis's turn, who performed it with a good grace, and who succeeded in procuring a few pistoles, as he said, by selling his theological books.

Then they, as usual, had recourse to M. de Tréville, who made some advances on their pay; but these advances could not go far with three musketeers who were already much in arrears, and a guardsman who as yet had no pay at all.

At length, when they found they were likely to be quite in want, they got together, by a final effort, eight or ten pistoles, with which Porthos went to the gaming-table. Unfortunately luck ran against him. He lost ail, together with twenty-five pistoles for which he pledged his word.

Then the embarrassment became distress. The hungry friends, followed by their lackeys, were seen haunting the quays and guard-rooms, picking up among their friends abroad all the dinners they could meet with; for, according to the advice of Aramis, it was prudent to sow repasts right and left in prosperity in order to reap a few its time of need.

D'Artagnan was racking his brain to find a direction with which, as with Archimedes's lever, he had no doubt that they should succeed in moving the world, when some one topped gently at his door.

A man was introduced, of rather simple mien, who had the appearance of a tradesman.

D'Artagnan dismissed Planchet, and requested his visitor to be seated.

"I have heard M. d'Artagnan spoken of as a very brave young man," said the bourgeois; "and this reputation, which he justly enjoys, has determined me to confide a secret to him."

"Speak, sir, speak," said D'Artagnan, who instinctively scented something advantageous.

The bourgeois made a fresh pause, and continued,

"I have a wife who is seamstress to the queen, sir, and who is not deficient in either good conduct or beauty. I was induced to marry her about three years ago, although she had but very little dowry, because M. de la Porte. the queen's cloak-bearer, is her godfather, and befriends her—"

"Well, sir?" asked D'Artagnan.

"Well," resumed the bourgeois— "well, sir, my wife was carried off yesterday morning, as she was coming out of her workroom."

"And by whom was your wife carried off?"

"I do not know whether I ought to tell you what I suspect—"

"Sir, I beg you to observe that I ask you absolutely nothing. It is you who have come to me. It is you who have told me that you had a secret to confide to me. Act, then, as you think proper; there is still time to retreat."

"No, sir, no; you appear to be an honest young man, and I will place confidence in you. I believe, then, that it is not on account of any intrigues of her own that my wife has been carried off, but that it has been done on account of the amours of a much greater lady than she is."

"Ah, ah! can it be on account of the amours of Madame de Bois-

Tracy?" said D'Artagnan, wishing to have the air, in the eyes of the bourgeois, of being up in court affairs.

"Higher, sir, higher. "

"Of Madame d'Aiguillon?"

"Higher still."

"Of Madame de Chevreuse?"

"Higher, much higher."

"Of the—" D'Artagnan stopped.

"Yes, sir," replied the terrified bourgeois, in a tone so low that he was scarcely audible.

"And with whom?"

"With whom can it be, if not with the Duke of—"

"The Duke of—"

"Yes, sir," replied the bourgeois, giving a still lower intonation to his voice.

"But how do you know all this?"

"How do I know it?"

"Yes, how do you know it? No half-confidence, or you understand!"

"I know it from my wife, sir—from my wife herself."

"And she knows it, she herself, from whom?"

"From M. de la Porte. Did I not tell you that she was the god-daughter of M. de la Porte, the queen's confidential agent? Well, M. de la Porte placed her near her Majesty, in order that our poor queen might at least have some one in whom she could place confidence, abandoned as she is by the king, watched as she is by the cardinal, betrayed as she is by everybody.

"Ah, ah! it begins to grow clear," said D'Artagnan.

"And the queen believes—"

"Well, what does the queen believe?"

"She believes that some one has written to the Duke of Buckingham in her name."

"In the queen's name?"

"Yes, to make him come to Paris; and when once in Paris, to draw him into some snare."

"The devil! But your wife, sir, what has she to do with all this?"

"Her devotion to the queen is known, and they wish either to remove her from her mistress, or to intimidate her, in order to obtain her Majesty's secrets, or to seduce her and make use of her as a spy."

"That is all very, probable," said D'Artagnan; "but the man who has carried her off—do you know him?"

"I have told you that I believe I know him."

"His name?"

"I do not know that. What I do know is that he is a creature of the cardinal's, his ready tool."

"But you have seen him?"

"Yes, my wife pointed him out to me one day."

"Has he anything remarkable about him by which he may be recognized?"

"Oh, certainly. He is a noble of lofty carriage, black hair, swarthy complexion, piercing eye, white teeth, and a scar on his temple."

"A scar on his temple!" cried D'Artagnan; "and also white teeth, a piercing eye, dark complexion, black hair, and haughty carriage. Why, that's my man of Meung."

"He is your man, do you say?"

"Yes, yes; but that has nothing to do with it. No I am mistaken. It simplifies the matter greatly, on the contrary. If your man is mine, with one blow I shall obtain two revenges, that's all. But where is this man to be met with?"

"I cannot inform you."

"Have you no information respecting his dwelling?"

"None. One day, as I was conveying my wife back to the Louvre, he was coming out as she was going in, and she showed him to me."

"The devil, the devil!" murmured D'Artagnan. "All this is vague enough. From whom did you learn the abduction of your wife?"

"From M. de la Porte."

"Did he give you any of the particulars?"

"He knew none himself."

"And you have learned none from any other quarter?"

"Yes, I have received—"

"What?"

"I fear I am committing a great imprudence."

"You still keep harping upon that; but I beg leave to observe to you that this time it is too late to retreat."

"I do not retreat, 'sdeath!" cried the bourgeois, swearing to keep his courage up. "Besides, by the word of Bonacieux—"

"Your name is Bonacieux?" interrupted D'Artagnan.

"Yes, that is my name."

"You said, then, by the word of Bonacieux! Pardon me for interrupting you, but it appears to me that that name is familiar to me."

"Very possibly, sir. I am your landlord."

"Ah, ah!" said D'Artagnan, half rising and bowing; "you are my landlord?"

"Yes, sir, yes. And as it is three months since you came, and, engaged as you must be in your important occupations, you have forgotten to pay me my rent—as, I say, I have not tormented you a single instant, I thought you would appreciate my delicacy."

"How can it be otherwise, my dear Bonacieux?" replied D'Artagnan. "Believe me, I am wholly grateful for such conduct; and if, as I have told you, I can be of any service to you—"

"And then I thought that owing me three months' rent, which I have said nothing about—"

"Yes, yes; you have already given me that reason, and I find it excellent"

"And, besides, considering that as long as you do me the honour to remain in my house I shall never speak to you about your future rent"

"Very good!"

"And adding to this, if necessary, that I mean to offer you fifty pistoles, if, against all probability, you should be short at the present moment"

"Admirable! But you are rich, then, my dear Monsieur Bonacieux?"

"I am comfortably off, sir, that's all. I have scraped together something like an income of two or three thousand crowns in the haberdashery business, and especially by investing some capital in the last voyage of the celebrated navigator Jean Mocquet; so that you understand, sir. But—" cried the bourgeois.

"What?" demanded D'Artagnan.

"Whom do I see yonder?"

"Where?"

"In the street, in front of your window, on the sill of that door—a man wrapped in a cloak."

"It is he!" cried D'Artagnan and the bourgeois, each at the same time having recognized his man.

"Ah, this time;" cried D'Artagnan, leaping towards his sword—"this time he shall not escape me!"

Drawing his sword from the sheath, he rushed out of the apartment.

On the staircase he met Athos and Porthos, who were coming to see him. They separated, and D'Artagnan rushed between them like an arrow.

"Where the devil are you going?" cried the two musketeers in a breath.

"The man of Meung!" replied D'Artagnan, and disappeared.

D'Artagnan had more than once related to his friends his adventure with the unknown, as well as the apparition of the beautiful foreigner, to whom this man had confided some important letter.

They understood, then, from the few words which escaped from D'Artagnan, what affair was in hand; and as they thought that after having overtaken his man or lost sight of him D'Artagnan would return to his rooms again, they kept on their way.

When they entered D'Artagnan's chamber it was empty. The landlord, dreading the consequences of the meeting which was doubtless about to take place between the young man and the unknown, had, consistently with the character he had given himself, judged it most prudent to decamp.

CHAPTER 9

D'Artagnan's Character Unfolds

As Athos and Porthos had foreseen, at the expiration of half an hour D'Artagnan returned. He had this time again missed his man, who had disappeared as if by enchantment. D'Artagnan had run, sword in hand, through all the neighbouring streets, but had found nobody resembling him whom he was looking for.

While D'Artagnan was running through the streets and knocking at doors, Aramis had joined his companions, so that on returning home D'Artagnan found the reunion complete.

"Well?" cried the three musketeers all together, on seeing D'Artagnan enter with his brow covered with perspiration and his face clouded with anger.

"Well" cried he, throwing his sword upon the bed; "this man must be the devil in person. He has disappeared like a phantom, like a shade, like a spectre."

He then told his friends, word for word, all that had passed between him and his landlord, and how the man who had carried off the wife of his worthy landlord was the same with whom he had had a difference at the hostelry of the Franc-Meunier.

"And did the mercer," rejoined Athos, "tell you, D'Artagnan, that the queen thought that Buckingham had been brought over by a forged letter?"

"She is afraid so."

"Wait a minute, then," said Aramis.

"What for?" demanded Porthos.

"Gentlemen," cried Aramis, "listen to this."

"Listen to Aramis," said his three friends.

"Yesterday I was at the house of a learned doctor of theology whom sometimes consult about my studies."

Athos smiled.

"This doctor has a niece;" continued Aramis.

"A niece, has he?" interrupted Porthos.

"A very respectable lady," said Aramis.

The three friends began to laugh.

"Ah, if you laugh, or doubt what I say," replied Aramis, "you shall know nothing."

"We are as stanch believers as Mohammedans, and as mute as catafalques," said Athos.

"I will go on, then," resumed Aramis. "This niece comes sometimes to see her uncle, and by chance was there yesterday at the same time that I was, and I could do no less than offer to conduct her to her carriage."

"Oh, oh! Then this niece of the doctor's keeps a carriage, does she?" interrupted Porthos, one of whose faults was a great looseness of speech. "A very nice acquaintance, my friend!"

"Porthos," replied Aramis, "I have already had occasion to observe to you more than once that you are very indiscreet, and that this injures you with women."

"Gentlemen, gentlemen," cried D'Artagnan, who began to get a glimpse of the result of the adventure, "the thing is serious. Endeavour, then, not to joke, if possible. Go on, Aramis, go on."

"All at once a tall, dark man, with the manner of a gentleman— Come! the same style as yours, D'Artagnan."

"The same, perhaps," said he.

"Possibly," continued Aramis—"came towards me, accompanied by five or six men, who followed at about ten paces behind him; and in the politest tone, 'Duke,' said he to me, 'and you, madame,' continued he, addressing the lady, who had hold of my arm—"

"The doctor's niece?"

"Hold your tongue, Porthos," said Athos; "you are insupportable."

"'Be so kind as to get into this carriage, and that without offering the slightest resistance or making the least noise.'"

"He took you for Buckingham!" cried D'Artagnan.

"I believe so," replied Aramis.

"But the lady?" asked Porthos.

"He took her for the queen!" said D'Artagnan.

"Just so," replied Aramis.

"The Gascon is the devil!" cried Athos; "nothing escapes him."

"The fact is," said Porthos, "Aramis is of the same height and something of the form of the handsome duke; but it nevertheless appears to me that the uniform of a musketeer—"

"I wore a very large cloak," said Aramis.

"In the month of July, the devil!" said Porthos. "Is the doctor afraid you should be recognized?"

"I can understand that the spy may have been deceived by your figure; but your face—"

"I had a very large hat on," said Aramis.

"Oh, good Lord!" cried Porthos, "how many precautions in order ¤o study theology!"

"Gentlemen, gentlemen," said D'Artagnan, "do not let us lose our time in jesting. Let us separate, and let us seek the mercer's wife; that is the key of the intrigue."

"A woman of such inferior condition! Do you believe it, D'Artagnan?" said Porthos, protruding his lip contemptuously.

"She is goddaughter to La Porte, the confidential valet of the queen. Have I not told you so, gentlemen? Besides, it has perhaps been a scheme of her Majesty's to have sought on this occasion for such lowly support. High heads can be seen from a distance; and the cardinal is far—sighted."

"Well," said Porthos, "in the first place, make a bargain with the mercer, and a good bargain, too."

"That's useless," said D'Artagnan; "for I believe if he does not pay us, we shall be well enough paid by another party."

At this moment a sudden noise of footsteps was heard upon the stairs, the door was thrown violently open, and the unfortunate mercer rushed into the chamber in which the council was being held.

"Save me, gentlemen, save me!" cried he. "There are four men come to arrest me! Save me! for the love of Heaven, save me!"

Porthos and Aramis arose.

"One moment," cried D'Artagnan, making them a sign to replace their half-drawn swords—"one moment. On this occasion we don't need courage; we need prudence."

At this moment the four guards appeared at the door of the antechamber; but seeing the four musketeers standing with swords at their sides, they hesitated to advance farther.

"Come in, gentlemen, come in. You are here in my apartment, and we are all faithful servants of the king and the cardinal."

"Then, gentlemen, you will not oppose our executing the orders we have received?" asked the one who appeared to be the leader of the party.

"On the contrary, gentlemen, we would assist you if it were necessary."

"What is he saying?" grumbled Porthos.

"That you are a simpleton," said Athos. "Hold your tongue."

"But you promised me—"said the poor mercer, in a very low voice.

"We can save you only by being free ourselves," replied D'Artagnan in a low and hurried tone; "and if we appear inclined to defend you, they will arrest us with you."

"It seems to me, nevertheless—"

"Come in, gentlemen, come in!" called out D'Artagnan; "I have no motive for defending the gentleman. I saw him to-day for the first time, and he can tell you on what occasion. He came to demand the rent of my lodging.—Is that not true, M. Bonacieux? Answer."

"That's the very truth," cried the mercer; "but the gentleman does not tell you—"

"Silence with respect to me; silence with respect to my friends; silence about the queen, above all, or you will ruin everybody without saving yourself.—Now, gentlemen, come, take away this man!"

And D'Artagnan pushed the half-stupefied mercer among the guards, saying to him,

"You are a shabby old fellow, my dear. You come to demand money of me—of a musketeer!—To prison with him. Gentlemen, once more, fake him to prison, and keep him under key as long as possible; that will give me time to pay him."

The officers were full of thanks, and took away their prey.

"Why, what devilish villainy have you done there," said Porthos, when the head policeman had rejoined his companions, and the four friends were left alone. "Shame, shame, for four musketeers to allow an unfortunate devil who cried out for help to be arrested in their midst. And a gentleman to hobnob with a bailiff!"

"Porthos," said Aramis, "Athos has already told you you are a simpleton, and I am quite of his opinion.—D'Artagnan, you are a great man, and when you occupy M. de Tréville's place, I will come and ask your influence to secure me an abbey."

"Well, I am quite lost!" said Porthos. "Do you approve of what D'Artagnan has just done?"

"Zounds! indeed I do!" said Athos. "I not only approve of what he has done, but I congratulate him upon it."

"And now, gentlemen," said D'Artagnan, without stopping to explain his conduct to Porthos, "all for one, one for all; that is our motto, is it not?"

"And yet—" said Porthos.

"Hold out your hand and swear!" cried Athos and Aramis at the same tune.

Overcome by example, grumbling to himself, Porthos stretched out his hand, and the four friends repeated with one voice the formula dictated by D'Artagnan.

"All for one, one for all."

"That's well! Now let every one retire to his own house," said D'Artagnan, as if he had done nothing but command all his life; "and attention! for from this moment we are at war with the cardinal."

Chapter 10

A Seventeenth-Century Mouse-Trap

The invention of the mouse-trap does not date from our day: as soon as society, in developing, had invented any kind of police, that police in its turn invented mouse-traps.

As perhaps our readers are not familiar with the slang of the Rue de Jerusalem, and as, in all the fifteen years we have been writing, we now for the first time apply this word to the thing, let us explain to them what a mouse-trap is.

When in a house, of whatever kind it may be, an individual suspected of any crime is arrested, the arrest is kept secret. Four or five men are placed in an ambuscade in the first apartment; the door is opened to all who knock; it is closed after them, and they are arrested; so that at the end of two or three days they have in their power almost all the frequenters of the establishment. And this is a mouse-trap.

The apartment of M. Bonacieux, then, became a mouse-trap, and whoever appeared there was taken and examined by the cardinal's people. It goes without saying that as a private passage led to the first floor, on which D'Artagnan lodged, those who called to see him were exempt from all search.

As to D'Artagnan, he did not stir from his apartment. He had converted his chamber into an observatory. From his windows he saw all who came and were caught; then, having removed some of the tiles of his floor and dug into the planking, and nothing remaining but a simple ceiling between him and the room beneath, in which the examinations were made, he heard all that passed between the inquisitors and the accused.

The examinations, preceded by a minute search of the persons arrested, were almost all conceived in this manner:

"Has Madame Bonacieux given anything to you for her husband, or any other person?

"Has Monsieur Bonacieux given anything to you for his wife, or for any other person?

"Has either the one or the other confided anything to you by word of mouth?"

On the evening of the day after the arrest of poor Bonacieux, as Athos had just left D'Artagnan to go to M. de Tréville, as nine o'clock had just struck, and as Planchet, who had not yet made the bed, was beginning his task, a knocking was heard at the street door. The door was instantly opened and shut: some one was caught in the mouse-trap.

D'Artagnan flew to his peek-hole, and laid himself down on the floor at full length to listen.

Cries were soon heard, and then moans, which some one was endeavouring to stifle. There were no questionings.

"The devil!" said D'Artagnan to himself; "it's a woman—they are searching her—she resists—they use force—the scoundrels!"

In spite of all his prudence, D'Artagnan had as much as he could do not to take part in the scene that was going on below.

"But I tell you that I am the mistress of the house, gentlemen! I tell you I am Madame Bonacieux! I tell you I belong to the queen!" cried the unfortunate woman.

"Madame Bonacieux!" murmured D'Artagnan. "Can I have been so lucky as to have found what everybody is looking for?"

"You are the very one we were waiting for," replied the examiners.

The voice became more and more indistinct; a tumultuous movement shook the wainscoting. The victim was resisting as much as one woman can resist four men.

"Pardon, gentlemen, par—"murmured the voice, which could now be heard only in inarticulate sounds.

"They are gagging her, they are going to drag her away," cried D'Artagnan to himself, springing from the floor. "My sword! Good! it is by my side. Planchet!"

"Sir."

"Run and get Athos, Porthos, and Aramis. One of the three will certainly be at home perhaps all three are. Tell them to arm, to come here, and be quick about it! Ah, I remember; Athos is at M. de Tréville's."

"But where are you going, sir, where are you going?"

"I am going down by the window, in order to be there the sooner," cried D'Artagnan. "Do you put back the tiles, sweep the floor, go out at the door, and run where I bid you."

"O sir, sir, you will kill yourself!" cried Planchet.

"Hold your tongue, you stupid fellow," said D'Artagnan; and laying g hold of the window-ledge, he let himself fall from the first story, which luckily was not far, without even scratching himself.

He then went straight to the door and knocked, murmuring,

"I will go and be caught in the mouse-trap in my turn, but woe be o the cats that shall pounce upon such a mouse!"

The knocker had scarcely sounded under the hand of the young man than the tumult ceased, steps approached, the door opened, and D'Artagnan, sword in hand, rushed into M. Bonacieux's apartment, the door of which doubtless moved by a spring, closed after him of itself.

Then those who were still living in Bonacieux's unfortunate

house, together with the nearest neighbours, heard loud cries, stamping of feet, clashing of swords, and much breaking of furniture. Then a moment after those who, surprised by this tumult, had gone to their windows to learn the cause of it, could see the door open, and four men, clothed in black, not come out of it, but fly, like so many frightened crows, leaving on the ground, and on the corners of the furniture, feathers from their wings—that is to say, portions of their clothes and fragments of their cloaks.

D'Artagnan was conqueror, without much trouble, it must be confessed, for only one of the bailiffs was armed, and he defended himself only for form's sake. It is true that the three others had endeavoured to knock the young man down with chairs, stools, and crockery; but two or three scratches made by the Gascon's blade terrified them. Ten minutes had sufficed for their defeat, and D'Artagnan remained master of the field of battle.

The neighbours who had opened their windows, with the indifference peculiar to the inhabitants of Paris in those times of perpetual riots and disturbances, closed them again as soon as they saw the four men in black fly away, their instinct telling them that for the moment all was over.

Besides, it began to grow late, and in those days, as at the present, people went to bed early in the Luxembourg quarter.

On being left alone with Madame Bonacieux, D'Artagnan turned towards her. The poor woman had fallen back upon an armchair in a half-fainting state. D'Artagnan examined her with a rapid glance.

She was a charming woman, of twenty-five or twenty-six years of age, with dark hair, blue eyes, a slightly turned-up nose, admirable teeth, and a pink and opal complexion. There, however, the signs stopped which might have confounded her with a lady of rank. Her hands were white, but pudgy; her feet did not bespeak the woman of quality. Fortunately, D'Artagnan had not yet reached the point of minding these details.

While D'Artagnan was examining Madame Bonacieux, and was, as we have said, close to her, he saw on the ground a fine cambric handkerchief, which he naturally picked up, and on the corner of which he recognized the same cipher that he had seen on the handkerchief, which had nearly caused him and Aramis to cut each other's throats.

From that time D'Artagnan had been cautious with respect to handkerchiefs having arms on them, and he therefore, without a remark, placed the one he had just picked up in Madame Bonacieux's pocket.

At that moment Madame Bonacieux recovered her senses. She opened her eyes, looked around her with terror, saw that the apartment was empty, and that she was alone with her liberator. She immediately held out her hands to him with a smile. Madame Bonacieux had the sweetest smile in the world.

"Ah, sir!" said she, "you have saved me. Allow me to thank you."

"Madame," said D'Artagnan, "I have only done what every gentleman would have done in my place. You owe me, then, no thanks."

"Yes I do, sir, yes I do; and I hope to prove to you that you have not aided an ungrateful person. But what could these men, whom I at first took for robbers, want of me, and why is M. Bonacieux not here?"

"Madame, those men were much more dangerous than any robbers could have been, for they are the agents of the cardinal; and as to your husband, M. Bonacieux, he is not here, because he was yesterday evening taken away to the Bastille."

"My husband in the Bastille!" cried Madame Bonacieux. "Oh, my God, what can he have done? Poor, dear man—he is innocence itself!

And something like a faint smile glided over the still terrified features of the young woman.

"What has he done, madame?" said D'Artagnan. "I believe that his only crime is to have at the same time the good fortune and the misfortune to be your husband."

"But, sir, you know then—"

"I know that you have been carried off, madame. But how did you escape?"

"I took advantage of a moment when they left me alone; and as I had known since morning what to think of my abduction, with the help of my sheets I let myself down from the window; then, as I thought my husband would be at home, I hastened here."

"To place yourself under his protection?"

"Oh no, poor, dear man, I knew very well that he was incapable of defending me; but as he could be otherwise useful to us, I wished to inform him."

"Of what?"

"Oh, that is not my secret; I therefore cannot tell you."

"Besides," said D'Artagnan—"pardon me, madame, if, guard as I am, I remind you of prudence—sides, I believe we are not here in a very proper place for imparting confidences. The men I have tit to flight will return reinforced; if they find us here, we are lost. I have sent, to be sure, for three of my friends, but who knows whether they are at home?"

"Yes, yes; you are right," cried the terrified Madame Bonacieux; "let us fly, let us escape!"

At these words she passed her arm under that of D'Artagnan, and pulled him forward eagerly.

"But whither shall we fly—where escape to?"

"Let us in the first place get away from this house; when clear of it we shall see."

And the young woman and the young man, without taking the trouble to shut the door after them, descended the Rue des Fossoyeurs rapidly, turned into the Rue des Fosses—Monsieur-le-Prince, and did not stop till they came to the Place Saint-Sulpice.

"And now what are we to do, and where do you wish me to take you?" asked D'Artagnan.

"I am quite at a loss how to answer you, I confess," said Madame Bonacieux. "My intention was to inform M. de la Porte, by means of my husband, in order that M. de la Porte might tell us exactly what has taken place at the Louvre in the course of the last three days, and whether there were any danger in presenting myself there."

"But I," said D'Artagnan, "can go and inform M. de la Porte."

"No doubt you could; only there is one drawback in it, and this is that M. Bonacieux is known at the Louvre, and would be allowed to pass; whereas you are not known there, and the gate would be closed against you."

"Ah, bah!" said D'Artagnan; "there is no doubt you have at some wicket of the Louvre a porter who is devoted to you, and who, thanks to a password, would—"

Madame Bonacieux looked earnestly at the young man.

"And if I give you this password," said she, "would you forget it as soon as you had made use of it?"

"By my honour, by the faith of a gentleman!" said D'Artagnan, with an accent so truthful no one could mistake it.

"Then I believe you. You appear to be a brave young man; besides, your fortune, perhaps, will be the result of your devotion."

"I will do, without a promise, and conscientiously, all that I can do to serve the king and be agreeable to the queen. Use me, then, as a friend."

"But I—where shall I go in the meanwhile?"

"Do you know no one to whose house M. de la Porte can go to get you?"

"No, I will trust nobody."

"Stop," said D'Artagnan; "we are near Athos's door. "Yes, here it is." "Who is this Athos?"

"One of my friends."

"But if he should lie at home and see me?"

"He is not at home; and I will carry away the key, after having placed you in his apartment."

"But if he should return?"

"Oh, he won't return; and if he should, he will be told that I have brought a lady with me, and that lady is in his apartment."

"But that will compromise me sadly, you know."

"Of what consequence can it be to you? Nobody knows you. Beside, we are in a situation in which we must not be too particular."

"Come, then, let us go to your friend's house. Where does he live?" "Rue Férou, two steps from here."

"Come, then."

And both resumed their way. As D'Artagnan had foreseen, Athos was not at home. He took the key, which was usually given him as

one of the family, ascended the stairs, and introduced Madame Bonacieux into the little apartment.

"Make yourself at home," said he. "Wait here, fasten the door
inside, and open it to nobody unless you hear three taps like these."
And he taped thrice—two taps close together and pretty hard, the
other after an interval, lighter.

"That is all right," said Madame Bonacieux. "Now it is my turn
to give you my orders."

"I am all attention."

"Present yourself at the wicket of the Louvre, towards the Rue
de l'Echelle, and ask for Germain."

"Well, and then?"

"He will ask you what you want, and you will answer by these two
words—'Tours' and 'Brussels.' He will immediately put himself
under your orders."

"And what shall I order him to do?"

"To go and fetch M. de la Porte, the queen's valet."

"And when he shall have found him, and M. de la Porte has come?"

"You will send him to me."

"Very well; but where and how shall I see you again?"

"Do you, then, wish very much to see me again?"

"Certainly I do."

"Well, let that care be mine, and do not worry."

"I depend upon your word."

"Certainly."

"Very well. Count on me for bringing this about, and have no
fear."

"I may depend on your word?"

"You may."

D'Artagnan bowed to Madame Bonacieux, darting at her the
most loving glance that he could possibly concentrate upon her
charming little person; and while he descended the stairs he heard
the door closed behind him and double-locked. In two bounds he
was at the Louvre. As he entered the wicket of l'Echelle ten o'clock
struck. All the events we have just described had taken place within
half an hour.

Everything happened as Madame Bonacieux said it would. On hearing the password, Germain bowed; ten minutes after La Porte was at the lodge; with two words D'Artagnan told him what was going on, and informed him where Madame Bonacieux was. La Porte assured himself, by having it twice repeated, of the exact address, and set off at a run. He had, however, scarcely gone ten steps before lie returned.

"Young man," said he to D'Artagnan, "I have a piece of advice to give you."

"What is it?"

"You may get into trouble by what has taken place."

"Do you think so?"

"Yes. Have you any friend whose clock is too slow?"

"What then?"

"Go and call upon him, in order that he may give evidence of your having been with him at half-past nine. In law that is called an alibi."

D'Artagnan found this advice prudent. He took to his heels, and was soon at M. de Tréville's; but instead of going into the drawing-room with everybody, he asked to be introduced to M. de Tréville's office. As D'Artagnan was one of the frequenters of the hotel, no difficulty was made in complying with his request, and a servant went to inform M. de Tréville that his young compatriot, having something important to communicate, solicited a private audience. Five minutes after, M. de Tréville was asking D'Artagnan what he could do for him, and to what he was indebted for his visit at so late an hour.

"Pardon me, sir," said D'Artagnan, who had profited by the moment he had been left alone to put back M. de Tréville's clock three-quarters of an hour; "I thought, as it was yet only twenty-five minutes past nine, it was not too late to wait upon you."

"Twenty-five minutes past nine!" cried M. de Tréville, looking at the clock; "why, that's impossible!"

"Look, rather, sir," said D'Artagnan; "the clock shows it."

"That's true," said M. de Tréville; "I should have thought it was later. But what can I do for you?"

Then D'Artagnan told M. de Tréville a long history about the queen. He expressed to him the fears he entertained with respect to her Majesty; he related to him what he had heard of the projects of the cardinal with regard to Buckingham; and all with a tranquillity and sereneness which deceived M. de Tréville the more because he had himself, as we have said, observed something new between the cardinal, the king, and the queen.

As ten o'clock was striking D'Artagnan left M. de Tréville, who thanked him for his information, recommended him to have she service of the king and queen always at heart, and returned to the drawing-room. But at the foot of the stairs D'Artagnan remembered he had forgotten his cane. He consequently rushed up again, re-entered the office, with a turn of his finger set the clock right again, that they might not perceive the next day it had been tampered with; and sure henceforth that he had a witness to prove his alibi, he ran downstairs and soon gained the street.

CHAPTER 11

The Plot Thickens

His visit to M. de Tréville being paid, D'Artagnan, quite thoughtful, took the longest way homewards.

Of what was D'Artagnan thinking, that he strayed thus from his path, gazing at the stars in the heavens, and sometimes sighing, sometimes smiling?

He was thinking of Madame Bonacieux. For an apprentice musketeer the young woman was almost an ideal of love. Pretty, mysterious, initiated into almost all the secrets of the court, which reflected such a charming gravity over her pleasing features, he suspected her of not being insensible to wooing, which is an irresistible charm for novices in love. Besides, D'Artagnan had delivered her from the hands of the demons who wished to search and maltreat her; and this important service had established between them one of those sentiments of gratitude which so easily take on a more tender character.

D'Artagnan, reflecting on his future loves, addressing himself to the beautiful night and smiling at the stars, went up the Rue Cherche-Midi, Chasse-Midi, as it was then called. As he fund himself in the quarter in which Aramis lived, he took it into his head to pay his friend a visit, in order to explain to him why he had sent Planchet to him with a request that he would come instantly to the mouse-trap. Now, Aramis was at home when Planchet came to his abode, he had doubtless hastened to the Rue des Fossoyeurs, and finding nobody but his two companions there, perhaps they would not be able to conceive, any of them, what all this meant. This result required an explanation; at least, so D'Artagnan thought.

D'Artagnan had just passed the Rue Cassette, and already caught sight of the door of his fiend's house, shaded by a mass of sycamore and clematis, which formed a vast arch above it, when he perceived something like a shadow issuing from the Rue Servandoni. This something was enveloped in a cloak, and D'Artagnan at first believed it was a man; but by the smallness of the form, the hesitation of the gait, and the indecision of the step, he soon discovered that it was a woman. Further, this woman, as if not certain of the house she was seeking, lifted up her eyes to look around her, stopped, went a little back, and then returned again. D'Artagnan was perplexed.

The young woman continued to advance, for, in addition to the lightness of her step, which had betrayed her, she had just given a slight cough which betrayed a clear, sweet voice. D'Artagnan believed this cough to be a signal.

Nevertheless, whether this cough had been answered by an equivalent signal which had driven away the hesitation of the nocturnal seeker, or whether she had recognized that she had arrived at the end of her journey, she boldly drew near to Aramis's shutter, and tapped at three equal intervals with her bent finger.

The three blows were scarcely struck when the inside casement was opened, and a light appeared through the panes of the shutter.

At the end of some seconds two sharp taps were heard on the inside. The young woman in the street replied by a single tap, and the shutter was opened a little way.

D'Artagnan then saw that the young woman took from her pocket a white object which she unfolded quickly, and which took the form of a handkerchief. She made her interlocutor look at the corner of this unfolded object.

This immediately recalled to D'Artagnan's mind the handkerchief he had found at the feet of Madame Bonacieux, which had reminded him of the one he had dragged from under Aramis's foot.

"What the devil could that handkerchief mean?"

Placed where he was, D'Artagnan could not see the face of Aramis. We say the face of Aramis, because the young man entertained no doubt that it was his friend who held this dialogue inside with the lady outside. Curiosity prevailed over prudence, and taking advantage of the preoccupation in which the sight of the handkerchief appeared to have plunged the two personages now on the scene, he stole from his hiding—place, and quick as lightning, but stepping with the utmost caution, he went and placed himself close to the angle of the wall, from which his eye could plunge into the interior of the apartment.

Upon gaining this advantage D'Artagnan came near uttering a cry of surprise. It was not Aramis who was conversing with the nocturnal visitor; it was a woman! D'Artagnan, however, could only see enough to recognize the form of her vestments, not enough to distinguish her features.

At the same instant the woman of the apartment drew a second handkerchief from her pocket, and exchanged it for the one which had just been shown to her. Then some words were pronounced by the two women. At length the shutter was closed. The woman who was outside the window turned round, and passed within four steps of D'Artagnan, pulling down the hood of her cloak; but the precaution was too late. D'Artagnan had already recognized Madame Bonacieux.

It must be, then, for some very important affair; and what is the affair of the greatest importance to a pretty woman of twenty-five? Love.

But was it on her own account or on account of another person that she exposed herself to such risks? This was a question the young man asked himself, the demon of jealousy already gnawing at his heart, neither more nor less than at the heart of an accepted lover.

There was, besides, a very simple means of satisfying himself where Madame Bonacieux was going. This was to follow her. The means was so simple that D'Artagnan employed it quite naturally and instinctively.

But at the sight of the young man, who came out from the wall like a statue walking from its niche, and at the noise of the steps which she heard resound behind her, Madame Bonacieux uttered a little cry and fled.

D'Artagnan ran after her. It was not a very difficult thing for him to overtake a woman embarrassed with her cloak. He came up to her before she had traversed a third of the street. The unfortunate woman was exhausted, not by fatigue, but by terror; and when D'Artagnan placed his hand upon her shoulder, she sank upon one knee, crying in a choking voice,

"Kill me, if you will; you shall know nothing!"

D'Artagnan raised her by passing his arm round her waist; but as he felt by her weight she was on the point of fainting, he made haste to reassure her by protestations of devotion. These protestations were nothing for Madame Bonacieux, for such protestations may be made with the worst intentions in the world; but the voice was all. The young woman thought she recognized the sound of that voice. She opened her eyes, cast a quick glance upon the man who had terrified her so, and at once perceiving it was D'Artagnan, she uttered a cry of joy.

Oh, it is you, it is you! Thank God, thank God!"

"Yes, it is I," said D'Artagnan—"it is I, whom God has sent to watch over you."

"Was it with that intention you followed me?"

"No," said D'Artagnan—"no, I confess it; it was chance that threw me in your way. I saw a female knocking at the window of one of my friends."

"One of your friends?" interrupted Madame Bonacieux.

"Without doubt; Aramis is one of my most intimate friends."

"Aramis! Who is he?"

"Come, come, you won't tell me you don't know Aramis?"

"This is the first time I ever heard his name."

"This is the first time, then, that you ever went to that house?"

"Certainly it is."

"And you did not know that it was inhabited by a young man?"

"No."

"My dear Madame Bonacieux, you are charming; but at the same time you are the most mysterious of women."

"Do I lose much by that?"

"No; you are, on the contrary, adorable!"

"Give me your arm, then."

"Most willingly. And now?"

"Now take me with you."

"Where?"

"Where I am going."

"But where are you going?"

"You will see, because you will leave me at the door."

"Shall I wait for you?"

"That will be useless."

"You will return alone, then?"

"Yes."

"Well, madame, I perceive I must act in accordance with your wishes."

D'Artagnan offered his arm to Madame Bonacieux, who took it; half laughing, half trembling, and both went up Rue la Harpe. When they reached there the young woman seemed to hesitate, as she had before done in the Rue Vaugirard. Nevertheless, by certain signs she appeared to recognize a door; and approaching that door,

"And now, sir," she said, "it is here I have business. A thousand thanks for your honourable company, which has saved me from all the dangers to which, alone, I might have been exposed. But the moment has come for you to keep your word; I have reached the place of my destination."

"If you could see my heart," said D'Artagnan, "you would there read in it so much curiosity that you would pity me, and so much love that you would instantly satisfy my curiosity. We have nothing to fear from those who love us."

"You speak very soon of love, sir!" she said, shaking her head.

"That is because love has come suddenly upon me, and for the first tine, and because I am not twenty years old."

"Sir," said the young woman, supplicating him and clasping her hands together—"sir, in the name of Heaven, by a soldier's honour, by the courtesy of a gentleman, depart! There! hear midnight striking; that is the hour at which I am expected."

"Madame," said the young man, bowing, "I can refuse nothing asked of me thus. Be satisfied; I will go."

And as if he felt that only a violent effort would give him the strength to detach himself from the hand he held, he sprang away, running; while Madame Bonacieux knocked, as she had done at the shutter, three slow regular taps. Then, when he had gained the corner of the street, he looked around. The door had been opened and shut again; the mercer's pretty wife had disappeared.

D'Artagnan pursued his way. He had given his word not to watch Madame Bonacieux, and if his life had depended upon the place to which she was going, or the person who should accompany her, D'Artagnan would still have returned home, since he had promised that he would do so. In five minutes he was in the Rue des Fossoyeurs.

"Poor Athos!" said he; "he will never guess what all this means. He must have fallen asleep waiting for me, or else he must have returned home, where he will have learned that a woman had been there. A woman at Athos's house! After all," continued D'Artagnan, "there was certainly one in Aramis's house. All this is very strange; I should like to know how it will all end."

"Badly, sir, badly!" replied a voice, which the young man recognized as Planchet's; for, soliloquizing aloud, as very preoccupied people do, he had entered the alley, at the end of which were the stairs which led to his chamber.

"How badly? What do you mean by that, you stupid fellow?" asked D'Artagnan. "What has happened, then?"

"All sorts of misfortunes."

"What?"

"In the first place, M. Athos is arrested."

"Arrested! Athos arrested! What for?"

"He was found in your lodging; they took him for you."

"And who arrested him?

"The guard brought by the men in black whom you put to flight."

"Why did he not tell them his name? Why did he not tell them he knew nothing about this affair?"

"He took care not to do so, sir. On the contrary, he came up to me, and said, 'It is your master who needs his liberty at this moment, and not I, since he knows everything and I know nothing. They will believe he is arrested, and that will give him time. In three days I will tell them who I am, and they cannot fail to set me at liberty again.'"

"Bravo, Athos! noble heart!" murmured D'Artagnan.

And his legs, already a little fatigued with running about during the day, carried D'Artagnan as fast as they could towards the Rue du Colombier.

M. de Tréville was not at his hotel. His company was on guard at the Louvre; he was at the Louvre with his company.

He must get at M. de Tréville; it was important that he should be informed of what was going on. D'Artagnan resolved to endeavour to get into the Louvre. His costume of a guard in the company of M. des Essarts would, he thought, be a passport for him.

As he was arriving at the end of the Rue Guénégaud he saw, coming out of the Rue Dauphine, two persons whose appearance struck his attention. One was a man, and the other a woman.

The woman had Madame Bonacieux's figure, and the man resembled Aramis so much as to be mistaken for him.

Besides, the woman had on that black cloak, which D'Artagnan could still see outlined upon the shutter of the Rue de Vaugirard, and upon the door of the Rue de la Harpe.

And still further, the man wore the uniform of the musketeers.

The woman's hood was pulled down, and the man held his handkerchief up to his face. Both, as this double precaution indicated—both had an interest, then, in not being recognized.

They followed the bridge. That was D'Artagnan's road, since

D'Artagnan was going to the Louvre. D'Artagnan followed them.

He had not gone twenty steps before he became convinced that the woman was really Madame Bonacieux, and the man Aramis.

He felt at that instant all the suspicions of jealousy agitating his heart.

He was doubly betrayed—by his friend, and by her whom he already loved as a mistress. Madame Bonacieux had sworn by all that was holy that she did not know Aramis, and a quarter of an hour after she had taken this oath he found her hanging on Aramis's arm.

The young man and woman had perceived they were followed, and had redoubled their speed. D'Artagnan hastened on, passed them, then turned on them at the moment they were before the Samaritaine, which was illuminated by a lamp that threw its light over all this part of the bridge.

D'Artagnan stopped before them, and they stopped before him.

"What do you want, sir?" demanded the musketeer, drawing back a step, and with a foreign accent which proved to D'Artagnan that he was deceived in one part of his conjectures at least.

"It is not Aramis!" cried he.

"No, sir, it is not Aramis; and by your exclamation, I perceive you have mistaken me for another, and pardon you."

"You pardon me!" cried D'Artagnan.

"Yes," replied the unknown. "Allow me, then, to pass on, since it is not with me you have anything to do."

"You are right, sir; it is not with you I have anything to do. It is with madame here."

"With madame! You do not know her!" replied the stranger.

"You are mistaken, sir; I know her very well."

"Ah," said Madame Bonacieux, in a tone of reproach—"ah, sir, I had the promise of a soldier and the word of a gentleman. I thought I might have depended upon them!"

"And I, madame!" said D'Artagnan, embarrassed; "you promised me—"

"Take my arm, madame," said the stranger, "and let us proceed on our way."

D'Artagnan, however, stupefied, cast down, annihilated by all

that had happened, stood, with his arms crossed, before the musketeer and Madame Bonacieux.

The musketeer advanced a step or two and pushed D'Artagnan
aside with his hand.

D'Artagnan made a spring backwards, and drew his sword.

At the same time, and with the rapidity of lightning, the
unknown drew his.

"In the name of Heaven, milord!" cried Madame Bonacieux,
throwing herself between the combatants, and seizing the swords
with her hands.

"Milord!" cried D'Artagnan, enlightened by a sudden idea—
"milord! Pardon me, sit, but are you not—"

"Milord, the Duke of Buckingham!" said Madame Bonacieux
In an undertone; "and now you may ruin us all."

"Milord—madame—I ask a hundred pardons. But I love her,
milord, and was jealous. You know what it is to love, milord. Pardon
me, and then tell me how I can risk my life to serve your grace."

"You are a good young man!" said Buckingham, holding out his
hand to D'Artagnan, who pressed it respectfully. "You offer me your
services; I accept them. Follow us at a distance of twenty paces to
the Louvre, and if any one watches us, slay him!"

D'Artagnan placed his naked sword under his arm, allowed she
duke and Madame Bonacieux to proceed twenty steps, and ten followed them, ready to carry out to the letter the instructions of the
noble and elegant minister of Charles I.

But fortunately the young seid had no opportunity to give the
duke this proof of his devotion, and the young woman and the handsome musketeer entered the Louvre by the wicket of l'Echelle without any interference.

As for D'Artagnan, he immediately repaired to the tavern of the
Pomme de Pin, where he found Porthos and Aramis, who were waiting for him. But, without giving them any explanation of the inconvenience he had caused them, he told them that he had himself terminated the affair in which he had thought for a moment he should
need their assistance.

And now, carried away as we are by our story, we must leave our three friends to return each to his own home, and follow the Duke of Buckingham and his guide through the windings of the Louvre.

CHAPTER 12

George Villiers, Duke Of Buckingham

Madame Bonacieux and the duke entered the Louvre without difficulty. Madame Bonacieux was known to belong to the queen; the duke wore the uniform of the musketeers of M. de Tréville, who, as we have said, were that evening on guard.

Buckingham, on being left alone, walked towards a mirror. His musketeer's uniform became him wonderfully well.

At this instant a door concealed in the tapestry was opened, and a woman appeared. Buckingham saw this apparition in the glass. He uttered a cry. It was the queen!

Anne of Austria advanced two steps. Buckingham threw himself at her feet, and before the queen could prevent him, kissed the hem of her robe.

"Duke, you already know that it is not I who caused you to be written to."

"Yes, yes, madame! yes, your Majesty!" cried the duke. "I know that I must have been mad, senseless, to believe that snow would become animated or marble warm. But what then? They who love easily believe in love; besides, this journey is not wholly lost, since I see you."

"Yes," replied Anne; "but you know why and how I see you, milord? Because, insensible to all my sufferings, you persist in remaining in a city where, by remaining, you run the risk of your own life, and make me run the risk of losing my honour. I see you to tell you that everything separates us—the depths of the sea, the enmity of kingdoms, the sanctity of vows. It is sacrilege to struggle against so many things, milord. In short, I see you to tell you that we must never see each other again."

"Speak on, madame, speak on, queen," said Buckingham; "the

sweetness of your voice covers the harshness of your words. You talk of sacrilege; but the sacrilege lies in the separation of two hearts formed by God for each other."

"Milord," cried the queen, "you forget that I have never told you I loved you."

"Silence, silence!" cried the duke. "If I am happy in an error, do not have the cruelty to deprive me of it. You have told me yourself, madame, that I have been drawn into a snare; and I, perhaps, shall leave my life in it—for, strangely enough, I have for some time had a presentiment that I shall shortly die." And the duke smiled, with a smile at once sad and charming.

"Oh, my God!" cried Anne of Austria, with an accent of terror which proved how much greater was the interest she took in the duke than she ventured to tell.

"I do not tell you this, madame, to terrify you; no, what I say to you is even ridiculous; and, believe me, I do not heed such dreams. But the words you have just spoken, the hope you have almost given me, will have richly paid for all, were it even my life."

"Oh, but I," said Anne— "I, duke, have had presentiments like-wise; I have had dreams. I dreamed that I saw you lying bleeding, wounded."

"In the left side, was it not, and with a knife?" interrupted Buck-ingham.

"Yes, it was so, milord, it was so—in the left side, and with a knife. Who can possibly have told you I had had that dream? I have imparted it to no one but my God, and only then in my prayers."

"I ask for no more. You love me, madame. It is enough."

"I love you! I?"

"Yes, yes. Would God send the same dreams to you as to me if you did not love me? Should we have the same presentiments if our exis-tences did not meet in our hearts? You love me, my queen, and you will weep for me?"

"Oh, my God, my God!" cried Anne of Austria, "this is more than I can bear. In the name of Heaven, duke, leave me—go! do not know whether I love you or do not love you, but what I know is, that I will not be a perjured woman. Take pity on me, then, and go. Oh, if you are struck in France, if you die in France, if I could imagine that your love for me was the cause of your death, nothing could ever console me; I should go mad. Depart, then; go, I implore you!"

"Oh, how beautiful you are so! Oh, how I love you!" said Buckingham.

"Oh, but go—go back, I implore you, and return later on! Come as ambassador, come as minister, come surrounded with guards who will defend you, with servants who will watch over you, and then, then I shall no longer fear for your life, and I shall be happy in seeing you again."

"Oh, is this true, is what you say true?"

"Yes."

"Then, some pledge of your indulgence, some object which, coming from you, may assure me that I have not dreamed; something you have worn, and that I may wear in my turn—a ring, a necklace, a chain!"

"Will you go then, will you go, if I give you what you ask fox?"

"Yes."

"Thus very instant?"

"Yes."

"You will leave France, you will return to England?"

"I will, I swear to you I will."

"Wait, then, wait."

And Anne of Austria went into her apartment, and came out again almost immediately, holding a casket in her hand made of rosewood, with her monogram incrusted in gold.

"Here, milord, here," said she; "keep this in memory of me."

Buckingham took the casket, and fell a second time on his knees.

"You promised me you would go back," said the queen.

"And I keep my word. Your hand, madame, your hand, and depart."

Anne of Austria stretched forth her hand, closing her eyes, and leaned the other upon Estefana, for she felt her strength was about to fail her.

Buckingham pressed his lips passionately to that beautiful hand, and then rising, said,

"Within six months, if I am not dead, I shall have seen you again, madame, even if I have upset the whole world for it."

And, faithful to the promise he had made, he rushed out of the apartment.

In the corridor he met Madame Bonacieux, who was waiting for him, and who, with the same precautions and the same good fortune, led him out of the Louvre.

Chapter 13

The Man Of Meung

There was in all this, as may have been noticed, one personage of whom, notwithstanding his precarious position, we have appeared to take but very little notice. This personage was M. Bonacieux, the respectable martyr of the political and amorous intrigues which were Pelting into such a tangle in this gallant and chivalric period.

The officers who had arrested him conducted him straight to the Bastile, where, all of a tremble, he was made to pass before a platoon of soldiers who were loading their muskets.

Thence, introduced into a half-subterranean gallery, he became, on the part of those who had brought him, the object of the grossest insults and the harshest treatment. The bailiffs perceived that they had not to deal with a nobleman, and they treated him like a very beggar.

At the end of half an hour, or thereabouts, an officer came to put an end to his tortures, but not to his anxiety, by giving the order to lead M. Bonacieux to the examination chamber.

Ordinarily, prisoners were questioned in their own cells, but with M. Bonacieux they did not use so many formalities.

In the evening, at the moment when he had made his mind up to lie down upon the bed, he heard steps in his corridor. These steps drew near to his cell, the door was thrown open, and the guards appeared.

"Follow me," said an officer, who came behind the guards.

"Ah, my God, my God!" murmured the poor mercer, "now, indeed, I am lost!"

And, mechanically and without resistance, he followed the guards who came for him.

He passed along the corridor, crossed a first court, then a second art of the building. At length, at the gate of the outer court, he found a carriage surrounded by four guards on horseback. They made him get into this carriage, the officer placed himself by his side, the door was locked, and both were left in a rolling prison.

The carriage was put in motion as slowly as a funeral car. Through the padlocked gratings the prisoner could see the houses and the pavement, that was all; but, true Parisian as he was, Bonacieux could recognize every street by the mounting stones, the sings, and the lamps.

The carriage, which had been stopped for a minute, resumed its way, threaded the Rue Saint Honoré, turned the Rue des Bons Enfants, and stopped before a low door.

The door opened, two guards received Bonacieux in their arms from the officer who supported him. They carried him along an alley, up a flight of stairs, and deposited him in an antechamber.

All these movements had been effected mechanically, as far as he was concerned. He had moved along as if in a dream; he had had a glimpse of objects as though through a fog; his ears had perceived sounds without comprehending them; he might have been executed at that moment without his making a single gesture in his own defence, or his uttering a cry to implore mercy.

He therefore remained upon the bench, with his back leaning against the wall and his hands hanging down, exactly on the spot where the guards had placed him.

On looking round him, however, as he could see no threatening object, as nothing indicated that he ran any real danger, as the bench was comfortably covered with a well-stuffed cushion, as the wall was ornamented with beautiful Cordova leather, and as large red damask curtains, held back by gold fastenings, floated before the window, he perceived by degrees that his fear was exaggerated, and he began to turn his head to the right and the left, upwards and downwards.

At this movement, which nobody opposed, he gained a little

courage, and ventured to draw up one leg and then the other. At length, with the help of both hands, he raised himself up upon the bench, and found himself upon his feet.

At that moment an officer of pleasant appearance opened a door, continued to exchange some words with a person in the next room and then came up to the prisoner.

"Is your name Bonacieux?" said he.

"Yes, officer," stammered the mercer, more dead than alive, "at your service."

"Come in," said the officer.

And he moved aside to let the mercer pass. The latter obeyed without reply, and entered the room, where it appeared he was expected.

It was a large, dose, and stifling cabinet, the walls furnished with, arms offensive and defensive, and where there was already a fire, although it was scarcely the end of September. A square table, covered with books and papers, upon which was unrolled an immense plan of the city of Rochelle, occupied the centre of the apartment.

Standing before the fireplace was a man of middle height, of a haughty, proud mien, with piercing eyes, a broad brow, and a thin face, which was made still longer by a royal (or imperial, as it is now called), surmounted by a pair of moustaches. Although this man was scarcely thirty-six or thirty-seven years of age, hair, moustaches, and royal all were growing grey. This man, though without a sword, had all the appearance of a soldier; and his buff leather boots, still slightly covered with dust, showed that he had been on horseback in the course of the day.

This man was Armand Jean Duplessis, Cardinal Richelieu.

At first sight nothing indicated the cardinal, and it was impossible for those who did not know his face to guess in whose presence they were.

"Is this Bonacieux?" asked he, after a moment of silence.

"Yes, monseigneur," replied the officer.

"Very well. Give me those. papers, and leave us."

The officer took the papers pointed out from the table, gave them ate him who asked for them, bowed to the ground, and retired.

"Do you know who carried off your wife?" said the cardinal.

"No, monseigneur."

"You have suspicions, nevertheless?"

"Yes, monseigneur."

"Your wife has escaped. Did you know that?"

"No, monseigneur."

"When you went to fetch your wife from the Louvre, did you always return directly home?"

"Scarcely ever. She had business to transact with linen-drapers, to whose shops I escorted her."

"And how many were there of these linen-drapers?'

"Two, monseigneur."

"And where did they live?"

"One Rue de Vaugirard, the other Rue de la Harpe."

"Did you go into these houses with her?"

"Never, monseigneur; I waited at the door."

"And what excuse did she make for thus going in alone?"

"She gave me none. She told me to wait, and I waited."

"Should you know those doors again?"

"Yes."

"Do you know the numbers?"

"Yes."

"What are they?"

"No. 25 in the Rue de Vaugirard; 75 in the Rue de la Harpe."

"Very well," said the cardinal.

At these words he took up a silver bell and rang it. The officer entered.

"Go," said he in a subdued voice, "and find Rochefort. Tell him to come to me immediately, if he has returned."

"The Count is here," said the officer, "and wishes to speak instantly with your Eminence."

"Let him come in, then—let him come in, then!" said the cardinal eagerly.

The officer rushed out of the apartment with that alacrity which all the cardinal's servants displayed in obeying him.

"To your Eminence!" murmured Bonacieux, rolling his eyes round in astonishment.

Five seconds had not elapsed after the disappearance of the officer when the door opened and a new personage entered.

"It is he!" cried Bonacieux.

"He! What he?" asked the cardinal.

"The man who took away my wife!"

The cardinal rang a second time. The officer reappeared

"Place this man in the care of his two guards, and let him wait till I send for him."

The officer took Bonacieux by the arm, and led him into the antechamber, where he found his two guards.

The newly-introduced personage followed Bonacieux impatiently with his eyes till he was gone out, and the moment the door closed he advanced eagerly toward the cardinal and said,

"They have seen each other."

"Who?" asked his Eminence.

"He and she."

"The queen and the duke?" cried Richelieu.

"Yes."

"How did it take place?"

"At half-past twelve the queen was with her women—"

"Where?"

"In her bedchamber—"

"Go on."

"When some one came and brought her a handkerchief from her *dame de lingerie.*"

"And then?"

"The queen immediately exhibited strong emotion, and, in spite of the rouge which covered her face, grew pale."

"Go on, go on! "

"She, however, rose, and with a trembling voice, 'Ladies,' she said, 'wait for me ten minutes; I shall soon return.' She then opened the door of her alcove and went out."

"Did none of her women accompany her?"

"Only Doña Estefana."

"And she afterwards returned?"

"Yes; but only to take a little rosewood casket, with her monogram upon it, and to go out again immediately."

"And when she finally returned, did she bring that casket with her?"

"No."

"Does Madame de Lannoy know what was in that casket?"

"Yes; the diamond studs which his Majesty gave the queen."

"And she came back without this casket?"

"Yes."

"Madame de Lannoy, then, is of the opinion that she gave them to Buckingham?"

"She is sure of it."

"Do you know where the Duchesse de Chevreuse and the Duke of Buckingham were concealed?"

"No, monseigneur. My people could tell me nothing positive in regard to that."

"But I know."

"You, monseigneur?"

"Yes, or at least I suspect. They were, one in the Rue de Vaugirard, No. 25, the other in the Rue de la Harpe, No. 75."

"Does your Eminence wish them both to be arrested?"

"It is too late; they will be gone."

"But still we can make sure of it."

"Take ten men of my guards, and search both houses thoroughly."

"Instantly, monseigneur."

The cardinal, upon being left alone, reflected for an instant, and then rang the bell a third time.

The same officer appeared.

"Bring the prisoner in again," said the cardinal.

M. Bonacieux was introduced anew, and upon a sign from the cardinal the officer retired.

"You have deceived me!" said the cardinal sternly.

"I," cried Bonacieux—"I deceive your Eminence!"

"Your wife, when going to Rue de Vaugirard and Rue de la Harpe, did not go to any linen-drapers."

"Then where, in God's name, did she go?"

"She went to the house of the Duchesse de Chevreuse, and she went to the Duke of Buckingham's."

"Yes," cried Bonacieux, recalling all the circumstances—"yes, that's it. Your Eminence is right. I told my wife several times that it was surprising that linen-drapers should live in such houses—in houses that had no signs—and every time she began to laugh. Ah, monseigneur!" continued Bonacieux, throwing himself at his Eminence's feet "ah, how truly you are the cardinal, the great cardinal, the man of genius whom all the world reveres!"

However contemptible might be the triumph gained over so vulgar a being as Bonacieux, the cardinal did not the less enjoy it for an instant. Then, almost immediately, as if a new thought had entered his mind, a smile passed over his lips, and reaching out his hand to the mercer,

"Rise, my friend," said he; "you are an honest man."

"The cardinal has touched me with his hand! I have touched the hand of the great man!" cried Bonacieux. "The great man has called me his friend!"

"Yes, my friend, yes," said the cardinal, with that paternal tone which he sometimes knew how to assume, but which deceived only those who did not know him; "and as you have been unjustly suspected—well, you must be indemnified. Here!, take this purse of a hundred pistoles, and pardon me."

"I pardon you, monseigneur!" said Bonacieux, hesitating to take the purse, fearing, doubtless, that this pretended gift was only a joke. "But you are free to have me arrested, you are free to have me tortured, you are free to have me hung. You are the master, and I should not have the least word to say about it. Pardon you, monseigneur! you cannot mean that."

"Ah, my dear Monsieur Bonacieux, you are generous in this matter, and I thank you for it. So you will take this purse, and you will go away without being too much dissatisfied with your treatment?"

"I shall go away enchanted."

"Farewell, then—that is to say, for the present, for I hope we shall meet again."

"Whenever monseigneur wishes. I am always at his Eminence's orders."

"And that will be frequently, I assure you, for I have found something extremely agreeable in your conversation."

"O monseigneur!"

"Au revoir, Monsieur Bonacieux, *au revoir!"*

And the cardinal made him a sign with his hand, to which Bonacieux replied by bowing to the ground. He then backed himself out, and when he was in the antechamber the cardinal heard him, in his enthusiasm, crying aloud, "Long life to monseigneur! Long life to his Eminence! Long life to the great cardinal!" The cardinal listened with a smile to this vociferous manifestation of M. Bonacieux's enthusiasm; and then, when Bonacieux's cries were no longer audible, "Good!" said he; "here's a man who, henceforward, would lay down his life for me."

Left alone, the cardinal sat down again, wrote a letter, which he sealed with his private seal, then rang the bell. The officer entered for the fourth time.

"Have Vitray sent to me," said he, "and tell him to be ready for a journey."

An instant after the man he required was before him, booted and spurred.

"Vitray," said he, "you will go with all speed to London. You must not stop an instant on the way. You will deliver this letter to milady. Here is an order for two hundred pistoles; call upon my treasurer and get the money. You shall have as much again if you are back within six days, and have executed your commission well."

The messenger, without replying a single word, bowed, took the letter, with the order for the two hundred pistoles, and went out.

These were the contents of the letter:

"Milady,—Be at the first ball at which the Duke of Buckingham shall be present. He will wear on his doublet twelve diamond studs, Get as near to him as you can, and cut off two of them.

"As soon as these studs are in your possession, inform me."

CHAPTER 14

Magistrates And Soldiers

It is well known how violent the king's prejudices were against the queen, and how skilfully these prejudices were kept up by the cardinal, who, in affairs of intrigue, mistrusted women much more than men. One of the principal causes of this prejudice was the friendship of Anne of Austria for Madame de Chevreuse. These two women gave him more uneasiness than the war with Spain, the quarrel with England, or the embarrassment of the finances. In his eyes and to his perfect conviction, Madame de Chevreuse not only served the queen in her political intrigues, but—and this troubled him still more—in her love affairs.

At the first word the cardinal uttered concerning Madame de Chevreuse— who, though exiled to Tours, and believed to be in that city, had come to Paris, remained there five days, and had outwitted the police—the king flew into a furious passion. Although capricious and unfaithful, the king wished to be called Louis the Just and Louis the Chaste. Posterity will have a difficulty in understanding this character, which history explains only by facts and never by reasonings.

But when the cardinal added that not only Madame de Chevreuse had been in Paris, but also that the queen had communicated with her by the means of one of those mysterious correspondences which at that tune was called a cabal, Louis XIII could contain himself no longer; he took a step toward the queen's apartment, showing that pale and mute indignation which, when it broke out, led this prince to the commission of the coldest cruelty.

And yet, in all this, the cardinal had not yet said a word about the Duke of Buckingham. But deeming that the moment was now right, he said: "Sire, Buckingham has been in Paris five days, and left it only this morning"

It is impossible to form an idea of the impression these few words made upon Louis XIII. He grew pale and red alternately.

"Buckingham in Paris!" cried he; "and what does he come to do there?"

"To conspire, no doubt, with your enemies, the Huguenots and the Spaniards."

"No, zounds, no! To conspire against my honour with Madame de Chevreuse, Madame de Longueville, and the Condés."

"O sire, what an idea! The queen is too prudent, and, besides, loves your Majesty too well."

"Woman is weak, cardinal," said the king; "and as to loving me much, I have my own opinion respecting that love."

"I none the less maintain," said the cardinal, "that the Duke of Buckingham came to Paris for a project purely political."

"And I am sure that he came for quite another purpose, cardinal. But if the queen be guilty, let her tremble!"

"I believe, and I repeat it to your Majesty, that the queen conspires against her king's power, but I have not said against his honour."

"And I—I tell you against both; I tell you the queen does not love me; I tell you she loves another; I tell you she loves that infamous Buckingham! Why did you not have him arrested while he was in Paris?"

"Arrest the duke! arrest the prime minister of King Charles II. Can you think of it, sire? What a scandal! And suppose, then, the suspicions of your Majesty, which I still continue to doubt, should prove to have any foundation, what a terrible disclosure, what a earful scandal!"

"But since he played the part of a vagabond or a thief, he should have been—"

Louis XIII stopped, terrified at what he was to say; while Richelieu, stretching out his neck, waited in vain for the word which had died on the lips of the king.

"He should have been—"

"Nothing," said the king, "nothing. But all the time he was in Paris you, of course, did not lose sight of him?"

"No, sire."

"Where did he lodge?"

"Rue de la Harpe, No. 75"

"Where is that?"

"Towards the Luxembourg."

"And you are certain that the queen and he did not see each other?"

"I believe the queen to have too high a sense of her duty, sire. And there is a simple way to make sure."

"What is that?"

"Give a ball; you know how much the queen loves dancing." Then the cardinal added,—"By the way, sire, do not forget to tell her Majesty, the evening before the ball, that you would like to see how her diamond studs become her."

CHAPTER 15

Bonacieux's Household

When the cardinal mentioned the diamond studs, Louis XIII was struck with his insistence, and began to fancy that this recommendation concealed some mystery.

He went, then, to the queen, and, according to his custom, approached her with new threats against those who surrounded her. Anne of Austria hung down her head, allowed the torrent to flow on without replying, and hoped that it would finally cease of itself. But this was not what Louis XIII wanted. Louis XIII wanted a discussion, from which some light or other might break, convinced as he was that the cardinal was practising some dissimulation, and was preparing for him one of those terrible surprises which his Eminence was so skilful in getting up. He arrived at this end by his persistence in accusation.

"But," cried Anne of Austria, tired of these vague attacks—"but, sire, you do not tell me all that you have in your heart. What have I done, then? Let me know what crime I have committed."

The king, attacked in so direct a manner, did not know what to answer. He thought that this was the moment to express the desire which he was to make only on the eve of the ball.

"Madame," said he, with dignity, "there will shortly be a ball at the City Hall. I wish that, in honour to our worthy provosts, you should appear at it in state dress, and particularly ornamented with the diamond studs which I gave you on your birthday. That is my answer."

It was a terrible answer. She became excessively pale, leaned her beautiful hand upon a stand, a hand which then appeared like one of wax, and looking at the king, with terror in her eyes, she was unable to reply by a single syllable.

"You hear, madame," said the king, who enjoyed this embarrassment to its full extent, but without guessing the cause—"you hear, madame?"

"Yes, sire, I hear," stammered the queen.

"Very well," said the king, retiring— "very well; I count on it."

The queen made a curtsy, less from etiquette than because her knees were sinking under her.

"I am lost," murmured the queen, "lost! for the cardinal knows all, and it is he who urges on the king, who as yet knows nothing, but will soon know everything. I am lost! My God, my God!"

She knelt upon a cushion and prayed, with her head buried between her palpitating arms.

Thus, while contemplating the misfortune which threatened her and the abandonment in which she was left, she broke out into sobs and tears.

"Can I be of no service to your Majesty?" said all at once a voice full of sweetness and pity.

The queen turned quickly round, for there could be no mistake in the tone of that voice. It was a friend who spoke thus.

In fact, at one of the doors which opened into the queen's apartment appeared the pretty Madame Bonacieux. She had been engaged in arranging the dresses and linen in a closet when the king entered. She could not get out, and had heard all.

The queen uttered a piercing cry at finding herself discovered, for in her trouble she did not at first recognize the young woman who had been given to her by La Porte.

"Oh, fear nothing, madame I" said the young woman, clasping her hands, and weeping herself at the queen's sorrow; "I am your Majesty's, body and soul, and however far I may be from you, however inferior may be my position, I believe I have discovered a means of extricating your Majesty from your trouble."

"You! O heaven, you!" cried the queen; "but look me in the face. I am betrayed on all sides. Can I trust in you?"

"O madame!" cried the young woman, falling on her knees, "upon my soul, I am ready to die for your Majesty."

This expression came from tie very bottom of the heart, and, like the first, there was no mistaking it.

"Yes," continued Madame Bonacieux — "yes, there are traitors here; but by the holy name of the Virgin, I swear that none is more devoted to your Majesty than I am. Those studs which the king speaks of, you gave them to the Duke of Buckingham, did you not? Those studs were in a little rosewood box, which he held under his arm? Am I mistaken? Is it not so, madame?"

"Yes."

"Well, those studs," continued Madame Bonacieux, "we must have them back again."

"Yes, without doubt, it is necessary," cried the queen. "But what can be done? How can it be effected?"

"Some one must be sent to the duke."

"But who, who? In whom can I trust?"

"Place confidence in me, madame. Do me that honour, my queen, and I will find a messenger."

"But I must write."

"Oh yes; that is indispensable. Two words from the hand of your Majesty and your own private seal."

The queen ran to a little table, upon which were pens, ink, and paper. She wrote two lines, sealed the letter with her private seal and gave it to Madame Bonacieux.

"And now," said the queen, "we are forgetting one very necessary thing."

"What is that, madame?'

"Money."

Madame Bonacieux blushed.

Anne of Austria ran to her jewel-case.

"Here," said she—"here is a ring of great value, as I have been told. It came from my brother, the king of Spain. It is mine, and I am at liberty to dispose of it. Take this ring, and turn it into money."

"In an hour you shall be obeyed, madame."

"You see the address," said the queen, speaking so low that Madame Bonacieux could hardly hear what she said—"To my Lord Duke of Buckingham, London."

"The letter shall be given to him."

"Generous girl!" cried Anne of Austria.

Madame Bonacieux kissed the queen's hands, concealed the paper in the bosom of her dress, and disappeared with the lightness of a bird.

Ten minutes afterwards she was at home. As she had not seen her husband since his liberation, she was ignorant of the change that had taken place in him with respect to the cardinal—a change which had since been strengthened by two or three visits from the Comte de Rochefort, who had become Bonacieux's best friend, and who hard persuaded him without great difficulty that nothing culpable had been intended by the carrying off of his wife, but that it was only a piece of political precaution.

She found Bonacieux alone.

Madame Bonacieux offered him her forehead to kiss.

"Let us talk a little," said she.

"What!" said Bonacieux, astonished.

"Yes; I have something of great importance to tell you."

"What!, What brings you to me? Is it not the desire of seeing a husband again from whom you have been separated for a week?" asked the mercer, very much piqued.

"Yes, that first, and other things afterwards."

"Speak, then."

"You must set out immediately. I will give you a paper which you must not part with on any account, and which you will deliver into the proper hands."

"And where am I to go?"

"London."

"I go to London! You are joking. I have nothing to do in London."

"But others require that you should go there."

"But who are those others? I warn you that I will never again work in the dark, and that I will know not only to what I expose myself, but for whom I expose myself."

"An illustrious person sends you, an illustrious person awaits you. The recompense will exceed your expectations; that is all I promise you."

"More intrigues! nothing but intrigues! Thank you, madame; I am aware of them now. The cardinal has enlightened me on that head."

"The cardinal?" cried Madame Bonacieux. "Have you seen the cardinal?"

"He sent for me," answered the mercer proudly.

"He ill-treated you, then? He threatened you?"

"He gave me his hand, and he called me his friend—his friend! Do you hear that, madame? I am a friend of the great cardinal!"

"Of the great cardinal!"

"I am sorry for it, madame, but I acknowledge no other power than that of the great man whom I have the honour to serve."

"Ah, you are a cardinalist, then, sir, are you?" cried she; "and you serve the party of those who ill—treat your wife and insult your queen?"

"Private interests are as nothing before the interests of all. I am for those who are saving the state," said Bonacieux emphatically.

"And do you know what that state is you talk about?" demanded Madame Bonacieux, shrugging her shoulders. "Be satisfied with being a plain, straightforward bourgeois, and turn your attention toward that side which holds out the greatest advantages."

"Eh, eh!" said Bonacieux, slapping a plump, round bag, which gave back a silvery sound; "what do you think of this, my lady preacher?"

"Where does that money come from?"

"Can't you guess?"

"From the cardinal?"

"From him, and from my friend the Comte de Rochefort. But what do you require of me then? Come, let us see."

"I have told you. You must set out instantly, sir; you must accomplish loyally the commission with which I deign to charge you; and on that condition I pardon everything, I forget everything; and still further"—and she held out her hand to him—"I give you my love again."

"But, my dear love, reflect a little upon what you require of me. London is far from Paris, very far, and perhaps the commission with which you charge me is not without dangers?"

"Of what consequence is that, if you avoid them?"

"Well, then, Madame Bonacieux," said the mercer—"well, then, I positively refuse. Intrigues terrify me."

Bonacieux fell into a profound reflection. He turned the two angers in his brain—the cardinal's and the queen's. The cardinal's predominated enormously.

"Well, I will give it up, then," said the young woman, sighing. "It is well as it is; say no more about it."

"Supposing, at least, you should tell me what I should have to do in London," replied Bonacieux.

"It is of no use for you to know anything about it," said the young woman, who drew back now by an instinctive mistrust. "It was about one of those follies of interest to women, a purchase by which much might have been gained."

But the more the young woman fought shy of committing herself, the more important Bonacieux conceived to be the secret which she declined to communicate to him. He resolved, then, that instant to hasten to the Comte de Rochefort, and tell him that the queen was looking for a messenger to send to London.

"Pardon me for leaving you, my dear Madame Bonacieux," said he; "but not knowing you would come to see me, I had made an engagement with a friend. I shall soon return; and if you will wait only x few minutes for me, as soon as I have concluded my business with that friend, I will come to get you; and as it is growing late, I will conduct you back to the Louvre."

"No, thank you, sir; you are not brave enough to be of any use to me whatever," replied Madame Bonacieux. "I shall return very safely to the Louvre by myself."

"As you please, Madame Bonacieux," said the mercer. "Shall I have the pleasure of seeing you soon again?"

"Yes; next week I hope my duties will afford me a little liberty, and I will take advantage of it to come and set things to rights here, as they must be somewhat upset."

"Very well; I shall expect you. You are not angry with me?"

"Who?—I? Oh, not the least in the world."

"Farewell till then."

"Till then."

Bonacieux kissed his wife's hand and set off at a quick pace.

"Well," said Madame Bonacieux, when her husband had shut the street door and she found herself alone, "the only thing still lacking that fool was to become a cardinalist! And I, who have answered for him to the queen—I, who have promised my poor mistress—ah, my God! my God! she will take me for one of those wretches who swarm the palace, and are placed about her as spies! Ah, Monsieur Bonacieux, I never did love you much, but now it is worse than ever. I hate you! and by my word you shall pay for this!"

At the moment she spoke these words a rap on the ceiling made her raise her head, and a voice which reached her through the ceiling cried,

"Dear Madame Bonacieux, open the little side door for me, and will come down to you."

CHAPTER 16

The Lover And The Husband

"Ah, madame," said D'Artagnan, as he entered by the door which the young woman had opened for him, "allow me to tell you that you have a sorry husband there."

"Then you overheard our conversation?" asked Madame Bonacieux eagerly, and looking at D'Artagnan with much uneasiness.

"The whole of it."

"But, my God I how could you do that?"

"By a method known to myself, and by which I likewise overheard the more animated conversation which you had with the cardinal's bailiffs."

"And what did you understand by what we said?"

"A thousand things. In the first place, that, fortunately, your husband is a simpleton and a fool. In the next place, that you are an trouble, of which I am very glad, as it gives me an opportunity of placing myself at your service; and God knows I am ready to throw myself into the fire for you. And that the queen wants a brave, intelligent, devoted man to make a journey to London for her. I have, at least, two of the three qualities you stand in need of, and here I am."

Madame Bonacieux made no reply, but her heart beat with joy, and a secret hope shone in her eyes.

"And what pledge can you give me," asked she, "if I consent to confide this message to you?"

"My love for you. Speak! command! What must I do?"

"But this secret is not mine, and I cannot reveal it in this manner."

"Why, you were going to confide it to M. Bonacieux," said D'Artagnan in vexation.

"As we confide a letter to the hollow of a tree, to the wing of a pigeon, or the collar of a dog."

"And yet—you see plainly that I love you."

"You say so."

"I am an honourable man."

"I believe so."

"I am brave."

"Oh, I am sure of that."

"Then put me to the proof."

"Listen," said she; "I yield to your protestations, I submit to your assurances. But I swear to you, before God who hears us, that if you betray me, and my enemies pardon me, I will kill myself while accusing you of my death."

"And I—I swear to you before God, madame," said D'Artagnan, "that if I am taken while accomplishing the orders you give me, I will die sooner than do anything or say anything that may compromise any one."

Then the young woman confided to him the terrible secret, a part of which had already been revealed to him, by chance, in front of the Samaritaine.

This was their mutual declaration of love.

D'Artagnan was radiant with joy and pride. This secret which he possessed, this woman whom he loved—confidence and love made him a giant.

"But still there is another thing," said Madame Bonacieux.

"What is that?" asked D'Artagnan, seeing that Madame Bonacieux hesitated to proceed.

"You have, perhaps, no money?"

"Perhaps is too much," said D'Artagnan, smiling.

"Then," replied Madame Bonacieux, opening a cupboard and taking from it the very bag which half an hour before her husband had caressed so affectionately, "take this bag."

"The cardinal's?" cried D'Artagnan, breaking into a loud laugh, he having heard, as may be remembered, thanks to his broken floor, every syllable of the conversation between the mercer and his wife.

"The cardinal's," replied Madame Bonacieux. "You see it makes a very respectable appearance."

"Zounds!" cried D'Artagnan, "it will be a doubly amusing affair to save the queen with his Eminence's money!"

"You are an amiable and charming young man!" said Madame Bonacieux. "Be assured you will not find her Majesty ungrateful."

"Oh, I am already more than recompensed!" cried D'Artagnan. "I love you; you permit me to tell you that I do; that is already more happiness than I dared to hope for."

"Silence!" said Madame Bonacieux, starting.

"What!"

"Some one is talking in the street."

"It is the voice of—"

"Of my husband! Oh yes, I recognized it!"

D'Artagnan ran to the door and pushed the bolt.

"He shall not come in before I am gone," said he; "and when I am gone, you can open the door for him."

"But I ought to be gone too. And the disappearance of this money—how am I to justify it if I am here?"

"You are right. We must go out."

"Go out? How? He will see us if we go out."

"Then you must come up into my room."

"Ah," said Madame Bonacieux, "you say that in a tone which terrifies me!"

Madame Bonacieux pronounced these words with tears in her eyes. D'Artagnan saw these tears, and much disturbed, softened, he threw himself at her feet.

"In my apartment you will be as sale as in a temple. I give you my word as a gentleman."

"Let us go, then. I place full confidence in you, my friend."

D'Artagnan carefully drew back the bolt, and both, light as shadows, glided through the interior door into the passage, ascended the stairs as quietly as possible, and entered D'Artagnan's apartment.

Once in his apartment, for greater security the young man barricaded the door. They both went up to the window, and through a slit in the shutter they saw M. Bonacieux talking with a man in a cloak.

At the sight of this man D'Artagnan started, half drew his sword, and sprang towards the door.

It was the man of Meung. D'Artagnan drew near the window and listened.

M. Bonacieux had opened his door, and seeing the apartment empty, had returned to the man in the cloak, whom he had left alone for an instant.

"She is gone," said he; "she must have gone back to the Louvre."

"You are sure," replied the stranger, "that she did not suspect the intention you had when you went out?"

"No," replied Bonacieux, with a self-sufficient air, "she is too superficial a woman."

"Let us walk into your apartment. We shall be safer there than in the doorway."

D'Artagnan raised the three or four tiles which made of his chamber another ear of Dionysius, spread a carpet, went down upon his knees, and made a sign to Madame Bonacieux to stoop down toward the opening, as he did.

"And you think that your wife—" said Rochefort.

"Has returned to the Louvre."

"Without speaking to any one but yourself?"

"I am sure of it."

"Please to understand that is an important point"

"So the news I brought you, then, has some value—"

"A very great value, my dear Bonacieux. I don't attempt to deny it."

"Then the cardinal will be pleased with me?"

"No doubt he will."

"The great cardinal!"

"Are you sure that in her conversation with you your wife mentioned no proper names?"

"I don't think she did."

"She did not name Madame de Chevreuse, the Duke of Buckingham, or Madame de Verne?"

"No; she only told me she wished to send me to London to further the interests of an illustrious personage."

"Oh, the traitor!" murmured Madame Bonacieux.

"Silence!" whispered D'Artagnan, taking a hand which, without thinking of it, she suffered him to retain.

"Nevertheless," continued the man in the cloak, "it was very silly of you not to have feigned to accept the mission. You would now be in possession of the letter; the state, which is now threatened, would be safe; and you—"

"I will go to the Louvre; I will ask for Madame Bonacieux; I will tell her I have reflected upon the matter; I will resume the affair, obtain the letter, and then hasten directly to the cardinal's."

"Well, begone then! Make all possible haste. I will shortly come back to learn the result of your plan."

The unknown went out.

"The wretch!" said Madame Bonacieux, addressing this other affectionate epithet to her husband.

"Silence, once more!" said D'Artagnan, pressing her hand still more tightly.

A terrible howling interrupted these reflections of D'Artagnan and Madame Bonacieux. It was her husband, who had discovered the disappearance of his money—bag, and was screaming out, "Thieves! thieves!"

Bonacieux cried for a long time. But as such cries, on account of their frequency, did not attract much notice in the Rue des Fossoyeurs, and as, besides, the mercer's house had not been for some time in very good repute, finding that nobody came, he went out, continuing to cry aloud, and his voice died away in the direction of the Rue du Bac.

"Now he is gone, it is your turn to go," said Madame Bonacieux. "Have courage, but above all, prudence, and remember that it is your duty to the queen!"

"To her and to you!" cried D'Artagnan. "Be satisfied, lovely Constance. I shall become worth of her gratitude, but shall I likewise return worthy of your love?

The young woman replied only by the vivid blush which mounted to her cheeks. A few moments later D'Artagnan went out in his turn, enveloped in a large cloak, which the sheath of a long sword held back cavalierly.

Madame Bonacieux followed him with her eyes, with that long, fond look with which a woman accompanies the man whom she feels she loves. But when he had turned the angle of the street she fell on her knees, and clasping her hands,

"Oh, my God!" cried she, "protect the queen, protect me!"

CHAPTER 17

Plan Of Campaign

D'Artagnan went straight to M. de Tréville's hotel. He had considered that in a few minutes the cardinal would be warned by this cursed unknown, who appeared to be his agent, and he rightly judged he had not a moment to lose.

The young man's heart overflowed with joy. An opportunity presented itself to him in which there would be both glory and money to be gained, and as a far higher encouragement still, had just brought him into close intimacy with the woman he adored. This chance was doing, then, for him, almost at once, more than he would have dared to ask of Providence.

"You have something to say to me, my young friend?" said M. de Tréville.

"Yes, sir," said D'Artagnan; "and you will pardon me, I hope, for having disturbed you when you know the importance of my business."

"Speak, then; I am all attention."

"It concerns nothing less," said D'Artagnan, lowering his voice, "than the honour, perhaps the life, of the queen."

"What are you saying?" asked M. de Tréville, glancing round to see if they were alone, and then fixing his scrutinizing look upon D'Artagnan.

"I say, sir, that chance has rendered me master of a secret—"

"Which you will keep, I hope, young man, with your life."

"But which I must impart to you, sir, for you alone can assist me in the mission I have just received from her Majesty."

"Is this secret your own?"

"No, sir; it is the queen's."

"Keep your secret, young man, and tell me what you wish."

"I wish you to obtain for me, from M. des Essarts, leave of absence for a fortnight."

"When?"

"This very night."

"You are leaving Paris?"

"I am going on a mission."

"May you tell me where?"

"To London."

"Has any one an interest in preventing your reaching there?'

"The cardinal, I believe, would give anything in the world to hinder me from succeeding."

"And you are going alone?"

"I am going alone."

"In that case you will not get beyond Bondy. I tell you so, by the word of De Tréville."

"How so, sir?"

"You will be assassinated."

"And I shall die in the performance of my duty."

"But your mission will not be accomplished."

"That is true," replied D'Artagnan.

"Believe me," continued Tréville, "in enterprises of this kind, four must set out, for one to arrive."

"Ah, you are right, sir," said D'Artagnan; "but you know Athos, Porthos, and Aramis, and you know whether I can make use of them."

"Without confiding to them the secret which I did not wish to know?"

"We are sworn, once and for ever, to implicit confidence and devotion against all proof. Besides, you can tell them that you have full confidence in me, and they will not be more incredulous than you."

"I can send to each of them leave of absence for a fortnight, that is all—Athos, whose wound still gives him inconvenience, to go to the waters of Forges; Porthos and Aramis to accompany their friend, whom they are not willing to abandon in such a painful position. Sending their leave of absence will be proof enough that I authorize their journey."

"Thanks, sir. You are a hundred times too good!"

"Go, then, and find them instantly, and let all be done tonight. Ah! but first write your request to M. des Essarts. You perhaps had a spy at your heels, and your visit—in that case already known to the cardinal—will be thus made regular."

D'Artagnan drew up his request, and M. de Tréville, on receiving it, assured him that before two o'clock in the morning the four furloughs should be at the respective domiciles of the travellers.

"Have the goodness to send mine to Athos's residence," said D'Artagnan. "I should fear some disagreeable encounter if I were to go home."

"I will. Farewell, and a prosperous journey! By the way," said M. de Tréville, calling him back.

D'Artagnan returned.

"Have you any money?"

D'Artagnan jingled the bag he had in his pocket.

"Enough?" asked M. de Tréville.

"Three hundred pistoles."

"Excellent! That would carry you to the end of the world. Go, then!"

D'Artagnan bowed to M. de Tréville, who held out his hand to him. D'Artagnan pressed it with a respect mixed with gratitude. Since his first arrival at Paris he had had constant occasion to honour this excellent man, whom he had always found worthy, loyal, and great.

CHAPTER 18

The Journey

At two o'clock in the morning our four adventurers left Paris by the gate St. Denis.

The lackeys followed, armed to the teeth.

All went well as far as Chantilly, where they arrived about eight o'clock in the morning. They needed breakfast, and alighted at the door of an inn recommended by a sign representing St. Martin giving half his cloak to a poor man.

They entered the public room, and seated themselves at table. A gentleman, who had just arrived by the route of Dammartin, was seated at the same table, and was taking his breakfast.

At the moment Mousqueton came to announce that the horses were ready, and they were rising from the table, the stranger proposed to Porthos to drink the cardinal's health. Porthos replied that he asked no better, if the stranger in his turn would drink the king's health. The stranger cried that he acknowledged no other king but his Eminence. Porthos told him he was drunk, and the stranger drew his sword.

"You have committed a piece of folly," said Athos, "but it can't be helped; there is no drawing back. Kill your man, and rejoin us as soon as you can."

And all three mounted their horses and set out at a good pace, while Porthos was promising his adversary to perforate him with all the thrusts known in the fencing schools.

And the travellers continued their route.

At Beauvais they stopped two hours, as much to breathe their horses a little as to wait for Porthos. At the end of the two hours, as Porthos did not come and they heard no news of him, they resumed their journey.

At a league from Beauvais, where the road was confined between two high banks, they fell in with eight or ten men who, taking advantage of the road being unpaved in this spot, appeared to be employed in digging holes and making muddy ruts.

Aramis, not liking to soil his boots with this artificial mortar, apostrophized them rather sharply. Athos wished to restrain him, but it was too late. The labourers began to jeer the travellers, and by their insolence disturbed the equanimity even of the cool Athos, who urged on his horse against one of them.

The men all immediately drew back to the ditch, from which each took a concealed musket. The result was that our seven travellers were outnumbered in weapons. Aramis received a ball which passed through his shoulder, and Mousqueton another ball which lodged in the fleshy parts at the lower portion of the back. Mousqueton alone fell from his horse, not because he was severely wounded, but from not being able to see the wound, he deemed it to be more serious than it really was.

"It is an ambuscade!" shouted D'Artagnan; "don't waste a shot! Forward!"

Aramis, wounded as he was, seized the mane of his horse, which carried him on with the others. Mousqueton's horse rejoined them, and galloped by the side of his companions.

"That horse will serve us for a relay," said Athos.

They continued at their best speed for two hours, although the horses were so fatigued that it was to be feared they would soon refuse service.

The travellers had chosen cross-roads, in the hope that they might meet with less interruption. But at Crèvecœur Aramis declared he could proceed no farther. In fact, it required all the courage which he concealed beneath his elegant form and polished manners to bear him so far. He grew paler every minute, and they were obliged to support him on his horse. They lifted him off at the door of an inn, left Bazin with him—who, besides, in a skirmish was more embarrassing than useful—and set forward again in the hope of sleeping at Amiens. They arrived at midnight, and alighted at the inn of the Golden Lily.

The host had the appearance of as honest a man as any on earth. He received the travellers with his candlestick in one hand and his cotton nightcap in the other.

"Grimaud can take care of the horses," said Planchet. "If you are willing, gentlemen, I will sleep across your doorway, and you will then be certain that nobody can come to you."

"And what will you sleep upon?" said D'Artagnan.

"Here is my bed," replied Planchet, producing a bundle of straw.

At four o'clock in the morning a terrible noise was heard in the stables. Grimaud had tried to waken the stable-boys, and the stable boys were beating him. When the window was opened the poor lad was seen lying senseless, with his head split by a blow with a fork-handle.

Planchet went down into the yard, and proceeded to saddle the horses. But the horses were all used up. Mousqueton's horse, which had travelled for five or six hours without a rider the day before, alone might have been able to pursue the journey. But, by an inconceivable error, a veterinary surgeon, who had been sent for, as it appeared, to bleed one of the host's horses, had bled Mousqueton's.

This began to be annoying. All these successive accidents were, perhaps, the result of chance, but they might, quite as probably, be the fruits of a plot. Athos and D'Artagnan went out, while Planchet was sent to inquire if there were not three horses for sale in the neighbourhood. At the door stood two horses, fresh, strong, and fully equipped. These were just what they wanted. He asked where their owners were, and was informed that they had passed the night in the inn, and were then settling with the master.

Athos went down to pay the reckoning, while D'Artagnan and Planchet stood at the street door. The host was in a low room at the back, to which Athos was requested to go.

Athos entered without the least mistrust, and took out two pistoles to pay the bill. The host was alone, seated before his desk, one of the drawers of which was partly open. He took the money which Athos offered to him, and after turning and turning it over and over in his hands, suddenly cried out that it was bad, and that he would have him and his companions arrested as counterfeiters.

"You scoundrel!" cried Athos, stepping towards him, "I'll cut your ears off!"

But the host stooped, took two pistols from the half-open drawer, pointed them at Athos, and called out for help.

At the same instant four men, armed to the teeth, entered by side doors, and rushed upon Athos.

"I am taken!" shouted Athos with all the power of his lungs. "Go on, D'Artagnan! spur! spur!" And he fired two pistols.

D'Artagnan and Planchet did not require twice bidding. They unfastened the two horses that were waiting at the door, leaped upon them, buried their spurs in their sides, and set off at full gallop.

And both, with free use of the spur, arrived at St. Omer without drawing bridle. At St. Omer they breathed their horses with their bridles passed under their arms, for fear of accident, and ate a hasty morsel standing in the road, after which they departed again.

At a hundred paces from the gates of Calais D'Artagnan's horse sank under him, and could not by any means be made to get up again, the blood flowing from both his eyes and his nose. There still remained Planchet's horse, but he had stopped short, and could not be started again.

Fortunately, as we have said, they were within a hundred paces of the city. They left their two horses upon the highway, and ran toward the port. Planchet called his master's attention to a gentleman who had just arrived with his lackey, and who was about fifty paces ahead of them.

They made all haste to come up to this gentleman, who appeared to be in a great hurry. His boots were covered with dust, and he was asking whether he could not instantly cross over to England.

"Nothing would be more easy," said the captain of a vessel ready to set sail, "but this morning an order arrived that no one should be allowed to cross without express permission from the cardinal."

"I have that permission," said the gentleman, drawing a paper from his pocket; "here it is."

"Have it signed by the governor of the port," said the captain, "and give me the preference."

"Where shall I find the governor?"

"At his country house."

"Where is that situated?"

"A quarter of a league from the city. Look, you may see it from here, at the foot of that little hill, that slated roof."

"Very well," said the gentleman.

And with his lackey he started for the governor's country house.

D'Artagnan and Planchet followed the gentleman at a distance of five hundred paces.

Once outside the city, D'Artagnan quickly overtook the gentleman as he was entering a little wood.

"Planchet," called out D'Artagnan, "take care of the lackey. I will manage the master."

Planchet, emboldened by his first exploit, sprang upon Lubin; and being strong and vigorous, he soon got him on his back, and placed his knee on his chest.

"Go on with your affair, sir," cried Planchet; "I have finished mine."

Seeing this, the gentleman drew his sword, and sprang upon D'Artagnan; but he had to deal with a tough customer.

In three seconds D'Artagnan had wounded him three times, exclaiming at each thrust,

"One for Athos! one for Porthos! and one for Aramis."

At the third thrust the gentleman fell like a log.

D'Artagnan believed hum to be dead, or at least insensible, and went toward him for the purpose of taking the order. But at the moment he stretched out his hand to search for it, the wounded man, who had not dropped his sword, pricked him in the breast, crying,

"And one for you!"

"And one for me—the best for the last!" cried D'Artagnan in a rage, nailing him to the earth with a fourth thrust through his body.

This time the gentleman closed his eyes and fainted. D'Artagnan searched his pockets, and took from one of them the order for the passage. It was in the name of the Comte de Wardes.

Then casting a glance on the handsome young man, who was scarcely twenty-five years of age, and whom he was leaving lying there unconscious and perhaps dead, he uttered a sigh over that unaccountable destiny which leads men to destroy one another for the interests of people who are strangers to them, and who often do not even know of their existence.

But he was soon roused from these reflections by Lubin, who uttered loud cries, and screamed for help with all his might.

Planchet grasped him by the throat, and pressed as hard as he could.

"Sir," said he, "as long as I hold him in this manner he can't cry, I'll be bound; but as soon as I let go, he will howl again as loud as ever. I have found out that he's a Norman, and Normans are obstinate."

In fact, tightly held as he was, Lubin endeavoured still to make a noise.

"Wait!" said D'Artagnan; and taking out his handkerchief, he gagged him.

"Now," said Planchet, "let us bind him to a tree."

This being properly done, they drew the Comte de Wardes close to his servant; and as night was approaching, and as the wounded man and the bound man were both at some little distance within the wood, it was evident they would remain there till the next day.

"And now," said D'Artagnan, "to the governor's house."

"But you appear to me to be wounded," said Planchet.

"Oh, that's nothing! Let us dispatch what is most pressing first, and we will attend to my wound afterwards; besides, it does not seem a very dangerous one."

And they both set forward as fast as they could towards the worthy functionary's country seat.

The governor signed the passport and delivered it to D'Artagnan, who lost no time in useless compliments, but thanked the governor, bowed, and departed.

Once out, he and Planchet set off as fast as they could, and by making a *détour*, avoided the wood, and re-entered the city by another gate.

The vessel was quite ready to sail, and the captain waiting on the wharf.

"Well?" said he, on perceiving D'Artagnan.

"Here is my pass, signed," said the latter.

"And that other gentleman?"

"He will not go to-day," said D'Artagnan; "but here, I'll pay you for us two."

"In that case we will be gone," said the captain.

"Yes; as soon as you please," replied D'Artagnan.

He leaped with Planchet into the boat. Five minutes after they were onboard.

D'Artagnan did not know London, he did not know one word of English, but he wrote the name of Buckingham on a piece of paper, and every one to whom he showed it pointed out to him the way to the duke's palace.

The duke was at Windsor hunting with the king.

D'Artagnan inquired for the duke's confidential valet, who, having accompanied him in all his travels, spoke French perfectly well. He told him that he came from Paris on an affair of life and death, and that he must speak with his master instantly.

The confidence with which D'Artagnan spoke convinced Patrick, which was the name of the minister's minister. He ordered two horses to be saddled, and himself went as the young guardsman's guide. As for Planchet, he had been lifted from his horse as stiff as a stake. The poor lad's strength was exhausted. D'Artagnan seemed to be made of iron.

On their arrival at the castle they inquired for the duke, and learned that he was hawking with the king in the marshes, two or three leagues away.

In twenty minutes they were at the place designated. Patrick soon caught the sound of his master's voice recalling his falcon.

"Whom shall I announce to my Lord Duke?" asked Patrick.

"The young man who one evening sought a quarrel with him on the Pont Neuf, opposite the Samaritaine."

"Rather a singular introduction!"

"You will find that it is as good as any other."

Patrick galloped off, reached the duke, and announced to him in these very words that a messenger awaited him.

Buckingham at once remembered the circumstance, and suspecting that something was going on in France, concerning which news was now brought to him, he took only the time to inquire where the messenger was, and recognizing at a distance the uniform of the guards, he put his horse into a gallop, and rode straight up to D'Artagnan. Patrick discreetly kept in the background.

"Has any misfortune happened to the queen?" cried Buckingham, throwing all his fear and love into the question.

"I believe not. Nevertheless, I believe she is in some great peril from which your Grace alone can extricate her."

"I!" cried Buckingham. "What is it? I should be but too happy to render her any service. Speak! speak!"

"Take this letter," said D'Artagnan.

"This letter! From whom does this letter come?"

"From her Majesty, as I think."

"From her Majesty!" said Buckingham, becoming so pale that D'Artagnan feared he was going to be ill; and he broke the seal.

"Just Heaven! what have I read?" cried the duke. —"Patrick, remain here, or rather join the king, wherever he may be, and tell his Majesty that I humbly beg him to excuse me, but an affair of the greatest importance calls me to London.—Come, sir, come!" And both set off toward the capital at full gallop.

CHAPTER 19

The Comtesse De Winter

As they rode along the duke learned from D'Artagnan, not all that had passed, but all that D'Artagnan himself knew. By adding what he got from the young man to his own recollections, he was enabled to form a pretty exact idea of a condition of things the seriousness of which the queen's letter, short and vague as it was, conveyed to him quite clearly.

The horses went like the wind, and they were soon at the gates of London.

On entering the court of his palace Buckingham sprang from his horse, and without caring what would become of him, threw the bridle on his neck and sprang toward the staircase.

The duke walked so fast that D'Artagnan had some trouble in keeping up with him. He passed through several apartments furnished with an elegance of which the greatest nobles of France had not even an idea, and arrived at length in a bedchamber which was at once a miracle of taste and of splendour. In the alcove of this chamber was a door, made in the tapestry, which the duke opened with a small gold key suspended from his neck by a chain of the same metal.

They then found themselves in a small chapel hung with a tapestry of Persian silk and embossed with gold, and brilliantly lit with a vast number of wax candles. Over a kind of altar, and beneath a canopy of blue velvet, surmounted by white and red plumes, was a life—size portrait of Anne of Austria, such a perfect likeness that D'Artagnan uttered a cry of surprise on beholding it. You might believe that the queen was about to speak.

On the altar, and beneath the portrait, was the casket containing the diamond studs.

The duke approached the altar, fell on his knees, as a priest might have done before a crucifix, then opened the casket.

"Here," said he, drawing from the casket a large bow of blue ribbon all sparkling with diamonds—"here," said he, "are the precious studs which I have taken an oath should be buried with me. The queen gave them to me; the queen takes them from me. Her will, like that of God, be done in all things."

Then he began to kiss, one after the other, those studs with which he was about to part. All at once he uttered a terrible cry.

"What is the matter?" exclaimed D'Artagnan anxiously; "what has happened to you, milord?"

"All is lost! all is lost!" cried Buckingham, turning as pale as death; "two of the studs are missing—there are but ten of them left!"

"Can you have lost them, milord, or do you think they have been stolen?"

"They have been stolen," replied the duke, "and it is the cardinal who has dealt me this blow. See!, the ribbons which held them have been cut with scissors."

"If milord suspects they have been stolen, perhaps the person who stole them still has them."

"Let me reflect," said the duke. "The only time I wore these studs was at a ball given by the king a week ago at Windsor. The Comtesse de Winter, with whom I had had a quarrel, became reconciled to me at that ball. That reconciliation was a jealous woman's vengeance. I have never seen her since. The woman is an agent of the cardinal's."

"Why, then, he has agents throughout the whole world!" cried D'Artagnan.

"Yes, yes," said Buckingham, mashing his teeth with rage; "he is a terrible antagonist! But when is the ball to take place?"

"Next Monday."

"Next Monday! Five days yet. That's more time than we need.— Patrick!" cried the duke, opening the door of the chapel—"Patrick!"

His confidential valet appeared.

"My jeweller and my secretary."

The valet went out with a mute promptness and silence that showed he was accustomed to obey blindly and without reply.

But although the jeweller had been summoned first, it was the secretary who first made his appearance. This was simple enough. He lived in the palace. He found Buckingham seated at a table in his bedchamber writing orders with his own hand.

"Master Jackson," said he, "go instantly to the lord chancellor, and tell him that I desire him to execute these orders. I wish them to be promulgated immediately."

The secretary bowed and retired.

"We are safe on that side," said Buckingham, turning toward D'Artagnan. "If the studs are not yet gone to Paris, they will not arrive till after you."

"How so, milord?"

"I have just placed an embargo on all vessels at present in his Majesty's ports, and without special permission not one will dare raise an anchor."

D'Artagnan was astonished to see by what fragile and unknown threads the destinies of a nation and the lives of men are sometimes suspended.

He was lost in these reflections when the goldsmith entered. He was an Irishman, one of the most skilful of his craft, and who himself confessed that he gained a hundred thousand pounds a year by the Duke of Buckingham.

"Master O'Reilly," said the Duke to him, leading him into the chapel, "look at these diamond studs, and tell me what they are worth apiece."

The goldsmith cast a glance at the elegant manner in which they were set, calculated, one with another, what the diamonds were worth, and without hesitation,

"Fifteen hundred pistoles each, your Grace," replied he.

"How many days would it require to make two studs exactly like them? You see there are two wanting."

"A week, your Grace."

"I will give you three thousand pistoles each if I can have them by the day after to-morrow."

"Your Grace, you shall have them."

An hour later the ordinance was published in London that no vessel bound for France should leave the ports—not even the packet-boat with letters. In the eyes of everybody this was a declaration of war between the two kingdoms.

On the day after the next, by eleven o'clock, the two diamond studs were finished; and they were such exact imitations, so perfectly like the others, that Buckingham could not tell the new ones from the old ones, and the most practised in such matters would have been deceived as he was.

He immediately called D'Artagnan.

"Here," said he to him, "are the diamond studs that you came to fetch; and be my witness that I have done all that human power could do."

"Rest assured, milord; I will tell what I have seen. But does your Grace mean to give me the studs without the casket?"

"The casket would only encumber you. Besides, the casket is

the more precious from being all that is left to me. You will say that I keep it."

"I will perform your commission word for word, milord."

"And now," resumed Buckingham, looking earnestly at the young man, "how shall I ever acquit myself towards you?"

"Let us understand each other, milord," replied D'Artagnan, "and let us weigh things well beforehand, in order that there may be no mistake. I am in the service of the king and queen of France, and form part of the company of M. des Essarts's guards, who, as well as his brother-in-law, M. de Tréville, is particularly attached to their Majesties. And, besides, it is very probable I should not have done anything of all this if it had not been to make myself agreeable to some one who is my lady, as the queen is yours."

"I understand," said the duke, smiling, "and I even believe that I know that other person. It is—"

"Milord, I have not named her!" interrupted the young man quickly.

"That is true," said the duke. "It is, then, to this person I am bound to discharge my debt of gratitude for your service. Go to the port, ask for the brig *Le Sund,* and give this letter to the captain. He will convey you to a little port where certainly no one is on the watch for you, and where only fishing-smacks ordinarily run in."

D'Artagnan bowed to the duke, and quickly made his way to the port opposite the Tower of London. He found the vessel that had been named to him, delivered his letter to the captain, who, after having it signed by the warden of the port, set sail at once.

Fifty vessels were waiting ready to sail.

As he was passing alongside of one of them D'Artagnan fancied he perceived on board the lady of Meung, the same whom the unknown gentleman had styled milady, and whom D'Artagnan had thought so handsome. But, thanks to the current of the river and a fair wind, his vessel passed so quickly that he lost sight of her in a moment.

The next day, about five o'clock in the morning, he landed at St. Valery. Four hours later he was in Neufchatel. At Pontoise he changed his horse for the last time, and at nine o'clock galloped into the court of M. de Tréville's hotel. He had covered nearly sixty leagues in twelve hours.

M. de Tréville received him as if he had seen him that same morning; only, when pressing his hand a little more warmly than usual, he informed him that M. des Essarts's company was on duty at the Louvre, and that he might repair to his post.

Chapter 20

The Ballet Of La Merlaison

The next day nothing was talked of in Paris but the ball which the provosts of the city were to give to the king and queen, and in which their Majesties were to dance the famous La Merlaison, the king's favourite ballet.

At midnight great cries and loud acclamations were heard. It was the king passing through the streets which led from the Louvre to the City Hall, and which were all illuminated with coloured lanterns.

A closet had been prepared for the king, and another for Monsieur. In each of these closets were placed masquerade dresses. The same had been done with respect to the queen and Madame la Présidente.

Half an hour after the king's entrance fresh acclamations were heard. These announced the queen's arrival. The provosts did as they lid done before, and, preceded by their sergeants, went out to receive their illustrious guest.

The king was the first to come out from his closet. He was attired in a most elegant hunting costume, and Monsieur and the other nobles were dressed as he was. This was the costume that was most becoming to the king, and when thus clothed he really appeared the first gentleman of his kingdom.

The cardinal drew near to the king and placed a casket in his hand. The king opened it, and found in it two diamond studs.

"What does this mean?" demanded he of the cardinal.

"Nothing," replied the latter; "only, if the queen has the studs—

but I very much doubt if she has—count them, sire, and if you find only ten, ask her Majesty who can have stolen from her the two studs that are here."

The king looked at the cardinal as if to ask him what it meant. But he had no time to put any question to him. A cry of admiration burst from every mouth. If the king appeared to be the first gentleman of his kingdom, the queen was assuredly the most beautiful woman in France.

True, her huntress habit was admirably becoming; she wore a beaver hat with blue feathers, a surtout of pearl-grey velvet fastened with diamond clasps, and a petticoat of blue satin embroidered in silver. On her left shoulder sparkled the diamond studs, on a bow of, the same colour as the plumes and the petticoat.

The king trembled with joy and the cardinal with vexation. However, at the distance they were from the queen, they could not count the studs. The queen had them; the only question was, had she ten or twelve?

At that moment the violins sounded the signal for the ballet. The king advanced toward Madame la Présidente, with whom he was to dance, and his Highness Monsieur with the queen. They took their places, and the ballet began.

The king danced facing the queen, and every time that he passed by her he devoured with his eyes those studs, the number of which he could not make out. A cold sweat covered the cardinal's brow.

The ballet lasted an hour. It had sixteen figures.

The ballet ended amid the applause of the whole assemblage, and every one led his partner to her place. But the king took advantage of the privilege he had of leaving his lady to hasten to the queen.

"I thank you, madame," said he, "for the deference you have shown to my wishes; but I think two of your studs are missing, and I bring them back to you."

At these words he held out to the queen the two studs the cardinal had given him.

"How, sire?" cried the young queen, affecting surprise; "you are giving me, then, two more. So now I shall have fourteen."

In fact, the king counted them, and the twelve studs were all on her Majesty's shoulder.

The king called the cardinal to him.

"What does this mean, cardinal?" asked the king in a severe tone.

"This means, sire," replied the cardinal, "that I was desirous of presenting her Majesty with these two studs, and that, not venturing to offer them myself, I adopted this means of inducing her to accept them.

"And I am the more grateful to your Eminence," replied Anne of Austria, with a smile that proved she was not the dupe of this ingenious piece of gallantry, "since I am certain these two studs have cost you as dearly as all the others cost his Majesty."

Then, after bowing to the king and the cardinal, the queen took her way to the chamber where she had dressed, and where she was to take off her ball costume.

The attention which we were obliged to give, at the beginning of this chapter, to the illustrious personages we have introduced to it diverted us for an instant from him to whom Anne of Austria owed the extraordinary triumph she had just obtained over the cardinal, and who, obscure, unknown, lost in the crowd gathered at one of the doors, was a witness of this scene, comprehensible only to four persons—the king, the queen, his Eminence, and himself.

The queen had just regained her chamber, and D'Artagnan was about to retire, when he felt a light touch on his shoulder. He turned round, and saw a young woman, who made him a sign to follow her. This young woman's face was covered with a black velvet mask, but notwithstanding this precaution, which was, in fact, taken rather against others than against him, he at once recognized his usual guide, the gay and witty Madame Bonacieux.

The haste which the young woman was in to convey to her mistress the fine news of her messenger's happy return prevented the two lovers from exchanging more than a few words. D'Artagnan, therefore, followed Madame Bonacieux, moved by a double sentiment, love and curiosity. At length, after a minute or two of turns and counterturns, Madame Bonacieux opened the door of a closet, which was entirely dark, and led the young man into it. There she made a fresh sign of silence, and opening a second door, concealed by a tapestry which as it was drawn aside let in a sudden flood of brilliant light, she disappeared.

D'Artagnan remained for a moment motionless, asking himself where he could be; but soon a ray of light penetrating from the chamber, the warm and perfumed air reaching even to him, the conversation of two or three ladies in language at once respectful and elegant, and the word "Majesty" many times repeated, clearly indicated to him that he was in a closet adjoining the queen's chamber.

The young man stood in the shadow and waited.

Although D'Artagnan did not know the queen, he soon distinguished her voice from the others, at first by a slightly foreign accent, and next by that tone of domination naturally impressed upon all royal words. He heard her approach and withdraw from the open door, and twice or three times he even saw the shadow of a body intercept the light.

At length a hand and an arm, surpassingly beautiful in form and whiteness, suddenly glided through the tapestry. D'Artagnan understood that this was his reward. He cast himself on his knees, seized the hand, and touched it respectfully with his lips; then the hand was withdrawn, leaving in his an object which he perceived to be a ring. The door immediately closed, and D'Artagnan found himself again in complete darkness.

D'Artagnan placed the ring on his finger, and again waited; it was evident that all was trot yet over. After the reward of his devotion; the reward of his love was to come. Besides, although the ballet was danced, the evening's pleasures had scarcely begun. Supper was to be served at three and the clock of St. John had struck three—quarters after two.

In fact, the sound of voices in the adjoining chamber diminished by degrees; the company was then heard departing; then the door of the closet in which D'Artagnan was was opened, and Madame Bonacieux entered quickly.

"You at last?" cried D'Artagnan.

"Silence!" said the young woman, placing her hand upon his lips —silence! and go the same way you came."

"But where and when shall I see you again?" cried D'Artagnan.

"A note which you will find at home will tell you. Go! go!"

And at these words she opened the door of the corridor and pushed D'Artagnan out of the closet. D'Artagnan obeyed like a child, without the least resistance or objection, which proves that he was really in love.

CHAPTER 21

The Rendezvous

D'Artagnan ran home immediately, and although it was after three o'clock in the morning, and he had the worst quarters of Paris to pass through, he met with no misadventure.

He found the door of his passage open, sprang up the stairs, and knocked softly, in a manner agreed upon between him and his lackey. Planchet, whom he had sent home two hours before from the City Hall, desiring him to sit up for him, came and opened the door.

"Has any one brought a letter for me?" asked D'Artagnan eagerly.

"No one has *brought* a letter, sir," replied Planchet; "but there is one come of itself."

"What do you mean by that, you stupid fellow?"

"I mean that when I came in, although I had the key of your apartment in my pocket and that key had never been out of my possession, I found a letter on the green table-cover in your bedroom."

"And where is that letter?"

"I left it where I found it, sir."

In the meantime the young man darted into his chamber and was opening the letter. It was from Madame Bonacieux, and was conceived in these terms:

"Warm thanks are to be offered to you, and to be transmitted to you. Be at St. Cloud this evening about ten o'clock, in front of the pavilion at the corner of M. d'Estrées's hotel.—C.B."

While reading this letter D'Artagnan felt his heart expand and close with that delicious spasm that tortures and caresses the hearts of lovers.

At seven o'clock in the morning he arose and called Planchet, who, at the second summons, opened the door, his countenance not yet quite free from the anxiety of the preceding night.

"Planchet," said D'Artagnan, "I am going out for all day, perhaps. You are, therefore, your own master till seven o'clock in the evening."

He took his way toward M. de Tréville's hotel. His visit the day before, we remember, had been very short, with little chances for confidential talk.

He found M. de Tréville in a most joyful mood. The king and queen had been charming to him" at the ball. The cardinal, however, had been particularly ill—tempered; he had retired at one o'clock under the pretence of being indisposed. Their Majesties did not return to the Louvre till six o'clock.

"Now," said M. de Tréville, lowering his voice and looking round at every corner of the apartment to see whether they were alone— "now let us talk about yourself, my young friend; for it is evident that your fortunate return has something to do with the king's joy, the queen's triumph, and the cardinal's humiliation. You must look out for yourself.

"What have I to fear," replied D'Artagnan, "so long as I have the good fortune to enjoy their Majesties' favour?"

"Everything, believe me. But, by the way," resumed M. de Tréville, "what has become of your three companions?"

"I was about to ask you if you had heard no news of them."

"None whatever, sir."

"Well, I left them on my road—Porthos at Chantilly, with a duel on his hands; Aramis at Crèvecœur, with a ball in his shoulder; and Athos at Amiens, detained by an accusation of counterfeiting."

"See there, now!" said M. de Tréville. "And how the devil did you escape?"

"By a miracle, sir, I must acknowledge, with a sword-thrust in my breast, and by nailing Comte de Wardes, on the road to Calais, like a butterfly on a tapestry."

"There again! De Wardes, one of the cardinal's men, a cousin of Rochefort's! But stop, my friend, I have an idea."

"Speak, sir."

"In your place, I would do one thing."

"What, sir?"

"While his Eminence was seeking for me in Paris, I should take, without sound of drum or trumpet, the road to Picardy, and should go and make some enquiries concerning my three companions. What the devil! they richly merit that piece of attention on your part."

"Your advice is good, sir, and to-morrow I will set out."

"To-morrow! And why not this evening?"

"This evening, sir, I am detained in Paris by urgent business."

"Ah, young man, young man! Some love affair. Take care, I repeat to you, take care! Woman was the ruin of us all, is the ruin of us all, and will be the ruin of us all, as long as the world stands. Take my advice and set out this evening."

"It is impossible, sir."

"You have given your word, then?"

"Yes, sir."

"Ah, that's quite another thing. But promise me, if you should not happen to be killed to-night, that you will go to-morrow."

"I promise you, sir. "

"Do you want money?"

"I still have fifty pistoles. That, I think, is as much as I shall need."

"But your companions?"

"I don't think they can be in need of any. We left Paris each with, seventy-five pistoles in his pocket."

"Shall I see you again before your departure?"

"I think not, sir, unless something new happens."

"Well, a pleasant journey to you, then."

"Thank you, sir."

And D'Artagnan left M. de Tréville, touched more than ever by his paternal solicitude for his musketeers.

He called successively at the abodes of Athos, Porthos, and Aramis. None of them had returned. Their lackeys likewise were absent, and nothing had been heard of either masters or servants.

He would have inquired after them of their mistresses, but he was not acquainted with Porthos's or Aramis's, and Athos had none.

D'Artagnan, being at bottom a prudent youth, instead of returning home, went and dined with the Gascon priest, who, at the time of the four friends' poverty, had given them a breakfast of chocolate.

Chapter 22

The Pavilion

At nine o'clock D'Artagnan was at the Hotel des Gardes. D'Artagnan had his sword, and placed two pistols in his belt; then mounted and departed quietly. It was quite dark, and no one saw him out.

D'Artagnan crossed the quays, went out by the gate of La Conference, and went along the road, much more beautiful then than it is now, leading to St. Cloud.

D'Artagnan reached St. Cloud; but instead of following the highway, he turned behind the chateau, reached a sort of retired lane, and found himself soon in front of the pavilion named. It was situated in a very private spot. A high wall, at the angle of which was the pavilion, ran along one side of this lane, and on the other a hedge protected from passers by a little garden, at the rear of which stood a small cottage.

He was now on the place appointed, and as no signal had been given hint by which to announce his presence, he waited.

His eyes were fixed upon the little pavilion situated at the angle of the wall, all the windows of which were closed with shutters, except one on the first story.

Through this window shone a mild light, silvering the trembling foliage of two or three linden trees that formed a group outside the park.

The clock on St. Cloud struck half-past ten.

It struck eleven!

At that moment he noticed the trees, on the leaves of which the light still shone; and as one of them drooped over the road, he thought that from its branches he might succeed in looking into the pavilion.

The tree was easy to climb. Besides, D'Artagnan was scarcely twenty, and consequently had not yet forgotten his schoolboy habits. In an instant he was among the branches, and his eyes penetrated through the clear glass into the interior of the pavilion.

One of the panes of glass was broken, the door of the room had been burst in, and hung, split in two, on its hinges; a table, which had been covered with an elegant supper, was overturned; the decanters, broken in pieces, and the crushed fruits, strewed the floor; everything in the apartment gave evidence of a violent and desperate struggle.

He hastened down into the street, with his heart throbbing frightfully.

The little soft light continued to shine in the calm of the night. D'Artagnan then perceived a thing that he had not before remarked, for nothing had led him to this scrutiny—that the ground, trampled here and hoof-marked there, presented confused traces of men and horses. Besides, the wheels of a carriage, which appeared to have come from Paris, had made a deep impression in the soft earth, not extending beyond the pavilion, but turning again towards Paris.

At length D'Artagnan, in following up his researches, found near the wall a woman's torn glove. Yet this glove, wherever it had not touched the muddy ground, was of irreproachable freshness. It was one of those perfumed gloves that lovers like to snatch from a pretty hand.

Then D'Artagnan became almost wild. He ran along the highway, retraced his steps, and coming to the ferry, closely questioned the boatman.

About seven o'clock in the evening, the boatman said, he had taken over a young woman, enveloped in a black mantle, who appeared to be very anxious not to be recognized.

There was then, as there is now, a crowd of pretty young women who came to St. Cloud, and who had good reasons for not being seen, and yet D'Artagnan did not for an instant doubt that it was Madame Bonacieux whom the boatman had noticed.

D'Artagnan took advantage of the lamp burning in the boatman's cabin to read Madame Bonacieux's note once again, and satisfy himself that he had not been mistaken, that the appointment was at St.

Cloud and not elsewhere, before M. d'Estrées's pavilion and not in another street.

He again ran back to the château. It appeared to him that something might have happened at the pavilion in his absence, and that fresh information was awaiting him.

The lane was still empty, and the same calm, soft light shone from the window.

D'Artagnan then thought of that mute, blind cottage: it must have seen, and perhaps could speak!

The gate was locked, but he leaped over the hedge, and in spite of the barking of a chained dog, went up to the cabin.

There was no answer to his first knocking. A deathlike silence reigned in the cottage as in the pavilion; but as the cottage was his last resource, he kept knocking.

It soon appeared to him that he heard a slight noise within, a timid noise, seeming itself to tremble.

Then D'Artagnan ceased to knock, and entreated with an accent so full of anxiety and promises, terror and persuasion, that his voice was of a nature to reassure the most timid. At length an old, worm-eaten shutter was opened, or rather pushed ajar, but closed again as soon as the light from a miserable lamp burning in the corner had shone upon D'Artagnan's baldric, sword-hilt, and pistol pommels. Nevertheless, rapid as the movement had been, D'Artagnan had had time to get a glimpse of an old man's head.

"In the name of Heaven," cried he, "listen to me! I have been waiting for some one who has not come. I am dying with anxiety. Could any misfortune have happened in the neighbourhood? Speak!"

The window was again opened slowly, and the same face appeared again. Only it was paler than before.

D'Artagnan related his story simply, with the omission of names. He told how he had an appointment with a young woman before that pavilion, and how, seeing she did not come, he had climbed the linden tree, and by the lamplight had seen the disorder of the chamber.

The old man read so much truth and so much grief in the young man's face that he made him a sign to listen, and speaking in a low voice, said,

"It was about nine o'clock when I heard a noise in the street, and was wondering what it could be, when, on coming to my gate, I found that somebody was endeavouring to open it. As I am poor, and am not afraid of being robbed, I went and opened the gate, and saw three men at a few paces from it. In the shade was a coach with horses, and some saddle-horses. These saddle-horses evidently belonged to the three men, who were dressed as cavaliers.

"'Ah, my worthy gentlemen,' cried I, 'what do you want?'

"'Have you a ladder?' said the one who appeared to be the leader of the party.

"'Yes, sir—the one with which I gather my fruit'

"'Lend it to us, and go into your house again. There is a crown for the trouble we cause you. Only remember this, if you speak a word of what you may see or hear (for you will look and listen, I am quite sure, however we may threaten you), you are lost'

"At these words he threw me a crown, which I picked up, and he took my ladder.

"Well, then, after I had shut the gate behind them, I pretended to go into the house again; but I immediately went out at a back door, and stealing along in the shade, I gained yonder clump of elder, from which I could see everything without being seen.

"The three men brought the carriage up quietly, and took out of it a little, short, stout, elderly man, poorly dressed in dark-coloured clothes. He climbed the ladder very carefully, looked slyly in at the window of the pavilion, came down as quietly as he had gone up, and whispered,

"'It is she!'

"Immediately the one who had spoken to me approached the door of the pavilion, opened it with a key he bad in his hand, closed tie door, and disappeared, while at the same time the other two men mounted the ladder. The little old man remained at the coach door, the coachman took care of his horses, a lackey held the saddle—horses.

"All at once loud screams resounded in the pavilion, and a woman ran to the window and opened it, as if to throw herself out of it; but as soon as she perceived the other two men, she sprang back, and they got into the chamber.

"Then I saw no more, but I heard the noise of breaking furniture. The woman screamed and cried for help, but her cries were soon stifled. Two of the men appeared, bearing the woman in their arms, and carried her to the carriage; the little old man entered it after her. The one who stayed in the pavilion closed the window, came out an instant after at the door, and satisfied himself that the woman was in the carriage. His two companions were already on horseback; he sprang into his saddle, the lackey took his place by the coachman, the carriage went off at a rapid pace, escorted by the three horsemen, and all was over. From that moment I have neither seen nor heard anything."

D'Artagnan, entirely overcome by such terrible news, remained motionless and mute, while all the demons of anger and jealousy were howling in his heart.

"But, my good gentleman," resumed the old man, upon whom this mute despair certainly produced a greater effect than cries and tears would have done, "do not take on so; they did not kill her— that's the main thing."

With a broken heart D'Artagnan again bent his way toward the ferry. Sometimes he could not believe it was Madame Bonacieux, and hoped he should find her next day at the Louvre; sometimes he feared she had been having an intrigue with some one else, who, in a jealous fit, had surprised her and carried her off. His mind was torn by doubt, grief, and despair.

"Oh, if I had my three friends here," cried he, "I should have, at least, some hopes of finding her; but who knows what has become of them?"

It was almost midnight; he decided to pass the night in an inn. D'Artagnan, be it remembered, was only twenty years old, and at that age sleep has imprescriptible rights, which it imperiously insists upon, even over the saddest hearts.

Chapter 23

Porthos

Instead of returning directly home, D'Artagnan alighted at M. de Tréville's door and quickly ran upstairs. This time he was determined to relate all that had passed.

M. de Tréville listened to the young man's account with a seriousness which proved that he saw something else in all this adventure than a love affair; and when D'Artagnan had finished,

"Hum!" said he; "all this smacks of his Eminence a league off."

"But what is to be done?" said D'Artagnan.

"Nothing, absolutely nothing at present, but to leave Paris, as I told you, as soon as possible. I will see the queen; I will relate to her the details of this poor woman's disappearance, of which she is, no doubt, ignorant. These details will guide her on her part, and on your return I shall perhaps have some good news to tell you. Count on me."

D'Artagnan knew that, although a Gascon, M. de Tréville was not in the habit of making promises, and that when by chance he did promise, he generally more than kept his word. He bowed to him, then, full of gratitude for the past and for the future; and the worthy captain, who, on his side, felt a lively interest in this young man who was so brave and resolute, pressed his hand affectionately, while wishing him a pleasant journey.

Determined instantly to put M. de Tréville's advice into practice, D'Artagnan rode toward the Rue des Fossoyeurs, in order to superintend the packing of, his portmanteau. On approaching the house he perceived M. Bonacieux, in morning costume, standing at his door.

"Well, young man," said he, "we appear to pass rather gay nights! Seven o'clock to the morning! Hang it! you seem to reverse ordinary customs, and come home at the hour when other people are going out."

"No one can reproach you for anything of the kind, M. Bonacieux," said the young man; "you are a model for sober people."

Bonacieux grinned a ghastly smile.

"Ah, ha!" said Bonacieux, "you are a jocular companion. But where the devil were you gadding last night, my young master? It does not appear to be very clean in the crossroads."

D'Artagnan glanced down at his boots, all covered with mud, but that same glance fell upon the mercer's shoes and stockings. It might have been said they had been dipped in the same mudhole. Both were stained with splashes of the very same appearance.

Then a sudden thought crossed D'Artagnan's mind. That little, short, stout, elderly man, that sort of lackey, dressed in dark clothes, treated without consideration by the men wearing swords who composed the escort, was Bonacieux himself! The husband had participated in the abduction of his wife!

"Ah, ha! but you are joking, my worthy man," said D'Artagnan. "It appears to me that if my boots want sponging, your stockings and shoes stand in equal need of brushing. May you not have been philandering a little also, M. Bonacieux? Oh, the devil! that's unpardonable in a man of your age, and who, besides, has such a pretty young wife as yours is!"

"O Lord, no!" said Bonacieux.

D'Artagnan left the mercer and at the top of the stairs he found Planchet.

"Are you not as anxious to get news of Grimaud, Mousqueton, and Bazin as I am to know what has become of Athos, Porthos, and Aramis?" said D'Artagnan.

"Oh yes, sir," said Planchet; "and I will go as soon as you please. Indeed, I think country air will suit us much better just now than the air of Paris. So then—"

"So then, pack up our necessaries, Planchet, and let us be off. On my part, I will go out ahead with my hands in my pockets, that nothing tray be suspected. You can join me at the Hôtel des Gardes."

D'Artagnan went out first, as had been agreed upon. Then, that he might have nothing to reproach himself with, he went for the last time to the residences of his three friends. No news had been received of them; only a letter, all perfumed, and of an elegant and delicate handwriting, had come for Aramis. D'Artagnan took charge of it. Ten minutes afterwards Planchet joined him at the stables of the Hôtel des Gardes. D'Artagnan, in order that there might be no time lost, had saddled his horse himself.

"All right," said he to Planchet, when the latter added the Portmanteau to the equipment.

As they left the Hôtel des Gardes they separated, going along the street in opposite directions, the one expecting to leave Paris by he gate of La Villette, and the other by the gate of Montmartre, with the understanding that they were to meet again beyond St. Denis. This, a strategic manoeuvre, was executed with perfect punctuality, and was crowned with the most fortunate results. D'Artagnan and Planchet entered Pierrefitte together.

Our two travellers arrived at Chantilly without any accident, and alighted at the hotel of the Great St. Martin, the same they had stopped at on their first trip.

The host, on seeing a young man followed by a lackey advanced respectfully to the door.

"I was thinking," said the host, "that it was not the first time I had had the honour of seeing you."

"Bah! I have passed, perhaps, ten times through Chantilly, and out of the ten times I have stopped at least three or four times at your house. Why, I was here only ten or twelve days ago. I was conducting some friends, musketeers, one of whom, by-the-bye, had a dispute with a manger, a man who, for some unknown reason, sought a quarrel with him."

"Ah, exactly so!" said the host; "I remember it perfectly. Is it not M. Porthos that your Lordship means?"

"Yes; that is my companions name. Good Heavens! my dear host, has any misfortune happened to him?"

"Your honour must have observed that he could not continue his journey."

"Why, but he promised to rejoin us, and we have seen nothing of him."

"He has done us the honour of remaining here."

"Well, can I see Porthos?"

"Certainly, sir. Take the stairs on your right; go up the first flight, and knock at No. 1. Only warn him that it is you."

"Warn him! Why should I do that?"

"Nobody enters his chamber except his servant."

"What!" Mousqueton is here, then?"

"Yes, sir; five days after his departure he came back in a very bad humour. It appears that he had also met with unpleasant experiences on his journey. Unfortunately he is more nimble than his master, so that for his master's sake he turns everything upside down; and as he thinks we might refuse what he asks for, he takes all he wants without asking at all."

"And what took place?"

"Oh, the affair was not long, I assure you. They placed themselves on guard. The stranger made a feint and a lunge, and that so rapidly that when M. de Porthos came to parry he had already three inches of steel in his breast. He fell on his back. The stranger immediately placed the point of his sword on his throat; and M. Porthos, finding himself at the mercy of his adversary, confessed himself conquered. Whereupon the stranger asked his name, and learning that it was Porthos, and not d'Artagnan assisted him to rise, brought him back to the hotel, mounted his horse, and disappeared."

"Very well. Now I know all that I wished to know. Porthos's room is, you say, on the first story, No. 1?"

Saying these words, D'Artagnan went upstairs. At the top of the stairs, on the most conspicuous door of the corridor, was traced in black ink a gigantic "No. 1." D'Artagnan knocked, and upon being told from inside to enter, went into the chamber.

Porthos was in bed, and was playing a game of lansquenet with Mousqueton, to keep his hand in, while a spit loaded with partridges was turning before the fire, and at each side of a large chimney-piece, over two chafing-dishes, were boiling two stewpans, from which exhaled a double odour of rabbit and garlic stews, very grateful to the olfactory nerves. In addition to this, he perceived that the top of a wardrobe and the marble of a stand were covered with empty bottles.

At the sight of his friend Porthos uttered a loud cry of joy; and Mousqueton, rising respectfully, yielded his place to him, and went to give an eye to the two stewpans, over which he appeared to have especial care.

"Ah, zounds! is that you?" said Porthos to D'Artagnan. "Welcome! Excuse my not coming to meet you. But," added he, looking at D'Artagnan with a certain degree of uneasiness, "you know what has happened to me?"

"Not exactly."

"Has the landlord told you nothing, then?"

"I asked after you, and came straight up."

Porthos seemed to breathe more freely.

"And what, then, has happened to you, my dear Porthos?" continued D'Artagnan.

"Why, on making a thrust at my adversary, whom I had already bit three tunes, and with whom I meant to finish by a fourth, my foot slipped on a stone, and I sprained my knee."

"Indeed!"

"Honour bright! Luckily for the rascal, for I should have left him dead on the spot, I assure you."

"And what became of him?"

"Oh, I don't know. He had enough, and set off without wanting any more. But you, my dear D'Artagnan, what has happened to you?"

"So that this sprain," continued D'Artagnan, "my dear Porthos, keeps you here in bed?"

"Really that's all! I shall be about again, however, in a few days."

While Porthos and Mousqueton were breakfasting with the appetites of convalescents, and with that brotherly cordiality which unites men in misfortune, D'Artagnan related how Aramis had been wounded, and was obliged to stop at Crèvecœur; how he had left Athos fighting at Amiens with four men, who accused him of being a counterfeiter; and how he, D'Artagnan, had been forced to pass over the Comte de Wardes's body in order to reach England.

But there D'Artagnan's disclosure ended.

At that moment Planchet entered. He informed his master that the horses were sufficiently refreshed, and that it would be possible to sleep at Clermont.

As D'Artagnan was tolerably reassured with regard to Porthos, and as he was anxious to obtain news of his two other friends, he held out his hand to the sick man, and told him he was going to resume his route in order to prosecute his researches. However, as he reckoned upon returning by the same road, if, in seven or eight days, Porthos were still at the hotel of the Great St. Martin, he would call for him on his way.

Porthos replied that, according to all probability, his sprain would snot permit him to depart during that time.

D'Artagnan, after having again recommended Porthos to the care of Mousqueton, and paid his reckoning to the landlord, resumed his route with Planchet.

Chapter 24

Aramis

D'Artagnan traversed the six or eight leagues between Chantilly and Crèvecœur.

This time not a host but a hostess received him. D'Artagnan was a physiognomist. His eye took in at a glance the plump, cheerful countenance of the mistress of the place, and he at once perceived there was no occasion for dissembling with her, or of fearing anything from such a jolly woman.

"My good dame," asked D'Artagnan, "could you tell me what has become of a friend of mine whom we were obliged to lease here about ten days ago?

"A handsome young man, of twenty-three or twenty-four, mild, amiable, and well made?"

"That's it."

"Wounded, moreover, in the shoulder?"

"Just so."

"Well, sir, he is still here."

"Ah, zounds! my dear dame," said D'Artagnan, springing from his horse and throwing the bridle to Planchet, "you restore me to life. Where is my dear Aramis? Let me embrace him! for, I confess it, am quite anxious to see him again."

"Well, you have only to take the right—hand staircase in the yard, and knock at No. 5 on the second floor."

D'Artagnan hastened in the direction pointed out, and turned to handle of the door No. 5.

The door opened, and D'Artagnan went into the chamber.

"Good-afternoon to you, dear D'Artagnan," said Aramis. "Believe me, I am very glad to see you."

"So am I delighted to see you," said D'Artagnan, and he added a reference to Aramis's wound.

"My wound, my dear D'Artagnan, has been a warning to me from Heaven."

"Your wound? Bah! it is nearly healed, and I am sure it is not that which at the present moment gives you the most pain."

"What wound?" asked Aramis, colouring.

"You have one in your heart, Aramis, deeper and more painful—a wound made by a woman."

The eye of Aramis kindled in spite of himself.

"Ah," said he, dissembling his emotion under a feigned carelessness, "do not talk of such things. What! I think of such things? I have love-pangs? *Vanitas vanitatum*! According to your idea, then, my brain is turned! And for whom? For some grisette, some chambermaid, whom I have courted in some garrison! Fie!"

"I crave your pardon, my dear Aramis, but I thought you aimed higher."

"Higher? And who am I, to nourish such ambition? A poor musketeer, a beggar and unknown, who hates slavery, and finds himself out of place in the world."

"Well, then, let us say no more about it," said D'Artagnan; "and let us burn this letter, which, no doubt, announces to you some fresh infidelity of your grisette or your chambermaid."

"What letter?" cried Aramis eagerly.

"A letter which was sent to your rooms in your absence, and which was given to me for you."

"But whom is that letter from?"

"Oh, from some tearful waiting-maid, some despairing grisette; from Madame de Chevreuse's chambermaid, perhaps, who must have been obliged to return to Tours with her mistress, and who, in order to make herself attractive, stole some perfumed paper, and sealed her letter with a duchess's coronet."

"What are you saying?"

"There! I really think I must have lost it," said the young man mischievously, while pretending to search for it. "But fortunately the world is a sepulchre; men, and consequently women also, are only shadows, and love is a sentiment upon which you cry, 'Fie, fie!'"

"D'Artagnan! D'Artagnan!" cried Aramis, "you are killing me!"

"At last, here it is!" said D'Artagnan. He drew the letter from his pocket.

Aramis sprang towards him, seized the letter, read it, or rather devoured it, his countenance absolutely beaming with delight.

"Your waiting-maid seems to have an agreeable style," said the carrier carelessly.

"Thanks, D'Artagnan, thanks!" cried Aramis, almost in a state of delirium. "She was forced to return to Tours; she is not faithless; she still loves me! Come, dear friend, come, let me embrace you; happiness stifles me!" And the two friends began to dance round.

At that moment Bazin entered.

"Be off, you scoundrel!" cried Aramis. "Order a larded hare, a fat capon, a leg of mutton with garlic, and four bottles of old Burgundy! 'Sdeath! let us drink while the wine is fresh. Let us drink heartily, and tell me something about what is going on in the world yonder."

Chapter 25

The Wife Of Athos

"Now we still have to get news of Athos," said D'Artagnan to the vivacious Aramis, when he had informed him of all that had passed since their departure from the capital, and when a good dinner had made one of them forget his woes and the other his fatigue.

"Do you think any harm can have happened to him?" asked Aramis. "Athos is so cool, so brave, and handles his sword so skilfully."

"There is no doubt of that. Nobody has a higher opinion of the courage and skill of Athos than I have; but I like better to hear my sword clang against lances than against staves. I fear lest Athos has been carried down by a mob of menials. Those fellows strike hard, and don't leave off in a hurry. This is my reason for wishing to set out again as soon as I possibly can."

"I will try to accompany you," said Aramis, "though I scarcely feel in a condition to mount on horseback. When do you set out?"

"To-morrow at daybreak."

"Till to-morrow, then," said Aramis; "for though you are made of iron you must need repose."

The next morning, when D'Artagnan entered Aramis's chamber, he found him standing at the window.

"My dear Aramis; take care of yourself," said he; "I will go alone in search of Athos."

"You are a man of bronze," replied Aramis.

"No, I have good luck, that is all. But how do you mean to pass your time till I come back?"

Aramis smiled. "I will make verses," said he.

"Yes, verses perfumed with the odour of the note from Madame de Chevreuse's serving-maid."

"Oh, make yourself easy on that head," replied Aramis; "you will find me ready to follow you."

They took leave of each other, and ten minutes later, after commending his friend to the care of Bazin and the hostess, D'Artagnan was trotting along in the direction of Amiens.

About eleven o'clock in the morning they perceived Amiens. At half-past eleven they were at the door of the cursed inn.

D'Artagnan related to Athos how he had found Porthos and Aramis. As he finished, the landlord entered with wine and a ham.

"Good!" said Athos, filling his glass and D'Artagnan's. "Here's to Porthos and Aramis! But, my friend, what is the matter with you, and what has happened to you personally? You don't look happy."

"Alas!" said D'Artagnan, "it is because I am the most unfortunate of all."

"You unfortunate!" said Athos. "Come! how the devil can you be unfortunate? Tell me that."

"Presently," said D'Artagnan.

"Presently! And why presently? Because you think I am drunk, D'Artagnan? Keep this in mind: my ideas are never so clear as when I have had plenty of wine. Speak, then; I am all ears."

D'Artagnan related his adventure with Madame Bonacieux. Athos listened to him without moving a muscle, and when he had finished,

"Trifles all that," said Athos—"nothing but trifles!" That was Athos's favourite expression.

"You always say trifles, my dear Athos," said D'Artagnan, "and that comes very ill from you, who have never been in love."

Athos's dull eye flashed suddenly, but it was only a flash; it became dull and vacant as before.

"True," said he quietly, "I have never been in love."

"Acknowledge, then, you stony-hearted man," said D'Artagnan, "that you have no right to be so hard on us whose hearts are tender."

"Your misfortune is laughable," said Athos, shrugging his shoulders. "I should like to know what you would say if I were to relate to you a real tale of love."

"Which concerns you?"

"Or one of my friends. What difference does it make?"

"Tell it, Athos, tell it."

"Let us drink! That will be better."

"Drink while you tell it!"

"Not a bad idea!" said Athos, emptying and filling his glass; "the two things go marvellously well together."

"I am all attention," said D'Artagnan.

Athos collected himself, and in proportion as he did so, D'Artagnan saw that he became paler. He was at that period of intoxication in which vulgar drinkers fall on the floor and go to sleep. But he dreamed aloud, without sleeping. This somnambulism of drunkenness had something frightful about it.

"You absolutely wish it?" he asked.

"I beg you to do it," said D'Artagnan.

"Be it, then, as you desire. A friend of mine—please to observe, a friend of mine, not myself," said Athos, interrupting himself with a gloomy smile—"one of the counts of my province (that is to say, of Berry), noble as a Dandolo or a Montmorency, when he was twenty-five years old fell in love with a girl of sixteen, beautiful as an angel. Through the ingenuousness of her age beamed an ardent mind—not a woman's mind, but a poet's. She did not please; she intoxicated. She lived in a small town with her brother, who was a vicar. Both had recently come into the country. Nobody knew where they came from; but on seeing her so lovely and her brother so pious, nobody thought of asking where they came from. They were said, however, to be of good extraction. My friend, who was lord of the country, might have seduced her; or he might have seized her forcibly, at his will, for he was master. Who would have come to the assistance of two strangers, two unknown persons? Unfortunately, he was an honourable man; he married her. The fool! the ass! the idiot!"

"How so, if he loved her?" asked D'Artagnan.

"Wait!" said Athos. "He took her to his château, and made her the first lady in the province; and in justice, it must be allowed she supported her rank becomingly."

"Well?" asked D'Artagnan.

"Well, one day when she was hunting with her husband," continued Athos, in a low voice, and speaking very quickly, "she fell from her horse and fainted. The count flew to her help; and as she appeared to be oppressed by her clothes, he ripped them open with his poniard, and in so doing laid bare her shoulder. Guess, D'Artagnan," said Athos, with a loud burst of laughter—"guess what she had on her shoulder."

"How can I tell?" said D'Artagnan.

"A list" said Athos. "She was branded!"

And Athos emptied at a single draught the glass he held in his hand.

"Horrors," cried D'Artagnan. "What are you telling me?"

"The truth. My friend, the angel was a demon. The poor young girl had been a thief."

"And what did the count do?"

"The count was a great noble. He had on his estates the right of life and death. He tore the countess's dress to pieces, tied her hands behind her, and hanged her on a tree!"

"Heavens, Athos, a murder!" cried D'Artagnan.

"Yes, a murder—nothing else," said Athos, pale as death. "But methinks I am left without wine!" And he seized by the neck the last bottle that remained, put it to his mouth, and emptied it at a single draught, as he would have emptied an ordinary glass.

Then he let his head fall on his two hands, while D'Artagnan sat facing him, overwhelmed with dismay.

"That has cured me of beautiful, poetical, and loving women," said Athos, getting to his feet, and neglecting to pursue the apologue of the count "God grant you as much! Let us drink!"

"Then she is dead?" stammered D'Artagnan.

"Zounds!" said Athos. "But hold out your glass. Some ham, my man!" cried Athos; "we can drink no longer!"

"And her brother?" asked D'Artagnan timidly.

"Her brother?" replied Athos.

"Yes, the priest."

"Oh, I inquired after him for the purpose of hanging him likewise; but he was beforehand with me—he had quitted the curacy instantly."

"Was it ever known who this miserable fellow was?"

"He was doubtless the fair lady's first lover and accomplice—a worthy man, who had pretended to be a curate for the purpose of getting his mistress married and securing her a position. He has been quartered before this time, I hope."

"My God! my God!" cried D'Artagnan, quire stunned by the relation, of this horrible, adventure.

"Pray eat some of this ham, D'Artagnan; it is exquisite," said Athos, cutting a slice, which he placed on the young man's plate. "What pity it is there are only four like this in the cellar! I could have drunk fifty bottles more."

D'Artagnan could no longer endure this conversation, which would have driven him crazy. He let his head fall on his hands and pretended to go to sleep.

"Young men no longer know how to drink," said Athos looking at him pityingly, "and yet this is one of the best of them, too!"

Their only anxiety now was to depart. D'Artagnan and Athos soon arrived at Crèvecœur. From a distance they perceived Aramis, seated in a melancholy manner at his window, looking out, like Sister Anne, at the dust in the horizon.

"Hello, ha, Aramis!" cried the two friends.

"Ah, it is you, D'Artagnan, and you, Athos," said the young man. "And so, my friends, we are returning, then, to Paris? Bravo! I am ready. We are going, then, to rejoin our good Porthos!"

They made a bait for an hour to refresh their horses. Aramis discharged his bill, and then set forward to join Porthos.

They found him up, not so pale as when D'Artagnan left him, and seated at a table, on which, though he was alone, was spread dinner enough for four persons. This dinner consisted of meats nicely dressed, choice wines, and superb fruit.

"Ah, by Jove!" said he, rising, "you came in the nick of time. Gentlemen, I was just at the soup, and you will dine with me."

The four friends, having set their minds at ease with regard to the future, did honour to the repast, the remains of which were abandoned to MM. Mousqueton, Bazin, Planchet, and Grimaud.

On arriving in Paris, D'Artagnan found a letter from M. de Tréville, informing him that, at his request, the king had just promised him his immediate admission into the musketeers.

As this was the height of D'Artagnan's worldly ambition—apart, of course, from his desire of finding Madame Bonacieux—he ran, full of joy, to seek his comrades, whom he had left only half an hour before. He found them very sad and deeply preoccupied. They were assembled in council at the residence of Athos, which always indicated an event of some seriousness.

M. de Tréville had just informed them that since it was his Majesty's fixed intention to open the campaign on the first of May, they must immediately get ready all their equipments.

The four philosophers looked at one another in a state of bewilderment. M. de Tréville never joked in matters relating to discipline.

"And what do you reckon your equipments will cost?" said D'Artagnan.

"Oh, we can scarcely venture to say. We have just made our calculations with Spartan niggardliness, and we each require fifteen hundred livres."

"Four times fifteen make sixty—ah! six thousand livres," said Athos.

"For my part, I think," said D'Artagnan, "with a thousand livres each—it is true I do not speak as a Spartan, but as a *procureur*—"

The word *procureur* roused Porthos.

"Stop!" said he; "I have an idea."

"Well, that's something. For my part, I have not the shadow of one," said Athos coolly. "But as to D'Artagnan, the hope of soon being one of us, gentlemen, has made him crazy. A thousand livres! I declare I want two thousand myself."

"Four times two make eight, then," said Aramis. "It is eight thousand that we want to complete our outfit."

"One thing more!" said Athos, waiting till D'Artagnan, who was going to thank M. de Tréville, had shut the door, "one thing more—that beautiful diamond which glitters on our friend's finger. What the devil! D'Artagnan is too good a comrade to leave his brothers in embarrassment while he wears a king's ransom on his middle finger."

CHAPTER 26

Milady

A Porthos had first found his idea, and had thought of it earnestly afterwards, he was the first to act. This worthy Porthos was a man of execution. D'Artagnan perceived him one day walking toward the church of St. Leu, and followed him instinctively. He entered the holy place. D'Artagnan entered behind him. Porthos went and leaned against one side of a pillar. D'Artagnan, still unperceived, leaned against the other side of it.

There happened to be a sermon, and this made the church very full of people. Porthos took advantage of this circumstance to ogle the women.

D'Artagnan observed, on the bench nearest to the pillar against which he and Porthos were leaning, a sort of ripe beauty, rather yellow and rather dry, but erect and haughty under her black hood. Porthos's eyes were furtively cast upon this lady, and then roved about at large over the nave.

On her side, the lady, who from time to time blushed, darted with the rapidity of lightning a glance toward the inconstant Porthos, and then immediately Porthos's eyes went wandering over the church anxiously. It was plain that this was a mode of proceeding that deeply piqued the lady in the black hood, for she bit her lips till they bled, scratched the end of her nose, and sat very uneasily in her seat.

Porthos, seeing this, began to make signals to a beautiful lady who was near the choir, and who was not only a beautiful lady, but also, no doubt, a great lady, for she had behind her a negro boy, who had brought the cushion on which she knelt, and a female servant, who held the emblazoned bag in which was placed the book from which she followed the service.

The lady of the red cushion produced a great effect—for she was very handsome—on the lady in the black hood, who saw in her a rival to be really dreaded; a great effect on Porthos, who thought her much prettier than the lady in the black hood; a great effect upon D'Artagnan, who recognized in her the lady of Meung, of Calais, whom his persecutor, the man with the scar, had saluted by the name of milady.

The sermon over, the solicitor's wife advanced toward the font of holy water. Porthos went before her, and instead of a finger, dipped his whole hand in.

"Eh, Monsieur Porthos, you don't offer me any holy water?"

Porthos, at the sound of her voice, started like a man awakening from a sleep of a hundred years.

"Ma—madame!" cried he, "is that you? How is your husband, our dear Monsieur Coquenard? Is he still as stingy as ever? Where can my eyes have been not to have even perceived you during the two hours the sermon has lasted?"

"I was within two paces of you, sir," replied the solicitor's wife; "but you did not perceive me, because you had eyes only for the pretty lady."

Porthos pretended to be confused.

"Ah," said he, "you have noticed—"

"I must have been blind if I had not."

"Yes," said Porthos carelessly, "that is a duchess of my acquaintance, whom I have great trouble to meet on account of her husband's jealousy, and who sent me word that she would come to-day, solely for the purpose of seeing me in this poor church, in his vile quarter."

"Monsieur Porthos," said the *procureuse*, "will you have the kindness to offer me your arm for five minutes? I have something to say to you."

"Certainly, madame," said Porthos, winking to himself, as a gambler does who laughs at the dupe he is about to pluck.

At that moment D'Artagnan was passing in pursuit of milady. He cast a glance at Porthos, and beheld his triumphant look.

"Ah, ha!" said he to himself, reasoning in accordance with the strangely easy morality of that gallant period, "here is one of us, at least, on the road to be equipped in time."

D'Artagnan had followed milady, without being perceived by her. He saw her get into her carriage, and heard her order the coachman to drive to St. Germain.

It was useless to endeavour to keep pace on foot with a carriage drawn by two powerful horses, so D'Artagnan returned to the Rue Férou.

In the Rue de Seine he met Planchet, who had stopped before a bake—shop, and was contemplating with ecstasy a cake of the most appetizing appearance.

D'Artagnan and Planchet got into the saddle, and cook the road to St. Germain.

Milady had spoken to the man in the black cloak. therefore she knew hire. Now, in D'Artagnan's opinion it was certainly the man in the black cloak who had carried off Madame Bonacieux the second time, as he had carried her off the first.

Thinking of all this, and from time to time giving his horse a touch of the spur, D'Artagnan completed his journey, and arrived at St. Germain. He was riding along a very quiet street, when from the ground floor of a pretty house, he saw a form appear that looked familiar. This person in question was walking along a kind of terrace, ornamented with flowers. Planchet recognized who it was first.

"Why, it is poor Lubin," said Planchet, "the lack of the Comte de Wardes, whom you so well accommodated a month ago at Calais, on the road to the governor's country house."

"So it is," said D'Artagnan; "I know him now. Do you think he would recollect you?"

"'Pon my word, sir, he was so greatly disturbed that I don't think he can have retained a very clear recollection of me."

"Well, go and get into conversation with him, and find out, if you can, whether his master is dead or not."

Planchet dismounted and went straight up to Lubin, who did not recognize him, and the two lackeys began to chat with the best understanding possible, while D'Artagnan turned the two horses into a lane, and went round the house so as to be present at the conference, coming back to take his place behind a hedge of hazels.

After a moment's watching from behind the hedge he heard the noise of a carriage, and saw milady's coach stop in front of him. He could not be mistaken; milady was in it. D'Artagnan bent over on his horse's neck in order to see everything without being seen.

Milady put her charming fair head out at the window, and gave some orders to her maid.

D'Artagnan followed the maid with his eyes, and saw her going toward the terrace. But it happened that some one in the house had called Lubin, so that Planchet remained alone, looking in all directions for D'Artagnan.

The maid approached Planchet, whom she took for Lubin, and holding out a little note to him,

"For your master," said she.

Thereupon she ran toward the carriage, which had turned round in the direction it had come; she jumped on the step, and the carriage drove off.

Planchet turned the note over and over; then, accustomed to passive obedience, he jumped down from the terrace, ran through the lane, and at the end of twenty paces met D'Artagnan, who, having seen all, was coming to him.

D'Artagnan opened the letter and read these words:

> "A person who takes more interest in you than she is willing to confess wishes to know on what day you will be in condition to walk in the forest. To-morrow, at the Hôtel Field of the Cloth of Gold, a lackey in black and red will wait for your reply."

"Oh, ho!" said D'Artagnan, "this is rather lively. It appears that milady and I are anxious about the health of the same person.— Well, Planchet, how is our good M. de Wardes? He is not dead, then?"

"Oh no, monsieur; he is as well as a man can be with four sword-wounds in his body—for you, without question, inflicted four upon the dear gentleman, and he is still very weak, having lost almost all his blood. As I told you, Lubin did not know me, and he related to me our adventure from one end to the other."

"Well done, Planchet! you are the king of lackeys. Now jump up on your horse, and let us overtake the carriage."

This they soon did. At the end of five minutes they perceived the carriage drawn up by the roadside. A cavalier richly dressed was close to the coach door.

The conversation between milady and the cavalier was so animated that D'Artagnan stopped on the other side of the carriage without any one but the pretty maid being aware of his presence. The conversation took place in English—a language which D'Artagnan could not understand; but by the accent the young man plainly saw that the beautiful Englishwoman was in a great rage. She terminated it by a gesture which left no doubt as to the nature of this conversation: this was a blow with her fan, applied with such force that the little feminine weapon flew into a thousand pieces.

The cavalier broke into a loud laugh, which appeared to exasperate milady.

D'Artagnan thought this was the moment to interfere. He approached the other door, and taking off his hat respectfully,

"Madame," said he, "will you permit me to offer you my services? This cavalier seems to have made you very angry. Speak one word, madame, and I will take it on myself to punish him for his lack of courtesy."

At the first word milady turned round, looking at the young man in astonishment; and when he had finished,

"Sir," said she, in very good French, "I should with great confidence place myself under your protection, if the person who is picking a quarrel with me were not my brother."

"Ah, excuse me, then," said D'Artagnan; "you must be aware that I was ignorant of, that, madame."

"What is that presumptuous fellow troubling himself about?" cried the cavalier whom milady had designated as her brother, stooping down to the height of the coach window, "and why does he not go on?"

"Presumptuous fellow yourself!" said D'Artagnan, also bending down on his horse's neck and answering through the carriage window. "I do not go on because it pleases me to stop here."

You might think that milady, timid as women are in general, would have interposed at this beginning of mutual provocations in order to prevent the quarrel from going too far; but, on the contrary, she threw herself back in her carriage, and called out coolly to the coachman, "Drive home!"

The pretty maid cast an anxious glance at D'Artagnan, whose good looks seemed to have produced an impression on her.

The carriage went on, and left the two men face to face, no material obstacle separating them any longer.

"Well, sir," said D'Artagnan, "you appear to be more presumptuous than I am, for you forget there is a little quarrel to arrange between us."

"You see well enough that I have no sword," said the Englishman. "Do you wish to play the braggart with an unarmed man?"

"I hope you have a sword at home," replied D'Artagnan. "But, at all events, I have two, and if you like I will throw with you for one of them."

"Quite unnecessary," said the Englishman; "I am well furnished with such sorts of playthings."

"Very well, my worthy gentleman," replied D'Artagnan; "pick out the longest, and come and show it to me this evening."

"Where?"

"Behind the Luxembourg. That's a charming place for such strolls as the one I propose to you."

"Very well; I will be there."

"Your hour?"

"Six o'clock. Now, then, who are you?" asked the Englishman.

"I am M. d'Artagnan, a Gascon gentleman, serving in the guards, in the company of M. des Essarts. And you?"

"I am Lord Winter, Baron of Sheffield."

"Well, then, I am your servant, baron," said D'Artagnan, "though your names are rather difficult to remember."

And touching his horse with his spur, he galloped back to Paris.

And D'Artagnan employed himself in arranging a little plan, the carrying out of which we shall see later on, and which promised him an agreeable adventure, as might be seen by the smiles which from time to time passed over his countenance, lighting up his thoughtful expression.

CHAPTER 27

English And French

The hour having come, he repaired to a yard behind the Luxembourg where goats were kept. He threw a piece of money to the goatkeeper to withdraw.

A silent party soon drew near to the same enclosure, and came into it.

"Sir," said D'Artagnan, "are we ready?"

"Yes!" answered the Englishman.

"On guard, then! " cried D'Artagnan.

And immediately two swords glittered in the rays of the setting sun, and the combat began with an animosity very natural to men who were enemies.

As to D'Artagnan, he fought purely and simply on the defensive. Then when he saw his adversary pretty well fatigued, with a vigorous side—thrust he knocked his sword from his grasp. The baron, finding himself disarmed, retreated two or three paces; but at this moment his foot slipped, and he fell backward.

D'Artagnan was on him at a bound, and placing his sword on his throat,

"I could kill you, sir," said he to the Englishman; "you are quite at my mercy, but I spare your life for pour sister's sake."

D'Artagnan was overjoyed. He had just realized the plan which he had conceived the development of which had occasioned the smiles we mentioned.

The Englishman, delighted at having to do with such a generous gentleman, pressed D'Artagnan in his arms, and paid a thousand compliments to him.

"And now, my young friend—for you will permit me, I hope, "to call you by that name," said Lord Winter—"on this very evening, if agreeable to you, I will present you to my sister, Lady Clarick. For I am desirous that she m her turn should take you into her good graces; and as she is in favour at court, perhaps, in the future, a word spoken by her might prove useful to you."

D'Artagnan reddened with pleasure and bowed his assent.

Lord Winter, on quitting D'Artagnan, gave him his sister's address. She lived at No. 6 Place Royale, then the fashionable quarter. Moreover, he promised to call and get him in order to present him. D'Artagnan appointed eight o'clock at Athos's residence.

Lord Winter arrived at the appointed time; but Athos, being warned of his coming, went into the other chamber. The Englishman accordingly found D'Artagnan alone, and as it was nearly eight o'clock, he took the young man with him.

An elegant coach below, drawn by two excellent horses, was waiting. They were soon at the Place Royale.

Milady Clarick received D'Artagnan seriously.

"You see," said Lord Winter, presenting D'Artagnan to his sister, "a young gentleman who has held my life in his hands, and who has not abused his advantage, although we were doubly enemies, since it was I who insulted him, and since I am an Englishman. Thank him, then, madame, if you have any affection for me."

Milady frowned slightly; a scarcely visible cloud passed over her brow, and such a peculiar smile appeared on her lips that the young man, observing this triple shade, almost shuddered at it.

"You are welcome, sir," said milady, in a voice the singular sweetness of which contrasted with the symptoms of ill-humour which D'Artagnan had just remarked; "you have to-day acquired eternal rights to my gratitude."

The pretty little maid whom D'Artagnan had already observed then came in. She spoke some words in English to Lord Winter, who immediately requested D'Artagnan's permission to retire, excusing himself on account of the urgency of the business that called him away, and charging his sister to obtain his pardon.

D'Artagnan shook hands with Lord Winter, and then returned to milady. Her countenance, with surprising mobility, had recovered its gracious expression.

The conversation took a cheerful turn. She told D'Artagnan that Lord Winter was only her brother-in-law, and not her brother. She had married a younger brother of the family, who had left her a widow with one child. This child was Lord Winter's sole heir, if Lord Winter did not marry. All this showed D'Artagnan that there was a veil hiding something, but he could not yet see under this veil.

Moreover, after half an hour's conversation D'Artagnan was convinced that milady was his compatriot. She spoke French with a purity and an elegance that left no doubt on that head.

He was profuse in gallant speeches and protestations of devotion. To all the nonsense which escaped our Gascon, milady replied with a smile of kindness. The hour for retiring arrived. D'Artagnan took leave of milady, and left the parlour the happiest of men.

On the stairs he met the pretty maid, who brushed gently against him as she passed, and then, blushing to the eyes, asked his pardon for having touched him in so sweet a voice that the pardon was granted instantly.

D'Artagnan came again on the morrow, and was even better received than on the day before. Lord Winter was not at home, and milady this time did all the honours of the evening. She appeared to take a great interest in him, and asked him where he was from, who were his friends, and whether he had not at sometimes thought of attaching himself to the cardinal.

D'Artagnan, who, as we have said, was exceedingly prudent for a young man of twenty, then remembered his suspicions regarding milady. He launched into a eulogy of his Eminence, and said that he should not have failed to enlist in the cardinal's guards instead of the king's if he had only known M. de Cavois instead of M. de Tréville.

Milady changed the conversation without any appearance of affectation, and asked D'Artagnan, in the most careless manner possible, if he had never been in England.

D'Artagnan replied that he had been sent there by M. de Tréville to bargain for some new horses.

At the same hour as on the preceding evening D'Artagnan retired. In the corridor he again met the pretty Kitty; that was the maid's name. She looked at him with an expression of good—will which it was impossible to mistake. But D'Artagnan was so preoccupied by her mistress that he noticed absolutely nothing which did not come from her.

D'Artagnan came again on the morrow and the day after that, and each day milady gave him a more gracious welcome.

Every evening, either in the antechamber, the corridor, or on the stairs, he met the pretty maid. But, as we have said, D'Artagnan paid no attention to poor Kitty's persistence.

CHAPTER 28

Maid And Mistress

In spite of the warnings of his conscience and the wise counsels of Athos, D'Artagnan hour by hour grew more and more deeply in love with milady. So the venturesome Gascon paid court to her every day, and he was convinced that sooner or later she could not fail to respond. One day when he arrived with his head in the air and as light at heart as a man who is expecting a shower of gold, he found the maid at the gateway of the hotel. But this time the pretty Kitty was not satisfied with merely touching him as he passed; she took him gently by the hand.

"Good!" thought D'Artagnan; "she is charged with some message to me from her mistress. She is about to appoint a meeting which she probably has not the courage to speak of." And he looked down at the pretty girl with the most triumphant air imaginable.

"I should like to speak a few words with you, Chevalier," stammered the maid.

"Speak, my dear, speak," said D'Artagnan; "I am all attention."

"Here? That's impossible. What I have to say is too long, and, still more, too secret."

"Well, what is to be done?"

"If you will follow me?" said Kitty timidly.

"Wherever you please."

"Come, then."

And Kitty, who had not let go D'Artagnan's hand, led him up a little dark, winding staircase, and, after ascending about fifteen steps, opened a door.

"Come in here, Chevalier," said she; "here we shall be alone, and can talk."

"And whose chamber is this, my pretty friend?"

"It is mine, Chevalier. It communicates with my mistress's by that door. But you need not fear; she will not hear what we say; she never goes to bed before midnight."

D'Artagnan glanced around him. The little apartment was charmingly tasteful and neat. But in spite of himself his eyes were directed to the door which Kitty said led to milady's chamber.

Kitty guessed what was passing in the young man's mind, and sighed.

"You love my mistress, then, very dearly, Chevalier?" said she,

"Oh, more than I can say, Kitty! I am madly in love with her!"

Kitty sighed again.

"Alas, sir," said she, "that is a great pity."

"What the devil do you see so pitiable in it?" said D'Artagnan.

"Because, sir," replied Kitty, "my mistress does not love you at all."

"Hah!" said D'Artagnan; "can she have charged you to tell me so?"

"Oh no, sir. Out of the regard I have for you I have taken on myself to tell you so."

"I am much obliged, my dear Kitty, but for the intention only—for the information, you must agree, is not very pleasant."

"That is to say, you don't believe what I have told you, do you?"

"We always have some difficulty in believing such things, if only from self-love."

"Then you don't believe me?"

" Why, I confess that unless you give me some proof of what you advance—"

"What do you say to this?"

And Kitty drew a little note from her bosom.

"For me?" said D'Artagnan, snatching the letter from her.

"No; for another."

"For another?"

"Yes."

"His name! his name!" cried D'Artagnan.

"Read the address."

"The Comte de Wardes."

The remembrance of the scene at St. Germain presented itself to the mind of the presumptuous Gascon. As quick as thought he tore open the letter, in spite of the cry which Kitty uttered on seeing what he was going to do, or rather what he was doing.

"Oh, good Lord! Chevalier," said she, "what are you doing?"

"I?" said D'Artagnan; "nothing." And he read,

> "You have not answered my first note. Are you indisposed, or have you forgot the glances you gave me at Madame de Guise's ball? You have an opportunity now, Count; do not allow it to escape."

D'Artagnan became very pale.

"Poor dear Monsieur d'Artagnan!" said Kitty, in a voice full of compassion, and pressing the young man's hand again.

"You pity me, my kind little creature?" said D'Artagnan.

"That I do, and with all my heart, for I know what it is to be in love."

"You know what it is to be in love?" said D'Artagnan, looking at her for the first time with some attention.

"Alas, yes."

"Well, then, instead of pitying me you would do much better to assist me in wreaking my revenge on your mistress."

"And what sort of revenge would you take?"

"I would triumph over her, and supplant my rival."

"I will never help you in that, Chevalier," said Kitty warmly.

"Why not?"

"For two reasons."

"What are they?"

"The first is, that my mistress will never love you. The second reason, Chevalier is, that in love, every one for herself!"

Then only D'Artagnan remembered Kitty's languishing glances and stifled sigh; how she constantly met him in the antechamber, in the corridor, or on the stairs; how she touched him with her hand every time she met him. But absorbed by his desire to please the great lady, he had disdained the maid. He who hunts the eagle heeds not the sparrow.

But this time our Gascon saw at a glance all the advantage that he might derive from the love which Kitty had just confessed so naively, or so boldly—the interception of letters addressed to the Comte de Wardes, bits of secret information, entrance at all hours into Kitty's chamber, which was near her mistress's. The perfidious fellow, as may be seen, was already sacrificing in idea the poor girl to obtain milady willingly or by force.

"Well, my dear Kitty," said he to the young girl, "do you want me to give you a proof of that love of which you doubt?"

"What love?" asked the girl.

"Of that which I am ready to feel for you."

"And what proof is that?"

"Do you want me to spend with you this evening the time I generally spend with your mistress?"

"Oh yes!" said Kitty, clapping her hands, "indeed I do."

"Well, then, my dear girl," said D'Artagnan, establishing himself in an armchair, "come here and let me tell you that you are the prettiest maid I ever saw."

And he told her so much, and so well, that the poor girl, who asked nothing better than to believe him, believed him. Nevertheless, to D'Artagnan's great astonishment, the pretty Kitty defended herself with considerable resolution.

Time passes very rapidly in attacks and repulses.

Twelve o'clock struck, and almost at the same time the bell was rung in milady's chamber.

"Great Heavens!" cried Kitty, "there is my mistress calling me! Go, go quick!"

D'Artagnan rose, took his hat as if it had been his intention to obey; then quickly opening the door of a large wardrobe, instead of the door of the staircase, he crouched down in the midst of milady's robes and dressing-gowns.

"What are you doing?" cried Kitty.

D'Artagnan, who had secured the key, locked himself into the wardrobe without replying.

"Well," cried milady, in a sharp voice, "are you asleep, that you don't answer when I ring?"

And D'Artagnan hear the communicating door opened violently.

"Here I am, milady, here I am!" cried Kitty, springing forward to meet her mistress.

Both went into the bedroom, and as the door remained open, D'Artagnan could hear milady for some time scolding her maid. Then at last she grew cooler, and the conversation turned upon him while Kitty was assisting her mistress to undress.

"Well," said milady, "I have not seen our Gascon this evening."

"What, milady! has he not been here?" said Kitty. "Could he be inconstant before having been made happy?"

"Oh no; he must have been prevented by M. de Tréville or M. des Essarts. I understand my game, Kitty. I have him safe."

"What are you going to do with him, madame?"

"Do with him? O Kitty, there is something between that man and me that he is quite ignorant of. He very nearly made me lose my credit with his Eminence. Oh, I will be revenged for that!"

"I thought you loved him."

"Love him? I detest him—a fool, who held Lord Winter's life in his hands and did not kill him, so that I missed three hundred thousand livres a year!"

"That's true," said Kitty; "your son was his uncle's only heir, and until his coming of age you would have had the enjoyment of his fortune."

D'Artagnan shuddered to his very marrow at hearing this gentle creature reproach him in that sharp voice, which she took such pains to conceal in conversation, for not having killed a man whom he had seen load her with kindnesses.

"Therefore," continued milady, "I should long ago have had my revenge on him, if the cardinal—I don't know why—had not requested me to treat him kindly."

"Oh yes; but you have not treated very kindly the little woman he was so fond of."

"What! the mercer's wife of the Rue des Fossoyeurs? Has he not already forgotten she ever existed? Fine vengeance that, 'pon my word!

A cold sweat broke from D'Artagnan's brow. This woman was a monster!

He resumed his listening, but unfortunately the toilet was completed.

"That will do," said milady. "Go into your own room, and tomorrow try again to get for me an answer to the letter I gave you."

"For M. de Wardes?" said Kitty.

"To be sure; for M. de Wardes."

"He is a man," said Kitty, "who appears to be quite different from that poor M. d'Artagnan."

"Go to bed, miss," said milady; "I don't like comments."

D'Artagnan heard the door close, then the noise of two bolts by which milady fastened herself in. Kitty on her side, as softly as possible, turned the key of the lock, and then D'Artagnan opened the closet door.

"O Heavens!" said Kitty, in a low voice, "what is the matter with you? How pale you are!"

"The abominable creature!" murmured D'Artagnan.

"Silence, silence! do go!" said Kitty. "There is nothing but a thin partition between my chamber and milady's; every word spoken in one can be heard in the other."

"That's just the reason I won't go," said D'Artagnan.

"What!" said Kitty, blushing.

"Or, at least, I will go—later."

And he drew Kitty to him. There was no way to resist—resistance makes so much noise. Therefore Kitty yielded. This was an impulse of vengeance on milady. D'Artagnan realized the truth of the saying that vengeance is the delight of the gods. Therefore, with a little natural affection, he might have been satisfied with this new conquest; but D'Artagnan knew only ambition and pride.

However, it must be said to his praise that the first use he made of his influence over Kitty was to try to learn from her what had become of Madame Bonacieux; but the poor girl swore on the crucifix to D'Artagnan that she was entirely ignorant in regard to that, her mistress never letting her know half her secrets. Only she believed she could say she was not dead.

D'Artagnan came the next day to milady's. As she was in a very ill humour, he suspected that the lack of an answer from M. de Wardes provoked her to be so. Kitty came in, but milady was very cross with her. She glanced at D'Artagnan, as much as to say, "See how I suffer on your account!"

Toward the end of the evening, however, the beautiful lioness became milder. She smilingly listened to D'Artagnan's soft speeches; she even gave him her hand to kiss.

When D'Artagnan took his departure he scarcely knew what to think; but as he was a youth not easily carried away by his emotions, even while he was continuing to pay court to milady he framed a little plan.

He found Kitty at the gate, and, as on the evening before, went up to her chamber. Kitty had been severely scolded; she was charged with negligence. Milady could not at all understand the Comte de Wardes's silence, and she ordered Kitty to come at nine o'clock in the morning to take a third letter to him.

D'Artagnan made Kitty promise to bring him that letter on the following morning. The poor girl promised all her lover desired; she was madly in love.

Everything occurred as it had the night before. D'Artagnan concealed himself in his wardrobe, milady called, undressed, sent Kitty away, and shut the door. As before, D'Artagnan returned home at five o'clock in the morning.

At eleven o'clock he saw Kitty coming; she held in her hand a fresh note from milady. This tithe the poor girl did not even hesitate at giving up the note to D'Artagnan. She let him do as he pleased. She belonged, body and soul, to her handsome soldier.

D'Artagnan opened the letter, and read as follows:

> "This is the third time I have written to you to tell you that I love you. Beware lest I write to you a fourth time to tell you that I detest you.
> "If you repent of the manner in which you have treated me, the young girl who brings you this note will tell you how a gentleman may obtain his pardon."

D'Artagnan coloured and grew pale several times as he read this note.

"Oh, you love her still," said Kitty, who had not for an instant taken her eyes off the young man's face.

"No, Kitty, you are mistaken; I do not love her, but I wish to revenge myself for her contempt of me."

"Oh yes, I know your vengeance! You told me!"

"What difference does it make to you, Kitty? You know f love only you."

"How can I be sure of that?"

"By the contempt I will cast on her."

D'Artagnan took a pen and wrote,

"Madame,—Until the present moment I could not believe that your two first letters were addressed to me, so unworthy did I feel myself of such an honour; besides, I was so seriously indisposed that I should, in any case, have hesitated to reply to them.

"But now I must believe in the excess of your kindness, since not only your letter but your servant assures me that I have the good fortune to be loved by you.

"She has no occasion to teach me the way in which a gentleman may obtain his pardon. I will come and ask mine at eleven o'clock this evening.

"To delay it a single day would be, in my eyes, now to commit a fresh offence.

"He whom you have rendered the happiest of men,

COMTE DE WARDES

D'Artagnan's plan was very simple. By Kitty's chamber he could gain her mistress's. He would take advantage of the first moment of surprise, shame, and terror to triumph over her.

The campaign was to open in a week, and he would be compelled to leave Paris. D'Artagnan had no time for a prolonged love-making.

"There!" said the young man, handing Bitty the letter sealed and addressed; "give this note to milady. It is the Comte de Wardes's reply."

Poor Kitty turned deathly pale: she suspected what the letter contained.

"But what does your note say?"

"Milady will tell you."

"Ah, you do not love me," cried Kitty, "and I am very wretched."

To such a reproach there is one answer that always deceives women. D'Artagnan replied in a way that left Kitty entirely convinced. Yet she wept a great deal before she could make up her mind to give the letter to milady. But at last she decided to do so, and that was all that D'Artagnan wanted.

Besides, he promised her that he would leave her mistress early that evening, and on coming out of the parlour would go up to Kitty's room. This promise completely consoled poor Kitty.

Chapter 29

Which Treats Of The Outfit Of Aramis And Porthos

Since the four friends had each been outfit-hunting they had had no regular meeting. They dined separately wherever they happened to be, or rather wherever they might find a dinner. Military duty likewise claimed its share of the precious time that was gliding away so swiftly.

They had agreed, however, to meet once a week about one o'clock at Athos's.

The day that Kitty went to see D'Artagnan was the day for their reunion.

Kitty had barely left him before D'Artagnan directed his steps toward the Rue Férou.

Porthos arrived a minute after D'Artagnan. Thus the four friends were all assembled.

Their four faces expressed four different feelings—Porthos's, tranquillity; D'Artagnan's, hope; Aramis's, anxiety; and Athos's, carelessness.

Bazin made his appearance at the door.

"What do you want of me, my friend?" said Aramis, with that mildness of language which was observable in him every time that his ideas led toward the church.

"A man is waiting for you at home," replied Bazin.

"Has he sent no special message for me?"

"Yes. 'If M. Aramis hesitates to come,' he said, 'tell him I am from Tours.'"

"From Tours!" cried Aramis. "A thousand pardons, gentlemen, but no doubt this man brings me the news I expected."

And instantly arising, he went off at a quick pace.

We will therefore leave the friends, who had nothing very important to say to each other, and follow Aramis.

On the news that the person who wanted to speak to him came from Tours, we saw with what rapidity the young man followed or rather hastened ahead of Bazin: he ran without stopping from the Rue Férou to the Rue de Vaugirard.

On entering, he found a man of short stature and intelligent eyes, but covered with rags.

"Did you ask for me?" said the musketeer.

"I wish to speak with Monsieur Aramis. Is that your name, sir?"

"Yes. You have brought me something?"

"Yes, if you can show me a certain embroidered handkerchief."

"Here it is," said Aramis, taking a key from his breast, and opening a little ebony box inlaid with mother-of-pearl—"here it is—look!"

The mendicant cast a rapid glance around him, in order to be sure that nobody could either see or hear him, and opening his ragged jacket, badly held together by a leather strap, he began to rip the upper part of his doublet, and drew a letter from it.

Aramis uttered a cry of joy at the sight of the seal, kissed the superscription, and with almost religious respect opened the letter, which contained the following:

> "Love,—Fate wills that we should be still for some time separated; but the delightful days of youth are not lost beyond return. Perform your duty in camp; I will do mine elsewhere. Accept what the bearer brings you; take part in the campaign like a true gentleman, and think of me, who tenderly kiss your black eyes!
> "Adieu! or, rather, *au revoir!*"

The mendicant kept ripping. He drew one by one from out his rags a hundred and fifty Spanish double pistoles, and laid them down on the table. Then he opened the door, bowed, and went out before the young man, stupefied, had a chance to address a word to him.

Aramis then re-read the letter, and perceived there was a postscript.

> "P.S.—You may welcome the bearer, who is a count and a grandee of Spain."

And he passionately kissed the letter, without even looking at the gold sparkling on the table.

Bazin was dazed at the sight of the gold, and forgot that he was coming to announce D'Artagnan, who, curious to know who the mendicant was, came to Aramis's residence on leaving Athos's.

Now, as D'Artagnan used no ceremony with Aramis, when he saw that Bazin forgot to announce him, he announced himself.

"The devil! my dear Aramis," said D'Artagnan, "if these are the prunes that are sent to you from Tours, you will make my compliments to the gardener who gathers them."

"You are mistaken, my dear," said Aramis, who was always discreet; "my bookseller has just sent me the price of that poem in one-syllable verse which I began yonder."

And having put two or three double pistoles into his pocket to answer the needs of the moment, he locked the others in the ebony box inlaid with mother-of-pearl, where he kept the famous handkerchief which served him as a talisman.

CHAPTER 30

At Night All Cats Are Grey

The evening so impatiently awaited by D'Artagnan at length arrived. D'Artagnan as usual, presented himself about nine o'clock at milady's house. He found her in a charming humour. Never had she received him so kindly. Our Gascon saw at the first glance that his note had been delivered and was doing its work.

Kitty entered, bringing some sherbet. Her mistress was very pleasant to her, and greeted her with her most gracious smile.

At ten o'clock milady began to appear uneasy. D'Artagnan understood what it meant. She looked at the dock, got up, sat down again, and smiled at D'Artagnan as much as to say, "You are doubtless very likeable, but you would be charming if you would go away."

D'Artagnan rose and took his hat; milady gave him her hand to kiss. The young man felt that she pressed his hand, and he understood that she did so, not out of coquetry, but from a feeling of gratitude at his departure.

This time Kitty was not waiting for him, either in the anteroom, or in the corridor, or under the gateway. D'Artagnan was obliged alone to find the staircase and the little chamber. Kitty was sitting down, her head hidden in her hands, and was weeping.

She heard D'Artagnan enter, but did not raise her head at all. The young man went up to her, took her hands; then she burst out into sobs.

As D'Artagnan had supposed, milady, on receiving the letter, had, in the delirium of her joy, told her maid everything. Then, as a reward for the manner in which she had this time done her errand, she had given Kitty a purse.

On returning to her room Kitty had flung the purse into a corner, where it was lying wide open, disgorging three or four gold coins on the carpet.

The poor girl lifted her head at D'Artagnan's caresses. He was terrified at the change in her countenance. She clasped her hands supplicatingly, but without venturing to speak a word.

At last, as the time for the interview with the count drew near, milady had all the lights extinguished, and dismissed Kitty with an injunction to introduce De Wardes the moment he arrived.

Kitty was not kept waiting long. Scarcely had D'Artagnan seen that the whole apartment was in darkness, when he sprang from his hidingplace just as Kitty was closing the door.

"What is that noise?" asked milady.

"It is I, the Comte de Wardes," replied D'Artagnan in a whisper.

"Well," said milady in a trembling voice, "why do you not come in? Count, count!" added she, "you well know I am waiting for you."

At this appeal D'Artagnan pushed Kitty gently aside and darted into the chamber.

"Yes, count," said milady, in her sweetest voice, and pressing his hand tenderly in hers—"yes, I am happy in the love which your looks and words have expressed to me each time we have met. I love you also. To-morrow, to-morrow, I wish some pledge from you to prove to me that you think of me. And lest you forget me, take this!"

She took a ring from her finger and put it on D'Artagnan's.

D'Artagnan remembered seeing that ring on milady's hand. It was a magnificent sapphire encircled by brilliants.

At that moment he felt ready to reveal everything. He opened his mouth to tell milady who he was, and with what revengeful purpose he had come, when she added,

"Poor dear angel, whom that monster of a Gascon came so near killing!"

The monster was himself!

"Do you suffer still from your wounds?" continued she.

"Yes, a great deal," said D'Artagnan, hardly knowing what to answer.

"Be assured," murmured she, "I will avenge you, and cruelly."

D'Artagnan needed some time to recover from this short dialogue. But all the ideas of vengeance he had brought had vanished completely. This woman exercised over him an unaccountable fascination: he hated her and adored her at the same moment.

But one o'clock had just struck, and they had to separate. D'Artagnan at the moment of leaving milady felt only a keen regret at departing, and in the passionate farewell they mutually bade each other a new interview was agreed upon for the following week. Poor Kitty hoped she might say some words to D'Artagnan when he came into her room; but milady herself guided him through the darkness, and left him only on the staircase.

The next morning D'Artagnan hastened to Athos's room. He had started on such a strange adventure that he wished to ask his advice. He told him everything. Athos frowned more than once. "Your milady," said he, "appears to me an infamous creature, but none the less did wrong in deceiving her. Now you have, in one way or another, a terrible enemy on your hands."

While talking to him Athos was gazing earnestly at the sapphire surrounded wi diamonds which had replaced on D'Artagnan's finger the queen's ring now carefully kept in a jewel-case.

"You are looking at my ring?" said the Gascon, proud of showing off such a rich gift before his friend.

"Yes," said Athos; "it reminds me of a family jewel."

"It is beautiful, isn't it?" said D'Artagnan.

"Magnificent!" replied Athos. "I did not think there existed two sapphires of such fine water. Did you exchange it for your diamond?"

"No," said D'Artagnan; "it is a gift from my beautiful English-woman, or rather from my beautiful Frenchwoman, for though I never have asked her, I am convinced she was born in France."

"This ring comes from milady!" cried Athos in a tone which revealed great emotion.

"From herself. She gave it to me last night."

"Show me your ring, I beg of you," said Athos.

"Here it is," replied D'Artagnan, drawing it from his finger.

Athos examined it and grew very pale. Then he tried it on the ring-finger of his left hand. It fitted his finger as if it had been made for it. A shadow of anger and vengeance passed over the nobleman's brow, usually so calm.

"It is impossible it can be she," said he. "How could that ring be in Milady Clarick's possession? And yet it is very difficult to find such an exact resemblance between two jewels."

"Do you know that ring?" asked D'Artagnan.

"I thought I did," said Athos; "but no doubt I was mistaken."

And he gave it back to D'Artagnan, without ceasing, however, to eye it.

"Come, D'Artagnan," said he after a moment, "take that ring off your finger, or turn the stone inside. It brings up to me such cruel memories that I could not keep cool enough to talk with you. Didn't you come to ask advice of me? Didn't you tell me you were in doubt what to do? But stop to let me take that sapphire again. The one I mentioned had one of its facets scratched in consequence of an accident."

D'Artagnan took the ring again from his finger and gave it to Athos.

Athos shuddered. "Ha!" said he; "look, isn't it strange?" And he showed D'Artagnan the scratches he remembered should be there.

"But from whom did you get this sapphire, Athos?"

"From my mother. As I tell you, it is an old family jewel, which never was to leave the family."

"And you—sold it?" asked D'Artagnan hesitatingly.

"No," replied Athos, with a singular smile; "I gave it away in a night of love, as it was given to you."

D'Artagnan became thoughtful in his turn. He seemed to see in milady's soul abysses the depths of which were full of darkness and mystery. He took back the ring, but put it in his pocket and not on his finger.

On reaching home D'Artagnan found Kitty waiting for him. A month of fever would not have changed the poor girl more than that night of sleeplessness and grief.

She was sent by her mistress to the false De Wardes. Her mistress was mad with love, intoxicated with joy. She wished to know when her lover would meet her again. And poor Kitty, pale and trembling, awaited D'Artagnan's reply.

As his reply he took a pen and wrote the following letter:

> "Do not depend upon me, madame, for the next meeting. Since my convalescence I have so many affairs of this kind on my hands that I am compelled to take them in a certain order. When your turn comes, I shall have the honour to inform you of it. I kiss your hands.

> COMTE DE WARDES

D'Artagnan handed the open letter to Kitty, who at first was unable to comprehend it, but who became almost wild with joy on reading it a second time. She could scarcely believe her happiness. She ran back to the Place Royale as fast as her feet could carry her.

Milady opened the letter with eagerness equal to Kitty's in bringing it. But at the first words she read she became livid. She crushed the paper in her hand, and turning with flashing eyes on Kitty,

"What is this letter?" cried she.

"The answer to yours, madame," replied Kitty, all in a tremble.

"Impossible!" cried milady. "It is impossible that a gentleman could have written such a letter to a woman."

She ground her teeth; she became ashen pale. She tried to take a step toward the window for air, but she could only stretch out her arms; her legs failed her, and she sank into an armchair.

CHAPTER 31

Dream Of Vengeance

That evening milady gave orders that when M. d'Artagnan came as usual, he should be immediately admitted. But he did not come.

The next day Kitty went to see the young man again, and related to him all that had passed the evening before. D'Artagnan smiled.

Milady's jealous anger was his revenge.

That evening milady was still more impatient than on the preceding one. She renewed the order relative to the Gascon; but, as before, she expected him in vain.

The next morning, when Kitty presented herself at D'Artagnan's, she was no longer joyous and alert, as she had been on the two preceding days, but, on the contrary, melancholy as death.

D'Artagnan asked the poor girl what was the matter; but her only reply was to draw a letter from her pocket and give it to him.

This letter was in milady's handwriting, only this time it was addressed to D'Artagnan, and not to M. de Wares.

He opened it and read as follows:

> "Dear Monsieur D'Artagnan,—It is wrong thus to neglect your friends, particularly when you are about to leave them for such a long time. My brother-in-law and myself expected you yesterday and the day before, but in vain. Will it be the same this evening?
> "Your very grateful
>
> LADY CLARICK

"It's very simple," said D'Artagnan; "I was expecting this letter. My credit rises by the Comte de Wardes's fall."

Instinct caused poor Kitty to guess a part of what was going to happen. D'Artagnan reassured her as well as he could, and promised to remain insensible to milady's seductions. He desired Kitty to tell her mistress that he was most grateful for her kindnesses, and that he would be obedient to her orders. But he dare not write, for fear of not being able sufficiently to disguise his writing to deceive such experienced eyes as milady's.

As nine o'clock was striking, D'Artagnan was at the Place Royale.

Milady assumed the most friendly air possible, and conversed with more than her usual brilliancy. At the same time the fever, which for an instant had left her, returned to give lustre to her eyes, colour to her cheeks, and vermilion to her lips. D'Artagnan was again in the presence of the Circe who had before surrounded him with her enchantment.

His love, which he believed to be extinct, but which was only asleep, awoke again in his heart. Milady smiled, and D'Artagnan felt that he could go to perdition for that smile.

There was a moment when he felt something like remorse.

By degrees milady became more communicative. She asked D'Artagnan if he had a mistress.

"Alas!" said D'Artagnan, with the most sentimental air he could assume, "can you be cruel enough to put such a question to me—to me who, from the moment I saw you, have only breathed and sighed by reason of you and for you!"

Milady smiled with a strange smile.

"Then you do love me?" said she.

"Have I any need to tell you so? Have you not perceived it?"

"Yes; but you know the prouder hearts are, the more difficult they are to be won."

"Oh, difficulties do not frighten me," said D'Artagnan. "I shrink before nothing but impossibilities."

"Nothing is impossible," replied milady, "to true love."

"Nothing, madame?"

"Nothing," repeated milady.

D'Artagnan impetuously drew his seat nearer to milady's.

"Well, now," she said, "let us see what you should do to prove this love of which you speak."

"All that could be required of me. Order; I am ready."

Milady remained thoughtful and apparently undecided for a moment; then, as if appearing to have formed a resolution,

"I have an enemy," said she.

"You, madame!" said D'Artagnan, affecting surprise; "is it possible? Heavens! good and beautiful as you are! "

"A mortal enemy."

"Really?"

"An enemy who has insulted me so cruelly that between him and me it is war to the death. May I count on you as my ally?"

D'Artagnan at once perceived what the vindictive creature was aiming at.

"You may, madame," said he, with emphasis. "My arm and my life are yours, as my love is."

"But," said milady, "how shall I repay such a service? I know what lovers are: they are men who will not do anything for nothing."

"You know the only reply that I desire," said D'Artagnan—"the only one worthy of you and of me!"

And he drew her gently to him.

She scarcely resisted.

"Selfish man!" cried she, smiling.

"Ah!" cried D'Artagnan, really carried away by the passion this woman had the power to kindle in his heart "ah! because my happiness appears so incredible to me, and because I am always afraid of seeing it fly away from me like a dream, I am anxious to make a reality of it."

"Well, deserve this pretended happiness, then!"

"I am at your disposal," said D'Artagnan.

"I love your devotion," said milady.

"Alas! is that all you love in me?" asked D'Artagnan.

"I love you also—you!" said she, taking his hand.

And the warm pressure made D'Artagnan tremble, as if the fever consuming milady communicated itself to him by the touch.

"You love me—you!," cried he. "Oh, if that were so, I should lose my reason I"

And he folded her in his arms. She made no effort to avoid the kiss which he pressed upon her lips, only she did not return it.

Her lips were cold; it appeared to D'Artagnan that he had kissed a statue.

He was not the less intoxicated with joy, electrified by love. He almost believed in milady's tenderness; he almost believed in De Wardes's crime. If De Wardes had at that moment been at hand, he would have killed him.

Milady seized her opportunity.

"His name is—"said she, in her turn.

"De Wardes; I know," cried D'Artagnan.

"And how do you know?" asked milady, seizing both his hands, and trying to read with her eyes to the bottom of his heart.

D'Artagnan felt that he had gone too far, and that he had made a mistake.

"Tell me! tell me! tell me, I say!" repeated milady; "how do you know?"

"How do I know?" said D'Artagnan.

"Yes."

"I know, because yesterday M. de Wardes, in a parlour where I was, displayed a ring which he said you gave him."

"Scoundrel!" cried milady.

The epithet, as may be easily understood, resounded to the very bottom of D'Artagnan's heart.

"Well?" continued she.

"Well, I will avenge you of this 'scoundrel,'" replied D'Artagnan, giving himself the airs of Don Japhet of Armenia.

"Thanks, my brave friend!" cried milady. "And when shall I be avenged?"

"To-morrow—immediately—when you please!"

Milady was about to cry out "immediately," but she reflected that such precipitation would not be very gracious toward D'Artagnan.

Besides, she had a thousand precautions to take, a thousand counsels to give to her defender, in order that he might avoid explanations with the count before witnesses. All this was answered by an expression of D'Artagnan's.

"To-morrow," said he, "you will be avenged."

She rang the bell. Kitty appeared.

"Go out this way," said she, opening a small private door, "and come back at eleven o'clock; we will then finish our conversation. Kitty will conduct you to my chamber."

The poor girl thought she should faint at hearing these words.

"Well, miss, what are you doing, standing there like a statue? Come, show the chevalier the way; and this evening at eleven o'clock—you understand!"

"It seems her appointments are all made for eleven o'clock," thought D'Artagnan. "That's a fixed habit."

Milady held out her hand to him, and he kissed it tenderly.

"There, now," said he, as he withdrew, scarcely heeding Kitty's reproaches—"there, I must not play the fool. This woman is certainly very bad. I must be on my guard."

CHAPTER 32

Milady's Secret

D'Artagnan left the hotel instead of going up at once to Kitty's chamber, as she tried to persuade him to do, and for this he had two reasons: the first, because in this way he avoided reproaches, recriminations, and entreaties; the second, because he was not sorry to have an opportunity to read his own thoughts, and, if possible, to fathom this woman's.

He walked six or seven times round the Place Royale, turning every ten steps to look at the light in milady's apartment, which was to be seen through the blinds. It was evident that this time the young woman was not in such haste to retire to her bedroom as she had been the first.

At length the light disappeared.

With this light was extinguished the last irresolution in D'Artagnan's heart. He recalled to his mind the details of the first night, and with beating heart and brain on fire he re-entered the hotel and rushed up to Kitty's chamber.

The young girl, pale as death, and trembling in all her limbs, wished to delay her lover; but milady, listening intently, had heard the noise made by D'Artagnan, and opening the door,

"Come," said she.

The door dosed after them.

She immediately came close to him again.

We cannot say how long the night seemed to milady, but D'Artagnan imagined he had been with her scarcely two hours when day bean to appear at the window-blinds, and soon invaded the chamber with its pallid light.

Then milady, seeing that D'Artagnan was about to quit her, recalled to his mind for the last time the promise he had made to avenge her on the Comte de Wardes.

"I am quite ready," said D'Artagnan; "but in the first place, I should like to be certain of one thing."

"What?"

"Whether you love me."

"I have proved to you that I do."

"Yes, and so I am yours body and soul. But if you love me as you say," continued he, "do you not feel a little fear on my account?"

"What have I to fear?"

" Why, that I may be dangerously wounded—even killed."

"Impossible!" cried milady; "you are such a valiant man, and such an expert swordsman."

"You would not, then, prefer a means," resumed D'Artagnan, "which would avenge you all the same, while rendering the combat useless?"

Milady looked at her lover in silence. The wan light of the first rays of day gave to her clear eyes a strangely baneful expression.

"Really," said she, "I believe you are now beginning to hesitate."

"No, I do not hesitate; but I really pity poor Comte de Wardes, since you have ceased to love him. And it seems to me that a man must be so severely punished merely by the loss of your love that he needs no other chastisement."

"Indeed!" said milady, with a look of some anxiety. "Explain yourself, for I really cannot tell what you mean."

And she looked at D'Artagnan, who held her in his arms, while his eyes seemed gradually to turn into flames.

"Yes; I am a man of honour," said D'Artagnan, determined to end the matter, "and since your love is mine, and I am sure I possess it—for I do possess it, do I not?"

"Absolutely and entirely. Go on."

"Well, I feel as if transformed—a confession weighs on my mind."

"Your confession," said she, growing paler—"what is this confession of yours?"

"You invited De Wardes on Thursday last to meet you here, in this very room, did you not?"

"I? No, certainly not!" said milady, in a tone so firm and with a face so unconcerned that if D'Artagnan had not been so absolutely certain he would have doubted.

"Do not tell a lie, my angel!" exclaimed D'Artagnan, smiling; "it would do no good."

"What do you mean? Speak! You frighten me to death!"

"Oh, reassure yourself; you are not guilty toward me, and I have already pardoned you."

"What more? what more?"

"De Wardes cannot boast of anything."

"How so? You yourself told me that my ring—"

"My love, I have your ring. The Duc de Wardes of last Thursday and the D'Artagnan of to-night are one and the same person."

The imprudent young man expected to see surprise mixed with shame—a slight storm resolving itself into tears. But he was strangely mistaken, and his error was of brief duration.

Pale and terrible, milady started up, repulsed D'Artagnan with a violent blow on the chest, and leaped from the bed. It was then almost broad daylight.

D'Artagnan held her back by her nightdress, of fine India muslin, in order to implore her pardon, but by a powerful and determined effort she struggled to escape. Then the cambric gave way, leaving her neck bare, and on one of her beautiful, white, round shoulders D'Artagnan, with an indescribable shock, recognized the fleur-de-lis, that indelible stamp imprinted by the executioner's debasing hand.

"Great God!" cried D'Artagnan, loosing his hold of her night-robe; and he remained on the bed, mute, motionless, and frozen.

But milady felt herself denounced by his very terror. Doubtless he had seen all. The young man now knew her secret, her terrible secret, of which every one, except him, was ignorant.

She turned on him, no longer a furious woman, but like a wounded panther.

"Ah, wretch," she cried, "you have basely betrayed me! And what is worse, you know my secret. You shall die!"

And she flew to a little marquetry casket standing on the toilet-table, opened it with a feverish, trembling hand, took out of it a small goldhandled poniard with a sharp, slender blade, and then half-naked flung herself on D'Artagnan with one bound.

Though the young man was brave, as we have seen, he was terrified at her wild face, her horribly staring eyes, her pale cheeks, her bleeding lips. He crept over to the farther side of the bed as he would have done if a viper had been crawling toward him, and as his hand, covered with sweat, touched his sword, he drew it from the scabbard.

But without heeding the sword, milady tried to climb on the bed again so that she might stab him, nor did she desist till she felt the keen point at her throat.

She then tried to seize the blade with her hands; but D'Artagnan kept it free from her grasp, and while presenting the point, sometimes at her eyes, sometimes at her breast, he slid off the bed, designing to make his escape by the door leading to Kitty's apartment.

Milady meantime kept rushing at him with horrible fury, screaming in a blood—curdling manner.

As all this, however, was like a duel, D'Artagnan soon began to recover himself.

"Very well, pretty lady, very well," said he; "but, by the gods, if you don't calm yourself, I will mark you with a second fleur-de-lis on one of those pretty cheeks!"

"Scoundrel! scoundrel!" howled milady.

But D'Artagnan, while approaching the door, kept all the time on the defensive.

At the noise they made, she in overturning the furniture in her efforts to get at him, he in screening himself behind the furniture to keep out of her reach, Kitty opened the door. D'Artagnan, who had constantly manoeuvred to gain this door, was not more than three paces from it. With one spring he flew from milady's chamber into the maid's, and, quick as lightning, shut the door, against which he leaned with all his weight, while Kitty bolted it.

"Quick, quick, Kitty!" said D'Artagnan, in a low voice, as soon as the bolts were fast, "let me get out of the hotel; for if we leave her time to turn round, she will have me killed by the servants!"

"But you can't go out so," said Kitty; "you have hardly any clothes on."

"That's true," said D'Artagnan, then, for the first time, taking note of the costume in which he appeared—"that's true. But dress me as well as you are able, only make haste. Think, my dear girl, it's life and death!"

Kitty was but too well aware of that. In a moment she muted him up in a flowered dress, a capacious— hood, and a cloak. She gave him some slippers, which he put on his naked feet, then she conducted him downstairs. It was time. Milady had already rung her bell, and roused the whole hotel. The porter had just opened the street door as milady, only half-dressed, was shouting down from her window,

"Don't open the door!"

CHAPTER 33

How, Without Incommoding Himself, Athos Got His Outfit

The young man made his escape while she was still threatening him with an impotent gesture. At the moment she lost sight of him milady sank back fainting into her bedroom.

D'Artagnan was so completely upset that, without considering what would become of Kitty, he ran at full speed across half Paris, and did not stop till he reached Athos's door.

Grimaud, his eyes swollen with sleep, came to open for him. D'Artagnan darted so violently into the room that he nearly knocked him over.

In spite of his habitual silence, the poor, fellow this time found his tongue.

"Helloa, there!" cried he; "what do you want, you strumpet? What's your business here, you hussy?"

"Grimaud," said Athos, coming out of his apartment in a dressing-gown—"Grimaud, I believe you are permitting yourself to speak?"

"Ah, monsieur, but—"

"Silence!"

Grimaud contented himself with pointing at D'Artagnan.

Athos recognizing his comrade, and phlegmatic as he was, he burst into a laugh made quite excusable by the strange masquerade before his eyes—hood askew, petticoats falling over shoes, sleeves tucked up, and moustaches stiff with agitation.

"Don't laugh, my friend!" cried D'Artagnan; "for Heaven's sake, don't laugh, for, on my soul, I tell you it's no laughing matter!"

"Well?" said Athos.

"Well," replied D'Artagnan, bending down to Athos's ear, and lowering his voice, "milady is marked with a fleur-de-lis on her shoulder!"

"Ah!" cried the musketeer, as if he had received a ball in his heart.

"Come, now," said D'Artagnan, "are you sure that the other is dead?"

"The other?" said Athos, in such a stifled voice that D'Artagnan scarcely heard him.

"Yes; she of whom you told me one day at Amiens."

Athos uttered a groan and let his head sink into his hands.

"This one is a woman of from twenty-six to twenty-eight years of age."

"Fair," said Athos, "is she not?"

"Very."

"Clear, blue eyes, of a strange brilliancy, with black eyelashes and eyebrows?"

"Yes."

"Tall, well-made? She has lost a tooth, next to the eye-tooth on the left?"

"Yes."

"The fleur-de-lis is small, rose-coloured, and somewhat faint from the coat of paste applied to it?"

"Yes."

"But you say she is an Englishwoman?"

"She is called milady, but she may be French. Lord Winter is only her brother-in-law."

"I will see her, D'Artagnan!" and he rang the bell.

Grimaud entered.

Athos made him a sign to go to D'Artagnan's residence and bring back same clothes.

Grimaud replied by another sign that he understood perfectly, and set off.

"Come, now, my dear friend, but this does not help toward your equipment," said Athos, "for if I am not mistaken, you have left all your clothes at milady's, and she certainly will not have the politeness to return them to you. Fortunately, you have the sapphire."

"The sapphire is yours, my dear Athos! Did you not tell me it was a family ring?"

"Yes; my father gave two thousand crowns for it, as he once told me. It formed part of the wedding present he made my mother, and it is magnificent. My mother gave it to me; and I, madman that I was, instead of keeping the ring as a holy relic, gave it to that wretched woman."

"Then, my dear, take back your ring, to which, it is plain, you attach much value."

"I take back the ring after it has passed through that infamous creature's hands! Never! D'Artagnan, this ring is defiled."

"Sell it, then."

"Sell a jewel that came from my mother! I confess I should regard it as a sacrilege."

"Pawn it, then. You can raise at least a thousand crowns on it. With such a sum you will be master of the situation. Then, when you get more money, you can redeem it, and have it back cleansed from its stains, for it will have passed through the usurer's hands."

Athos smiled.

"You are a capital comrade, my dear D'Artagnan," said he. "Your never-failing cheerfulness lifts up poor souls in affliction. Well, let us pawn the ring, but on one condition.

"What?"

"That five hundred crowns of it shall be yours and five hundred mine."

"Well, then, I will take it," said D'Artagnan.

At this moment Grimaud came in accompanied by Planchet, who was anxious about his master and curious to know what had happened to him, and so had taken advantage of the opportunity and brought the clothes himself. D'Artagnan dressed; Athos did the same. Then when both were ready to go out, Athos imitated the action of a person taking aim, and Grimaud immediately took down his musketoon and got ready to follow his master.

They arrived without mishap at the Rue des Fossoyeurs. Bonacieux was at the door; he looked banteringly at D'Artagnan.

"Ah, my dear tenants" said he. "Hurry up; you have a very pretty girl waiting at your room, and you know women don't like to be kept waiting."

"It's Kitty," said D'Artagnan to himself, and darted into the passage. In fact, there on the landing that led to his chamber he found the poor girl all of a tremble and crouching against the door.

As soon as she saw him,

"You promised me your protection; you promised to save me from her anger," said she. "Remember, you are the one who ruined me!"

"Yes, certainly I did," said D'Artagnan. "Be at ease, Kitty. But what happened after I left?"

"How can I tell?" said Kitty. "The lackeys came when they heard her cries. She was mad with anger. Every imaginable curse she poured forth against you. Then I thought she would remember that you went through my chamber into hers, and that then she would suppose I was your accomplice. So I took what little money I had, and the best of my things, and I ran away."

"Poor girl! But what can I do with you? I am going away the day after to-morrow."

"Do what you please, chevalier. Help me out of Paris; help me out of France!"

"I cannot take you, however, to the siege of Rochelle," said D'Artagnan.

"No; but you can get me a place in the provinces with some lady of your acquaintance—in your own country, for instance."

"Ah, my dear love, in my country the ladies do without chambermaids. But stop! I can manage it for you—Planchet, go and find M. Aramis. Have him come here immediately. We have something very important to say to him."

When Aramis arrived the matter was explained to him, and he was told that he must find a place for Kitty with some of his high connections.

Aramis reflected for a minute, and then said, colouring,

"Will it be rendering you a service, D'Artagnan?"

"I shall be grateful to you all my life."

"Very well. Madame de Bois-Tracy asked me, in behalf of a friend of hers who resides in the provinces, I believe, for a trustworthy chambermaid; and, my dear D'Artagnan, if you can answer for this young girl—"

"O sir, be assured that I shall be entirely devoted to the person who will afford me the means of leaving Paris."

"Then," said Aramis, "this turns out all for the best."

He sat down at the table and wrote a little note, which he sealed with a ring and gave to Kitty.

"And now, my dear girl," said D'Artagnan, "you know that it is not well for any of us to be here. Therefore let us separate. We shall meet again in better days."

"And whenever and wherever we meet again," said Kitty, "you will find that I love you as devotedly as I love you to-day."

"A gambler's vow!" said Athos, while D'Artagnan went to conduce. Kitty downstairs.

An instant afterwards the three young men separated, agreeing to meet again at four o'clock at Athos's residence, and leaving Planchet to guard the house.

Aramis returned home, and Athos and D'Artagnan went to see about pawning the sapphire.

As our Gascon had foreseen, they found no difficulty in obtaining three hundred pistoles on the ring. Still further, the Jew told them that he would give five hundred pistoles for it if they would sell it to him, as it would make a magnificent pendant for an earring.

Athos and D'Artagnan, with the activity of two soldiers, and the knowledge of two connoisseurs, spent scarcely three hours in purchasing the musketeer's entire outfit. Besides, Athos was very easy to please, and a great noble to his fingers' ends. Whenever anything suited him, he paid the price asked, without any thought of dickering. D'Artagnan would have remonstrated at this, but Athos put his hand on his shoulder with a smile, and D'Artagnan understood that it was all very well for such a little Gascon gentleman as himself to drive a bargain, but not for a man who had the bearing of a prince.

The musketeer found a superb Andalusian horse, black as jet, nostrils of fire, legs clean and elegant, rising six years. He examined him, and found him sound and without blemish. A thousand livres was asked for him.

He might, perhaps, have been bought for less; but while D'Artagnan was discussing the price with the dealer, Athos was counting the hundred pistoles on the table.

Grimaud had a stout, short Picard cob, which cost three hundred livres.

But when the saddle and arms for Grimaud were purchased, Athos had not a son left of his hundred and fifty pistoles. D'Artagnan offered his friend a part of his share, which he should return when convenient.

But Athos only replied to this proposal by shrugging his shoulders.

"How much did the Jew say he would give for the sapphire if he purchased it?" said Athos.

"Five hundred pistoles."

"That is to say, two hundred more—a hundred pistoles for you, and a hundred pistoles for me. Well, now, that would be a real fortune to us, my friend; let us go back to the Jew's again."

"What! will you—"

"This ring would certainly only recall very bitter remembrances. Then we shall never be masters of three hundred pistoles to redeem it, so that we really should lose two hundred pistoles by the bargain. Go, tell him the ring is his, D'Artagnan, and come back with the two hundred pistoles."

"Reflect, Athos!"

"We need ready money just now, and we must learn how to make sacrifices. Go, D'Artagnan, go; Grimaud will accompany you with his musketoon."

Half an hour afterwards D'Artagnan returned with the two thousand livres, and without having met with any accident.

Thus it was that Athos found at home resources which he did not expect.

CHAPTER 34

A Vision

At four o'clock the four friends were all assembled in Athos's apartments. Their anxiety about their outfits had all disappeared, and each face preserved now only the expression of its own secret anxieties, for behind all present happiness is concealed a fear for the future.

Suddenly Planchet entered, bringing two letters for D'Artagnan.

The one was a little note neatly folded, with a pretty seal in green wax, on which was impressed a dove bearing a green branch.

The other was a large square epistle, resplendent with the terrible arms of his Eminence the cardinal-duke.

At the sight of the little letter D'Artagnan's heart bounded, for he thought he recognized the writing; and though he had seen it but once, the memory of it remained at the bottom of his heart.

He therefore seized the little letter and opened it eagerly.

"On Thursday next, at seven o'clock in the evening," said the letter, "be on the road to Chartist. Look carefully into the carriages that pass; but if you value your own life, or the life of those who love you, do not speak a word, do not make a motion which may lead any one to believe that you recognize her who exposes herself to everything for the sake of seeing you for an instant only."

No signature.

"That's a snare," said Athos; "don't go, D'Artagnan."

"And yet," replied D'Artagnan, "I think I recognize the writing."

"But your second letter," said Athos—"you forget that. It appears to me, however, the seal shows it well deserves to be opened. For my part, I declare, D'Artagnan, I think it of much more consequence than the little piece of waste paper you have so slyly slipped into your bosom."

D'Artagnan grew red.

"Well," said the young man, "let us see, gentlemen, what his Eminence wants of me." And D'Artagnan unsealed the letter and read,

"M. D'Artagnan, of the king's guards, company Des Essarts, is expected at the Palais-Cardinal this evening at eight o'clock.
"LA HOUDENIÈRE, Captain of the Guards."

"The devil!" said Athos; "here's a rendezvous much more serious than the other."

"I will go to the second after attending the first," said D'Artagnan. "One is for seven o'clock, and the other for eight; there will be tune for both."

At this moment the clock of La Samaritaine struck six, and a short gallop brought D'Artagnan to the Chaillot road. The day was beginning to decline, carriages, were passing and repassing. D'Artagnan darted a scrutinizing glance into every carriage that appeared, but saw no face with which he was acquainted.

At length, after waiting a quarter of an hour, and just as it was quite twilight, a carriage appeared, coming at full speed, on the road to Sèvres. A presentiment instantly told D'Artagnan that this carriage contained the person who had appointed the rendezvous. The young man was himself astonished to feel his heart beating so violently. Almost instantly a woman put her head out at the window, with two fingers placed on her mouth, either to enjoin silence or to send him a kiss. D'Artagnan uttered a slight cry of joy. This woman, or rather this apparition—for the carriage passed with the rapidity of a vision was Madame Bonacieux.

By an involuntary movement, and in spite of the injunction given, D'Artagnan started his horse to a gallop, and in a few strides overtook the carriage. But the window was hermetically shut; the vision had disappeared.

D'Artagnan then remembered the injunction contained in the anonymous note: "If you value your own life, or the life of those who love you, do not speak a word, do not make a motion which may lead any one to believe that you recognize her who exposes herself to everything for the sake of seeing you for an instant only."

He stopped, therefore, trembling, not for himself, but for the poor woman who had evidently exposed herself to great danger by appointing this rendezvous.

The carriage pursued its way, still going at a full pace, till it dashed into Paris and disappeared.

D'Artagnan remained fixed to the spot, astounded, and not knowing what to think. If it was Madame Bonacieux, and if she was returning to Paris, why this fugitive interview? why this simple exchange of a glance? why this last kiss? If, on the other side, it was not she, which was still quite possible—for the little light that remained rendered a mistake easy—if it was not she, might it not be the beginning of some machination against him with the bait of this woman with whom it was known he was in love?

Half-past seven struck. The carriage was twenty minutes behind the time appointed. D'Artagnan remembered that he had a visit to pay.

He reached the Rue St. Honoré, and in the Place du Palais-Cardinal, he entered boldly at the front gate.

He entered the antechamber and placed his letter in the hands of the usher on duty, who showed him into the waiting-room and passed on into the interior of the palace.

The usher returned and made a sign to D'Artagnan to follow

him. He passed along a corridor, crossed a large drawing-room, entered a library, and found himself in the presence of a man seated at a desk and writing.

The usher introduced him and retired without speaking a word. D'Artagnan remained standing and examined this man.

D'Artagnan at first believed that he had to do with some judge examining his papers, but he perceived that the man at the desk was writing, or rather correcting, lines of unequal length by scanning the words on his fingers. He saw that he was in presence of a poet. In an instant the poet closed his manuscript, on the cover of which was written *Mirame, a Tragedy in Five Acts,* and raised his head.

D'Artagnan recognized the cardinal.

CHAPTER 35

A Terrible Vision

The cardinal leaned his elbow on his manuscript, his cheek on his hand, and looked at the young man for a moment. No one had a more searching eye than Cardinal Richelieu, and D'Artagnan felt this look run through his veins like a fever.

"Sit down there before me, Monsieur d'Artagnan; you are enough of a nobleman not to listen standing."

And the cardinal pointed with his finger to a chair for the young man, who was so amazed at what was going on that he waited for a second sign from the cardinal before he obeyed.

"You are brave, Monsieur d'Artagnan," continued his Eminence; "you are prudent, which is still better. I like men of head and heart. Don't be afraid," said he, smiling; "by men of heart I mean men of courage. But though you are young and have hardly entered on life, you have powerful enemies; if you do not take heed, they will destroy you!"

"Alas, monseigneur!" replied the young man, "very easily, no doubt; for they are strong and well supported, while I am alone."

"Yes, that's true. But alone as you are, you have already done much, and will do still more, I doubt not. And yet you need, I believe, to be guided in the adventurous career you have chosen, for, if I mistake not, you came to Paris with the ambitious idea of making your fortune."

"I am at the age of extravagant hopes, monseigneur," said D'Artagnan.

"There are no extravagant hopes save for fools, sir, and you are a man of brains. Now, what would you say to an ensign's commission in my guards, and a company after the campaign?"

"Ah, monseigneur!"

"You accept, do you not?"

"Monseigneur," replied D'Artagnan, with an embarrassed air.

"What! do you decline?" cried the cardinal, in astonishment.

"I am in his Majesty's guards, monseigneur, and I have no reason to be dissatisfied."

"But it seems to me that my guards are also his Majesty's guards, and whoever serves in a French corps serves the king."

"Monseigneur, your Eminence has misunderstood my words."

"That is to say, you refuse to serve me, sir," said the cardinal in a tone of vexation, through which, however, a sort of esteem manifested itself. "Remain free, then, and preserve your hatreds and your sympathies."

"Monseigneur—"

"Well, well!" said the cardinal, "I am not angry with you, but you are aware it is enough to defend and reward our friends; we owe nothing to our enemies. And yet I will give you a piece of advice: take good care of yourself, Monsieur d'Artagnan, for from the moment I withdraw my hand from you I would not give an obole for your life."

"I will try to do so, monseigneur," replied the Gascon, with a noble confidence.

"Remember by-and-by, at some moment when mischance may happen to you," said Richelieu pointedly, "that I came to seek you, and that I did all in my power to prevent this misfortune befalling you."

"Whatever may happen," said D'Artagnan, placing his hand on

his heart and bowing, "I shall entertain an eternal gratitude toward your Eminence for what you are now doing for me."

"Well, let it be, then, as you have said, Monsieur d'Artagnan; we shall meet again after the campaign. I will have my eye on you, for I shall be there," replied the cardinal, pointing with his finger to a magnificent suit of armour he was to wear; "and on our return—well, we will settle our account!"

"Ah, monseigneur!" cried D'Artagnan, "spare me the weight of your disfavour; remain neutral, monseigneur, if you find that I act as a gentleman ought to act."

"Young man," said Richelieu, "if I am able once again to say to you what I have said to you to-day, I promise you to do so."

This last expression of Richelieu's conveyed a terrible doubt; it alarmed D'Artagnan more than a threat would have done, for it was a warning. The cardinal, then, was trying to preserve him from some threatened misfortune. He opened his mouth to reply, but with a gesture the cardinal dismissed him.

D'Artagnan descended by the same staircase at which he had entered.

When he reached Athos's residence, Aramis and Porthos inquired as to the cause of this strange interview; but D'Artagnan confined himself to telling them that Richelieu had sent for him to propose to him to enter his guards with the rank of ensign, and that he had refused.

"And you were right," cried Aramis and Porthos, with one voice.

Athos fell into a deep reverie and made no remark. But when they were alone,

"You have done your duty, D'Artagnan," said Athos; "but yet perhaps you have done wrong."

D'Artagnan sighed deeply, for this voice responded to a secret voice of his soul, which told him that great misfortunes were awaiting him.

The whole of the next day was spent in preparations for departure, D'Artagnan went to take leave of M. de Tréville. At that time it was still believed that the separation of the musketeers and the guards would be only temporary, as the king was holding his parliament that very day, and proposed to set out the day after. M. de Tréville contented himself with asking D'Artagnan if he could do anything for him, but D'Artagnan answered that he was supplied with all he wanted.

That night all the comrades of the company of M. des Essarts's guards and of the company of M. de Tréville's musketeers who had struck up a mutual friendship came together. They were parting to meet again when it should please God, and if it should please God. The night, therefore, was a somewhat riotous one, as may be imagined, for in such cases extreme preoccupation can be combated only by extreme carelessness.

At the first sound of the morning trumpet the friends separated, the musketeers hastening to M. de Tréville's hotel, the guards to M. des Essarts's. Each of the captains then led his company to the Louvre, where the king reviewed them.

The review over, the guards set forward alone on their march, the musketeers waiting for the king.

Meantime, D'Artagnan was marching off with his company. On arriving at the Faubourg St. Antoine, he turned round to look gaily at the Bastille; but as he looked at the Bastille alone he did not observe milady, who, mounted upon a light bay horse, was pointing him out to two ill-looking men who immediately came close up to the ranks to take notice of him. To a questioning look milady signified that it was he. Then, certain that there could no longer be any mistake in the execution of her orders, she gave spurs to her horse and disappeared.

The two men then followed the company, and on leaving the Faubourg St. Antoine mounted two horses properly equipped, which a servant out of livery was holding in expectation of their coming.

CHAPTER 36

The Siege Of Rochelle

The siege of Rochelle was one of the great political events of Louis XIII's reign, and one of the cardinal's great military enterprises. It is therefore interesting and even necessary that we should say a few words about it; moreover, many details of this siege are connected in too important a manner with the story we have undertaken to relate to allow us to pass it over in silence.

The cardinal's political views when he undertook this siege were considerable. Let us unfold them first, and then we will pass on to his private views, which, perhaps, had not less influence on his Eminence than the former.

Of the important cities given up by Henry IV to the Huguenots as places of safety there remained only Rochelle. It became necessary, therefore, to destroy this last bulwark of Calvinism—a dangerous leaven, with which the ferments of civil revolt and foreign war were constantly mingling.

Rochelle, which had derived a new importance from the ruin of the other Calvinist cities, was then the focus of dissensions and ambitions. Moreover, its port was the last gateway in the kingdom of France open to the English, and by closing it against England the cardinal completed the work of Joan of Arc and the Duc de Guise.

The king was to follow as soon as his Bed of justice was held. But on rising from his Bed of justice on the 28th of June, he felt himself attacked by fever. He was, notwithstanding, anxious to set out; but his illness becoming more serious, he was obliged to stop at Villeroi.

Now, whenever the king stopped the musketeers stopped. The consequence was that D'Artagnan, who was still in the guards, found himself, for the time at least, separated from his good ends Athos, Aramis, and Porthos.

He arrived, however, without accident in the camp established before Rochelle toward the 10th of September, 1627.

Everything was unchanged. The Duke of Buckingham and his English, masters of the Isle of Ré, were still besieging, but unsuccessfully, the citadel of St. Martin and the fort of La Prée; and hostilities with Rochelle had begun, two or three days before, about a fort which the Duc d'Angoulême had just built near the city.

The guards, under M. des Essarts's command, took up their quarters at the Minimes.

But, as we know, D'Artagnan, preoccupied by the ambition of passing into the musketeers, had formed but few friendships among his comrades. He found himself isolated, and given over to his own reflections.

One day D'Artagnan was walking alone along a pretty little road leading from the camp to the village of Angoutin, when, in the last ray of the setting sun, he thought he saw a musket-barrel glittering behind a hedge.

He determined to direct his course as far away from it as he could, when, behind a rock on the opposite side of the road, he perceived the muzzle of another musket-barrel.

It was evidently an ambuscade.

The young man cast a glance at the first musket, and with a certain degree of anxiety saw that it was levelled in his direction; but as soon as he perceived that the mouth of the barrel was motionless, he threw himself flat on the ground. At the same instant the gun was fired, and he heard a ball whistle over his head.

No time was to be lost. D'Artagnan sprang up with a bound, and at the same instant the ball from the other musket tore up the stones on the very place on the road where he had thrown himself face to the ground.

And immediately taking to his heels, he ran towards the camp, with the swiftness of the young men of his country, so renowned for their agility; but great as was his speed, the one who had first fired, having had time to reload, fired a second shot, so well aimed this time that the bullet struck his hat and carried it ten paces from him.

However, as D'Artagnan had no other hat, he picked up this as he ran, and arrived at his quarters, very pale and quite out of breath. He sat down without saying a word to anybody, and began to reflect.

D'Artagnan took his hat, examined the hole made by the bulk and shook his head. The ball was not a musket-ball; it was an arquebuse-ball. The accuracy of the aim had first given him the idea that a particular kind of weapon had been employed. It could not, then, be a military ambuscade, as the ball was not of the regulation calibre.

It might be a kind remembrance of the cardinal's.

But D'Artagnan shook his head. For people against whom he had only to stretch out his hand, his Eminence had rarely recourse to such means.

It might be a vengeance of milady's.

That was the most probable.

At nine o'clock the next morning the drums beat the salute. The Duc d'Orléans was inspecting the posts. The guards ran to their arms, and D'Artagnan took his place in the midst of his comrades.

Monsieur passed along the front of the line. Then all the superior officers approached him to pay him their compliments, M. des Essarts, captain of the guards, among the rest.

It seems the Rochellais had made a sortie during the night, and had retaken a bastion which the royal army had gained possession of two days before; the point was to ascertain, by reconnoitring, how the enemy guarded this bastion.

In act, at the end of a few minutes, Monsieur raised his voice and said,

"I want for this mission three or four volunteers, led by a trusty man."

"As to the trusty man, I have him at hand, monseigneur," said M. des Essarts, pointing to D'Artagnan; "and as to the four or five volunteers, monseigneur has but to make his intentions known, and the men will not be wanting."

"Four gallant men who will risk being killed with me!" said D'Artagnan, raising his sword.

Two of his comrades of the guards immediately sprang forward, and two soldiers having joined them, the number was deemed sufficient; so D'Artagnan declined all others, as he was unwilling to injure the chances of those who came forward first.

It was not known whether, after taking the bastion, the Rochellais had evacuated it or left a garrison in it; so the object was to examine the place near enough to ascertain.

D'Artagnan set out with his four companions, and followed the trench.

Screened by the revetment, they came within a hundred paces of the bastion. There, on turning round, D'Artagnan perceived that the two soldiers had disappeared.

He thought that they had stayed behind from fear, and so he continued to advance.

At the turning of the counterscarp they found themselves within about sixty paces of the bastion.

No one was to be seen, and the bastion seemed abandoned.

The three men of the forlorn hope were deliberating whether to proceed any farther, when suddenly a circle of smoke enveloped the stone giant, and a dozen balls came whistling round D'Artagnan and his two companions.

They knew what they wanted to know: the bastion was guarded. A longer stay in this dangerous spot would therefore have been uselessly imprudent. D'Artagnan and his two companions turned their backs, and beat a retreat like a flight.

On arriving at the angle of the trench which was to serve them as a rampart, one of the guardsmen fell; a ball had passed through his breast. The other, who was safe and sound, kept on his way to camp.

D'Artagnan was not willing to abandon his companion thus, and stooped down to raise him and assist him in regaining the lines. But at this moment two shots were fired. One ball hit the head of the already wounded guardsman, and the other flattened itself against a rock, after passing within two inches of D'Artagnan.

The young man turned quickly round, for this attack could not come from the bastion, which was masked by the angle of the trench. The idea of the two soldiers who had abandoned him occurred to his mind, and reminded him of the assassins of two evenings before. So he resolved this time to satisfy himself on this point, and fell on his comrade's body as though he were dead.

He instantly saw two heads appearing above an abandoned work, within thirty paces of him; they were the heads of his two soldiers.

But as he might be merely wounded and might accuse them of their crime, they came up to him with the purpose of making sure of him. Fortunately, deceived by D'Artagnan's trick, they neglected to reload their guns.

When they were within ten paces of him, D'Artagnan, who in falling had taken great care not to let go his sword, suddenly got up, and with one leap came upon them.

The assassins realized that if they fled toward the camp without killing their man they should be accused by him; therefore their first idea was to desert to the enemy. One of them took his gun by the barrel, and used it as he would a club. He aimed a terrible blow at D'Artagnan, who dodged it by springing on one side; but by this movement he left free passage to the bandit, who at once darted off toward the bastion. As the Rochellais who guarded the bastion were ignorant of the intentions of the man they saw coming toward them, they fired at him, and he fell, struck by a ball which broke his shoulder.

Meantime D'Artagnan had thrown himself on the other soldier, attacking him with his sword. The struggle was not long. The wretch had nothing to defend himself with but his discharged arquebuse. The guardsman's sword slipped down the barrel of the now useless weapon, and pierced the thigh of the assassin, who fell.

D'Artagnan immediately placed the point of the weapon at his throat.

"Wretch," cried D'Artagnan, "see here, speak quickly! Who employed you to assassinate me?"

"A woman whom I don't know, but who is called milady."

"But if you don't know this woman, how do you know her name?"

"My comrade knew her and called her so. She made the bargain with him, and not with me; he has even now in his pocket a letter from that person, which must be of great importance to you, judging by what I have heard."

"But how are you concerned in this ambuscade?"

"He proposed to me to undertake it with him, and I agreed."

"And how much did she give you for this fine enterprise?"

"A hundred louis."

"Well, good enough!" said the young man, laughing; "she thinks I am worth something. A hundred louis! Well, that was a temptation for two miserable creatures like you. So I understand you accepted it, and I grant you my pardon, but on one condition."

"What is that?" said the soldier, uneasy at perceiving that all was not over.

"That you go and fetch me the letter your comrade has in his pocket."

"Why," cried the bandit, "that is fetch, another way of killing me. How can you wish me to go and fetch that letter under the fire from the bastion?"

Terror was so strongly painted on his face, covered with a cold sweat, that D'Artagnan took pity on him, and casting on him a look of contempt,

"Well," said he, "I will show you the difference between a man of true courage and a coward, as you are. Stay, I will go."

And with a light step, an eye on the watch, observing the movements of the enemy and taking advantage of all the aid afforded by the nature of the ground, D'Artagnan succeeded in reaching the second soldier.

There were two means of attaining his object—to search him on the spot, or to carry him away, making a buckler of his body, and then search him in the trench.

D'Artagnan preferred the second means, and lifted the assassin on his shoulders at the very moment the enemy fired.

A slight shock, the dull thud of three balls penetrating the flesh, a last cry, a convulsion of agony, proved to D'Artagnan that the man who had just tried to assassinate him had saved his life.

D'Artagnan regained the trench, and threw the body down by the wounded man, who was as pale as death.

He instantly began the search. Among some unimportant papers he found the following letter, the one which he had gone to get at the risk of his life:

> "Since you have lost track of that woman, and she is now in safety in the convent, which you should never have allowed her to reach, try, at least, not to miss the man. If you do, you know that my hand reaches far, and that you shall repay me very dearly the hundred louis you have had of me."

No signature. Nevertheless it was plain the letter came from milady. He consequently kept it as a piece of evidence, and as he was in safety behind the angle of the trench, he began to question the wounded man. He confessed that he had undertaken, with his comrade, the man just killed, to abduct a young woman about to leave Paris by the gate of La Villette; but having stopped to drink at a saloon, they had missed the carriage by ten minutes.

"But what were you to have done with the woman?" asked D'Artagnan, in great agitation.

"We were to have conveyed her to a hotel in the Place Royale," said the wounded man.

"Yes, yes," murmured D'Artagnan; "that's the place—milady's own residence."

Then the young man, shuddering, felt what a terrible thirst of vengeance impelled this woman to destroy him, as well as those who loved him, and how well acquainted she must be with affairs of the court, since she had discovered everything. Doubtless she owed this information to the cardinal.

But he also perceived, with a feeling of genuine joy, that the queen must have at last discovered the prison in which poor Madame Bonacieux was expiating her devotion, and that she had freed her from that prison. And the letter he had received from the young woman, and her passing along the Chaillot road like an apparition, were now explained.

He turned to the wounded man, who had watched with intense anxiety all the varying expressions of his countenance, and holding out his arm to him,

"Come," said he; "I will not abandon you thus. Lean upon me, and let us return to camp."

The guardsman who had returned at the first discharge had announced the death of his four companions. There was therefore much astonishment and delight inregiment when the young man was seen to come back safe and sound.

D'Artagnan explained the sword-wound of his companion by a sortie which he improvised. He told of the other soldier's death and the perils they had encountered. This recital was for him the occasion of a veritable triumph. The whole army talked of this expedition for a day, and Monsieur sent him his compliments on it.

CHAPTER 37

The Anjou Wine

D'Artagnan had become more tranquil. He felt only one uneasiness, and that was at not hearing from his three friends.

But one morning early in November everything was explained to him by this letter, dated from Villeroi:

> Monsieur D'artagnan,—MM. Athos, Porthos, and Aramis, after giving an entertainment at my house, and having a very gay time, created such a disturbance that the provost of the castle, a very rigid man, has had them confined for some days; but I fulfil the order they have given me by forwarding to you a dozen bottles of my Anjou wine, with which they are much taken. They are desirous that you should drink to their health in their favourite wine. I have done so, and am, sir, with great respect, your very humble and obedient servant,
>
> GODEAU, Steward of the Musketeers.

"That's good!" cried D'Artagnan; "they think of me in their pleasures, as I thought of them in my troubles. Well, I will certainly drink to their health with all my heart, but I will not drink alone."

And D'Artagnan went after two guardsmen with whom he had formed greater intimacy than with the others, to invite them to drink with him this delicious Anjou wine which had just been sent him from Villeroi.

One of the two guardsmen was engaged that evening, and the other for the next. So the meeting was fixed for the day after that.

Planchet, very proud of being raised to the dignity of butler, thought he would get everything ready, like an intelligent man; and with this object in mind called in the assistance of the lackey of one of his master's guests, named Fourreau, and the sham soldier who had tried to kill D'Artagnan, and who, belonging to no corps, had been in D'Artagnan's service, or rather Planchet's, ever since D'Artagnan saved his life.

The hour of the banquet having come, the two guests arrived, took their places, and the dishes were served on the table. Planchet waited, towel on arm; Fourreau uncorked the bottles, and Brisemont, as the convalescent was named, carefully poured into glass decanters the wine, which seemed to be rather muddy after the joltings of the journey. As the first bottle of this wine was a little thick at the bottom, Brisemont poured the dregs into a glass, and D'Artagnan allowed him to drink it, for the poor devil had not as yet much strength.

The guests, after having eaten their soup, were on the point of touching the first glass of wine to their lips, when suddenly the cannon roared from Fort Louis and Fort Neuf. Instantly the guardsmen, imagining this to be caused by some unexpected attack, either of the besieged or the English, sprang to their swords.

But scarcely were they out of the messroom when they learned the cause of the noise. Cries of "Hurrah for the king! hurrah for the cardinal!" were resounding on every side, and drums were beating in all directions.

In fact, the king had made forced marches, and had just arrived with all his household and a reinforcement of ten thousand troops.

His musketeers rode in front of him and behind him. D'Artagnan, standing with his company drawn up in line, saluted with an expressive gesture his friends, whom he followed with his eyes, and M. de Tréville, who instantly recognized him.

The ceremony of reception over, the four friends were soon in one another's arms.

"By Jove! cried D'Artagnan, "you could not have arrived more opportunely; the dinner cannot have had time to cool.—Can it, gentlemen?" added the young man, turning to the two guardsmen, whom he introduced to his friends.

"Ah, ha!" said Porthos, "so it seems we were feasting!"

"Is there any drinkable wine in your shanty?" asked Athos.

"Well, by Jove! there is your own, my dear friend," replied D'Artagnan.

"Our wine!" exclaimed Athos in astonishment.

"Yes, the wine you sent me."

"We sent you wine?"

"Yes; you know what I mean—the wine from the slopes of Anjou."

"Did you send this wine, Aramis?" said Athos.

"No; and you, Porthos?"

"No; and you, Athos?"

"No!"

"Well, but if it was not you, it was your steward," said D'Artagnan. "Our steward!"

"Here is his letter," said D'Artagnan, and he exhibited the note to his comrades.

"That is not his writing!" said Athos; "I know it. Before we left Villeroi I settled the accounts of our crowd."

"It is a forged letter," said Porthos. "We have not been under arrest."

D'Artagnan rushed towards the messroom, the three musketeers and the two guards following him.

The first object that met D'Artagnan's eyes on entering the dining room was Brisemont stretched on the ground and rolling in horrible convulsions.

Planchet and Fourreau, pale as death, were trying to aid him; but it was plain that all assistance was useless—all the features of the dying man were distorted with the death struggle.

"Ah!" cried he, perceiving D'Artagnan—"ah! I it is frightful! You pretend to pardon me, and you poison me!"

"I swear to you on the Gospel," said D'Artagnan, throwing himself down by the dying man, "that I didn't know the wine was poisoned, and I was going to drink of it as you did."

"I do not believe you," cried the soldier.

And he expired under redoubled torments.

"Oh, my friends," said D'Artagnan, "you come once more to save my life—not only mine, but the lives of these gentlemen.—Gentlemen," continued he, addressing the guardsmen, "I request you say nothing about this adventure. Great personages may have had a hand in what you have seen, and if talked about, the evil would only recoil on us."

"Ah, sir," stammered Planchet, more dead than alive—"ah, sir, what a narrow escape I have had!"

"Gentlemen," said D'Artagnan, addressing the guardsmen, "you will easily see that such a feast can only be very melancholy after what has lust taken place; so I beg you to accept my excuses, and put off the party till another day."

The two guardsmen courteously accepted D'Artagnan's excuses, and perceiving that the four friends desired to be alone, they retired.

When the young guardsman and the three musketeers were without witnesses, they looked at each other with an air which plainly expressed that each of them realized the seriousness of the situation.

"In the first place," said Athos, "let us leave this room; a dead man, especially the victim of a violent death, is not agreeable company."

The manager gave them another room, and served them with boiled eggs, while Athos went himself to draw water at the spring. In a few words Porthos and Aramis were informed of all that had occurred.

"Well," said D'Artagnan to Athos, "you see, dear friend, that it is war to the death!"

"Bah!" said Athos; "God has preserved us hitherto; God will preserve us still."

"Yes, He has. Besides, we are men; and all things considered, it is our lot to risk our lives. But she—"added D'Artagnan in an undertone.

"She? Who?" asked Athos.

"Constance."

"Madame Bonacieux! Ah, that's true!" said Athos. "My poor friend, I had forgotten."

"Well," said Aramis, "but have you not learned by the letter you found on the dead assassin that she is in a convent? One may be very comfortable in a convent; and as soon as the siege of Rochelle is over, I promise you, I take upon myself to get news of her."

"You, Aramis!" cried the three friends. "How?"

"By the queen's almoner, with whom I am very intimately acquainted."

And with this assurance the four friends, having finished their modest repast, separated, promising to meet again that evening. D'Artagnan returned to the Minimes, and the three musketeers repaired to the king's quarters, where they had to prepare their lodging.

CHAPTER 38

The Tavern Of The Red Dovecot

Meanwhile the king, who, although he had so recently arrived, was in such haste to face the enemy, and, with more reason than the cardinal, shared his hatred for Buckingham, desired every disposition to be made, first to drive the English from the Isle of Ré, and afterwards to press the siege of Rochelle.

As it is not our intention to write a journal of the siege, but, on the contrary, only to introduce such events of it as are connected with the story we are telling, we will content ourselves with saying in a word or two that the expedition succeeded, to the king's great astonishment and the cardinal's great glory. The English, driven back foot by foot, beaten in every skirmish, and overwhelmed in the passage of the Isle of Loix, were obliged to re-embark, leaving on the battlefield two thousand men, among whom were five colonels, three lieutenant-colonels, two hundred and fifty captains, and twenty gentlemen of rank, four pieces of cannon, and sixty colours, which were taken to Paris by Claude de St. Simon, and suspended with great pomp in the arches of Notre Dame.

The cardinal was left free to carry on the siege without having, at least for the moment, anything to fear from the English.

All the responsibility rested on the cardinal, for one cannot be a despotic minister without responsibility; therefore all the resources of his mighty genius were expended night and day engaged in listening to the slightest rumour heard in any of the great kingdoms of Europe.

The cardinal, to whom his most inveterate detractors have never denied personal bravery, was not prevented, however, from making excursions by night, sometimes to communicate to the Duc d'Angoulême important orders; sometimes to go and confer with the king; sometimes to have an interview with a messenger whom he did not wish to receive at his headquarters.

Now, one evening, when D'Artagnan, who was in the trenches, was not able to accompany them, Athos, Porthos, and Aramis, mounted on their war-horses, enveloped in their military cloaks, with their hands on their pistol-butts, were returning from an ale-house called the Red Dovecot, which Athos had discovered two days before on the road to La Jarrie. They were riding along on the road leading to the camp, and quite on their guard, as we have stated, for fear of an ambuscade, when, about a quarter of a league from the village of Boinar, they fancied they beard the trampling of horses approaching them. All three instantly halted, closed in, and waited, occupying the middle of the road. In an instant, just as the moon broke out from behind a cloud, they saw appear at a turn of the road two horsemen, who, on perceiving them, stopped in their turn, seemingly to deliberate whether they should continue their route or go back. Their hesitation aroused some suspicion in the three friends, and Athos, riding a few paces in advance of the others, cried in a firm voice,

"Who goes there?"

"Who goes there, yourselves?" replied one of the two horsemen.

"That is not an answer," replied Athos. "Who goes there? Answer, or else we charge."

"Your name" insisted the horseman, letting his cloak fall, and leaving his face uncovered.

"The cardinal!" cried the astonished musketeer.

"Your name?" cried his Eminence for the third time.

"Athos," said the musketeer.

The cardinal made a sign to his attendant, who drew near to him.

"These three musketeers shall follow us," said he in an undertone. "I do not wish it known I left the camp; and by following us we shall be certain; they will tell no one."

"We are gentlemen, monseigneur," said Athos; "put us on our honour, and give yourself no uneasiness. Thank God, we can keep a secret.

The cardinal fixed his keen eyes on the bold speaker.

"You have a quick ear, Monsieur Athos," said the cardinal; "but now listen to this: it is not from mistrust that I ask you to follow me, but for my security. No doubt your companions are MM. Porthos and Aramis."

"Yes, your Eminence," said Athos, while the two musketeers who had remained behind advanced, hat in hand.

"I know you, gentlemen," said the cardinal, "I know you. I know you are not altogether my friends, and I am sorry for it; but I know you are brave and loyal gentlemen, and that confidence may be reposed to you. Monsieur Athos, do me the honour of accompanying me, you and your two friends, and then I shall have an escort to excite envy in his Majesty, if we should meet him."

The three musketeers bowed to the necks of their horses.

"Well, on my honour," said Athos, "your Eminence is right in taking us with you; we have seen ill-looking faces on the road, and we have even had a quarrel at the Red Dovecot with four of them."

"And pray what was your quarrel about?"

"These fellows were drunk, said Athos, "and knowing that a lady had arrived at the tavern this evening, they were on the point of forcing her door."

"Forcing her door!" said the cardinal; "and for what purpose?"

"To do her violence, without doubt," said Athos. "I have had the honour of informing your Eminence that these wretches were drunk."

"And was the lady young and handsome?" asked the cardinal in some anxiety.

"We did not see her, monseigneur," said Athos.

"You did not see her! Ah, very well," replied the cardinal quickly; "you acted quite right in defending a woman's honour; and as I myself am going to the Red Dovecot, I shall know whether you have told me truth or not."

Athos bowed.

"And now, gentlemen, that's all very well," continued his Eminence. "I know what I wanted to know. Follow me."

The three musketeers fell behind his Eminence, who again

enveloped his face in his cloak and started up his horse, keeping at from eight to ten paces in advance of his four companions.

They soon reached the silent, solitary tavern. The landlord doubtless knew what illustrious visitor was coming, and had consequently sent intruders away.

At ten paces from the door the cardinal made a sign to his attendant and the three musketeers to halt. A saddled horse was fastened to the window-shutter. The cardinal knocked three times in a peculiar manner.

A man enveloped in a cloak immediately came out, and exchanged some rapid words with the cardinal; after which he got on horseback and set off in the direction of Surgères, which was likewise that of Paris.

"Advance, gentlemen," said the cardinal.

"You have told me the truth, gentlemen," said be, addressing the three musketeers, "and it will not be my fault if our meeting this evening be not advantageous to you; meanwhile follow me."

The cardinal alighted; the three musketeers followed big example. The cardinal threw the bridle of his horse to his attendant; the three musketeers fastened their horses to the shutters.

The landlord stood at the door; for him, the cardinal was only an officer coming to visit a lady.

"Have you a room on the ground floor where these gentlemen can fait, near a good fire?" the cardinal asked.

The landlord opened the door of a large room, in which a poor stove had just been replaced by a large and excellent fireplace.

"I have this, sir," said he.

"That will do," replied the cardinal.—"Come in, gentlemen, and be kind enough to wait for me; I shall not be more than half an hour."

And while the three musketeers were going into the ground-floor room, the cardinal, without asking further information, mounted the staircase like a man who has no need of his way being pointed out to him.

CHAPTER 39

The Utility Of Stove-Pipes

It was evident that without suspecting it, and actuated solely by their chivalric and adventurous characters, our three friends had just rendered a service to some one whom the cardinal honoured with his special protection.

Now who was that some one? This was the question the three musketeers put to each other. Then, seeing that none of the replies their wits could furnish was satisfactory, Porthos called the landlord and asked for dice.

Porthos and Aramis sat down at the table and began to play. Athos walked about in a contemplative mood.

While thinking and walking, Athos kept passing and re-passing before the stove-pipe, broken in half, the other end of which went into the upper chamber; and every time he passed he heard a murmur of words, which at length attracted his attention. Athos went close to it: and distinguished some words which undoubtedly seemed to deserve so deep an interest that he beckoned to his friends to be silent, remaining himself bent, with his ear placed against the opening of the lower orifice.

"Listen, milady," said the cardinal; "the affair is important. Sit down and let us talk."

"Milady!" murmured Athos.

"I am listening to your Eminence with the greatest attention," replied a woman's voice that made the musketeer start.

"A small vessel, with an English crew, whose captain is devoted to me, awaits you at the mouth of the Charente, at Fort de la Pointe. He will set sail to-morrow morning."

"I must go there to-night, then?"

"Instantly! That is to say, as soon as you have received my instructions. Two men, whom you will find at the door on going out will serve as your escort. You will let me leave first, and, half an hour after, you can go away in your turn."

"Yes, monseigneur. Now let us return to the mission in which you wish to employ me, and, as I desire to continue to merit your Eminence's confidence, deign to explain it to me in clear and precise so that I may not commit any error."

There was a moment of deep silence between the two speakers. It was evident the cardinal was weighing beforehand the terms in which he was about to speak, and that milady was collecting all the power of her mind to understand the things he was about to say, and to engrave them in her memory when they were spoken.

Athos took advantage of this moment to tell his two companions to fasten the door on the inside, and to beckon them to come and listen with him.

The two musketeers, who loved their ease, each brought a chair for himself and one for Athos. All three then sat down with their heads together and their ears alert.

"You will go to London," pursued the cardinal; "when you reach London you will seek out Buckingham."

"I must beg your Eminence to observe," said milady, "that since the affair of the diamond studs, about which the duke always suspected me, his Grace has been very mistrustful of me."

"Well, this time;" said the cardinal, "it is not a question of worming yourself into his confidence, but you will present yourself frankly and loyally as a negotiator.

"You will go to Buckingham in my behalf, and you will tell him I am acquainted with all the preparations he has made; but that they give me no uneasiness, since at the first step he takes I will ruin the queen."

"Will he believe that your Eminence is in a position to accomplish the threat you make him?"

"Yes, for I have the proofs."

"I must be able to present these proofs so as to convince him."

"Unquestionably. And you will tell him I will publish the report of Bois-Robert and of the Marquis de Beautru, regarding the interview with the queen which the duke had at the constable's residence, on the evening Madame la Connétable gave a masked ball. You will tell him, in order that be may not doubt anything, that he came there in the costume of the Great Mogul, which the Chevalier de Guise was to have worn, and which he bought for three thousand pistoles."

"Very well, monseigneur."

"All the details of his entrance and departure on the night when he was introduced into the palace in the character of an Italian fortune-teller you will tell him, in order that he may not doubt the correctness of my information."

"Is that all, monseigneur?"

"Tell him also that I am acquainted with all the details of the adventure at Amiens; that I will have a little romance made of it, wittily turned, with a plan of the garden and portraits of the principal actors in that nocturnal romance."

"I will tell him that."

"Then add that his Grace in his precipitation to quit the Isle of Ré forgot and left behind him in his lodging a letter from Madame de Chevreuse, which singularly compromises the queen, inasmuch as it proves not only that her Majesty can love the king's enemies, but that she can conspire with the enemies of France. You recollect perfectly rill I have told you, do you not?"

"Your Eminence will judge: Madame la Connétable's ball; the night at the Louvre; the evening at Amiens; the arrest of Montague; the letter of Madame de Chevreuse."

"That's it," said the cardinal— "that's it. You have an excellent memory, milady."

"But," resumed the lady to whom the cardinal had just addressed,this flattering compliment, "if, in spite of all these reasons, the duke does not yield, and continues to threaten France?"

"If he persists—" His Eminence made a pause, and resumed: "If he persists—well, then I shall hope for one of those events which change the destinies of states."

"If your Eminence would quote to me some one of these events in history," said milady, "perhaps I should partake of your confidence in the future."

"Well, here, then, for example," said Richelieu. "When in 1610, for a cause almost similar to the one that moves the duke, King Henry IV, of glorious memory, was about to invade Flanders and Italy at the same time, in order to attack Austria on both sides—well, did there not happen an event which saved Austria? Why should not the king of France have the same chance as the emperor?"

"Your Eminence means the knife-stab of the Rue de la Fer-ronnerie?"

"Exactly so," said the cardinal. "The only difficulty at this moment is to find some woman, handsome, young, and clever, who wants to get revenge on the duke. Such a woman may be found. The duke has had many love affairs, and if he has succeeded in many of his intrigues by his promises of eternal constancy, he must likewise have sown the seeds of many hatreds by his eternal infidelities."

"No doubt," said milady coolly, "such a woman may be found."

"Well, such a woman, who would put Jacques Clement's knife or Ravaillac's in a fanatic's hands, would save France."

"She is found," said milady.

"Then we must find the miserable fanatic who will serve as an instrument of God's justice."

"He will be found."

"Well," said the cardinal, "that is it."

"And now," said milady, without appearing to remark the change of the cardinal's tone toward her—"now that I have received your Eminence's instructions regarding your enemies, will monseigneur permit me to say a few words to him of mine?"

"Who are they?" replied the cardinal.

"In the first place, there is a little intriguing woman named Bona-cieux."

"She is in the prison of Nantes."

"That is to say, she was there," replied milady; "but the queen obtained an order from the king, by means of which she has been conveyed to a convent."

"And what convent?"

"I don't know; the secret has been well kept."

"But I will know!"

"And will your Eminence tell me in what convent this woman is?"

"I see nothing improper in that," said the cardinal.

"Well, now I have an enemy much more to be dreaded by me than this little Madame Bonacieux."

"Who is that?"

"Her lover."

"What is his name?"

"I mean that wretch D'Artagnan."

"He is a bold fellow," said the cardinal.

"And because he is a bold fellow he is the more to be feared."

"I must have," said the cardinal, "a proof of his connection with Buckingham."

"A proof! " cried milady; "I will find you ten."

"Well, then, it is the simplest thing in the world. Get me your proof, and I will send him to the Bastille."

"So far so good, monseigneur; but afterwards?"

"When one is in the Bastille there is no afterwards!" said the cardinal in a low voice. "Ah, by God!" continued he, "if it were as easy for me to get rid of my enemy as it is easy to get rid of yours, and if it were only against such people you required impunity—"

"Monseigneur," replied milady, "a fair exchange—life for life, man for man; give me one, I will give you the other."

"I don't know what you mean, nor do I even wish to know what you mean," replied the cardinal; "but I wish to please you, and see nothing out of the way in giving you what you ask for with respect to so mean a creature—the more so as you tell me this petty D'Artagnan is a libertine, a duellist, a traitor."

"An infamous scoundrel, monseigneur, an infamous scoundrel!"

"Give me paper, a pen, and some ink, then," said the cardinal.

"Here they are, monseigneur."

There was a moment of silence, which proved that the cardinal was engaged in seeking the terms in which he should write the note, or else in writing it. Athos, who had not lost a word of the conversation, took his two companions by the hand and led them to the other end of the room.

"Well," said Porthos, "what do you want, and why do you not let us listen to the end of the conversation?"

"Hush!" said Athos, speaking in a low voice; "we have heard all It was necessary for us to hear; besides, I don't prevent you from listening but I must be gone."

"You must be gone!" said Porthos; "and if the cardinal asks for you, what answer can we make?"

"You will not wait till he asks; you will speak first, and tell him that I am gone as a scout, because certain expressions of our landlord have made me think the road is not safe. I will say a word or two about it to the cardinal's attendant likewise. The rest concerns myself; don't be anxious about that."

"Be prudent, Athos," said Aramis.

"Don't be worried," replied Athos.

Porthos and Aramis resumed their places by the stove-pipe.

Athos went out without any mystery, took his horse, which was tied with those of his friends to the fastenings of the shutters, in four words convinced the attendant of the necessity of a vanguard for their return, carefully examined the priming of his pistol, drew his sword, and, like a forlorn hope, took the road to the camp.

CHAPTER 40

A Conjugal Scene

As Athos had foreseen, the cardinal soon came down. He opened the door of the room where the musketeers were, and found Porthos playing an earnest game at dice with Aramis. He cast a rapid glance round the room, and perceived that one of his men was missing.

"What has become of Monsieur Athos?" asked he.

"Monseigneur," replied Porthos, "he has gone on as a scout, owing to some expressions dropped by our landlord making him fear the road was not safe."

"And how have you been amusing yourself, M. Porthos?"

"I have won five pistoles from Aramis, monseigneur."

"Well; now will you return with me?"

"We are at your Eminence's orders."

"To horse, then, gentlemen, for it is getting late."

The attendant was at the door, holding the cardinal's horse by the bridle. A short distance away a group of two men and three horses appeared in the shade; these were the two men who were to conduct milady to Fort de la Pointe, and superintend her embarkation.

The attendant confirmed to the cardinal what the two musketeers had already said regarding Athos. The cardinal made an approving gesture, and started to return with the same precautions he had used in coming.

Let us leave him: to follow the road to the camp, protected by his attendant and the two musketeers, and return to Athos.

For a hundred paces he maintained the gait with which he started, but when once out of sight, he turned his horse to the right, made a circuit, and came back to within twenty paces, where, shielded by a coppice, he might watch the passage of the little troop. Having recognized his companions' laced hats and the golden fringe of the cardinal's cloak, he waited till the horsemen had turned the angle of the road, and having lost them from sight, he returned at a gallop to tire tavern, which was opened to him without hesitation.

The landlord recognized him.

"My officer," said Athos, "has forgotten to give a piece of very important information to the lady, and has sent me back to repair his forgetfulness."

"Go up," said the host; "she is still in her room."

Athos availed himself of the permission, mounted the stairs with his lightest step, gained the landing, and through the open door saw milady putting on her hat.

He went straight into the chamber and closed the door behind him.

At the noise he made in bolting it milady turned round.

Athos was standing before the door, enveloped in his cloak, with his hat pulled down aver his eyes. On seeing that figure, mute and motionless like a statue, milady was startled.

"Who are you, and what do you want?" cried she.

"There now!" murmured Athos; "it is certainly she!"

And dropping his cloak and raising his hat, he advanced toward milady.

"Do you know me, madame?" said he.

Milady took one step forward, and then grew pale, as though she saw a serpent.

"Come," said Athos. "Good! I see you know me."

"The Comte de la Fère!" murmured milady, drawing back till the wall prevented her going any farther.

"You believed me to be dead, did you not, as I believed you to be? And the name of Athos as well concealed the Comte de la Fère as the name of Lady Clarick concealed Anne de Beuil! Were you not so called when your honoured brother married us? Our position is truly strange," pursued Athos, laughing. "We have lived up to the present time only because we believed each other to be dead, and because a remembrance is less oppressive than a living creature, though sometimes a remembrance is a devouring thing!"

"But," said milady, in a hollow, faint voice, "what brings you back to me? and what do you want with me?"

"I wish to tell you that, though t have remained invisible to your eyes, I have not lost sight of you. I can tell you of your actions day by day from the time you entered the cardinal's service until this evening."

A smile of incredulity passed over milady's pale lips.

"You must be Satan!" cried she.

"Perhaps," said Athos. "But, at least, listen to what I say. Assassinate the Duke of Buckingham, or have him assassinated; it makes no difference to me. I don't know him; besides, he is an Englishman. But do not touch with the tip of your finger a single hair of D'Artagnan, who is a faithful friend, whom I love and defend, or I swear to you by my father's life the crime which you shall have committed shall be your last."

Athos was seized with a kind of vertigo. The sight of this creature, who had nothing womanly about her, recalled devouring remembrances. His desire for her death returned, burning, and pervaded him like a raging fever. He put his hand to his belt, drew out a pistol, and cocked it.

Milady, pale as a corpse, struggled to cry out; but her frozen tongue could utter only a hoarse sound, which had nothing human in it, and seemed a wild beast's rattle. Clinging to the dark tapestry, she appeared, with her hair in disorder, like the frightful image of terror.

Athos slowly raised his pistol, stretched out his arm, so that the weapon almost touched milady's forehead; and then, in a voice the more terrible from having the supreme calmness of an inflexible resolution,

"Madame," said he, "you will this instant deliver to me the paper the cardinal signed; or, on my soul, I will blow your brains out."

With another man, milady might have preserved some doubt; but she knew Athos, yet she remained motionless.

"You have one second to decide," said he.

Milady saw by the contraction of his countenance that he was about to pull the trigger; she put her hand quickly into her bosom, pulled out a paper, and held it toward Athos.

"Take it," said she, "and be damned! "

Athos took the paper, returned the pistol to his belt, approached the lamp to be assured that it was the right paper, unfolded it, and read,

"August 5, 1628.
"By my order, and for the good of the State, the bearer hereof has done what he has done.
RICHELIEU."

"And now," said Athos, taking up his cloak again and putting on his hat—"now that I have drawn your teeth, viper, bite if you can."

And he left the chamber without once looking behind him.

At the door he found the two men, and the horse which they held.

"Gentlemen," said he, "you know monseigneur's order is for you to conduct that woman, without losing time, to Fort de la Pointe, and not to leave her till she is on board."

As his words agreed exactly with the order they had received, they bowed in sign of assent.

Athos leaped lightly into his saddle, and set out at full gallop; only, instead of following the road, he took across the fields, urging his horse to the utmost, and stopping occasionally to listen.

In one of his halts he heard the trampling of several horses on the road. He had no doubt it was the cardinal and his escort. He immediately galloped on ahead, rubbed his horse down with some heather and leaves of trees, and then placed himself in the middle of the road, about two hundred aces from the camp.

"Who goes there?" cried he, as soon as he saw the horsemen coming.

"That is our brave musketeer, I think," said the cardinal.

"Yes, monseigneur," said Porthos, "it is he."

"Monsieur Athos," said Richelieu, "receive my thanks for the good guard yon have kept. Gentlemen, we are here; take the gate on the left. The watchword is 'King and Ré.'"

On saying these words the cardinal bent his head in salutation of the three friends, and took the right hand, followed by his attendant, for that night he himself was to sleep in camp.

"Well," said Porthos and Aramis together, as soon as the cardinal was out of hearing—"well, he signed the paper she asked for!"

"I know he did," said Athos, "and here it is."

And the three friends did not exchange another word till they got to their quarters, except to give the watchword to the sentinels.

But they sent Mousqueton to tell Planchet that his master was requested to come to the quarters of the musketeers the instant he left the trenches.

Milady, as Athos had foreseen, on finding the two men awaiting her, made no objection to going with them.

Consequently, after travelling all night, she was at seven o'clock at Fort de la Pointe; at eight o'clock she had embarked; and at nine the vessel, which, with letters of marque from the cardinal, was supposed to be going to Bayonne, raised anchor and set sail toward England.

CHAPTER 41

The Bastion St. Gervais

On rejoining his three friends, D'Artagnan found them assembled in the same room. Athos was meditating, Porthos was twirling his moustache, Aramis was reading prayers in a charming little Book of Hours, bound in blue velvet.

"By Jove," said he, "gentlemen, I hope what you have to tell me is worth the trouble; or else, I warn you, I will not pardon you for making me come here instead of getting a little rest, after a night spent in taking and dismantling a bastion. Ah! why were you not there, gentlemen? It was warm work."

"We were in a place where it was not very cold!" replied Porthos, giving his moustache a twirl that was peculiar to him.

"Hush!" said Athos.

"Oh, ho!" said D'Artagnan, comprehending the musketeer's slight frown; "it appears there is something new on hand."

"Aramis," said Athos, "you went to breakfast the day before yesterday at the tavern of the Infidel, I believe?"

"Yes."

"How did you fare?"

"For my part I ate but little. The day before yesterday was a fast-day, and they had nothing but meat."

"15th that is not quite what I asked you," replied Athos. "I want to know if you were left alone, and nobody interrupted you."

"Why, I think there were not many intruders. Yes, Athos, I know what you mean; we shall do very well at the Infidel."

"Let us go to the Infidel, then; for here the walls are like sheets of paper."

D'Artagnan, who was accustomed to his friend's manner of acting, and perceived immediately by a word, a gesture, or a sign from him that the circumstances were serious, took Athos's arm and went out with him without saying anything. Porthos followed, chatting with Aramis.

On their way they fell in with Grimaud. Athos beckoned him to come with them. Grimaud, as usual, silently obeyed; the poor lad had nearly come to the pass of forgetting how to speak.

They arrived at the taproom of the Infidel; it was seven o'clock in the morning, and daylight began to appear. The three friends ordered breakfast, and went into a room in which, the host said, they were not likely to be disturbed.

Unfortunately, the hour was badly chosen for a private conference. Reveille had just, been beaten; every one was shaking off the drowsiness of night, and, to dispel the humid morning air, came to take a drop at the bar. Dragoons, Swiss guardsmen, musketeers, light-horsemen succeeded one another with a rapidity which might answer the landlord's purposes very well, but agreed badly with the views of the four friends. Thus they replied very curtly to the salutations, healths, and jokes of their companions.

"Come," said Athos; "we shall get into some pretty quarrel or other, and we don't need one just now. D'Artagnan, tell us what sort of a night you had, and we will describe ours afterwards."

"Ah, yes!" said a light-horseman, lolling about with a glass of brandy in his hand, which he was leisurely sipping—"ah, yes! You gentlemen of the guards were in the trenches last night, and you had a bone to pick with the Rochellais."

D'Artagnan looked at Athos to know if he ought to reply to this intruder, who mixed unasked in their conversation.

"Well," said Athos, "don't you hear M. de Busigny, who does you the honour of addressing you? Relate what has passed during the night, since these gentlemen wish to know."

"Did you not take a bastion?" asked a Swiss, who was drinking rum out of a beer-class.

"Yes, sir," said D'Artagnan, bowing; "we had that honour. As you may have heard, we even put a, barrel of powder under one of the angles, which, when it blew up, made a very pretty breach —without reckoning that, as the bastion was not built yesterday, all the rest of the building was much shaken."

"And which bastion was it?" asked a dragoon, with his sabre run through a goose, which he was taking to have cooked.

"The bastion St. Gervais," replied D'Artagnan, "from behind which the Rochellais have been annoying our workmen."

"Was the affair hot?"

"Yes, moderately so. We lost five men, and the Rochellais eight or ten."

"Balzempleu!" said the Swiss, who, notwithstanding the admirable stock of oaths possessed by the German language, had acquired the habit of swearing in French.

"But," said the light-horseman, "probably they will send pioneers this morning to repair the bastion."

"Yes, probably," said D'Artagnan.

"Gentlemen," said Athos, "I have a wager to propose."

"Ah, ha! a vager!" cried the Swiss.

"What is it?" said the light-horseman.

"Stop a bit," said the dragoon, placing his sabre like a spit upon the two large iron dogs which held the firebrands on the hearth— "stop a bit; I am in it.—You dog of a landlord! a dripping-pan instantly, that I may not lose a drop of the fat of this estimable bird."

"You are quite right," said the Swiss; "koose-krease is koot vith bastry."

"There!" said the dragoon. "Now for the wager. We are all attention, M. Athos."

"Ah, now for the wager!" said the light-horseman.

"Well, Monsieur de Busigny, I will bet you," said Athos, "that my three companions MM. Porthos, Aramis, and D'Artagnan, and myself, will go and breakfast in the bastion St. Gervais, and will remain there an hour, by the watch, whatever the enemy may do to dislodge us."

Porthos and Aramis looked at each other; they began to understand.

"Well, but," said D'Artagnan, in Athos's ear, "you are going to get us all killed without mercy."

"We are much more likely to be killed," said Athos, "if we do not go."

"'Pon my word, gentlemen!" said Porthos, turning round upon his chair and twirling his moustache, "that's a fine bet, I hope."

"I take it," said M. de Busigny. "Now let us fix the stake."

"Why, you are four, gentlemen," said Athos, "and we are four: a dinner for eight. Will that do?"

"Capitally," replied M. de Busigny.

"Perfectly well," said the dragoon.

"Dat suits me," said the Swiss.

The fourth auditor, who during all this conversation had played a mute part, nodded to show that he acquiesced in the proposition.

"The breakfast for these gentlemen is ready," said the landlord.

"Well, bring it in," said Athos.

The landlord obeyed. Athos called Grimaud, pointed to a large basket standing in a corner, and made a sign to him to wrap the food up in the napkins.

And bowing to all the astonished spectators, the young men started off for the bastion St. Gervais, followed by Grimaud carrying the basket, ignorant of where he was going, but, in the passive obedience which Athos had taught him, not even thinking of asking.

As long as they were within the camp the four friends did not exchange a word; besides, they were followed by inquisitive loungers, who, hearing of the wager, were anxious to know how they would succeed. But when once they had passed the line of circumvallation, and found themselves in the open field, D'Artagnan, who was completely ignorant of what was going on, thought it was time to demand an explanation.

"And now, my dear Athos," said he, "do me the kindness to tell me where we are going."

"Why, you see plainly enough we are going to the bastion."

"But what are we going to do there?"

"We have some very important things to talk over, and it was impossible to talk five minutes in that tavern without being annoyed by all those importunate fellows, who keep coming in, saluting you, and addressing you. Yonder, at least," said Athos, pointing to the bastion, "they will not come and disturb us."

"It seems to me," said D'Artagnan, with that prudence which was so naturally allied with his extreme bravery—"it seems to me that we could have found some retired place on the downs or by the seashore."

"Where we should have been seen all four conferring together, so that at the end of a quarter of an hour the cardinal would have been informed by his spies that we were holding a council."

When they reached the bastion the four friends turned round.

More than three hundred soldiers of all kinds were assembled at the gate of the camp; and in a separate group they could distinguish M. de Busigny, the dragoon, the Swiss, and the fourth wagerer.

Athos took off his hat, put it on the end of his sword, and waved it in the air. All the spectators returned him his salute, accompanying this politeness with a loud hurrah, which they plainly heard. After which they all four disappeared in the bastion, where Grimaud had already preceded them.

CHAPTER 42

The Council Of The Musketeers

The bastion was occupied only by a dozen dead bodies, French and Rochellais.

"Gentlemen," said Athos, who had assumed the command of the expedition, "while Grimaud is laying out the breakfast, let us begin by getting together the guns and cartridges; we can talk while performing that task. These gentlemen," added he, pointing to the bodies, "will not hear us."

"But still we might throw them into the ditch," said Porthos, "after assuring ourselves they have nothing in their pockets."

"Yes," said Athos; "that's Grimaud's business."

"Well, then," cried D'Artagnan, "let Grimaud search them, and throw them over the walls."

"By no means," said Athos; "they may be useful to us."

"These dead bodies useful to us?" exclaimed Porthos. "Why, you are crazy, my dear friend."

"'Judge not rashly,' say the Gospels and the cardinal," replied Athos. How many guns, gentlemen?"

"Twelve," replied Aramis.

"How many cartridges?"

"A hundred."

"That's quite as many as we shall want. Let us load the guns."

The four musketeers went to work. As they were loading the last musket Grimaud signified that breakfast was ready.

Athos replied, still by gestures, that it was all right, and showed Grimaud a kind of pepper-box, making him understand that he was to stand as sentinel. Only, to alleviate the tedium of the duty, Athos allowed him to take a loaf, two cutlets, and a bottle of wine.

"And now, to table," said Athos.

The four friends sat down on the ground, with their legs crossed, like Turks or tailors.

"But the secret?" said D'Artagnan.

"The secret is," said Athos, "that I saw milady last night."

D'Artagnan was lifting a glass to his lips, but at the mention of milady his hand shook so that he put the glass on the ground again, for fear of spilling the contents.

"You saw your wi—"

"Hush!" interrupted Athos; "you forget, my dear D'Artagnan, that these gentlemen have not been initiated, as you have, into the secrets of my family affairs. I saw milady."

"And where?" demanded D'Artagnan.

"About two leagues from here, at the tavern of the Red Dove-cot." And Athos told D'Artagnan of the events that had taken place at the tavern.

"Do you know," said Porthos, "that to twist that damned milady's beck would be less of a sin than to twist the necks of these poor Huguenot devils, who have committed no other crimes than singing in French the Psalms that we sing in Latin?"

"What says the abbé?" asked Athos quietly.

"I say I am entirely of Porthos's opinion," replied Aramis.

"And I too," said D'Artagnan.

"Fortunately, she is a good way off," said Porthos, "for I confess she would make me very uncomfortable if she were here."

"She makes me uncomfortable in England as well as in France," said Athos.

"She makes me uncomfortable wherever she is," said D'Artagnan.

"But when you had her in your power, why did you not drown her, or strangle her, or hang her?" said Porthos. "It is only the dead who don't come back again."

"You think so, do you, Porthos?" replied the musketeer, with a sad smile, which D'Artagnan alone understood.

"I have an idea," said D'Artagnan.

"What is it?" cried the musketeers.

"To arms!" shouted Grimaud.

The young men sprang up and seized their muskets.

A small troop advanced, consisting of from twenty to twenty-five men; they were soldiers of the garrison.

"Shall we return to the camp?" suggested Porthos. "I don't think the sides are equal."

"Impossible, for three reasons," replied Athos. "The first is, that we have not finished breakfast; the second is, that we have still some very important things to talk about; and the third is, that it yet lacks ten minutes before the hour will be over."

"Well, then," said Aramis, "we must form a plan of battle."

"It's very simple," replied Athos. "As soon as the enemy are within range, we must fire on them. If they continue to advance, we must fire again. We must fire as long as we have loaded guns. Then, if the rest of the troop persist in mounting to the assault, we will allow the besiegers to reach the ditch, and then we will push down on their heads that strip of wall which seems to stand only by a miracle of equilibrium."

"Bravo!" cried Porthos. "Decidedly, Athos, you were born to be a general, and the cardinal, who fancies himself a great captain, is nothing to you."

"Gentlemen," said Athos, "no divided attention, I beg. Let each one pick out his man."

"I cover mine," said D' Artagnan.

"And I mine," said Porthos.

"And I *idem*," said Aramis.

"Fire, then!" said Athos.

The four muskets made but one report, but four men fell.

The drum immediately heat, and the little troop advanced double-quick.

Then the musket-shots were repeated without regularity, but always aimed with the same correctness. Nevertheless, as if they had been aware of the numerical weakness of the friends, the Rochellais continued to advance on the run.

At every three shots at least two men fell; but the approach of those who remained was not slackened.

On reaching the root of the bastion, there were still more than a dozen or fifteen of the enemy. A last discharge welcomed them, but did not stop them. They leaped into the ditch, and prepared to scale the breach.

"Now, my friends," said Athos, "finish them at a blow. To the wall! to the wall!"

And the four friends, aided by Grimaud, pushed with the barrels of their muskets an enormous side of the wall, which bent over as if swayed by the wind, and giving way from its base, fell with a horrible crash into the ditch. Then a fearful cry was heard, a cloud of dust mounted toward the sky, and all was over!

"Can we have destroyed them all, from the first to the last?" said Athos.

"Faith, it seems so," said D'Artagnan.

"No," cried Porthos; "there go three or four, limping away."

In fact, three or four of these unfortunate men, covered with dirt and blood, were escaping along the hollow way, and were making for the city. These were all that were left of the little troop.

Athos looked at his watch.

"Gentlemen," said be, "we have been here an hour, and our wager is won; but we will be fair players. Besides, D'Artagnan has not told us his idea yet."

And the musketeer, with his usual coolness, went and sat down again before the remains of the breakfast.

"My idea?" said D'Artagnan.

"Yes; you said you had an idea," said Athos.

"Oh, I remember now," said D'Artagnan. "Well, I will go to England again; I will go and find Buckingham."

"You shall not do that, D'Artagnan," said Athos coolly.

"And why not? Have I not been there once?"

"Yes; but at that period we were not at war. At that period Buckingham was an ally, and not an enemy. What you now contemplate doing would amount to treason."

D'Artagnan perceived the force of this reasoning, and was silent.

"Let us have your idea, Aramis," said Athos, who entertained great deference for the young musketeer.

"We must inform the queen."

"Ah, 'pon my word, yes," said Porthos and D'Artagnan at the same time. "I think we are getting at the proper means."

"Inform the queen!" said Athos. "And how? Have we any friends at court? Can we send any one to Paris without its being known in the camp? It is a hundred and forty leagues from here to Paris; before our letter reached Angers we should be in a dungeon."

"As to sending a letter safely to her Majesty," said Aramis, "I will take that on myself. I know a clever person at Tours—"

Aramis stopped on seeing Athos smile.

"Well, do you not adopt this means, Athos?" asked D'Artagnan.

"I do not reject it altogether," said Athos, "but I wish to remind Aramis that he cannot quit the camp, and that no one but one of us can be trusted; that two hours after the messenger has set out, all the capuchins, all the alguazils, all the black caps of the cardinal, will know your letter by heart, and you and your clever person will be arrested. Allow me to give Grimaud some indispensable orders."

Athos made a sign for his lackey to draw near.

"Grimaud," said Athos, pointing to the bodies which lay in the bastion, "take those gentlemen, set them up against the wall, put their hats on their heads, and their guns in their hands."

"Oh, great man!" cried D'Artagnan, "I understand now."

"This milady—this woman—this creature—this demon has a brother-in-law, as I think you have told me, D'Artagnan?"

"Yes, I know him very well; and I also believe that he has not a very warm affection for his sister-in-law."

"There is no harm in that; if he detested her, it would be all the better," replied Athos.

"In that case, we are as well off as we could wish."

"What is her brother-in-law's name?"

"Lord Winter."

"Where is he now?"

"He returned to London at the first rumour of war."

"Well, he's just the man we want," said Athos; "we must warn him. We will send him word that his sister-in-law is on the point of assassinating some one, and we will beg of him not to lose sight of her. There is in London, I hope, some establishment like that of the Magdalens, or of the Repentant Women. He will place his sister in one of these, and we are in peace."

"But I think it would be still better;" said Aramis, "to inform the queen and Lord Winter at the same time."

"Yes; but who is to carry the letter to Tours, and who the letter to London?"

"I answer for Bazin," said Aramis.

"And I for Planchet," said D'Artagnan.

"That is so," said Porthos; "if we cannot leave the camp, our lackeys may."

"To be sure they may," said Aramis; "and this very day we write the letters, we give them money, and they set out."

"We will give them money?" replied Athos. "Have you any money, then?"

The four friends looked at one another, and a cloud came over the brows which had been for an instant so cheerful.

"Quick!" cried D'Artagnan; "I see black points and red points moving yonder. It is a whole army!"

"'Pon my word," said Athos; "yes, there they are. Do you see the sneaks coming without drums or trumpets?—Ah! have you finished, Grimaud?"

Grimaud made a sign in the affirmative, and pointed to a dozen bodies which he had set up in the most picturesque attitudes—some carrying arms, others seeming to aim, and the rest sword in hand.

"Bravo!" said Athos; "that does honour to your imagination."

"Very good," said Porthos. "I should like, however, to understand."

"Let us get away first," said D'Artagnan; "and you can understand afterwards.

"Faith!" said Athos. "I have nothing more to say against a retreat. Our wager called for an hour: we have stayed an hour and a half. Nothing can be said; let us be off, gentlemen, let us be off!"

Grimaud bad already gone on with the basket and the dessert. The four friends followed.

An instant later a furious firing was heard.

"What's that?" asked Porthos; "what are they firing at now? I hear no balls, and I see no one!"

"They are firing on our dead men," replied Athos.

"But our dead men will not return their fire."

"You are right. Then they will fancy it is an ambuscade, they will deliberate; and by the time they find out the joke we shall be out of range. That's why it is useless to get a pleurisy by going too fast."

"Oh, I understand now," said the astonished Porthos.

"That's very lucky," said Athos, shrugging his shoulders.

The French, seeing the four friends returning leisurely, uttered shouts of enthusiasm.

At length a fresh discharge was heard, and this time the balls came rattling among the stones around the four friends, and whistling sharply in their ears. The Rochellais had just taken possession of the bastion.

"What bunglers!" said Athos. "How many have we killed of them—a dozen?"

"Or fifteen.""

"How many did we crush under the wall?"

"Eight or ten."

"And in exchange for all that, not a scratch! Ah! but what is the matter with your hand, D'Artagnan? It seems to me it is bleeding."

"Oh, it's nothing," said D'Artagnan.

"A spent ball?"

"Not even that."

"What is it, then?"

We have said that Athos loved D'Artagnan as though he was his son, and this sombre and inflexible character sometimes felt a parent's anxiety for the young man.

"Only grazed a little," replied D'Artagnan. "My fingers were caught between the stone of the wall and the stone of my ring, and the skin was broken."

"That comes of wearing diamonds, my master," said Athos disdainfully.

"Ah, to be sure." cried Porthos; "there is really a diamond. Why the devil, then, do we plague ourselves about money when there is a diamond?"

"Well, then," said D'Artagnan gaily, "let us sell the diamond, and say no more about it."

The fusillade was still going on; but the friends were out of range, and the Rochellais only fired to soothe their consciences.

"Faith! it was time that idea came into Portho's head. Here we are in camp; therefore, gentlemen, not a word more of this affair. We are observed; they are coining to meet us; we shall be borne in in triumph."

In fact, as we have said, the whole camp was in commotion. More than two thousand persons had been present, as at a play, at this fortunate escapade of the four friends—an escapade of the real motive of which no one had a suspicion. Nothing was heard but cries of "Hurrah for the musketeers! Hurrah for the guards!" M. de Busigny was the first to come and shake Athos by the hand, and acknowledge that the wager was lost. The dragoon and the Swiss followed him, and all their comrades followed the dragoon and the Swiss. There was no end to the congratulations, pressures of the hand, and embraces; there was inextinguishable laughter at the Rochellais. The tumult at length became so great that the cardinal fancied there was a riot, and sent La Houdinière, his captain of the guards, to find out what was going on.

The affair was described to the messenger with all the effervescence of enthusiasm.

"Well?" asked the cardinal, on seeing La Houdinière, return.

"Well, monseigneur," replied the latter, "three musketeers and a guardsman laid a wager with M. de Busigny that they would go and breakfast in the Bastion St. Gervais, and while breakfasting they held it for two hours against the enemy, and have killed I don't know how many Rochellais."

"Did you inquire the names of the three musketeers?"

"Yes, monseigneur."

"What are their names?"

"MM. Athos, Porthos, and Aramis."

"Always my three brave fellows!" murmured the cardinal. "And the guard?"

"M. d'Artagnan."

"Still my young scapegrace. Positively, these four men must be mine."

That same evening the cardinal spoke to M. de Tréville of the morning's exploit, which was the tails of the whole camp. M. de Tréville, who had received the account of the adventure from the very mouths of the heroes of it, related it in all its details to his Eminence, not forgetting the episode of the napkin.

"Very well, Monsieur de Tréville," said the cardinal; "pray let me have that napkin. I will have three fleurs-de-lis embroidered on it in gold, and will give it to your company as a standard."

"Monseigneur," said M. de Tréville, "that will hardly be doing justice to the guards. M. d'Artagnan is not mine; he serves under M. des Essarts."

"Well, then, take him," said the cardinal; "when four men are so much attached to one another, it is only fair that they should serve in the same company."

That same evening M. de Tréville announced this good news to the three musketeer; and D'Artagnan, inviting all four to breakfast with him next morning.

D'Artagnan was beside himself with joy. We know that the dream of his life had been to become a musketeer.

The three friends were likewise greatly delighted.

That evening D'Artagnan went to present his compliments to M. des Essarts, and to inform him of his promotion.

M. des Essarts, who esteemed D'Artagnan, offered to aid him in any way, as this change of corps would entail expenses for outfit.

D'Artagnan respectfully declined, but thinking the opportunity a good one, he begged him to nave the diamond he put into his hand valued, as he wished to turn it into money.

By eight o'clock next morning M. des Essarts's valet came to D'Artagnan's lodging, and gave him a purse containing seven thousand livres.

This was the price of the queen's diamond.

CHAPTER 43

A Family Affair

Athos had invented the phrase, *family affair*. A family affair was not subject to the cardinal's investigation; a family affair concerned no one; people might employ themselves in a family affair before all the world.

Thus Athos had discovered the words, *family affair*.

Aramis had discovered the idea, the lackeys.

Porthos had discovered the means, the diamond.

D'Artagnan alone had discovered nothing—he, ordinarily, the most inventive of the four; but it must also be said that the mere mention of milady paralyzed him.

Oh no! we were mistaken; he had discovered a purchaser for his diamond.

The breakfast at M. de Tréville's was delightfully gay. D'Artagnan was already in his uniform, for as he was nearly of the same size as Aramis, and as Aramis had bought two of everything, he furnished his friend with a complete outfit.

D'Artagnan would have been at the height of his wishes if he had not constantly seen milady, like a dark cloud, on the horizon.

After breakfast it was agreed that they should meet again in the evening at Athos's lodging, and would there end the affair.

D'Artagnan passed the day in exhibiting his musketeer's uniform in every street of the camp.

In the evening, at the appointed hour, the four friends met. There remained only three things to be decided on—what they should write to milady's brother; what they should write to the clever person at Tours; and which should be the lackeys to carry the letters.

"Draw up this note for us, Aramis," said D'Artagnan. "But be concise."

"I ask nothing better," said Aramis, with that ingenuous self-confidence which every poet has; "but let me know what I am about. I have heard, in one way and another, that Lord Winter's sister-in-law was vile. It was even proved to me when I overheard her conversation with the cardinal."

"Worse than vile, ye gods!" said Athos.

"But," continued Aramis, "the details escape me."

D'Artagnan told him all he needed to know about milady.

Aramis accordingly took the pen, reflected for a few moments, wrote eight or ten lines in a charming little feminine hand, and then, in a soft, slow voice, as if, each word had been scrupulously weighed, he read the following:

> "Milord.—The person who writes these lines had the honour of crossing swords with you in a little yard near the Rue d'Enfer. As you have several times since been kind enough to call yourself that person's friend, he thinks it his duty to respond to your friendship sending you important information. Twice you have almost been the victim of a neat relative whom you believe to be your heir, because you do not know that before she contracted a marriage in England she was already married in France. But the third time, which is this, you may succumb. Your relative left Rochelle for England during the night. Be on the watch for her arrival, for she has great and terrible projects. If you absolutely insist on knowing what she is capable of, read her past history upon her left shoulder."

"Well, now, that's wonderfully well done," said Athos; "really, my dear Aramis, you have the pen of a secretary of state. Lord Winter will now be upon his guard, if the letter should reach him; and even if it should fall into the cardinal's hands, we shall not be compromised. But as the lackey who goes may make us believe he has been to London and may stop at Châtellerault, let us give him only half the sum with the letter, promising that he shall have the other half in exchange for the reply. Have you the diamond?" continued Athos. "I have what is still better: I have the value of it."

And D'Artagnan threw the purse on the table. At the sound of the gold Aramis raised his eyes and Porthos started; Athos remained unmoved.

"How much is there in that purse?"

"Seven thousand livres, in louis of twelve francs."

"Seven thousand livres!" cried Porthos—"that wretched little diamond was worth seven thousand livres?"

"It seems so," said Athos, "since here they are. I don't suppose that our friend D'Artagnan has added any of his own."

"But, gentlemen, in all this," said D'Artagnan, "we have no thought of the queen. Let us look a little after her dear Buckingham's heath. That is the least we owe her."

"You are right," said Athos; "but that falls to Aramis."

"Well," relied the latter, "what must I do?"

"Oh, it's simple enough," replied Athos. "Write a second letter for hat clever personage who lives at Tours."

Aramis resumed his pen, reflected a little more, and wrote the following lines, which he immediately submitted to his friends' approbation,

"My dear cousin."

"Ah, ha!" said Athos; "this clever lady is your relative, then?"

"She is my cousin-german."

"Good—for your cousin, then!"

Aramis continued:

> "My dear cousin,—His Eminence the cardinal, whom God preserve for the happiness of France and the confusion of the enemies of the kingdom, is on the point of finishing up with the heretic rebels of Rochelle; it is probable that the aid of the English fleet will never even arrive in sight of the place. I will even venture to say that I am certain the Duke of Buckingham will be prevented from starting for there by some great event. His Eminence is the most illustrious politician of times past, of times present, and probably of times to come. He would extinguish the sun, if the sun incommoded him. Give these happy tidings to your sister, my dear cousin. I have dreamed that that cursed Englishman was dead. I cannot recollect whether it was by steel or by poison; only I am sure of this: I have dreamed he was dead, and you know my dreams never deceive me. Be assured, then, of seeing me soon return."

"Capital," cried Athos; "you are the king of poets, my dear Aramis. You speak like the Apocalypse, and you are as true as the gospel. There is nothing now for you to do but to put the address on your letter."

"That's easily done," said Aramis.

He folded the letter coquettishly, took it, and wrote,

"To Mademoiselle Michon, seamstress, Tours."

The three friends looked at each other and laughed; they were caught.

"Now," said Aramis, "you understand, gentlemen, that Bazin is the only person who can carry this letter to Tours. My cousin knows no one but Bazin, and places confidence in no one else; any other person would fail. Besides, Bazin is ambitious and learned; Bazin has read history, gentlemen. He knows that Sixtus V. became pope after having tended pigs. Then, as he means to enter holy orders at the same time as myself, he does not despair of becoming a pope in his turn, or at least a cardinal. You understand that a man who has such views will never allow himself to be taken, or if taken, will undergo martyrdom rather than speak."

"Well, well," said D'Artagnan, "I grant you Bazin with all my heart, but let me have Planchet. Milady one day had him turned out of doors, with a sound caning. Now Planchet has an excellent memory, and I will be bound that if he can see possible means of vengeance, he will let himself be beaten to death rather than fail. If your affairs of Tours are your affairs, Aramis, those of London are mine. I beg, then, that Planchet may be chosen, especially as he has already been to London with me, and knows how to say very correctly, *London, sir, if you please,* and, *My master, Lord d'Artagnan.* With that, you may be satisfied, he can make his way, both going and returning."

"In that case," said Athos, "Planchet must receive seven hundred livres for going, and seven hundred livres for coming back; and Bazin, three hundred livres for going, and three hundred livres for coming back. That will reduce the sum to five thousand livres. We will each take a thousand livres, to be employed as seems good to each, and we will leave a fund of a thousand livres, in the guardianship of the abbé here, for extraordinary occasions or common necessities. Does that suit you?"

"My dear Athos," said Aramis, "you speak like Nestor."

Planchet was sent for, and instructions were given him. He had already been notified by D'Artagnan, who had shown him first the glory, next the money, and then the danger.

"I will carry the letter in the lining of my coat," said Planchet, "and if I am taken I will swallow it."

"Well, but then you will not be able to fulfil your commission," said D'Artagnan.

"You will give me a copy of it this evening, and I will know it by heart before morning."

D'Artagnan looked at his friends, as if to say, "Well, what did I promise you?"

"Now," continued he, addressing Planchet, "you have eight days to get to Lord Winter, you have eight days to return in—in all sixteen days; if on the sixteenth day after your departure, at eight o'clock in the evening, you are not here, no money, even if it be but five minutes past eight."

"Ah, sir!" said Planchet, "I will succeed, or I will consent to be quartered; and if they quarter me, be assured that not a morsel of me will speak."

In the morning, as he was mounting his horse, D'Artagnan, who felt at the bottom of his heart a partiality for the duke, took Planchet aside.

"Listen," said he to him. "When you have given the letter to Lord Winter, and he has read it, you will further say to him, 'Watch over his Grace, Lord Buckingham, for there is a plot to assassinate him.' But, Planchet, you see this is so serious and important that I have not informed my friends that I would entrust this secret to you; and for a captain's commission I would not write it."

"Be at rest, sir," said Planchet; "you shall see whether confidence can be placed in me or not."

And mounted on an excellent horse, which he was to leave at the end of twenty leagues to take the post, Planchet set off at a gallop.

Bazin set out the next day for Tours, and was allowed a week in which to perform his commission.

On the morning of the eighth day Bazin, fresh as ever and smiling as usual, entered the tavern of the Infidel as the four friends were sitting down to breakfast, saying, as had been agreed upon,

"Monsieur Aramis, here is your cousin's answer."

Aramis took the letter, which was in a large, coarse hand, and ill-spelt.

"Good gracious!" cried he, laughing, "I really despair of my poor Michon; she will never write like M. de Voiture."

Aramis read the letter, and passed it to Athos.

"See what she writes to me, Athos," said he.

Athos cast a glance over the epistle, and, to dissipate all the suspicions that might have been created, read aloud,

> "My Cousin,—My sister and I are very skilful in interpreting dreams, and even entertain great fear of them; but of ours it may be said, I hope, every dream is an illusion. Farewell! Take care of yourself, and act so that we may, from time to time, hear you spoken of.
>
> MARIE MICHON

On the sixteenth day signs of anxiety were so manifest in D'Artagnan and his three friends that they could not remain quiet in one place, and they wandered about like ghosts on the road by which Planchet was expected.

The day, however, passed away, and the evening came on slower than ever, but it came. The taprooms were filled with drinkers. Athos, who had pocketed his share of the diamond, seldom quitted the Infidel. He had found in M. de Busigny—who, by the way, had given them a magnificent dinner—a partner worthy of his company. They were laying together as usual when seven o'clock struck; the patrols were heard passing to double the posts. At half-past seven tattoo was sounded.

"We are lost," said D'Artagnan in Athos's ear.

"You mean we have lost," said Athos quietly, drawing four pistoles from his pocket and flinging them on the table. "Come, gentlemen," said he, "they are beating the tattoo; to bed, to bed!"

And Athos went out of the Infidel, followed by D'Artagnan. Aramis came behind, giving his arm to Porthos. Aramis mumbled verses, and Porthos from time to time pulled a hair or two from his moustache, as a sign of despair.

But behold! suddenly a shadow appears in the darkness, the outline of which is familiar to D'Artagnan, and a well-known voice says,

"Sir, I have brought your cloak, for it is chilly this evening."

"Planchet!" cried D'Artagnan intoxicated with joy.

"Planchet!" repeated Aramis and Porthos.

"Well, certainly Planchet" said Athos; "what is there astonishing in that? He promised to be back by eight o'clock, and eight is just now striking. Bravo, Planchet! you are a lad of your word, an if ever you leave your master I promise you a place in my service."

"Oh no, never!" said Planchet. "I will never leave M. d'Artagnan."

At the same lime D'Artagnan felt Planchet slipping a note into his hand.

"I have a note," said he to Athos and his friends.

"Very well," said Athos; "let us go home and we will read it."

The note burned in D'Artagnan's hand. He wished to hasten; but Athos took his arm and passed it under his own, and the young man was obliged to regulate his pace by his friend's.

At length they reached the tent, lit a lamp, and whilst Planchet stood at the entrance, so that the four friends might not be surprised, D'Artagnan with a trembling hand broke the seal and opened the letter so anxiously expected.

It contained half a line in a thoroughly British hand, and of thoroughly Spartan brevity:

"Thank you. Be easy."

Athos took the letter from D'Artagnan's hands, drew near to the lamp, set fire to it, and did not let it go till it was reduced to ashes.

Then calling Planchet,

"Now, my lad," said he, "you may claim your seven hundred livres; but you did not run much risk with such a note as that."

"'Twas not from lack of trying every means to compass it," said Planchet.

"Well," cried D'Artagnan, "tell us about it."

"Ah, sir, it's a very long story."

"You are right, Planchet," said Athos; "besides, tattoo has been sounded, and we should be observed if we kept a light burning longer than the others."

"So be it," said D'Artagnan. "Let us go to bed. Planchet, sleep soundly."

"Faith, sir, it will be the first time I have done so these sixteen days!"

"Or I either!" said D'Artagnan.

"Or I either!" said Porthos.

"Or I either!" said Aramis.

"Well, if I must tell you the truth—or I either!" said Athos.

CHAPTER 44

Fatality

Meantime, milady, drunk with rage, roaring on the deck of the vessel like a lioness embarked, had been tempted to leap into the sea in order to regain the coast, for she could not get rid of the idea that she had been insulted by D'Artagnan and threatened by Athos, and after all was leaving France without being revenged on either.

But milady continued her voyage, and on the very day that Planchet embarked at Portsmouth for France, his Eminence's messenger entered the port in triumph.

All the city was stirred by an extraordinary commotion: four large ships, recently built, had just been launched. Standing on the jetty, his clothes bedizened with gold, glittering as usual with diamonds and precious stones, his hat ornamented with a white feather which drooped on his shoulder, Buckingham was seen, surrounded by a staff almost as brilliant as himself.

They entered the roadstead; but as they were making ready to cast anchor, a little cutter, formidably armed and purporting to be a coast-guard, approached the merchant vessel, and dropped into the sea its

gig, which directed its course to the ladder. The gig contained an officer, a boatswain, and eight oarsmen. The officer alone got on board,
where he was received with all the deference inspired by a uniform.

The officer conversed a few moments with the captain, had him
read several papers of which he was the bearer; and on the merchant-
captain's order, all on board, both passengers and crew, were called
on deck.

After this kind of summons had been given, the officer inquired
aloud about the place of the brig's departure, of her route, of her land-
ings; and all these questions the captain answered without hesitation and without difficulty.

Then the officer began to pass in review all the individuals, one
after the other; and stopping in front of milady, surveyed her very
closely, but without addressing a single word to her. He then went
up to the captain, again said a few words to him, and, as if from that
moment the vessel was under his command, he ordered a manoeuvre which the crew immediately executed.

Then the vessel resumed her course, still escorted by the little
cutter, which sailed side by side with it, threatening her side with the
mouths of its six cannon, while the boat followed in the wake of
the ship.

While the officer made his scrutiny of milady, milady, as may
well be imagined, had been sharply eyeing him. But great as was
the power of this woman, with eyes of flame, in reading the hearts
of those whose secrets she wished to divine, she met this time with
a face so impenetrable that no discovery followed her investigation.
The officer who had stopped before her and silently studied her with
so much care might have been twenty-five or twenty-six years old.
He had a pale complexion, with clear blue eyes, rather deeply set;
his mouth, fine and well cut, remained motionless in its correct
lines; his chin, strongly set, denoted that strength of will which, in
the ordinary Britannic type, usually stands only for obstinacy; a
brow a little receding, as is proper for poets, enthusiasts. and soldiers, was scarcely shaded by short thin hair, which, like the heard
covering the lower part of his face, was of a beautiful deep-chestnut
colour.

When they entered the port it was already nightfall. The fog made the darkness still denser, and formed round the beacons and the lantern of the jetty a circle like that which surrounds the moon when the weather threatens to become rainy. The air they breathed was gloomy, damp, and cold.

Milady, courageous as she was, shivered in spite of herself.

The officer desired to have milady's luggage pointed out to him, ordered it to be placed in the boat; and when this operation was completed, he offered her his hand and invited her to descend.

Milady looked at the man and hesitated.

"Who are you, sir," she asked, "that you are so kind as to busy yourself so particularly on my account?"

"You must see, madame, by my uniform, that I am an officer in the English navy," replied the young man.

"But is it the custom for officers in the English navy to give their services to their female compatriots who land at a port of Great Britain, and to carry their gallantry so far as to bring them ashore?"

"Yes, madame, it is our custom, not from gallantry, but prudence, in time of war, to bring foreigners to certain hotels, in order that they may be under the eye of the government until full information can be obtained about them."

These words were spoken with the most exact politeness and the most perfect calmness. Nevertheless, they had not the power of convincing milady.

"But I am not a foreigner, sir," said she, with an accent as pure as ever was heard between Portsmouth and Manchester; "my name is Lady Clarick, and this measure—"

"This measure is general, madame, and you would not succeed in escaping from it."

"I will follow you, then, sir."

And accepting the officer's hand, she began to climb down the ladder, at the foot of which the gig was awaiting her. The officer followed her. A large cloak was spread in the stern. The officer had her sit down on the cloak, and placed himself beside her.

"Give way!" said he to the sailors.

The eight oars fell at once into the sea, making but a single sound.

giving a single stroke, and the gig seemed to fly over the surface of the water.

At the end of five minutes they reached shore.

The officer sprang on the quay and offered milady his hand.

A carriage was in waiting.

"Is this carriage for us?" asked milady.

"Yes, madame," replied the officer.

"So the hotel is at some distance?"

"At the other end of the town."

"Very well," said milady; and she got resolutely into the carriage.

The officer saw that the baggage was fastened carefully behind the carriage; and when this operation was over, he took his place beside milady, and shut the door.

Instantly, without any order being given, or place of destination indicated, the coachman set off at a gallop, and plunged into the streets of the town.

Such a strange reception naturally gave milady ample matter for reflection; so, seeing that the young officer did not seem at all disposed to talk, she recline in her corner of the carriage, and passed in review all the suppositions which presented themselves, one after the other, to her mind.

At length, after nearly an hour's ride, the carriage stopped before an iron gate, which shut in a sunken avenue leading to a castle severe in form, massive, and isolated. Then, as the wheels rolled over a fine gravel, milady could hear a dull roar, which she recognized as the noise of the sea dashing against a rock-bound coast.

The carriage passed under two arched gateways, and at length stopped in a dark, square court. Almost immediately the carriage door was opened, the young man sprang lightly to the ground, and gave milady his hand. She leaned on it, and to her turn alighted quite calmly.

"Still, the fact is I am a prisoner," said milady, looking around her, and then fixing her eyes on the young officer with a most gracious smile; "but I feel assured it will not be for long," added she. "My own conscience and your politeness, sir, are the guarantees of that."

Flattering as this compliment was, the officer made no reply, but drawing from his belt a little silver whistle, such as boatswains use in ships of war, he whistled three times, with three different modulations. Several men then appeared, unharnessed the smoking horses, and put the carriage into a coach-house.

The officer, always with the same calm politeness, invited his prisoner to enter the house. She, always with the same smiling countenance, took his arm, and passed with him under a low arched door, which, by a vaulted passage, lighted only at the farther end, led to a stone staircase turning round a stone column. Then they paused before a massive door, which, after the young officer had inserted a key into the lock, turned heavily on its hinges, and disclosed the chamber destined for milady.

With a single glance the prisoner took in the apartment in its minutest details.

It was a chamber the furniture of which was at once suited to a prison or the dwelling of a free man; yet the bars at the windows and the outside bolts on the door decided the question in favour of the prison. For an instant all this creature's strength of mind abandoned her. She sank into an armchair, with her arms folded, her head hanging down, and expecting every instant to see a judge enter to question her.

But no one entered except two marines, who brought in her trunks and packages, deposited them in a corner of the room, and retired without speaking.

The officer presided over all these details with the same calmness milady had always observed in him, never uttering a word, and making himself obeyed by a gesture of his hand or a sound of his whistle.

One might have said that between this man and his inferiors spoken language did not exist, or had become useless.

At length milady could hold out no longer. She broke the silence.

"In the name of Heaven, sir," cried she, "what is the meaning of all this? Put an end to my doubts. I have courage enough for any danger I can foresee, for any misfortune I can comprehend. Where am I, and why am I here? If I am free, why these bars and these doors? If I am a prisoner, what crime have I committed?"

"You are here in the apartment destined for you, madame. I received orders to go and take charge of you at sea, and to conduct you to this castle. This order, I believe, I have accomplished with all a soldier's strictness, but also with all the courtesy of a gentleman. Here ends, at least for the present, the duty I had to fulfil toward you; the rest concerns another person."

"And who is this other person?" asked milady. "Can you not tell me his name?"

At that moment a great jingling of spurs was heard on the stairs. People talking together went by, the sounds of voices died away, and the noise made by a single footstep approached the door.

"Here he is, madame," said the officer, leaving the entrance clear, and drawing himself up in an attitude of respect and submission.

At the same time the door opened; a man appeared on the threshold.

He had no hat on, wore a sword at his side, and was crushing a handkerchief in his hand.

Milady thought she recognized this shadow in the gloom; she leaned with one hand on the arm of the chair, and protruded her head as if to meet a certainty.

Then the stranger advanced slowly, and as he advanced into the circle of light projected by the lamp, milady involuntarily drew back.

Then, when she had no longer any doubt—

"What!" my brother!" cried she, at the culmination of her amazement; "is it you?"

"Yes, fair lady," replied Lord Winter, making a bow, half courteous, half ironical; "it is I, myself."

"Then this castle?"

"Is mine."

"This room?"

"Is yours."

"I am your prisoner, then?"

"Nearly so."

"But this is a frightful abuse of power!"

"No high-sounding words. Let us sit down and talk calmly, as brother and sister ought to do."

Then turning toward the door, and seeing that the young officer was waiting for his last orders,

"It is all right," said he; "I thank you. Now leave us alone, Mr. Felton."

CHAPTER 45

Brother and sister

While Lord Winter was shutting the door, closing a shutter, and drawing a chair near to his sister-in-law's armchair, milady was thoughtfully plunging her glance into the depths of possibility, and discovered the whole plot, not even a glimpse of which she could get long as she was ignorant into whose hands she had fallen. She knew her brother-in-law was a worthy gentleman, a bold huntsman, an intrepid player, enterprising with women, but with less than average skill in intrigues. How could he have discovered her arrival and caused her to be seized? Why did he detain her?

Athos had indeed said some words which proved that the conversation she had had with the cardinal had fallen into others' ears; but she could not suppose that he had dug a counter-mine so promptly and so boldly. She feared, rather, that her preceding operations in England had been discovered. Buckingham might have guessed that it was she who had cut off the two studs, and avenged himself for that little treachery. But Buckingham was incapable of going to any excess against a woman, particularly if that woman was supposed to have acted from a feeling of jealousy.

This supposition appeared to her the most reasonable: it seemed to her that they wanted to revenge the past, and not to anticipate the future. At all events, she congratulated herself on having fallen into the hands of her brother-in-law, with whom she reckoned she could come off easily, rather than into the hands of an avowed and intelligent enemy.

"Yes, let us talk, brother," said she, with a kind of sprightliness, now that she had decided to get from the conversation, in spite of all dissimulation Lord Winter could bring to it, the information of which she stood in need for regulating her future conduct.

"So you decided to come to England again," said Lord Winter, "in spite of the resolutions you so often manifested in Paris never to set your foot again on British soil?"

Milady replied to this question by another question.

"Before everything," said she, "tell me how you had me watched so closely as to be aware in advance not only of my arrival, but, still more, of the day, the hour, and the port at what I should arrive?"

Lord Winter adopted the same tactics as milady, thinking that as his sister-in-law employed them they must be good.

"But tell me, my dear sister," replied he—"what have you come to do in England?"

"Why, to see you," replied milady, without knowing how much she aggravated by this reply the suspicions which D'Artagnan's letter had given birth to in her brother-in-law's mind, and only desiring to gain her auditor's good-will by a falsehood.

"Ah, to see me?" said Lord Winter craftily.

"Yes."

"Well, I reply that your every wish should be fulfilled, and that we should see each other every day."

"Am I, then, to remain here eternally?" demanded milady in some terror.

"Yes, at present," continued Lord Winter, "you will remain in this castle. The walls of it are thick, the doors strong, and the bars solid. Moreover, your window opens immediately over the sea. The men of my crew, who are devoted to me for life and death, mount guard around this apartment, and watch all the passages leading to the castle yard. The officer who commands alone here in my absence you have seen, and therefore already know him. As you must have observed, he knows how to obey orders, for I am sure you did not come from Portsmouth here without trying to make him speak. What do you say to that? Could a statue of marble have been more impassive and more mute? You have already tried the power of your seductions on many men, and, unfortunately, you have always succeeded. Try them on him. By God! if you succeed with him, I pronounce you the demon himself."

He went to the door and opened it hastily.

"And now, madame, try to make your peace with God, for you are judged by men!"

Milady let her head sink, as if she felt herself crushed by this sentence. Lord Winter went out and shut the door.

An instant after, the heavy step of a marine was heard in the corridor, serving on sentinel's duty, with his axe in his girdle and his musket on his shoulder.

Milady remained for some minutes in the same position, for she thought they might perhaps be watching her through the keyhole.

Then she slowly raised her head, and assuming a formidable expression of menace and defiance, ran to the door to listen, looked out of her window, and returning to bury herself again in her large armchair, she reflected.

CHAPTER 46

Officer

Meanwhile the cardinal was anxiously looking for news from England; but no news arrived, except what was annoying and threatening.

One day when the cardinal, oppressed by mortal weariness of mind, hopeless of the negotiations with the city, without news from England, had gone out with no other aim than to ride, accompanied only by Cahusac and La Houdinière, skirting the beach and mingling the immensity of his dreams with the immensity of the ocean, he came ambling along to a hill, from the top of which he perceived, behind a hedge, reclining on the sand, in the sun so rare at this period of the year, seven men surrounded by empty bottles. Four of these men were our musketeers, preparing to listen to a letter one of them had just received. This letter was so important that it caused them to abandon their cards and their dice on a drumhead.

The other three were occupied in uncorking an enormous demijohn of Collioure wine; they were the gentlemen's lackeys.

The cardinal was, as we have said, in very low spirits; and when he was in that state of mind, nothing increased his depression so much as gaiety in others. Besides, he had another strange fancy, which was always to believe that the causes of his sadness created the gaiety of others. Making a sign to La Houdinière and Cahusac to stop, he alighted from his horse, and went toward these suspected merrymakers, hoping, by means of the sand which deadened the sound of his steps, and of the hedge which concealed his approach, to catch some words of a conversation which seemed so interesting. Ten paces from the hedge he recognized the Gascon prattle, and as he had already perceived that these men were musketeers, he had no doubt that the three others were those called "the inseparables"—that is to say, Athos, Porthos, and Aramis.

As may well be supposed, his desire to hear the conversation was increased by his discovery. His eyes took on a strange expression, and with the step of a cat he advanced toward the hedge. But he had not been able as yet to make out anything more than vague syllables without any positive sense, when a short, sonorous cry made him start, and attracted the attention of the musketeers.

"Officer!" cried Grimaud.

"I believe you are speaking, you rascal!" said Athos, rising on his elbow, and fascinating Grimaud with his flashing eyes.

Grimaud therefore said not a word more, but contented himself with pointing his index finger at the hedge, signifying by this gesture the presence of the cardinal and his escort.

With a single bound the musketeers were on their feet, and saluted respectfully.

The cardinal seemed furious.

"It seems that the musketeers set sentinels for themselves," said he. "Are the English expected by land, or do the musketeers consider themselves officers of rank?"

"Monseigneur," replied Athos, for amidst the general alarm he alone had preserved that calmness and *sang froid* which never forsook him —"monseigneur, the musketeers, when they are not on duty, or when their duty is over, drink and play at dice, and they are officers of very high rank to their lackeys."

"Lackeys!" grumbled the cardinal. "Lackeys who are ordered to warn their masters when any one passes are not lackeys; they are sentinels."

"Your Eminence may perceive that if we had not taken this precaution, we should have been in danger of letting you pass without presenting you our respects, or offering you our thanks for the favour you have done us in uniting us.—D'Artagnan," continued Athos, "you were only just now so anxious for such an opportunity for expressing your thanks to monseigneur. Here it is; avail yourself of it."

These words were pronounced with that perfect imperturbability which distinguished Athos in the hour of danger, and with that excessive politeness which made of him at certain moments a king more majestic than kings by birth.

D'Artagnan came forward and stammered out a few words of thank which soon expired under the cardinal's gloomy looks.

"No matter, gentlemen," continued the cardinal, without appearing to be in the least diverted from his first intention by the incident which Athos had raised—"no matter, gentlemen. I do not like simple soldiers, because they have the advantage of serving in a privileged corps, thus to play the great lords; and discipline is the same for them as for everybody else."

Athos allowed the cardinal to finish his sentence completely, and bowing in sign of assent, he replied in his turn,

"Discipline, monseigneur, has in no way, I hope, been forgotten by us. We are not on duty, and we believe that, as we are not on duty, we are at liberty to dispose of our time as we please. If we are so fortunate as to have some particular command from your Eminence, we are ready to obey you. Your Eminence may perceive," continued Athos, frowning, for such an investigation began to annoy him, "that we have come out with our arms, so as to be ready for the least alarm."

And he showed the cardinal the four muskets stacked near the drum, on which were the cards and dice.

"We beg your Eminence to believe," added D'Artagnan, "that we should have come to meet you, if we could have supposed it was you coming toward us with so few attendants."

"Do you know what you look like, always together, as you are, armed, and sentinelled by your lackeys?" said the cardinal. "You look like four conspirators."

"Oh, so far, monseigneur, it's true," said Athos; "we do conspire, as your Eminence might have seen the other day, only we conspire against the Rochellais."

"Eh, politicians! replied the cardinal, frowning in his turn; "the secret of many things unknown might perhaps be found in your brains, if we could read in them as you were reading that letter which you concealed when you saw me coming."

The colour mounted to Athos's face, and he made a step toward his Eminence.

"One would think that you really suspected us, monseigneur, and that we are undergoing a cross-examination. If it be so, we trust your Eminence will deign to explain yourself, and we shall then at least be acquainted with our real position."

"And if it were an examination," replied the cardinal, "others beside you have undergone such, Monsieur Athos, and have replied to them."

"So, monseigneur, I have told your Eminence that you had but to question us, and we are ready to reply."

"What was that letter you were about to read, Monsieur Aramis, and which you concealed?"

"A woman's letter, monseigneur."

"Oh, I understand. We must be discreet with such letters. But nevertheless we may show them to a confessor, and you know I have taken orders."

"Monseigneur," said Athos, with a calmness all the more terrible that he risked his life when he made this reply, "the letter is a woman's, but it is neither signed Marion de Lorme nor Madame d'Arguillon."

The cardinal became as pale as death. A flash of fire darted from his eyes. He turned round as if to give an order to Cahusac and Hou-dinière, Athos saw the movement; he took a step toward the muskets, on which the other three friends had fixed their eyes like men ill-disposed to allow themselves to be arrested. The cardinal's party consisted of only three; the musketeers, lackeys included, numbered seven. He judged that the match would be so much the less equal if Athos and his companions were really plotting; and by one of those quick changes which he always had at command, all his anger faded away into a smile.

"Come, come!" said he, "you are brave young men, proud in daylight, faithful in darkness; no fault can be found with you for watching over yourselves when you watch so carefully over others. Gentlemen, I have not forgotten the night in which you served me as an escort to the Red Dovecot. If there were any danger to be apprehended on the road I am going, I should request you to accompany me; but as there is none, remain where you are, finish your bottles, your game, and your letter. Farewell, gentlemen!"

And remounting his horse, which Cahusac had led to him, he saluted them with his hand and rode away.

The four young men, standing motionless, followed him with their eyes without speaking a single word until he had disappeared.

Then they looked at one another.

All showed their consternation and terror in their faces; for notwithstanding his Eminence's friendly farewell, they plainly perceived that the cardinal went away with rage in his heart.

Athos alone smiled with a self-possessed, disdainful smile.

When the cardinal was out of hearing and sight,

"That Grimaud kept but tardy watch!" cried Porthos, anxious to visit his ill-humour on some one.

Grimaud was about to excuse himself. Athos lifted his finger, and Grimaud was silent.

"Would you have given up the letter, Aramis?" said D'Artagnan.

"I," said you in his most flute-like tone—"I had made up my mind. If he had insisted on the letter being given up to him, I would have presented the letter to him with one hand, and with the other I would have run my sword through his body."

"I expected as much," said Athos; "and that was why I interfered between you and him. Truly, this man is very unwise to talk in this way to other men; one would say he had never had to do with any but women and children."

"My dear Athos," said D'Artagnan, "I admire you very much, but, nevertheless, we were in the wrong, after all."

"How in the wrong?" exclaimed Athos. "Whose, then, is the air we breathe? Whose is the ocean on which we look? Whose is the sand on which we were reclining? Whose is that letter of your mistress's? The cardinal's? 'Pon my honour, this man fancies the world belongs to him. There you stood, stammering, stupefied, confounded. One might have supposed that the Bastille appeared before you, and that the gigantic Medusa was converting you into stone. Come, now, is to be in love conspiring? You are in love with a woman whom the cardinal has caused to be shut up, and you wish to get her out of the cardinal's hands. That's a game you are playing with his Eminence; this letter is your hand. Why should you show your hand to your adversary? That is never done. If he finds it out, well and good. We are finding out his, aren't we?"

"In truth, what you say has sense in it, Athos," said D'Artagnan.

"In that case let there be no more question of what has just occurred, and let Aramis resume the letter from his cousin where the cardinal, interrupted him."

Aramis took the letter from his packet, the three friends surrounded him, and the three lackeys grouped themselves again near the demijohn.

"You had only read a line or two," said D'Artagnan, "so begin the setter over again."

"Willingly," said Aramis.

> "My dear Cousin,—I think I shall decide to set out for Béthune, where my sister has placed our little servant in the convent of the Carmelites. This poor child is resigned; she knows she cannot live elsewhere without risking the salvation of her soul. However, if the affairs of our family are settled, as we hope they will be, I believe she will run the risk of being damned, and will return to those whom she misses, particularly as she knows they are always thinking of her. In the meanwhile, she is not altogether wretched;

what she most desires is a letter from her intended I know that such commodities pass with difficulty through the gratings; but after all, as I have proved to you, my dear cousin, I am not unskilled, and I will take charge of the commission. My sister thanks you for your good and eternal remembrance. She underwent for a moment considerable anxiety; but she is now at length a little reassured, having sent her secretary yonder, in order that nothing may happen unexpectedly.

"Farewell, my dear cousin. Let us hear from you as often as possible—that is to say, whenever you can send with safety. I embrace you.

MARIE MICHON

"Oh, what do I not owe you, Aramis?" cried D'Artagnan. "Dear Constance! I have at length, then, news of her. She lives; she is in safety in a convent; she is at Béthune! Where do you suppose Béthune is, Athos?"

"Why, upon the frontiers of Artois and of Flanders. When the siege is once over we shall be able to make a tour in that direction."

"And that will not be long, it is to be hoped," said Porthos; "for this morning they hung a spy who confessed that the Rochellais had come to the leather of their shoes. Supposing that after having eaten the leather they eat the soles, I cannot see what they have left, unless they eat one another."

"Poor fools!" said Athos, emptying a glass of excellent Bordeaux wine, which, without having at that period the reputation it now enjoys, no less merited it—"poor fools! As if the Catholic religion was not the most agreeable of all religions! All the same," resumed he, after having smacked his tongue against his palate, "they are brave fellows. But what the devil are you about, Aramis?" continued Athos. "Why, you are squeezing that letter into your pocket!"

"Yes," said D'Artagnan, "Athos is right; it must be burnt. Who knows whether the cardinal has not a secret for examining ashes?"

"He must have one," said Athos.

"What are you going to do with the letter, then?" asked Porthos.

"Come here, Grimaud," said Athos.

Grimaud got up and obeyed.

"As a punishment for having spoken without permission, my friend, you will please eat this piece of paper. Then, to recompense you for the service you will have rendered us, you shall afterwards drink this glass of wine. Here is the letter. First, chew vigorously."

Grimaud smiled; and with his eyes fixed on the glass which Athos had just filled to the brim, he crushed the paper and swallowed it.

"Bravo, Master Grimaud!" said Athos. "And now take this. Good K! I excuse you from saying "Thank you."

Grimaud silently swallowed the glass of Bordeaux wine; but his eyes, raised toward heaven during the whole time this delicious occupation lasted, spoke a language which, though mute, was none the less expressive.

"And now," said Athos, "unless the cardinal should form the ingenious idea of ripping up Grimaud, I think we may be almost free from anxiety."

Meantime his Eminence was continuing his melancholy ride, murmuring between his moustaches what he so often said before,

"These four men must positively be mine."

CHAPTER 47

Days of Captivity

Let us return to milady, whom our eyes, turned toward the coast of France have lost from sight for an instant.

We shall find her in the despairing attitude in which we left her, plunged in an abyss of dismal reflections, a dismal hell, at the gate of which she has almost left hope behind; for now for the first time she doubts, for the first time she fears.

On two occasions her fortune has failed her, on two occasions she has found herself discovered and betrayed; and on both these occasions she failed before the fatal genius sent doubtlessly by Heaven to combat her: D'Artagnan has conquered her—her, the invincible power of evil.

He has deceived her love, humbled her pride, thwarted her ambition; and now he is ruining her fortune, depriving her of liberty, and even threatening her life. Moreover, he has lifted the corner of her mask—that ægis with which she covered herself, and which rendered her so strong.

From Buckingham, whom she hates as she hates all she has loved, D'Artagnan averted the tempest with which Richelieu threatened him in the person of the queen. D'Artagnan had passed himself off on her as De Wardes, for whom she had conceived one of those invincible tigress-like fancies common to women of her character. D'Artagnan knows the terrible secret which she has sworn no one should know without dying. Finally, just as she has obtained from Richelieu a signed permit by means of which she is going to take vengeance on her enemy, this paper is torn from her hands, and D'Artagnan holds her prisoner, and is about to send her to some filthy Botany Bay, some infamous Tyburn of the Indian Ocean.

For all this, doubtless, D'Artagnan is responsible. From whom can come so many disgraces heaped on her head, if not from him? He alone could have transmitted to Lord Winter all these frightful secrets, which he has discovered, one after another, in consequence of Fate. He knows her brother-in-law; he must have written to him.

"Come, come! I must have been mad to be carried away so," says she, plunging into the glass, which reflects back the burning glance by which she seems to question herself. "No violence; violence is a proof of weakness. In the first place, I have never succeeded by that means. Perhaps if I employed my strength against women, I should have a chance to find them weaker than myself, and consequently to conquer them. But I battle with men, and for them I am only a woman. Let me battle like a woman, then. My strength is in my weakness."

Then, as if to render an account to herself of the changes she could impose upon her countenance, so mobile and so expressive, she made it assume successively all expressions, from passionate anger, which convulsed her features, to the sweetest, most affectionate, and most seducing smile. Then her hair in turn, under her skilful hands, took on all the undulations she thought might assist the charms of her face. At length she murmured, satisfied with herself,

"Come, nothing is lost. I am still beautiful."

In fact, as was shown by this last reflection—this instinctive return to hope—sentiments of weakness or fear did not dwell long in that deep soul. Milady sat dawn to table, ate of several dishes, drank a little Spanish wine, and felt all her resolution return.

Before she went to bed she had commented on, analyzed, turned on all sides, examined on all points, the words, the gestures, the signs, and even the silence of the two men; and the result of her commentary, her analysis, her study, was that Felton, everything considered, was decided to be the more vulnerable of her two persecutors.

"Weak or strong," repeated milady, "that man has a spark of pity in his soul. Of that spark I will make a flame that shall devour him. As to the other, he knows me, he fears me, and knows what he has to expect of me if ever I escape from his hands. So it is useless to attempt anything with him. But Felton—that's another thing. He is an ingenuous, pure, and apparently virtuous young man, there is a way of getting him."

And milady went to bed, and fell asleep with a smile on her lips. Any one who had seen her sleeping might have said she was a young girl dreaming of the crown of feowers she was to wear on her brow at the next fête.

Milady dreamed that she at length had D'Artagnan in her power, that she was present at his execution; the sight of his odious blood, flowing beneath the executioner's axe, spread that charming smile upon her lips.

She slept as a prisoner sleeps who is rocked by his first hope.

In the morning when they entered her chamber she was still in bed. Felton remained in the corridor. He brought with him the woman of whom he had spoken the evening before, and who had just arrived; this woman entered, and approaching milady's bed, offered her services.

Milady was habitually pale. Her complexion might therefore deceive a person who saw her for the first time.

"I am in a fever," said she; "I have not slept a single instant during all this long night; I am in frightful pain. Will you be more humane to me than others were to me yesterday? Besides, all I ask is permission to stay in bed."

"Would you like a physician sent for?" asked the woman.

Felton listened to this dialogue without speaking a word.

Milady reflected that the more people she had around her, the more she should have to work upon, and the stricter would be the watch Lord Winter kept over her. Besides, the physician might declare the malady was feigned; and milady, having lost the first game, was not willing to lose the second.

"Send for a physician!" said she. "What would be the good of that? These gentlemen declared yesterday that my illness was a comedy; it would be just the same to-day, no doubt, for since yesterday evening they have had plenty of time to send for a doctor."

"Then," said Felton, becoming impatient, "say yourself, madame, what treatment you wish followed."

"Eh I how can I tell? My God! I know that I am in pain, that's all. Give me anything you like; it is of very little consequence to me."

"Go, get Lord Winter," said Felton, tired of these eternal complaints.

"Oh no, no!" cried milady; "no sir, do not call him, I conjure you. I am well, I want nothing; do not call him."

She put such prodigious vehemence, such irresistible eloquence, into this exclamation that Felton, in spite of himself, advanced some steps into the room.

"He has come!" thought milady.

"Now, of you are really in pain," said Felton, "a physician shall be sent for; and if you deceive us—well, why, it will be so much the worse for you. But at least we shall not have to reproach ourselves with anything."

Milady made no reply, but turning her beautiful head over on her pillow, she burst into sears, and sobbed as though her heart would break.

Felton surveyed her for an instant with his usual coolness; then, seeing that the crisis threatened to be prolonged, he left the room. The woman followed him, and Lord Winter did not appear.

"I fancy to begin to see my way," murmured milady, with a savage joy, burying herself under the clothes to conceal from anybody who might be watching her this burst of inward satisfaction.

Two hours passed away.

"Now it is time that the malady should be over," said she; "let me get up and obtain some success this very day. I have but ten days, and this evening two will be gone."

On entering milady's room in the morning they had brought her breakfast; now she thought it could not be long before they would come to clear the table, and that she should see Felton.

Milady was not mistaken. Felton reappeared again, and without observing whether she had or had not touched her repast, he made a sign for the table to be carried out of the room, as it was brought in all set.

Felton remained behind; he held a book in his hand.

Milady, reclining in an armchair near the fireplace, beautiful, pale, and resigned, looked like a holy virgin awaiting martyrdom.

Felton approached her, and said,

"Lord Winter, who is a Catholic, as well as yourself, madame, thinking that the privation of the rites and ceremonies of your church might be painful to you, has consented that you should read every day the ordinary of your mass, and here is a book which contains the ritual of it."

At the manner in which Felton laid the book on the little table near which milady was sitting, at the tone in which he pronounced the two words "your mass," at the disdainful smile with which he accompanied them, milady raised her head and looked more attentively at the officer.

Then, by the plain arrangement of his hair, by his costume of exaggerated simplicity, by his brow polished like marble, but hard and impenetrable like it, she recognized one of those gloomy Puritans she had so often met with, both at the court of King James and at the court of the king of France, where, in spite of the remembrance of St. Bartholomew's, they sometimes came to seek refuge.

She then had one of those sudden inspirations which only people of genius have in great crises, in the supreme moments which are to decade their fortunes or their lives.

Those two words, "your mass," and a simple glance cast on Felton, revealed to her all the importance of the reply she was about to make.

But with that rapidity of intelligence which was peculiar to her, this reply, ready arranged, presented itself to her lips,

"I," said she, with an accent of disdain struck in unison with that which she had remarked in the young officer's voice—"I, sir? My mass? Lord Winter, the corrupted Catholic, knows very well that I am not of his religion, and this is a snare he wishes to set for me!"

"And of what religion are you, then, madame?" asked Felton.

"I will tell," cried milady, with a feigned enthusiasm, "on the day when I shall have suffered sufficiently for my faith."

Felton's look revealed to milady the full extent of the space she had just opened for herself by this single word.

The young officer, however, remained mute and motionless. His look alone had spoken.

"I am in the hands of mine enemies," continued she, with that tone of enthusiasm which she knew was familiar to the Puritans. "Well, let my God save me, or let me perish for my God! That is the reply I beg you to make to Lord Winter. And as to this book," added she, pointing to the ritual with her finger, but without touching it, as though she would be contaminated by the touch, "you may carry It back and make use of it yourself; for doubtless you are doubly Lord Winter's accomplice—the accomplice in his persecutions, the accomplice in his heresies."

Felton made no reply, took the book with the same appearance of repugnance which he had before manifested, and retired thoughtfully.

Then size threw herself upon her knees and bean to pray.

"My God, my God!" said she, "Thou knowest in what holy cause I suffer; give me, then, the strength to suffer."

The door opened gently; the beautiful suppliant pretended not to hear the noise, and in a voice broken by tears she continued,

"God of vengeance! God of goodness! wilt Thou allow this man's frightful projects to be accomplished?"

Then only did she feign to hear the sound of Felton's steps; and rising quick as thought, she blushed, as if ashamed of being surprised on her knees.

"I do not like to disturb those who pray, madame," said Felton seriously; "do not disturb yourself on my account, I beseech you."

"How do you know I was praying, sir?" said milady, in a voice choked by sobs. "You were mistaken, sir; I was not praying."

"Do you think, then, madame," replied Felton, in the same serious voice, but in a milder tone—"do you think I assume the right of preventing a creature from prostrating herself before her Creator? God forbid! Besides, repentance is becoming to the guilty. Whatever crimes they may have committed, for me the guilty are sacred at the feet of God."

"Guilty!—I?" said milady, with a smile which might have disarmed the angel of the last judgment. "Guilty! Oh, my God, Thou knowest whether I am guilty! Say I am condemned, sir, if you please; but you know that God, who loves martyrs, sometimes permits the innocent to be condemned."

"Were you condemned, were you innocent, were you a martyr," replied Felton, "the greater would be the need of prayer; and I myself will aid you with my prayers."

"Oh, you are just a man!" cried milady, throwing herself on her knees at his feet. "I can stand it no longer, for I fear I shall be wanting in strength in the moment at which I shall be forced to undergo the struggle and confess my faith. Listen, then, to the supplication of a despairing woman. You are made a tool of, sir; but that is not the question. I ask you only one favour, and if you grant it me, I will bless you in this world and in the world to come."

"Speak to the master, madame," said Felton; "happily I am not charged with the power either of pardoning or punishing. God has laid this responsibility on one higher placed than I am."

"To you—no, to you alone! Listen to me rather than contribute to my destruction, rather than contribute to my ignominy."

"If you have deserved this shame, madame, if you have incurred this ignominy, you must submit to it as an offering to God."

"What do you say? Oh, you do not understand me! When I speak of ignominy, you think I speak of some punishment or other, of imprisonment or death! Would to Heaven it were no worse! Of what consequence to me is imprisonment or death?"

"I no longer understand you, madame," said Felton.

"Or, rather, you pretend not to understand me, sir!" replied the prisoner, with a doubting smile.

"No, madame, on the honour of a soldier, on the faith of a Christian."

"What! You are ignorant of Lord Winter's designs on me?"

"I am."

"Impossible! You are his confidant!"

"I never lie, madame."

"Oh, he makes too little concealment of them for you not to guess them."

"I seek to guess nothing, madame; I wait till I am confided in; and apart from what Lord Winter has said to me before you, he has confided nothing to me."

"Why, then," cried milady, with an incredible accent of truthfulness —"why, then, you are not his accomplice; you do not know that he destines me to a disgrace which all the punishments of the world cannot equal in horror?"

"You are mistaken, madame," said Felton, reddening; "Lord Winter is not capable of such a crime."

"Good!" said milady to herself; "without knowing what it is, he calls it a crime!"

Then aloud,

"The friend of the infamous is capable of everything."

"Whom do you call the infamous?" asked Felton.

"Are there, then, in England two men to whom such an epithet can be applied?"

"You mean George Villiers?" said Felton, and his eyes flashed fire.

"Whom pagans and infidel gentiles call the Duke of Buckingham," replied milady. "I could not have thought that there was an Englishman in all England who would have required so long an explanation to understand of whom I was speaking."

"The hand of the Lord is stretched over him," said Felton; "he will not escape the chastisement he deserves."

Felton only expressed regarding the duke the execration which all the English felt for a man whom the Catholics themselves called the extortioner, the pillager, the profligate, and whom the Puritans styled simply Satan.

"Oh, my God, my God!" cried milady; "when I supplicate Thee to pour on this man the chastisement which is his due, Thou knowest that I pursue not my own vengeance, but that I pray for the deliverance of a whole nation!"

"Do you know him, then?" asked Felton.

"At length he questions me!" said milady to herself, at the height of joy at having obtained so quickly such a great result. "Oh, do I know him? Yes; to my misfortune, to my eternal misfortune!"

And milady wrung her hands, as if she had reached the very paroxysm of grief.

Felton no doubt felt within himself that his strength was deserting him, and he took several steps toward the door; but the prisoner, whose eye was never off him, sprang after him and stopped him.

"Sir," cried she, "be kind, be clement, listen to my prayer. That knife, which the baron's fatal prudence deprived me of, because be knows the use I would make of it—Oh, hear me to the end! That knife—give it to me for a minute only, for mercy's, for pity's sake! I will embrace your knees! You shall shut the door, that you may be certain I am not angry with you! My God! the idea of being angry with you, the only just, good, and compassionate being I have met with!—you, my saviour perhaps! One minute, that knife, one minute, a single minute, and I will restore it to you through the grating of the door; only one minute, Mr. Felton, and you will have saved my honour."

"To kill yourself?" cried Felton, in terror, forgetting to withdraw his hands from the hands of the prisoner—"to kill yourself?"

"I have said, sir," murmured milady, lowering her voice, and allowing herself to sink overpowered to the ground—"I have told my secret! He knows all!—My God, I am lost!"

Felton remained standing, motionless and undecided.

"He still doubts," thought milady; "I have not been sufficiently genuine."

Some one was heard walking in the corridor. Milady recognized Lord Winter's step.

Felton recognized it also, and took a step toward the door.

Milady sprang forward.

"Oh, not a word," said she, in a concentrated voice—"not a word to this man of all I have said to you, or I am lost, and it would be you—you—"

Then as the steps drew near she became silent for fear of being heard, applying, with a gesture of infinite terror, her beautiful hand to Felton's mouth.

Felton gently pushed milady from him, and she sank into an easy-chair.

Lord Winter passed before the door without stopping, and they heard the sound of his footsteps in the distance.

Felton, as pale as death, remained some instants with his ear alert and listening; then, when the sound had entirely died away, he breathed like a man awaking from a dream, and rushed out of the apartment.

"Ah," said milady, listening in her turn to the noise of Felton's steps, which faded away in a direction opposite to Lord Winter's— "ah, at length thou art mine!"

The next day, when Felton entered milady's apartment he found her standing upon a chair, holding in her hands a cord made of several cambric handkerchiefs torn into strips, twisted together into a kind of rope, and tied at the ends. As the noise Felton made in opening the door milady leaped lightly to the ground and tried to hide behind her the improvised cord she held in her hand.

The young man was even paler than usual, and his eyes, inflame by lack of sleep, showed that he had passed a feverish night.

Nevertheless, his brow was armed with a sternness more severe than ever.

He advanced slowly toward milady, who had sat down, and taking one end of the murderous rope, which, by mistake or perhaps by design, she allowed to appear,

"What is this, madam" he asked coldly.

"This? Nothing," said milady, smiling with that melancholy

expression which she knew so well how to give to her smile. *"Ennui* is the mortal enemy of prisoners; I was blue, and I amused myself with twisting a rope.

Felton turned his eyes toward that part of the wall of the apartment before which he had found milady standing in the chair in which she was now seated, arid over her head he perceived a gilt-headed screw, fixed in the wall for the purpose of hanging up clothes or arms.

He started, and the prisoner saw that start; for though her eyes were cast down, nothing escaped her.

"And what were you doing standing on that chair?" asked he.

"What difference does that make to you?" replied milady.

"But," replied Felton, "I wish to know."

"Do not question me," said the prisoner; "you know that we true Christians are forbidden to tell falsehoods."

"Well, then," said Felton, "I will tell you what you were doing, or rather what you were going to do: you were going to finish the fatal work you cherish in your mind. Remember, madame, if our God forbids us to tell falsehoods, He much more severely forbids suicide."

"When God sees one of His creatures unjustly persecuted, placed between suicide and dishonour, believe me, sir," replied milady, in a tone of deep conviction, "God pardons suicide, for then suicide is martyrdom."

"You say either too much or too little. Speak, madame; in Heaven's name, explain yourself."

"They have eyes," repeated milady, with an accent of indescribable relief, "but they see not; ears have they, but they hear not."

"But," cried the young officer, "speak, speak, then!"

"Confide my shame to you!" cried milady, with the blush of modesty on her face—"for often the crime of one becomes the shame of another —confide my shame to you, a man, and I a woman! Oh," continued she placing her hand modestly over her beautiful eyes, "never! never!—I could not."

Milady had achieved a half-triumph, and the success obtained doubled her strength.

"You promised me something."

"What? My God!" said the young man, who, in spite of his self-command, felt his knees tremble and the sweat start from his brow.

"You promised to bring a knife, and to leave it with me after our conversation."

"Say no more of that, madame," said Felton. "There is no situation, however terrible, that can authorize one of God's creatures to inflict death upon itself. I have reflected that I could never become guilty of such a sin."

"Ah, you have reflected!" said the prisoner, sitting down in her armchair with a smile of disdain; "and I also have reflected."

"About what?"

"That I can have nothing to say to a man who does not keep his word."

"Oh, my God!" murmured Felton.

"You may retire," said milady. "I shall not speak."

"Here is the knife," said Felton, drawing from his pocket the weapon which, according to his promise, he had brought, but which he hesitated to give to his prisoner.

"Let me see it," said milady.

"For what purpose?"

"On my honour I will instantly return it to you. You shall place it on that table, and you may remain between it and me."

Felton handed the weapon to milady, who examined the temper of it attentively, and tried the point on the tip of her finger.

"Well," said she, returning the knife to the young officer, "this is fine and good steel. You are a faithful friend, Felton."

Felton took back the weapon and laid it on the table, in accordance with his agreement with his prisoner.

Milady followed him with her eyes, and made a gesture of satisfaction.

"Now," said she, "listen to me."

The recommendation was useless. The young officer was standing before her, awaiting her words as if to devour them.

"Felton," said milady, with a solemnity full of melancholy, "if your sister, your father's daughter, said to you,

"While still young, unfortunately beautiful, I was dragged into a snare. I resisted. Ambushes, acts of violence, were multiplied around me. I resisted. The religion I serve, the God I adore, were blasphemed because I called to my aid my religion and my God. I resisted. Then outrages were heaped upon me, and when they could not ruin my soul they determined to defile my body for ever. Finally—"

Milady, stopped, and a bitter smile passed over her lips.

"Finally," said Felton—"finally, what did they do?"

"Finally, one evening, they resolved to paralyze my unconquerable resistance. One evening a powerful narcotic was mixed with my water. Scarcely had I finished my repast when I felt myself sink by degrees into a strange torpor. Though I was without suspicion, a vague fear seized me, and I tried to struggle against sleep. I arose. I endeavoured to run to the window and call for help, but my legs refused to carry me. It seemed as if the ceiling were sinking down on my head and crushing me under its weight. I stretched out my arms; I tried to speak; I could only utter inarticulate sounds. An irresistible faintness came over me. I supported myself by an armchair, feeling that I was about to fall, but this support was soon insufficient for my weak arms. I fell on one knee, then on both. I tried to pray, but my tongue was frozen. God, doubtless, neither heard nor saw me, and I sank down on the floor, a prey to a sleep which was like death.

"Of all that passed during my sleep, or the time that glided away while it lasted, I have no recollection. The only thing I recollect is, that I woke in bed, in a round chamber, the furniture of which was sumptuous and into which light penetrated only by an opening in the ceiling. Moreover, no door seemed to give entrance to the room. It might have been called a magnificent prison.

"It was long before I could make out where I was, or could take account of the details I describe. My mind seemed to strive in vain to shake off the heavy darkness of the sleep from which I could not rouse myself. I had vague perceptions of a space travelled over, of the rolling of a carriage, of a horrible dream in which my strength was exhausted; but all this was so dark and so indistinct in my mind that these events seemed to belong to another life than mine, and yet mixed with mine by a fantastic duality.

"For some time the state into which I had fallen appeared so strange that I thought I was dreaming. I arose tremblingly. My clothes were near me on a chair. I neither remembered having undressed myself, nor going to bed. Then little by little the reality broke upon me, full of chaste terrors. I was no longer in the house where I had been dwelling. As well as I could judge by the light of the sun, the day was already two-thirds gone. It was the evening before that I had fallen asleep; my sleep, then, must have already lasted nearly twenty-four hours! What had happened during this long sleep?

"I dressed myself as quickly as possible. My slow and stiff motions all attested that the effects of the narcotic were still not entirely dissipated. The chamber was evidently furnished for a woman's reception; and the most finished coquette could not have formed a wish which, on looking round the apartment, she would not have found gratified.

"Certainly I was not the first captive who had been shut up in this splendid prison. But you understand, Felton, the more superb the prison, the greater was my terror.

"Yes, it was a prison, for I vainly tried to get out of it. I sounded all the walls in the hopes of discovering a door, but everywhere the walls returned a full, dull sound.

"I made the circuit of the room perhaps twenty times, in search of an outlet of some kind; there was none, I sank exhausted with fatigue and terror into an armchair.

"In the meantime night was rapidly coining on, and with night my terrors increased. I did not know but I had best remain where I was seated. I seemed to be surrounded by unknown dangers, into which I was likely to fall at every step. Although I had eaten nothing since the evening before, my fears prevented me from feeling hungry.

"No noise from without by which I could measure the time reached me. I only supposed it might be seven or eight o'clock in the evening, for it was October and quite dark.

"All at once a door, creaking on its hinges, made me start. A globe of fire appeared above the glazed opening of the ceiling, casting a strong light into my chamber, and I perceived with terror that a man was standing within a few paces of me.

"A table, with two covers, bearing a supper ready prepared, stood, as if by magic, in the middle of the apartment.

"That man was he who had pursued me during a whole year, who lead vowed my dishonour, and who, by the first words that issued from his mouth, gave me to understand he had accomplished it the preceding night."

"The scoundrel!" murmured Felton.

"Oh yes, the scoundrel!" cried milady, seeing the interest which the young officer, whose soul seemed to bang on her lips, took in her strange story—"oh yes, the scoundrel! He believed that, by having triumphed over me in my sleep, all was completed. He came, hoping that I should accept my shame, since my shame was consummated. He came to offer his fortune in exchange for my love.

"Alas! my desperate resistance could not last long. I felt my strength fail, and this time it was not my sleep that enabled the scoundrel to prevail, but my swooning."

Felton listened without making any sound but a kind of suppressed roar. Only the sweat streamed down his marble brow, and his hand, under his coat, tore his breast.

"My first impulse on coming to myself was to feel under my pillow for the knife I had not been able to reach. If it had not come into play for defence, it might at least serve in expiation.

"'Ah, ha!' cried he, seizing my arm, and wresting from me the weapon, 'you want to take my life, do you, my pretty Puritan? But this is more than dislike, this is ingratitude! Come, come, calm yourself, my sweet girl! I thought you were become kinder. I am not one of those tyrants who detain women by force. You don't love me. With my usual fatuity, I doubted it; now I am convinced. To-morrow you shall be free.'

"I had but one wish, and that was that he should kill me.

"'Beware!' said I for my liberty is your dishonour.'

"'Explain yourself, my pretty sibyl.'

"'Yes; for no sooner shall I have left this place than I will tell everything. I will proclaim the violence you have used toward me. I will describe my captivity. I will denounce this palace of infamy. You are placed very high, my lord, but tremble! Above you there is the king. Above the king there is God."

"Perfect master as he seemed over himself, my persecutor allowed a movement of anger to escape him. I could not see the expression of his face, but I felt the arm on which my hand was placed tremble.

"'Then you shall not go from here,' said he.

"At these words he retired. I heard the door open and shut, and I remained overwhelmed, yet less, I confess, by my grief than by the shame of not having avenged myself."

CHAPTER 48

Device of Classical Tragedy

After a moment's silence, employed by milady in observing the young man who was listening to her, milady continued her recital.

"When evening came I was so weak that almost every instant I fainted, and every time that I fainted I thanked God, for I thought I was going to die.

"In the midst of one of these fainting fits I heard the door open. Terror recalled me to myself.

"He entered the apartment, followed by a man in a mask. He himself was masked, but I knew his step, I knew his voice. I knew him by that imposing carriage which hell stowed on his person for the curse of humanity.

"'Well,' said he to me, 'have you made up your mind?'"

"'You have said Puritans have but one word. Mine you have heard, and that is to pursue you on earth before the tribunal of men, in heaven before the tribunal of God.'

"'You persist, then?'

"'I swear it before the God who hears me. I will take the whole world, as a witness of your crime, and that until I have found an avenger.'

"'Executioner,' said he, 'do your duty.'"

"Oh, his name, his name!" cried Felton; "tell it me!"

"Then in spite of my cries, in spite of my resistance—for I began to realize that for me there was a question of something worse than death —the executioner seized me, threw me on the floor, bruised me with his rough grasp. Suffocated by sobs, almost without consciousness, invoking God, who did not listen to me, I suddenly uttered a frightful cry of pain and shame. A burning fire, a red-hot iron, the iron of the executioner, was imprinted on my shoulder."

Felton uttered a groan.

"Here," said milady, rising with the majesty of a queen—"here, Felton, behold the new martyrdom invented for a young girl, pure, and yet the victim of a scoundrel's brutality. Learn to know the hearts of men, and henceforth make yourself less easily the instrument of their unjust revenges."

Milady, with a swift gesture, opened her dress, tore the cambric that covered her bosom, and, red with feigned anger and simulated modesty, showed the young man the ineffaceable impression which dishonoured her beautiful shoulder.

"But," cried Felton, "it is a fleur-de-lis which I see there."

"And therein consisted the infamy," replied milady. "The brand of England!—it would have been necessary to prove what tribunal had imposed it on me, and I could have made a public appeal to all the tribunals of the kingdom; but the brand of France!—oh, by that, by that I was branded indeed!"

This was too much for Felton.

Pale, motionless, overwhelmed by this frightful revelation, dazzled by the superhuman beauty of this woman, who unveiled herself before ham with a shamelessness which appeared to him sublime, he ended by falling on his knees.

"Pardon!, pardon!" cried Felton; "oh, pardon!"

Milady read in his eyes, "Love! love!"

"Pardon for what?" asked she.

"Pardon me for having joined your persecutors."

Milady held out her hand to him.

"So beautiful! so young!" cried Felton, covering that hand with his kisses.

Milady cast on him one of those looks which make a slave into a king.

Felton was a Puritan. He dropped this woman's hand to kiss her feet.

He more than loved her; he adored her.

When this crisis was past; when milady seemed to have recovered her self-control, which she had not lost even for an instant; when Felton had seen her cover again with the veil of chastity those treasures of love which were concealed from him only to make him desire them the more ardently,

"Ah, now! " said he, "I have only one thing to ask of you—that is, the name of your true executioner. For in my eyes there is but one. The other was the instrument, that was all."

"What, brother!" cried milady; "must I name him? Have you not yet divined who he is?"

"What!" cried Felton; "he!—he again!—he always! What!—the seal culprit!"

"The real culprit," said milady, "is the ravager of England, the persecutor of true believers, the cowardly ravisher of the honour of so many women—he who, to satisfy a caprice of his corrupt heart, is about to make England shed so much blood, who protects the Protestants to-day and will betray them to-morrow—"

"Buckingham! Then it is Buckingham!" cried Felton, in exasperation.

Milady hid her face in her hands, as if she could not endure the shame which this name recalled to her.

"Buckingham, the executioner of this angelic creature!" cried Felton. "And Thou hast not hurled Thy thunder at him, my God! And Thou hast left him noble, honoured, powerful, for the ruin of us all!"

"God abandons him who abandons himself," said milady, "But He will draw down on his head the punishment reserved for the damned!" said Felton, with increasing excitement. "He wishes that human vengeance should precede heavenly justice."

"Men fear him and spare him."

"I," said Felton—"I do not fear him, nor will I spare him!"

Milady felt her soul bathed in a hellish joy.

Severn knocks resounded on the door. This time milady really pushed him away from her.

"Hark!" said she; "we have been overheard. Some one is coming! All is over! We are lost!"

"No," said Felton; "it is only the sentinel warning me that they are about to change guard."

"Then run to the door and open it yourself."

Felton obeyed. This woman was already his whole thought, his whole soul.

He found a sergeant in command of a watch patrol.

"Well, what is the matter?" asked the young lieutenant.

"You told me to open the door if I heard any one cry out," said the soldier; "but you forgot to leave me the key. I heard you cry out without understanding what you said. I tried to open the door, but it was locked inside; then I called the sergeant."

"And here I am," said the sergeant.

Felton, bewildered, almost mad, stood speechless.

Milady, perceiving that it was now her turn to come forward, ran to the table, and seizing the knife which Felton had laid down,

"And what right have you to prevent me from dying?" said she.

"Great God!" exclaimed Felton, on seeing the knife glitter in her hand.

At that moment a burst of ironical laughter resounded through the corridor. Attracted by the noise, the baron, in his dressing-gown, his sword under his arm, was standing in the doorway.

"Ah, ha!" said he; "here we are, at the last act of the tragedy. You see, Felton, the drama has gone through all the phases I named. But be at ease; no blood will flow."

Milady perceived that all was lost unless she gave Felton an instant and terrible proof of her courage.

"You are mistaken, my lord—blood will flow; and may that blood fall back on those who cause it to flow!"

Felton uttered a cry and rushed toward her. He was too late; milady had stabbed herself.

But the knife had very fortunately, we should say skilfully, come in contact with the steel busk which at that period, like a cuirass, defended women's bosoms; it had glided down it, tearing her dress, and had penetrated slantingly between the flesh and the ribs.

Milady's robe was none the less stained with blood in a second. Milady fell backward and seemed to have fainted.

Felton snatched away the knife.

"See, my lord," said he, in a deep, gloomy tone, "here is a woman who was under my guard, and who has killed herself!"

"Do not worry, Felton," said Lord Winter. "She is not dead; demons do not die so easily. Do not worry, but go wait for me in my chamber."

"But my lord—"

"Go, sir; I command you."

At this injunction from his superior, Felton obeyed; but as he went out he put the knife into his bosom.

Lord Winter contented himself with calling the woman who waited on milady, and when she came he recommended the prisoner, who was still in a swoon, to her care, and left her alone with her.

But as the wound after all might be serious, he immediately sent off a man on horseback to fetch a doctor.

Chapter 49

Escape

As Lord Winter had thought, milady's wound was not dangerous. So soon as she was left alone with the woman whom the baron had summoned, and who hastened to her, she opened her eyes.

It was necessary, however, to affect weakness and pain, but this was not a very difficult task for an actress like milady. Thus the poor woman was completely the prisoner's dupe, and notwithstanding her entreaties, she persisted in watching all night.

But this woman's presence did not prevent milady from thinking.

There was no longer any doubt that Felton was convinced; Felton was hers. If an angel appeared to that young man to accuse milady, he would certainly, in the disposition of mind he was then in, regard him as a messenger from the demon.

Milady smiled at this thought, for Felton was henceforth her only hope, her only means of safety.

But Lord Winter might have suspected him! But Felton himself might now be watched!

Toward four o'clock in the morning the doctor came. Since milady had stabbed herself the wound had already closed. The doctor could therefore measure neither its direction nor depth. He only recognized by milady's pulse that her case was not serious.

In the morning milady, under the pretence of not having slept during the night and wanting rest, sent away the woman who attended her.

She had one hope—that Felton would appear at the breakfast hour; but Felton did not come.

Were her fears realized? Was Felton, suspected by the baron, about to fail her at the decisive moment? She had only one day left. Lord Winter had announced her embarkation for the 23rd, and it was now the morning of the 22nd.

Nevertheless she still waited patiently till the dinner hour.

Though she had eaten nothing in the morning, the dinner was brought in at its usual time. Milady then perceived with terror that the uniform of the soldiers who guarded her was changed.

Then she ventured to ask what had become of Felton.

She was told that he had left the castle an hour before on horseback. She inquired whether the baron was still at the castle. The soldier replied that he was, and that he had given orders to be informed if the prisoner wished to speak to him.

Milady replied that she was too weak at present, and that her only desire was to be left alone.

The soldier went out, leaving the dinner served.

Felton was sent away; the marines were changed. Felton, then, was mistrusted!

This was the last blow to the prisoner.

Left alone, she got up. The bed in which she had remained for prudence, and in order that she might be believed to be seriously wounded, burnt her like a blazing fire. She cast a glance at the door. The baron had had a plank nailed over the grating. He feared, no doubt, that through this opening she might still, by some diabolical means, succeed in corrupting her guards.

At six o'clock Lord Winter came in. He was armed to the teeth. This man, in whom milady till that time had only seen a rather silly gentleman, had become an admirable jailer. He appeared to foresee everything, to divine everything, to anticipate everything.

A single look at milady informed him of all that was passing in her mind.

"Ay!" said he, "I see; but you will not kill me to-day either. You have no longer a weapon; and besides, I am on my guard. You began to pervert my poor Felton. He was already yielding to your infernal influence. But I amend to save him. He wilt never see you again; all is over. Get your clothes together; to-morrow you will go. I had fixed the embarkation for the 24th. But I have reflected that the more promptly the affair takes place, the more certain it will be. To-morrow at noon I shall have the order for your exile, signed Buckingham." *Au revoir*, then. That is all I have to say to you to-day. To-morrow I will see you again, to take my leave of you."

And at these words the baron went out.

The supper was served. Milady felt that she needed all her strength. She did not know what might take place during this night, which was approaching portentously, for enormous clouds were rolling over the face of the sky, and distant lightning announced a storm.

Suddenly she heard a tap at her window, and by the help of a flash of lightning she saw the face of a man appear behind the bars.

She ran to the window and opened it.

"Felton!" cried she. "I am saved!"

"Yes," said Felton; "but be silent, be silent! I must have time to file through these bars. Only take care that they do not see me through the grating of the door."

"Oh, it is a proof that the Lord is on our side, Felton!" replied milady. "The grating is closed with a board."

"That is well; God has made them mad!" said Felton.

Milady shut the window, extinguished the lamp, and went to lie down on the bed. Amid the moaning of the storm she heard the grinding of the file on the bars, and by the light of every flash she saw Felton's shadow behind the panes.

She spent an hour scarcely breathing, panting, with a cold sweat on her brow, and her heart oppressed by frightful agony at every movement she heard in the corridor.

There are hours that last a year.

At the end of an hour Felton tapped again.

Milady sprang out of bed and opened the window. Two bars removed made an opening large enough for a man to pass through.

"Are you ready?" asked Felton.

"Yes. Must I take anything with me?"

"Money, if you have any."

"Yes; fortunately they have left me all I had."

"So much the better, for I have expended all mine in hiring a vessel."

"Here!" said milady, placing a bag full of louis in Felton's hands. Felton took the bag and threw it to the foot of the wall.

"Now," said he, "will you come?"

"I am here."

Milady climbed on a chair, and leaned the upper part of her body through the window. She saw the young officer suspended over the abyss by a rope ladder. For the first time a feeling of terror reminded her that she was a woman. The dark space frightened her.

"I expected this," said Felton.

"Oh, it's nothing, it's nothing!" said milady; "I will descend with my eyes shut."

"Have you confidence in me?" said Felton.

"Can you ask me such a question?"

"Put your two hands together. Cross them; that's right!"

Felton fastened her two wrists together with a handkerchief, and then tied a cord over the handkerchief.

"What are you doing?" asked milady in surprise.

"Put your arms round my neck, and fear nothing."

"But I shall make you lose your balance, and we shall both be dashed to pieces."

"Don't be afraid. I am a sailor."

Not a second was to be lost. Milady put her arms round Felton's neck, and let herself slip out of the window.

Felton began to descend the ladder slowly, step by step. In spite of the weight of their bodies, the blast of the hurricane trade them swing to and fro in the air.

"Now," said Felton, "we are safe!"

Milady breathed a deep sigh and fainted.

Felton continued to descend. When he reached the bottom of the ladder, and found no more support for his feet, he clung to it with his hands. At length, coming to the last round, he hung by his hands and touched the ground. He stooped down, picked up the bag of money, and took it in his teeth.

Then he seized milady in his arms, and set off briskly in the direction opposite to the one the patrol had taken. He soon left the beat, climbed across the rocks, and when he reached the shore of the sea, whistled.

A similar signal replied to him, and five minutes after a boat appeared, rowed by four men.

"To the sloop," said Felton, "and give way lively."

A black speck was rocking on the sea. It was the sloop.

While the boat was advancing with all the speed, its four oarsmen could give it, Felton untied the cord, and then the handkerchief that bound milady's hands together.

They drew near to the sloop. A sailor on watch hailed the boat; the boat replied.

"What vessel is this?" asked milady.

"One I hired for you."

"Where is it going to carry me?"

"Wherever you please, after you have landed the at Portsmouth."

"What are you going to do at Portsmouth?" asked milady.

"Fulfil Lord Winter's orders," said Felton, with a gloomy smile.

"What orders?" insisted milady.

"Do you not understand?" asked Felton.

"No; explain yourself, I beg of you."

"As he mistrusted me, he determined to guard you himself, and sent me in his place to get Buckingham to sign the order for your transportation."

"But if he mistrusted you, how could he confide such an order to you?"

"Could I be supposed to know what I was the bearer of?"

"True! And you are going to Portsmouth?"

"I have no time to lose. To-morrow is the 23rd, and Buckingham, sets sail to-morrow with his fleet."

"He sets sail to-morrow! Where for?"

"For Rochelle."

"He must not sail!" cried Milady, forgetting her usual presence of mind.

"Do not worry I" replied Felton; "he will not sail."

Milady started with joy. She had just read to the depths of this young man's heart: Buckingham's death was written there at full length.

"Felton," cried she, "you are as great as Judas Maccabaeus! If you die, I will die with you; that is all I can say to you."

"Silence!" cried Felton; "we are here."

In fact they were grazing the sloop.

Felton climbed up the ladder first, and gave milady his hand, while the sailors supported her, for the sea was still very turbulent.

An instant after they were on the deck.

"Captain," said Felton, "this is the lady of whom I spoke to you, and whom you must convey safe and sound to France."

"In the meanwhile," said Felton, "convey me to the little bay of—; you know it was agreed you should put in there."

The captain replied guy ordering the necessary manoeuvres, and toward seven o'clock in the morning the little vessel was casting anchor in the designated bay.

During this passage Felton related everything to milady—how, instead of going to London, be had hired the little vessel; how he had returned; how he had scaled the wall by fastening cramps in the interstices of the stones as he ascended, to give him foothold; and how, when he had reached the bars, he fastened his ladder. Milady knew the rest.

Milady tried to encourage Felton in his project, but at the first word that issued from her mouth she plainly saw that the young fanatic stood more in need of being moderated than urged on.

It was agreed that milady should wait for Felton till ten o'clock. If he did not return by ten o'clock, she was to sail without him.

Then, in case he was free, he was to rejoin her in France, at the convent of the Carmelites, at Béthune.

CHAPTER 50

What Took Place At Portsmouth, August 23, 1628

Felton took leave of milady as a brother about to go for a mere walk takes leave of his sister—by kissing her hand.

He entered Portsmouth about eight o'clock in the morning. The whole population was on foot. Drums were beating in the streets and in the port. The troops about to be embarked were marching toward the sea.

Felton arrived at the palace of the Admiralty covered with dust and streaming with perspiration. His face, usually so pale, was purple with heat and passion. The sentinel was about to keep him away, but Felton called to the officer of the post, and drawing from his pocket the letter of which he was the bearer,

"A pressing message from Lord Winter," said he.

At the name of Lord Winter, who was known to be one of his Grace's most intimate friends, the officer of the post gave orders to pass Felton, who, indeed, wore a naval officer's uniform.

Felton darted into the palace.

At the moment he entered the vestibule another man was entering, likewise, covered with dust and out of breath, leaving at the gate a post-horse, which, as soon as he had alighted from it, sank down exhausted.

Felton and he addressed Patrick, the duke's confidential valet, at the same moment. Felton named Lord Winter. The stranger would give no name, and asserted that he could make himself known to the duke alone. Each insisted on being admitted before the other.

Patrick, who knew Lord Winter had official dealings and friendly relations with the duke, gave the preference to the one who came in his name. The other was forced to wait, and it was easy to see how he cursed the delay.

The valet led Felton through a large hall, in which were waiting the deputies from Rochelle, headed by the Prince de Soubise, and introduced him into a closet, where Buckingham, just out of the bath, was finishing his toilet, on which, as usual, he was bestowing extraordinary attention.

"Lieutenant Felton, from Lord Winter," said Patrick.

"From Lord Winter!" repeated Buckingham. "Let him come in."

Felton entered. He held the knife with which milady had stabbed herself open in his bosom. With one bound he was on the duke.

At that moment Patrick entered the room, crying,

"A letter from France, my lord!"

"From France!" cried Buckingham, forgetting everything on thinking from whom that letter came.

Felton took advantage of this moment, and plunged the knife into his side up to the handle.

"Ah, traitor!" cried Buckingham, "thou hast killed me!"

"Murder!" screamed Patrick.

Felton cast his eyes round for means of escape, and seeing the door free, he rushed into the next chamber, in which, as we said, the deputies from Rochelle were waiting, crossed it as quickly as possible, and sprang toward the staircase. But on the first step he met Lord Winter, who, seeing him pale, wild, livid, and stained with blood, both on his hands and face, seized him by the throat, crying,

"I knew it! I guessed it! A minute too late! Oh, unfortunate; unfortunate that I am!"

Felton made no resistance. Lord Winter placed him in the hands of the guards, who led him, until they should receive fresh orders, to a little terrace looking out over the sea; and then he rushed into Buckingham's room.

At the cry uttered by the duke and Patrick's scream the man whom Felton had met in the antechamber darted into the closet.

He found the duke lying on a sofa, with his hand pressed convulsively over the wound.

"La Porte," said the duke in a faint voice— "La Porte, do you come from her?"

"Yes, monseigneur," replied Anne of Austria's faithful cloak-bearer, "but too late, perhaps."

"Silence, La Porte; you may be overheard.—Patrick, let no one enter. —Oh, I shall not know what she says to me!—My God! I am dying!"

And the duke fainted.

The duke, however, was not dead. He recovered a little, opened his eyes, and hope revived in all hearts.

"Gentlemen," said he, "leave me alone with Patrick and La Porte.—Ah, is that you, De Winter? You sent me a strange madman this morning. See what a condition he has brought me to!"

"Oh, my lord!" cried the baron, "I shall never console myself for it."

"And you would be quite wrong, my dear De Winter," said Buckingham, holding out his hand to him; "I do not know the man who deserves being regretted during the whole of another man's life. But leave us, I pray you."

The baron went out sobbing.

Only the wounded duke, La Porte, and Patrick remained in the closet. A surgeon had been sent for, but none could be found.

"You will live, my lord, you will live!" repeated Anne of Austria's faithful servant, on his knees before the duke's sofa.

"What did she write me?" said Buckingham feebly, streaming with blood and suppressing his frightful agony to speak of her he loved; "what did she write me? Read me her letter."

"Oh, my lord!" said La Porte.

"Obey, La Porte. Do you not see I have no time to lose?"

La Porte broke the seal and placed the paper before the duke's eyes; but Buckingham tried in vain to make out the writing.

"Read it!" said he—"read it! I cannot see. Read, then! for soon, perhaps, I shall not hear, and I shall die without knowing what she has written me."

La Porte made no further objection, and read,

"Milord,—By what I have suffered by you and for you since I have known you, I conjure you, if you have any care for my repose, to interrupt those great armaments which you are preparing against France, to put an end to a war the ostensible cause of which in publicly said to be religion, and the hidden and real cause of which is privately whispered to be your love for me. This war may bring not only great catastrophes on England and France, but misfortunes on you, milord, for which I should never console myself.

"Be careful of your life, which is threatened, and which will be dear to me from the moment I am not obliged to see an enemy in you.—Your affectionate

ANNE

Buckingham collected all his remaining strength to listen to the reading of the letter. Then when it was ended, as if he had met with a bitter disappointment in it,

"Have you nothing else to say to me verbally, La Porte?" asked he.

"Yes, monseigneur. The queen charged me to bid you be on your guard, for she has been informed that your assassination would be attempted."

"And is that all, is that all?" replied Buckingham impatiently.

"She likewise charged me to tell you that she still loved you."

"Ah," said Buckingham, "God be praised! My death, then, will not be to her as the death of a stranger."

La Porte burst into tears.

"Patrick," said the duke, "bring me the casket in which the diamond studs were kept."

Patrick brought the object desired, which La Porte recognized as having belonged to the queen.

"Now the white satin sachet on which her monogram is embroidered in pearls."

Patrick again obeyed.

"Here, La Porte," said Buckingham, "these are the only remembrances I ever received from her—this silver casket and these two

letters. You will restore them to her Majesty and as a last memorial"
—he looked round for some valuable object—"you will add to
them—"

He still looked; but his eyes, darkened by death, saw only the
knife which had fallen from Felton's hand, still steaming with the
red blood spread over its blade.

"And you will add to them this knife," said the duke, pressing
the hand of La Porte.

He had just strength enough to place the sachet at the bottom of
the silver casket, and to let the knife fall into it, making a sign to La
Porte that he was no longer able to speak. Then in a last convulsion,
which he had no longer the power to resist, he slipped from the sofa
to the floor.

Patrick uttered a loud cry.

Buckingham tried to smile a last time, but death checked his
wish, which remained graven on his brow like a last kiss of love.

As soon as Lord Winter saw Buckingham was dead he ran to Felton, whom the soldiers were still guarding on the terrace of the
palace.

"Miserable wretch!" said he to the young man, who since Buckingham's death had regained the coolness and self-possession which
was never again to abandon him—"miserable wretch! What hast
thou done?"

"I have avenged myself" said he.

"Avenged yourself!" said the baron. "Rather say that you have
served as an instrument for that cursed woman. But I swear to you
that this crime shall be her last."

"I don't know what you mean," replied Felton quietly, "and I am
ignorant of whom you are speaking, my lord. I killed the Duke of
Buckingham because he twice refused your request to have me
appointed captain. I punished him for his injustice, that is all."

De Winter, stupefied, looked on while the soldiers bound Felton,
and did not know what to think of such insensibility.

"Be punished *alone,* in the first place, miserable man!" said Lord
Winter to Felton, "but I swear to you, by the memory of my brother
whom I loved so much, that your accomplice is not saved."

Felton hung down his head without pronouncing a syllable.

Lord Winter descended the stairs rapidly, and went to the port.

Chapter 51

In France

During all this time nothing new happened in the camp at Rochelle. Only the king, who was much bored as usual, but perhaps, a little more so in the camp than elsewhere, resolved to go incognito and spend the festival of St. Louis at St. Germain, and asked the cardinal to order him an escort of twenty musketeers only. The cardinal, who was sometimes affected by the king's unrest, granted this leave of absence with great pleasure to his royal lieutenant, who promised to return about the 15th of September.

M. de Tréville, on being informed by his Eminence, packed his portmanteau, and as, without knowing the cause, he knew the great desire and even imperative need that his friends had of returning to Paris, he fixed on them, of course, to form part of the escort.

The four young men heard the news a quarter of an hour after M. de Tréville, for they were the first to whom he communicated it. Then D'Artagnan appreciated the favour the cardinal had conferred on him by transferring him at last to the musketeers, for had it not been her that circumstance, he would have been forced to remain in the camp while his companions left it.

His impatience to return toward Paris, of course, had for its cause the danger which Madame Bonacieux would run of meeting at the convent of Béthune. with milady, her mortal enemy. Aramis, therefore, as we have said, had written immediately to Marie Michon, the seamstress at Tours, who had such fine acquaintances, to obtain from the queen permission for Madame Bonacieux to leave the convent, and to retire either into Lorraine or Belgium. They had not long to wait for an answer, and eight or ten days later Aramis received the following letter:

"My dear cousin,—Here is my sister's permission to withdraw our little servant from the convent of Béthune, the air of which you think does not agree with her. My sister sends you her permission with great pleasure, for she is very fond of the little girl, to whom she intends to be more serviceable hereafter.—I salute you,

MARIE MICRON

In this letter was enclosed an order conceived in these terms:

"The superior of the convent of Béthune will place in the hands of the person who shall present this note to her the novice who entered the convent on my recommendation and under my patronage.
"At the Louvre, August 10th, 1628.

ANNE

Their joy was great. They sent their lackeys on in advance with the baggage, and set out on the morning of the 16th.

The cardinal accompanied his Majesty from Surgères to Mauzé, and there the and his minister took leave of each other with great demonstration friendship.

At length the escort passed through Paris on the 23rd, in the night. The king thanked M. de Tréville, and permitted him to give out furloughs of four days, on condition that not one of those so favoured should appear in an, public place, under penalty of the Bastille.

The first four furloughs granted, as may be imagined, were to our friends. Moreover, Athos obtained of M. de Tréville six days instead of four, and got these six days lengthened by two nights more, for they set out on the 24th at five o'clock in the evening, and as a further kindness, M. de Tréville post-dated the furlough to the morning of the 25th.

On the evening of the 25th, as they were entering Arras, and as

D'Artagnan was dismounting at the tavern of the Golden Harrow to drink a glass of wine, a horseman came out of the post-yard, where he had lust had a relay, starting off at a gallop, with a fresh horse, on the road to Paris. At the moment he was passing through the gateway into the street the wind blew open the cloak in which he was wrapped, though it was August, and lifted his hat, which the traveller seized with his hand just as it left his head, and pulled it down quickly over his eyes.

D'Artagnan, who had his eyes fixed on this man, became very pale, and let his glass fall.

"What is the matter, sir?" asked Planchet.—"Oh, come, gentlemen, gentlemen! My master is ill!"

The three friends hastened to D'Artagnan, but instead of finding him ill, met him running for his horse. They stopped him at the door.

"Now, where the devil are you going in this way?" cried Athos.

"It is he!" cried D'Artagnan, pale with passion, and with the sweat on his brow; "It is he! Let me overtake him!"

"He—who?" asked Athos.

"He—my man!"

"What man?"

"That cursed man, my evil genius, whom I have always seen when threatened by some misfortune; he who accompanied the horrible woman when I met her for the first time; he whom I was seeking when I offended our friend Athos; he whom I saw on the very morning of the day Madame Bonacieux was carried off! I just saw him! It is he! I recognized him when his cloak blew open!"

"The devil!" said Athos musingly.

"To horse, gentlemen, to horse! Let us pursue him! We shall overtake him!"

"My dear friend," said Aramis, "remember that he's gone in an opposite direction to that in which we are going; that he has a fresh horse, and ours are fatigued; that consequently we shall disable our own horses without even the chance of overtaking him. Let the man go, D'Artagnan; let us save the woman."

"Hello, sir"" cried an hostler, running out and looking after the unknown—"hello, sir! here is a paper which dropped out of your hat. Hello, sir! Hello! "

"Friend," said D'Artagnan, "a half-pistole for that paper!"

"Faith, sir, with great pleasure! Here it is!"

The hostler, delighted with the good day's work he had done, went into the yard again. D'Artagnan unfolded the paper.

"Well?" eagerly demanded all his three friends, surrounding him.

"Only one word!" said D'Artagnan.

"Yes," said Aramis; "but that one word is the name of some town or village."

"*Armentières!*" read Porthos—"Armentières! I don't know it."

"And that name of a town or village is written in her hand!" cried Athos.

"Come on! come on!" said D'Artagnan; "let us keep that paper carefully; perhaps I have not lost my last pistole. To horse, my friends, to horse!"

And the four friends galloped off on the road to Béthune.

CHAPTER 52

The Carmelite Convent at Béthune

Great criminals carry with them a kind of predestination, causing them to surmount all obstacles, causing them to escape all dangers up to the moment which Providence, exhausted has designated as the reef of their impious fortunes.

Thus it was with milady. She passed through the cruisers of both nations, and reached Boulogne without accident.

On landing at Portsmouth milady was an Englishwoman, driven from Rochelle by the persecutions of the French. On landing at Boulogne, after a two days' passage, she claimed to be a Frenchwoman, whom the English persecuted at Portsmouth, out of their hatred for France.

Milady had likewise the most efficacious of passports—her

beauty, her noble appearance, and the generosity with which she scattered pistoles. Freed from the usual formalities by the affable smile and gallant manners of an old governor of the port, who kissed her hand, she only stayed long enough at Boulogne to post a letter, conceived in the following terms:

> "To his Eminence Monseigneur Cardinal Richelieu, in his camp before Rochelle:
> "Monseigneur, let your Eminence be reassured: his Grace the Duke of Buckingham *will not set out* for France.
> "Boulogne, evening of the 25th.
>
> "LADY DE —.
>
> "P.S.—According to your Eminence's desire, I am going to the convent of the Carmelites at Béthune, where I will await your orders."

In fact, that same evening milady began her journey. Night overtook her. She stopped and slept at an inn. At five o'clock the next morning she was on her way again, and three hours later entered Béthune.

She inquired for the Carmelite convent, and went to it immediately.

The superior came to meet her. Milady showed her the cardinal's order. The abbess assigned her a chamber, and had breakfast served.

After breakfast the abbess came to pay her a visit. There are very few distractions in the cloister, and the good mother-superior was eager to make acquaintance with her new inmate.

Milady wished to please the abbess. Now this was an easy matter for a woman so really superior as she was. She tried to be agreeable. She was charming, and won the good nun by her varied conversation, and by the graces of her whole person.

But here she was greatly embarrassed. She slid not know whether the abbess was a royalist or a cardinalist; she therefore confined herself to a prudent middle course. But the abbess on her part maintained a still more prudent reserve, contenting herself with making a profound inclination of the head every time that the fair traveller pronounced his Eminence's name.

Milady began to think she should be very greatly bored in the convent; so she resolved to risk something, in order immediately to know how to act afterwards. Desirous of seeing how far the good abbess's discretion would go, she began to tell a scandal, carefully veiled at first, but very circumstantial afterwards, about the carding, relating the minister's amours with Madame d'Aiguillon, Marion de Lorme, and several other women of easy virtue.

The abbess listened more attentively, grew animated by degrees, and smiled.

"Good!" thought milady; "she likes my conversation. If she is a cardinalist, she has no fanaticism, at least, in it."

She then went on to describe the persecutions wreaked by the cardinal on his enemies. The abbess only crossed herself without approving or disapproving. This confirmed milady in her opinion that the nun was rather a royalist than a cardinalist. Milady, therefore, continued colouring her narrations more and more.

"I am very ignorant about all these matters," said the abbess at length; "but though we are distant from the court and remote from the interests of the world, we have very sad examples of what you have related; and one of our inmates has suffered much from the cardinal's vengeance and persecution."

"One of your inmates!" said milady. "O Heavens! Poor woman, I pity her, then!"

"And you are right, for she is much to be pitied. Imprisonment, threats, ill-treatment—she has suffered everything. But after all," resumed the abbess, "the cardinal has perhaps plausible motives for acting thus; and though she has the look of an angel, we must not always judge people by appearances."

"The cardinal does not only pursue crimes," said milady, "there are certain virtues which he pursues more severely than certain offences."

"Permit me, madame, to express my surprise," said the abbess.

"At what?" asked milady naively.

"At the language you use."

"What do you find so astonishing in my language?" asked milady, smiling.

"You are the cardinal's friend, for he sends you here, and yet—"

"And yet I speak ill of him," replied milady, finishing the mother-superior's thought.

"At least, you don't speak well of him."

"That is because I am not his friend," said she, sighing, "but his victim!"

"Then, madame," said the abbess, smiling, "be reassured. The house in which you are will not be a very hard prison, and we will do all in our power to make you love your captivity. You will find here, moreover, that young woman who is persecuted, no doubt, in consequence of some court intrigue. She is amiable and courteous."

"And when can I see this young lady, for whom I already feel great a sympathy?" asked milady.

"Why, this evening," said the abbess; "even during the day. But you told me you had been travelling these four days. This morning you rose at five o'clock; you must need rest. Go to bed and sleep; at dinner-time we will wake you."

Though milady would very willingly have gone without sleep, sustained as she was by all the excitements that a fresh adventure was awakening in her heart, ever thirsting for intrigues, she nevertheless accepted the mother-superior's advice. During the preceding twelve fifteen days she had experienced so many different emotions that if her iron frame was still capable of supporting fatigue, her mind required repose. She therefore took leave of the abbess and went to bed.

She was awakened by a gentle voice sounding at the foot of her bed. She opened her eyes, and saw the abbess, accompanied by a young woman with light hair and a delicate complexion, who was giving lace a look full of benevolent curiosity.

The young woman's face was quite unknown to her. Each examine the other with great attention while exchanging the customary compliments. Both were very handsome, but of quite different styles of beauty. Milady, however, smiled on observing that she excelled the young woman by far in her noble air and aristocratic bearing. To be sure, the novices habit which the young woman wore was not very advantageous in sustaining a contest of this kind.

The abbess introduced them to each other. Then when this formality was accomplished, as her duties called her to the church, she left the two young women alone.

Suddenly realization came to milady.

"I know you," she said. "You are Madame Bonacieux."

The young woman drew back in surprise and terror.

"Oh, do not deny it! Answer! " continued milady.

"Well, yes, madame!" said the novice.

Milady's face was illumined by such a savage joy that in any other circumstances Madame Bonacieux would have fled in terror. But shy was absorbed by her jealousy.

"Speak, madame!" resumed Madame Bonacieux, with an energy of which one would not have thought her capable.

"Do you not understand?" said milady, who had already overcome her agitation and recovered all her presence of mind.

"How can I understand? I know nothing."

"Can you not understand that M. d'Artagnan, being my friend, might take me into his confidence?"

"Indeed!"

"Do you not perceive that I know all—your being carried off from the little house at St. Germain, his despair, that of his friends, and their useless inquiries from that moment? How could I help being astonished when, without having the least expectation of such a thing, I meet you face to face—you of whom we have so often spoken together, you whom he loves with all his soul, you whom he had taught me to love before I had seen you! Ah, dear Constance, I have found you, then; I see you at last!"

And milady stretched out her arms to Madame Bonacieux, who, convinced by what she had just said, saw nothing in this woman but a sincere and devoted friend.

At that moment the galloping of a horse was heard.

"Oh!" cried Madame Bonacieux, darting to the window, "can it be he already?"

Milady stayed in bed, petrified by surprise. So many unexpected things were happening to her all at once that for the first time she was at a loss.

"D'Artagnan!" murmured she; "can it be he?" And she remained in bed with her eyes staring.

"Hush!" said Madame Bonacieux; "some one is coming."

In fact, the door opened, and the mother-superior entered.

"Did you come from Boulogne?" demanded she of milady.

"Yes, I did," replied she, trying to recover her self-possession. "Who wants me?"

"A man who will not tell his name, but who comes from the cardinal."

"And wishes to speak with me?" asked milady.

"He wishes to speak to a lady just come from Boulogne."

"Then let him come in, if you please."

"Oh, my God, my God!" cried Madame Bonacieux; "can it be any bad news?"

"I am afraid so."

"I will leave you with this stranger; but as soon as he is gone, if you will permit me, I will return."

"Certainly! I beg you will."

The mother-superior and Madame Bonacieux retired.

Milady was left alone, with her eyes fixed on the door. An instant after the jingling of spurs was heard on the stairs, then steps approached, the door opened, and a man appeared.

Milady uttered a cry of joy. This man was the Comte de Rochefort, the cardinal's personal agent.

"Ah!" cried milady and Rochefort together, "so it is you?"

"Yes, it is."

"And you come?" asked milady.

"From Rochelle. And you?"

"From England."

"Buckingham?"

"Dead or desperately wounded, as I was leaving without having succeeded in obtaining anything from him. A fanatic assassinated him."

"Ah!" said Rochefort, with a smile, "this is a piece of good luck—one that will delight his Eminence! Have you informed him of it?"

"I wrote to him from Boulogne. But what brings you here?"

"His Eminence was uneasy, and sent me to inquire after you."

"What did the cardinal say with respect to me?"

"I was to take your dispatches, written or verbal, to return post-haste; and when he shall know what you have done, he will think of what you have to do."

"So I must remain here?"

"Here, or in the neighbourhood."

"You cannot take me with you?"

"No; the order is imperative. Near the camp you might be recognized; and your presence, you must be aware, would compromise his Eminence."

"You are right. Now, will you make me a report of all that has happened?"

"Why, I have related the events to you. You have a good memory; repeat what I have told you. A paper may get lost."

"You are right; only let me know where to find you, so that I may not lose time in hunting for you about the neighbourhood."

"You are right; wait."

"Do you want a map?"

"Oh, I know this country well."

"You will wait for me, then, at—"

"Let me reflect a moment. Oh yes, at Armentières."

"What is Armentières?"

"A little town upon the Lys. I shall only have to cross the river, and I shall be in a foreign country."

"Capital! But it is understood you will cross the river only in case of danger."

"Certainly."

"And you say you will wait for me at Armentières?"

"At Armentières."

"Write that name on a piece of paper, lest I forget it. That is not compromising; a name of a town, is it?"

"Eh! who knows? No matter," said milady, writing the name on a half sheet of paper; "I will run the risk."

"Good!" said Rochefort, taking the paper from milady, folding it, and placing it in the lining of his hat. "Besides, do not worry. I will do as children do, and in case I lose the paper, I will repeat the name as I go along. Now, is that all?"

"Good! When do you start?"

"In an hour-time to eat a morsel while I am sending for a post-horse."

"Capital. Farewell, chevalier!"

"Farewell, countess!"

"Recommend me warmly to his Eminence!"

"Recommend me to Satan!"

Milady and Rochefort exchanged a smile and separated.

An hour afterwards Rochefort set out at his horse's best speed; five hours after that he was passing through Arras.

Our readers already know how he was recognized by D'Artagnan, and how the fact, by suggesting fears to the four musketeers, gave fresh activity to their journey.

CHAPTER 53

The Drop of Water

Rochefort had scarcely departed when Madame Bonacieux came back. She found milady with a smiling countenance.

"Come and sit down close to me," said milady.

Milady arose and went to the door, opened it, looked down the corridor, and then returned and seated herself near Madame Bonacieux.

"That man," said milady, lowering her voice, "is my brother!"

"Your brother!" cried Madame Bonacieux.

"Well, no one must know this secret, my dear, but yourself. If you reveal it to any one at all I shall be lost, and you also, perhaps."

"O Heavens!"

"Listen to me. This is what has happened: My brother, who was coming to my assistance, to take me away by force if it were necessary, fell in with the cardinal's emissary coming in search of me. He followed him. Reaching a solitary and retired part of the road, he drew his sword and required the messenger to deliver up to him the papers of which he was the bearer. The messenger resisted; my brother killed him."

"Oh!" said Madame Bonacieux, with a shudder.

"Remember that was the only way. Then my brother determined to substitute cunning for force. He took the papers, and presented himself here as the cardinal's emissary, and in an hour or two a carriage will come to take me away by order of his Eminence."

"I understand. Your brother sends the carriage."

"Exactly so."

"But D'Artagnan is coming!"

"Do not be deceived. D'Artagnan and his friends are detained at the siege of Rochelle."

"How do you know that?"

"My brother met some of the cardinal's emissaries in the uniform of musketeers. You would have been summoned to the gate; you would have thought you went to meet friends; you would have been carried off and taken back again to Paris."

"Dear lady," said Madame Bonacieux, "pardon me for interrupting you, but what do you advise me to do? Good Heavens! You have more experience than I have. Speak! I will listen."

"There would be a very simple way, very natural—"

"What? Say!"

"To wait, concealed in the neighbourhood, until you satisfied yourself who the men were who came to ask for you."

"But where can I wait?"

"Oh, there is no difficulty in that. I shall stop and conceal myself at a few leagues from here, till my brother can rejoin me. Well, I will take you with me. We can conceal ourselves and wait together."

"Oh yes, yes; you are right. In this way all will go well—all will be for the best; but do not go far from here."

Milady was wrong in fearing that Madame Bonacieux would

have any suspicions. The poor young woman was too innocent to suppose that any woman could be guilty of such perfidy. Besides, the name of the Countess Winter, which she had heard the abbess pronounce, was perfectly unknown to her, and she was even ignorant that she had so great and so fatal a share in the misfortunes of her life.

"You see," said she, "everything is ready. The abbess suspects nothing. Take a mouthful to eat, drink a swallow of wine, and let us go."

"Yes," said Madame Bonacieux mechanically; "let us go."

Milady made her a sign to sit down before her, poured out a small glass of Spanish wine for her, and helped her to some of the breast of a chicken.

Madame Bonacieux ate a few mouthfuls mechanically, and just touched the glass to her lips.

"Come, come!" said milady, lifting hers to her mouth, "do as I do."

But just as she was putting hers to her mouth her hand remained suspended. She had heard something on the road which sounded like the far-off beat of hoofs approaching; then, almost at the same time, it seemed to her that she heard the neighing of horses.

This noise roused her from her joy as a storm awakens the sleeper in the midst of a beautiful dream. She grew pale and ran to the window, while Madame Bonacieux, rising all of a tremble, supported herself on her chair to avoid falling.

Nothing was yet to be seen, only they heard the galloping constantly draw nearer.

"O Heavens!" cried Madame Bonacieux, "what is that noise?"

"It is either our friends or our enemies," said milady, with her terrible coolness. "Stay where you are. I will tell you."

Madame Bonacieux remained standing, mute, pale, and motionless.

The noise became louder; the horses could not be more than at hundred paces distant. If they were not yet to be seen, it was because the road made a bend. Yet the noise became so distinct that the horses might be counted by the sharply defined sound of their hoofs.

Milady gazed with all her eyes; it was just light enough for her to recognize those who were coming.

Suddenly, at a turn of the road, she saw the glitter of laced hats and the waving of plumes; she counted two, then five, then eight horsemen. One of them was two lengths of his horse in advance of the others.

Milady uttered a stifled groan. In the first horseman she recognized D'Artagnan.

"O Heavens, Heavens!" cried Madame Bonacieux, "what is it? what is it?"

"It is the cardinal's guards—not an instant to be lost!" cried milady. "Let us fly! let us fly!"

"Yes, yes, let us fly!" repeated Madame Bonacieux, but without being able to take a step, fixed to the spot as she was by terror.

They heard the horsemen riding under the windows.

"Come on, then! do come on!" cried milady, striving to drag the young woman along by the arm. "Thanks to the garden, we yet can escape. I have the key. But let us make haste. In five minutes it will he too late!"

Madame Bonacieux tried to walk, took two steps, and sank on her knees.

Milady strove to lift her up and carry her, but could not succeed.

At this moment they heard the rolling of the carriage, which as soon as the musketeers were seen set oft at a gallop. Then three or four shots were fired.

"For the last time, will you come?" cried milady.

"Oh, my God, my God!" You see my strength fails me. You see plainly I cannot walk. Escape yourself."

"Escape myself, and leave you here! No, no, never!" cried milady.

All at once she stopped; a livid flash darted from her eyes. She ran to the table, poured into Madame Bonacieux's glass the contents of a ring which she opened with singular quickness.

It was a grain of a reddish colour, which instantly melted.

Then taking the glass with a firm hand,

"Drink," said she; "this wine will give you strength—drink!"

And she put the glass to the lips of the young woman, who drank mechanically.

"This is not the way I wanted to avenge myself," said milady, setting the glass on the table with an infernal smile, "but, faith! one does what one can." And she rushed out of the room.

Madame Bonacieux saw her go without being able to follow her. She was like those people who dream they are pursued, and who vainly struggle to walk.

A few moments passed. A frightful noise was heard at the gate. Every instant Madame Bonacieux expected to see milady, but she did not return.

At length she heard the grating of the hinges of the opening gates; the noise of boots and spurs resounded on the stairs. There was a great murmur of voices coming nearer and nearer; it seemed to her she heard her own name pronounced.

All at once she uttered a loud cry of joy, and darted toward the door. She had recognized D'Artagnan's voice.

"D'Artagnan! D'Artagnan!" cried she, "is it you? This way! this way!"

"Constance! Constance!" replied the young man, "where are you? My God!"

At the same moment the door of the cell yielded to a shock, rather than opened. Several men rushed into the room. Madame Bonacieux had sunk into an armchair, without the power of moving.

D'Artagnan threw down a pistol, still smoking, which he held in his band, and fell on his knees before his mistress. Athos replaced his in his belt. Porthos and Aramis, who held their drawn swords in their hands, returned them to their scabbards.

"O D'Artagnan! my beloved D'Artagnan! You have come, then, at last. You have not deceived me! It is indeed you!"

"Yes, yes, Constance!—reunited!"

"Oh, how foolish *she* was to tell me you would not come! I hoped silently. I was not willing to flee. Oh, how rightly I have acted! How happy I am!"

At the word *she,* Athos, who had quietly seated himself, suddenly got up.

"*She!* Who?" asked D'Artagnan.

"Why, my companion. She who, out of friendship for me, wished to save me from my persecutors. She who, mistaking you for the cardinal's guards, has just made her escape."

"Your companion!" cried D'Artagnan, becoming paler than his mistress's white veil. "What companion do you mean?"

"She whose carriage was at the gate; a woman who calls herself your friend, D'Artagnan; a woman to whom you have told everything."

"But her name, her name!" cried D'Artagnan; "my God! don't you know her name?"

"Yes, it was pronounced before me. Stop—but—it is strange—oh, my God! my head swims—I cannot see!"

"Help, friends, help! Her hands are like ice!" cried D'Artagnan; "she is ill! Great God, she is growing unconscious!"

While Porthos was calling for help at the top of his voice, Aramis ran to the table to get a glass of water. But he stopped at seeing the horrible alteration that had taken lace in the face of Athos, who, standing before the table, his hair rising from his head, his eyes fixed in stupor, was looking at one of the glasses, and seemed a prey to the most horrible doubt.

"Oh," said Athos, "oh no! It is impossible! God would not permit such a crime!"

Madame Bonacieux opened her eyes under D'Artagnan's kisses.

"She revives!" cried the young man.

"Madame," said Athos—"madame, in Heaven's name, whose empty glass is this?"

"Mine, sir," said the young woman, in a dying voice.

"But who poured out for you the wine that was in this glass?"

"*She.*"

"But who is she?"

"Oh, I remember," said Madame Bonacieux; "the Countess Winter."

The four friends uttered one and the same cry, but the cry of Athos dominated over all the rest.

At that moment Madame Bonacieux's face grew livid, a stifled agony overcame her, and she sank panting into the arms of Porthos and Aramis.

D'Artagnan seized Athos's hand with anguish difficult to describe.

"What! do you believe—"

His voice was stifled by sobs.

"I believe everything," said Athos.

"D'Artagnan! D'Artagnan!" cried Madame Bonacieux, "where art thou? Do not leave me! Thou seest that I am dying!"

D'Artagnan let fall Athos's hand, which he stir held convulsively clasped in his, and hastened to her.

Her beautiful face was distorted, her glassy eyes were fixed, a convulsive shuddering shook her body, the sweat stood on her brow.

"In Heaven's name, run, call! Aramis! Porthos! call for help!"

"Useless!" said Athos, "useless! For the poison which she pours out there is no antidote."

"Yes, yes! help, help!" murmured Madame Bonacieux—"help!"

Then collecting all her strength, she took the young man's head between her hands, looked at him for an instant as if her whole soul had passed into her look, and pressed her lips to his.

"Constance! Constance!" cried D'Artagnan wildly.

A sigh escaped from Madame Bonacieux's mouth and dwelt for an instant on D'Artagnan's lips. That sigh was her soul, so chaste and so loving, reascending to heaven.

D'Artagnan held only a corpse pressed to his heart.

The young man uttered a cry, and fell by his mistress's side as pale and as cold as she was.

Porthos wept, Aramis lifted his hand toward heaven, Athos made the sign of the cross.

At that moment a man appeared in the doorway, almost as pale as those in the room, looked round him, saw Madame Bonacieux dead and D'Artagnan fainting.

He appeared just at that moment of stupor which follows great catastrophes.

"I was not mistaken," said he. "Here is M. d'Artagnan, and you are his three friends, MM. Athos, Porthos, and Aramis."

"Gentlemen," continued the stranger, "since you will not recognize a man who probably owes his life to you twice, I must name myself. I am the Lord Winter—that woman's brother-in-law."

The three friends uttered a cry of surprise.

Athos rose and offered him his hand.

"You are welcome, milord," said he; "you are one of our friends."

"I left Portsmouth five hours after her," said Lord Winter. "I arrived three hours after her at Boulogne. I missed her by twenty minutes at St. Omer. At last at Liliers I lost trace of her. I was going about at haphazard, inquiring of every one, when I saw you gallop by. I recognized M. d'Artagnan. I called to you; you did not answer. I tried to follow you, but my horse was too tired to go at the same rate as yours. And yet it seems that, in spite of all your diligence, you still arrived too late."

At that moment D'Artagnan opened his eyes.

He tore himself from the arms of Porthos and Aramis, and threw himself like a madman on his tress's dead body.

Athos rose, walked up to his friend with a slow and solemn step, kissed him tenderly, and as he burst into violent sobs, said to him, with his noble and persuasive voice,

"Friend, be a man! Women weep for the dead; men avenge them!"

And affectionate as a father, consoling as a priest, great as a man who has suffered much, he drew away his friend.

All five, followed by their lackeys leading their horses, took their way to the town of Béthune, the outlying houses of which they saw, and stopped at the first inn to which they came.

"But," said D'Artagnan, "are we not to pursue that woman?"

"Presently," said Athos; "I have certain measures to take."

"She will escape us," replied the young man—"she will escape us, Athos, and it will be your fault."

"I will answer for her," said Athos.

D'Artagnan had such trust in his friend's word that he bowed hip head, and entered the inn without making a reply.

Porthos and Aramis looked at each other, not at all understanding Athos's confidence.

Lord Winter thought he spoke in this way to assuage D'Artagnan's sorrow.

"Now, gentlemen," said Athos, when he had ascertained there were five vacant rooms in the hotel, "let us each retire to his own chamber. D'Artagnan needs to be alone, to weep and to sleep. I take charge of everything. Do not worry."

"It seems to me, however," said Lord Winter, "that if there are any measures to be taken against the countess, it concerns me; she is my sister-in-law."

"Me also!" said Athos; "she is my wife."

D'Artagnan smiled, for he realized that Athos was sure of his vengeance since he revealed such a secret. Porthos and Aramis looked at each other. Lord Winter thought Athos was mad.

"Now, all go to your rooms," said Athos, "and leave me to act. You must perceive that in my quality of a husband this concerns me. Only, D'Artagnan, if you have not lost it, give me the piece of paper which fell from that man's hat. The name of the village of—is written on it."

"Ah!" said D'Artagnan, "I understand now. That name written in her hand—"

"You see," said Athos, "there is a God in heaven!"

CHAPTER 54

The Man In The Red Cloak

Athos's despair had given place to a concentrated grief, which made this man's brilliant mental faculties keener than ever.

Possessed lay a single thought—that of the promise he had made, and of the responsibility he had assumed—he was the last to retire to his room. He begged the host to get him a map of the province, bent over it, examined the lines traced on it, perceived that there were four different roads from Béthune to Armentières?" and called the valets.

Planchet, Grimaud, Bazin, and Mousqueton presented themselves, and received Athos's clear, positive, and serious orders. They were to set out the next morning at daybreak, and to go to Armentières—each by a different route. Planchet, the most intelligent of the four, was to follow the road by which had passed the carnage on which the four friends had fired, and which was accompanied, as will be remembered, by Rochefort's servant.

All four were to meet the next day at eleven o'clock. If the had discovered milady's retreat, three were to remain on guard; the fourth was to return to Béthune, to inform Athos and serve as a guide to the four friends.

When these arrangements were made the lackeys retired.

Athos then arose from his chair, girded on his sword, enveloped himself in his cloak, and left the hotel. It was nearly ten o'clock. At ten o'clock in the evening, we know, the streets in provincial towns are very little frequented.

Athos reached the suburb, situated at the end of the city, opposite where he and his friends had entered it. Here he appeared uneasy and embarrassed, and stopped.

Fortunately, a beggar passed and came up to Athos to ask charity. Athos offered him a crown to accompany him where he was going. The beggar hesitated at first, but at the sight of the piece of silver glittering in the darkness he consented, and walked on before Athos.

Reaching the corner of a street, he showed in the distance a small house isolated, solitary, dismal. Athos went to the house, while the beggar, having received his reward, hurried away as fast as he could walk.

Athos went round the house before he could distinguish the door from the reddish colour in which the house was painted. No light shone through the chinks of the shutters; no sound gave reason to believe that a was inhabited. It was dark and silent as a tomb.

Three times Athos knocked and no one responded. At the third knock, however, the door was half opened, and a man of lofty stature, pale complexion, and black hair and beard appeared.

Athos and he exchanged some words in a low voice. Then the

tall man made a sign to the musketeer that he might come in. Athos immediately took advantage of the permission, and the door closed after him.

Then be explained to him the cause of his visit, and the service he required of him. But scarcely had he expressed his request when the unknown, who had remained standing before the musketeer, drew back in terror, and refused. Then Athos took from his pocket a small paper, on which were written two lines, accompanied by a signature and a seal, and presented them to him who had been too premature in showing these signs of repugnance. The tall man had scarcely read the two lines, seen the signature, and recognized the seal, when he bowed to denote that he had no longer any objection to make, and that he was ready to obey.

Athos required no more. He arose, bowed, went out, returned by the carne way he had come, re-entered the hotel, and shut himself up in his room.

At daybreak D'Artagnan came to him, and asked him what was to be done.

"Wait!" replied Athos.

Some minutes later the mother-superior of the convent sent to inform the musketeers that the funeral would take place at noon.

At the hour appointed Lord Winter and the four friends repaired to the convent. The bells were tolling solemnly, the chapel was open, the grating of the choir was closed. In the centre of the choir the body of the victim, clothed in her novitiate dress, was exposed.

At the chapel door D'Artagnan felt his courage failing him again, and turned to look for Athos, but Athos had disappeared. He had returned to the hotel and found Planchet impatiently waiting for him.

Everything was as Athos had foreseen.

Planchet took the short cut, and by seven o'clock in the morning was at Armentières.

There was but one hotel, the Post. Planchet went and presented himself as a lackey out of a place, who was in search of a job. He had not chatted ten minutes with the people of the tavern before he knew that a lady had come there about eleven o'clock the night before alone, had taken a room, had sent for the steward, and told him that she wanted to stay some time in that neighbourhood.

Planchet did not need to know any more. He hastened to the rendezvous, found the three lackeys at their posts, placed them as sentinels at all the doors of the hotel, and came to find Athos, who was just hearing the last of the report when his friends returned.

All their faces were melancholy and anxious, even Aramis's mild fare.

"What is to be done?" asked D'Artagnan.

"Wait," replied Athos.

Each one went to his own room.

At eight o'clock in the evening Athos ordered the horses to be saddled, and had Lord Winter and his friends notified to be prepared for the expedition.

In an instant all five were ready. Each examined his arms, and put them in order. Athos was last to come down, and found D'Artagnan already on horseback and impatient.

"Patience!" cried Athos; "one of us is still lacking."

The four gentlemen looked round them in astonishment, for they vainly wondered who this some one lacking could be.

At this moment Planchet brought Athos's horse. The musketeer leaped lightly into the saddle.

"Wait for me," cried he; "I will be back."

And he set off at a gallop.

In a quarter of an hour he returned, accompanied by a tall man, masked, and enveloped in a large red cloak.

Lord Winter and the three musketeers looked at one another inquiringly. None of them could give the others any information, for all were ignorant who this man was. Nevertheless, they felt that this was as it should be, since the thing was done by Athos's order.

At nine o'clock, guided by Planchet, the little cavalcade set out, following the route the carriage had taken.

It was a melancholy sight, that of these six men, riding silently, each plunged is his own thoughts, sad as despair, sombre as punishment.

CHAPTER 55

Judgment

It was a dark and stormy night. Monstrous clouds were flying across the sky, concealing the light of the stars. The moon would not rise before midnight.

Occasionally, by the light of a lightning flash gleaming along the horizon, the road could be seen stretching before them, white and solitary. Then when the flash became extinct, all relapsed into darkness.

Just as the little troop had passed Goskal, and were approaching the Post, a man sheltered under a tree stepped out from its trunk, with which he had been confounded in the darkness, and advanced into the middle of the road, with his finger on his lips.

Athos recognized Grimaud.

"What's the matter?" cried Athos; "has she left Armentières?"

Grimaud nodded. At a movement made by D'Artagnan,

"Silence, D'Artagnan!" said Athos. "I have taken this whole affair myself, so it is my right to question Grimaud.

"Where is she?" asked Athos.

Grimaud stretched out his hands in the direction of the Lys.

"Far from here?" asked Athos.

Grimaud showed his master his forefinger bent.

"Alone?" asked Athos.

Grimaud made a sign that she was.

By a flash of lightning they saw the village of Enguinghem.

"Is she there, Grimaud?" asked Athos.

Grimaud shook his head.

And the troop continued their route.

Another flash gleamed. Grimaud stretched out his arm, and by the livid light of the fire-serpent they distinguished a little isolated house on the banks of the river, within a hundred paces of a ferry.

One window was lighted.

"Here we are!" said Athos.

At this moment a man who had been crouching in a ditch

jumped up. It was Mousqueton. He pointed his finger to the lighted window.

"She's there," said he.

"And Bazin?" asked Athos.

"While I was watching the window, he was watching the door."

"Good!" said Athos; "you are all faithful servants."

Athos leaped down from his horse, gave the bridle to Grimaud, and advanced toward the window, after having made a sign to the rest of the troop to go toward the door.

The little house was surrounded by a quickset hedge two or three feet high. Athos sprang over the hedge and went up to the window, which was without shutters, but had the half-curtains closely drawn.

He got upon the stone coping, in order to see over the top of the curtain.

By the light of the lamp he saw a woman wrapped in a dark mantle sitting on a stool near a dying fire. Her elbows rested on a mean table, and she leaned her head on her two hands, which were white as ivory.

Her face was not distinguishable, but an ominous smile passed over Athos's lips. There was no mistaking. It was indeed she whom he sought.

At this moment a horse neighed. Milady raised her head, saw Athos's pale face close to the window, and screamed.

Athos saw he was recognized, pushed the window with his knee and hand. It yielded; the panes broke.

And Athos, like the spectre of vengeance, sprang into the room.

Milady ran to the door and opened it; but paler and more threatening still than Athos, D'Artagnan stood on the threshold.

Milady drew back, uttering a cry. D'Artagnan, believing she might have means of flight, and fearing lest she should escape them, drew a pistol from his belt. But Athos raised his hand.

"Put back your weapon, D'Artagnan," said he; "this woman must be judged and not assassinated. Wait but a moment longer, my friend, and you shall be satisfied. Come in, gentlemen."

D'Artagnan obeyed, for Athos had the solemn voice and the mighty gesture of a judge sent by the Lord Himself. So behind

D'Artagnan entered Porthos, Aramis, Lord Winter, and the man in the red cloak.

The four lackeys guarded the door and the window.

Milady had sunk into a chair, with her hands extended, as if to conjure away this terrible apparition. On perceiving her brother-in-law she uttered a terrible cry.

"What do you want?" screamed milady.

"We want," said Athos, "Charlotte Backson, who first was called Comtesse de la Fère, and afterwards Lady Winter, Baroness of Sheffield."

"I am she! I am she!" murmured she, at the height of terror. "What do you want of me?"

"We intend to judge you according to your crimes," said Athos. "You shall be free to defend yourself. Justify yourself if you can.—Monsieur d'Artagnan, it is for you to accuse her first."

D'Artagnan stepped forward.

"Before God and before men," said he, "I accuse this woman of poisoning Constance Bonacieux, who died yesterday evening."

He turned to Porthos and Aramis.

"We bear witness to this," said the two musketeers, with one impulse D'Artagnan continued,

"Before God and before men, I accuse this woman of having tried to poison me by wine which she sent me from Villeroi, with a forged letter, purporting that the wine came from my friends. God preserved me, but a man named Brisemont died in my place."

"We bear witness to this," said Porthos and Aramis, in the same voice.

"Before God and before men, I accuse this woman of having urged me to murder the Baron de Wardes. But as no one is present to bear witness to the truth of this accusation, I attest it myself. I have done."

And M. d'Artagnan passed to the other side of the room with Porthos and Aramis.

"It is your turn, milord," said Athos.

The baron came forward.

"Before God and before men," said he, "I accuse this woman of having caused the assassination of the Duke of Buckingham."

"The Duke of Buckingham assassinated!" cried all present with one voice.

"Yes," said the baron, "assassinated. On receiving the warning letter you wrote to me, I had this woman arrested, and put her in the charge of a loyal servant. She corrupted this man she placed the dagger in his hand, she made him kill the duke. And at this moment, perhaps, Felton is paying with his life for this fury's crime!"

A shudder crept through the judges at the revelation of these crimes of which they had not yet heard.

"This is not all," proceeded Lord Winter. "My brother, who made you his heir, died in three hours of a strange disorder, which left livid traces over all his body. Sister, how did your husband die?"

"Horror!" cried Porthos and Aramis.

"Buckingham's assassin, Felton's assassin, my brother's assassin; I demand justice upon you, and I swear that if it be not granted to me, I will execute it myself."

And Lord Winter ranged himself by D'Artagnan's side, leaving his place free for another accuser.

Milady buried her face in her two hands, and tried to recall her ideas, confused in a mortal vertigo.

"It is my turn," said Athos, himself trembling as the lion trembles at the sight of the serpent—"it is my turn. I married this woman when she was a young girl. I married her in spite of all my family. I gave my wealth, I gave her my name; and one day I discovered that this woman was branded—this woman was marked with a fleur-de-lis on her left shoulder."

"Oh," said milady, "I defy you to find the tribunal which pronounced that infamous sentence upon me. I defy you to find him who executed it."

"Silence!" said a voice. "It is for me to reply to that!"

And the man in the red cloak came forward in his turn.

"Who is this man? who is this man?" cried milady. She was suffocated by terror; her hair, which had become undone, seemed to stand up over her livid countenance as if it were alive.

All eyes were fixed on this man, for to all except Athos he was unknown.

Even Athos looked at him with as much stupefaction as the others, for he knew not how he could in any way be mixed up with the horrible drama which was at that moment coming to its climax.

After approaching milady with a slow and solemn step, so that the table alone separated them, the unknown took off his mask.

Milady for some time examined with increasing terror his pale face, framed in its black hair and beard, and the only expression of which was icy sternness. Then all at once,

"Oh no, no!" cried she, rising and retreating to the very wall; "no, no! it is an infernal apparition! It is not he! Help, help!" she screamed in a hoarse voice, turning to the wall as if she could tear an opening in it with her hands.

"But who are you, then?" cried all the witnesses of this scene.

"Ask this woman," said the man in the red cloak, "for you see well enough she knows me!"

"The executioner of Lille! the executioner of Lille!" cried milady, a prey to wild terror, and clinging with her hands to the wall to avoid failing.

Everyone drew back, and the man in the red cloak remained standing alone in the middle of the room.

"Oh, forgive me, pardon, pardon!" cried the wretched woman, falling on her knees.

The unknown waited for silence.

"I told you so—that she knew me," he went on to say. "Yes, I am the executioner of the city of Lille, and here is my story."

All eyes were fixed upon this man; his words were awaited with anxious eagerness.

"This young woman when she was a young maiden was as beautiful as she is now. She was a nun in the convent of the Benedictines of Templemar. A young priest, of a simple and believing heart, was the chaplain of that convent. She undertook to seduce him, and succeeded; she would have seduced a saint.

"The vows of both were sacred—irrevocable. Their intrigue could not last long without ruining both. She prevailed on him to leave the country; but for them to leave the country, to escape together, to reach another part of France, where they might live at ease because there they would be unknown, money was necessary. Neither of them had any. The priest stole the sacred utensils and sold them. But as they were preparing to escape together, they were both arrested.

"Within a week she seduced the jailer's son and escaped. The young priest was condemned to ten years in chains, and to be branded. I was executioner of the city of Lille, as this woman has said. I was obliged to brand the guilty man; and the guilty man, gentlemen, was my brother!

"I then swore that this woman who had ruined him, who was more than his accomplice, since she had spurred him on to commit the crime, should share at least his punishment. I suspected the place where she was concealed. I followed her, I caught her, I bound her, and I imprinted the same disgraceful mark on her that I had imprinted on my poor brother.

"The day after my return to Lille, my brother in his turn succeeded in making his escape. I was accused of complicity, and was condemned to stay in prison in his place till he should be again a prisoner. My poor brother was ignorant of my condemnation. He had rejoined his woman. They fled together into Berry, and there he obtained a little curacy. This woman passed for his sister.

"The ford of the estate on which the curate's church was situated saw this pretended sister, and fell in love with her so sincerely that he offered to marry her. Then she left the man whom she had ruined! for the man whom she was destined to ruin, and became the Comtesse de la Fère—"

All eyes were turned toward Athos, whose real name this was. He bowed his head in token that all that the executioner had said was true.

"Then," resumed the other, "mad, desperate, determined to get rid of an existence from which she had taken away everything, both honour and happiness, my poor brother returned to Lille, and learning the sentence that had condemned me in his place, gave himself up, and hanged himself that same night from the airhole of his dungeon cell.

"I must say in justice that they who had condemned me kept their word. As soon as the identity of the body was proved, I was set at liberty.

"That is the crime of which I accuse her. That is the cause of her being branded."

"Monsieur d'Artagnan," said Athos, "what penalty do you demand against this woman?"

"The penalty of death," replied D'Artagnan.

"Milord de Winter," continued Athos, "what penalty do you demand against this woman?"

"The penalty of death," replied Winter.

"MM. Porthos and Aramis," repeated Athos, "you who are her judges, what penalty do you pronounce on this woman?"

"The penalty of death," replied the musketeers in a hollow voice.

Milady uttered a frightful shriek, and dragged herself along on her knees several paces toward her judges.

Athos stretched out his hand toward her.

"Charlotte Backson, Comtesse de la Fire, Milady de Winter," said he, "your crimes have wearied men on earth and God in heaven. If you know any prayer, say it; for you are condemned, and you shall die."

At these words, which left her no hope, milady rose to her full height and tried to speak, but her strength failed her. She felt that a powerful and implacable hand was seizing her by the hair, and was dragging her away as irrevocably as fate drags man. She did not, therefore, even attempt to make any resistance, and went out of the cottage.

Lord Winter, D'Artagnan, Athos, Porthos, and Aramis followed her. The lackeys followed their masters, and the room was left desolate, with its broken window, its open door, and its smoky lamp burning forlornly on the table.

CHAPTER 56

Execution

It was almost midnight. The moon, hollowed by its waning, and red as blood under the last traces of the storm, was rising behind the little town of Armentières, which outlined against its pallid light the dark silhouette of its houses and the skeleton of its high carved belfry. In front of them the Lys was rolling its waters like a river of molten lead; while on the other bank could be seen a black mass of trees, outlined against a stormy sky, which was invaded by huge coppery clouds creating a kind of twilight amid the night.

Two of the lackeys dragged milady along, each taking one of he arms. The executioner walked behind them, and Lord Winter, D'Artagnan, Porthos, and Aramis walked behind the executioner.

When they reached the banks of the river the executioner approached milady and bound her hands and her feet.

Athos took a step toward milady.

"I pardon you," said he, "the ill you have done me; I pardon you for my blasted future, my lost honour, my defiled love, and my salvation for ever compromised by the despair into which you have cast me. Die in peace!"

Lord Winter advanced next.

"I pardon you," said he, "the poisoning of my brother, the assassination of his Grace the Duke of Buckingham; I pardon you poor Felton's death; I pardon you the attempts on me personally. Die in peace!"

"And I," said D'Artagnan— "pardon me, madame, for having by deceit, unworthy of a gentleman, provoked your anger; and in exchange I pardon you the murder of my poor sweetheart and your cruel vengeance against me. I pardon you, and I weep for you. Die in peace!"

"I am lost!" murmured milady in English; "I must die!"

Then she rose of her own accord, and cast around her one of those keen looks which seemed to dart from a flaming eye.

She saw nothing.

She listened; she heard nothing.

She had only enemies around her.

"Where am I to die?" she asked.

"On the other bank," replied the executioner.

Then he made her enter the boat.

The boat moved off toward the left bank of the Lys, bearing the guilty woman and the executioner. All the others remained on the right bank, where they had fallen on their knees.

The boat glided along the ferry-rope under the gleam of a pale cloud which hung over the water at the moment.

It was seen reaching the opposite bank; the figures were outlined in black against the red-tinted horizon.

Milady during the passage had contrived to untie the cord which fastened her feet; on reaching the bank, she jumped lightly on shore and took to flight.

But the soil was moist. When she reached the top of the bank she slipped and fell on her knees.

A superstitious idea struck her: she realized that Heaven denied its aid, and she remained in the attitude in which she had fallen, with her head drooping and her hands clasped.

Then from the other bank the executioner was seen to raise both his arms slowly. A moonbeam fell on the blade of his broadsword. His two arms fell; they heard the hissing of the scimitar and the victim's cry; then a truncated mass sank under the blow.

The executioner then took off his red cloak, spread it on the ground, laid the body in it, threw in the head, tied it by the four corners, lifted it on his shoulder, and got into the boat again.

In the middle of the stream he stopped the boat, and holding his burden over the water,

"Let the justice of God be done!" cried he, in a loud voice.

And he let the body drop into the depths of the waters, which closed over it.

Three days later the four musketeers were in Paris again. They had not exceeded their leave of absence, and that same evening went to pay their customary visit to M. de Tréville.

"Well, gentlemen," asked the excellent captain, "have you enjoyed your excursion?"

"Prodigiously!" replied Athos for himself and his companions.

Conclusion

On the sixth of the following month the king, in compliance with the promise he had made the cardinal to leave Paris and to return to Rochelle, departed from his capital, unable to recover from his amazement at the news which was just beginning to spread abroad that Buckingham had been assassinated.

The return to Rochelle was profoundly dull. Our four friends in particular astonished their comrades. They travelled together, side by side, with melancholy eyes and hanging heads. Athos alone from time to time raised his broad brow. A flash kindled in his eyes, a bitter smile passed over his lips. Then, like his comrades, he again resumed his reveries.

When the escort arrived in a city, as soon as they had escorted the king to his lodgings the four friends either retired to their own quarters or to some secluded tavern, where they neither drank nor played. They only conversed in a low voice, looking around attentively that no one overheard them.

One day, when the king had halted on the way to fly the magpie, and the four friends, according to their custom, instead of following the sport, had stopped at a tavern on the turnpike, a man, riding full speed from Rochelle, pulled up at the door to drink a glass of wine, and glanced into the room where the four musketeers were sitting at table.

"Hello, Monsieur d'Artagnan!" said he, "isn't it you I see there?"

D'Artagnan raised his head and uttered a cry of joy. It was the man he called his phantom; it was the stranger of Meung, of the Rue des Fossoyeurs, and of Arras.

D'Artagnan drew his sword and sprang toward the door.

But this time, instead of eluding him, the stranger leaped from his horse and advanced to meet D'Artagnan.

"Ah, sir!" said the young man, "I meet you, then, at last! This time you shall not escape me!"

"Neither is it my intention, sir, for this time I was seeking you. I arrest you in the name of the king. I tell you that you must surrender your sword to me, sir, and that without resistance. Your life depends upon it. I warn you."

"But who are you?" demanded D'Artagnan, lowering the point of his sword, but without yet surrendering it.

"I am the Chevalier de Rochefort," answered the stranger, "Cardinal Richelieu's equerry, and I have orders to conduct you to his Eminence."

"We are returning to his Eminence, chevalier," said Athos, advancing; "and you will be good enough to accept M. d'Artagnan's word that he will go straight to Rochelle."

"I must place him in the hands of guards who will take him to camp."

"We will serve as his guards, sir, on our word as gentlemen; but, on our word as gentlemen, likewise," added Athos, "M. d'Artagnan shall not leave us."

The Chevalier de Rochefort cast a glance backward, and saw that Porthos and Aramis had taken their places between him and the door. He perceived that he was completely at the mercy of these four men.

"Gentlemen," said he, "if M. d'Artagnan will surrender his sword to me and join his word to yours, I shall be satisfied with your promise to convey M. d'Artagnan to the cardinal's quarters."

"You have my word sir, and here is my sword."

"This suits me all the better," said Rochefort, "as I must continue my journey."

"If it is to rejoin milady," said Athos coolly, "it is useless. You will not find her."

"What has become of her?" asked Rochefort eagerly.

"Come back with us to the camp and you shall know."

Rochefort remained thoughtful for a moment then, as they were only a day's journey from Surgères, where the cardinal was coming to meet the king, he resolved to follow Athos's advice and go back with them.

Besides, this return gave him the advantage of watching over his prisoner.

They resumed their route.

At three o'clock the next afternoon they reached Surgères. The cardinal, on returning in the evening to his headquarters at the bridge of La Pierre, found D'Artagnan, without his sword, and the three musketeers armed, standing before the door of the house which he was occupying.

This time, as he was well attended, he looked at them sternly, and made a sign with his eye and hand for D'Artagnan to follow him.

D'Artagnan obeyed.

"We shall wait for you, D'Artagnan," said Athos, loud enough for he cardinal to hear him.

His Eminence kept on his way without uttering a single word.

D'Artagnan entered after the cardinal, and behind D'Artagnan the door was guarded.

His Eminence went to the room which served him as a study, and made a sign to Rochefort to bring in the young musketeer.

Rochefort obeyed and retired.

D'Artagnan remained alone before the cardinal. This was his second interview with Richelieu, and he afterwards confessed that he felt sure it would be his last.

Richelieu remained standing leaning against the mantelpiece. A table was between him and D'Artagnan.

"Sir," said the cardinal, "you have been arrested by my orders."

"So I have been told, monseigneur."

"Do you know why?"

"No, monseigneur, for the only thing for which I could be arrested is still unknown to your Eminence."

Richelieu looked steadfastly at the young man.

"You are charged with having corresponded with the enemies of the kingdom. You are charged with having surprised state secrets. You are charged with having tried to thwart your general's plans."

"And who charges me with this, monseigneur?" said D'Artagnan, who suspected the accusation came from milady—"a woman branded by the law of the country; a woman who was married to one man in France and to another in England; a woman who poisoned her second husband, and who attempted to poison me!"

"What is all this, sir?" cried the cardinal, astonished; "and what woman are you speaking of thus?"

"Of Milady de Winter," replied D'Artagnan—"yes, of Milady de Winter, of whose many crimes your Eminence was doubtless ignorant when you honoured her with your confidence."

"Sir," said the cardinal, "if Milady de Winter has committed the crimes which you say, she shall be punished."

"She is punished, monseigneur."

"And who has punished her?"

"We."

"Is she in prison?"

"She is dead."

"Dead!" repeated the cardinal, who could not believe what he heard. "Dead! Did you say she was dead?"

D'Artagnan then related the poisoning of Madame Bonacieux in the Carmelite convent of Béthune, the trial in the lonely house, and the execution on the banks of the Lys.

"So," said the cardinal, in a tone the mildness of which contrasted with the severity of his words, "you have constituted yourselves judges, forgetting that they who punish without licence to punish are assassins?"

"Another might reply to your Eminence that he had his pardon in his pocket. I shall content myself with saying, Command, monseigneur; I am ready."

"Your pardon?" said Richelieu, surprised.

"Yes, monseigneur," said D'Artagnan.

"And signed by whom? By the king?"

And the cardinal pronounced these words with a singular expression of contempt.

"No; by your Eminence."

"By me? You are mad, sir!"

"Monseigneur will doubtless recognize his own writing."

And D'Artagnan presented to the cardinal the precious paper which Athos had forced from milady, and which he had given to D'Artagnan to serve him as a safeguard.

His Eminence took the paper and read in a slow voice, dwelling on every syllable:

> August 5, 1628.
>
> By my order, and for the good of the State, the bearer hereof has done what he has done.
>
> RICHELIEU

The cardinal, after reading these two lines, fell into deep thought, but he did not return the paper to D'Artagnan. At last he raised his head, fixed his eagle look upon D'Artagnan's frank, loyal, intelligent face, and reflected for the third or fourth time what a future this young man had before him, and what resources his activity, his courage, and his understanding could devote to a good master.

On the other hand, milady's crimes, her strength of mind, and her infernal genius had more than once terrified him. He felt something like a secret joy at being for ever rid of such a dangerous accomplice.

The cardinal went to the table, and without sitting down, wrote a few lines on a parchment, two-thirds of which was already filled up, and axed his seal to it.

"Here, sir," said the cardinal to the young man; "I have taken from you one signed blank, and I give you another. The name is wanting in this commission, and you yourself will write it in."

D'Artagnan took the paper hesitatingly, and cast his eyes over it.

It was a lieutenant's commission in the musketeers.

D'Artagnan fell at the cardinal's feet.

"Monseigneur;" said he, "my life is yours! Henceforward dispose of it. But I do not deserve this favour which you bestow on me. I have three friends who are more meritorious and more worthy—"

"You are an honest fellow, D'Artagnan," interrupted the cardinal, taping him familiarly on the shoulder, charmed at having subdued thus rebellious nature. "Do with this commission what you will. Only remember that though the name is left blank I give it to you."

"I shall never forget it," replied D'Artagnan. "Your Eminence may be certain of that."

The cardinal turned round and said in a loud voice,

"Rochefort! "

The chevalier, who doubtless was behind the door, entered immediately.

"Rochefort." said the cardinal, ":you see M. d'Artagnan. I receive him among the number of my friends. Shake hands, then, and be prudent, if you wish to preserve your heads."

Rochefort and D'Artagnan saluted each other distantly, but the cardinal was there observing them with his vigilant eye.

They left the chamber at the same time.

"We shall meet again, shall we not, sir?"

"When you please," said D'Artagnan.

"An opportunity will offer," replied Rochefort.

"What's that?° said the cardinal, opening the door.

The two men smiled at each other, shoo hands, and bowed to his Eminence.

"We were beginning to grow impatient," said Athos.

"Here I am, friends," replied D'Artagnan—"not only free, but in favour."

"Will you tell us about it?"

"This evening."

Accordingly, that same evening D'Artagnan repaired to *the quarters* of Athos, whom he found in a fair way of emptying his bottle of Spanish wine, an occupation which he religiously fulfilled every night.

He related what had taken place between the cardinal and himself, and drawing the commission from his pocket,

"Here, my dear Athos," said he; "this naturally belongs to you."

Athos smiled his sweet, fascinating smile.

"My friend," said he, "for Athos this is too much, for the

Comte de la Fère it is too little. Keep the commission; it is yours. Alas! my God! It has cost you enough."

D'Artagnan left Athos's room and went to Porthos's.

He found him dressed in a magnificent coat covered with splendid embroidery, looking at himself in a &lass.

"Ah, ha!" exclaimed Porthos; "it is you, dear friend. How do you think these garments fit me?"

"Wonderfully well," said D'Artagnan. "But I have come to offer you a dress which will suit you still better."

"What's that?" asked Porthos.

"That of a lieutenant in the musketeers."

D'Artagnan related to Porthos his interview with the cardinal, and taking the commission from his pocket,

"Here, my dear," said he; "write your name in it, and become my officer."

Porthos cast his eyes over the commission, and returned it to D'Artagnan, to the young man's great astonishment.

"Yes," said he—"yes, that would flatter me very much, but I should not have time enough to enjoy the distinction. During our expedition to Béthune. my duchess's husband died; so that, my dear, since the coffer of the defunct is holding out its arms to me, I am going to marry the widow. Look here! I was trying on my wedding suit. Keep your lieutenancy, my dear, keep it."

The young man entered Aramis's apartment.

He found him kneeling before a praying-desk, with his head leaning on an open prayer-book.

He described to him his interview with the cardinal, and for the third time drawing his commission from his Pocket,

"You, our friend, our intelligence, our invisible protector," said he, `accept this commission. You have deserved it more than any one by your wisdom and your counsels, which were always followed by such happy results."

"Alas l; dear friend," said Aramis, "our recent adventures have entirely disgusted me with life and with the sword. This time my determination is irrevocably taken. After the siege I shall enter the house of the Lazarists. Keep tire commission, D'Artagnan.

The profession of arms suits you. You will be a brave and gallant captain."

D'Artagnan, his eye moist with gratitude and beaming with joy, went back to Athos, whom he found still at table, contemplating the charms of his last lass of Malaga by the light of his lamp.

"Well," said he, they also have refused this commission!"

"Because, dear friend, no one is more worthy of it than yourself."

And he took a pen, wrote D'Artagnan's name on the commission, and returned it to him.

"I shall then no longer have any friends," said the young man. "Alas! nothing more, only bitter recollections."

And he let his head sink into his hands, while two tears rolled down his cheeks.

"You are young," replied Athos, "and your bitter recollections have time to be changed into sweet memories."

Epilogue

Rochelle, deprived of the aid of the English fleet and the reinforcements promised by Buckingham, surrendered after a siege of a year. On the 28th of October, 1628, the capitulation was signed.

The king made his entrance into Paris on December 23, the same year. He was received in triumph, as if he came from conquering an enemy and not Frenchmen. He entered by the Faubourg St. Jacques with magnificent display.

The procession, led by symbolical cars, passed under a dozen triumphal arches, on which all the gods of Olympus were celebrating the unnumbered virtues of Louis the Victorious. An immense throng, stationed along the whole route of the procession, rent the air with their enthusiastic acclamations, greeting the conqueror's return.

D'Artagnan took possession of his rank. Porthos left the service, and during the following year married Madame Coquenard. The coffer so eagerly coveted contained 800,000 livres.

Mousqueton had a magnificent livery, and enjoyed the satisfaction for which he had yearned all his life—that of standing behind a gilded carriage.

Aramis, after a long absence in Lorraine, suddenly disappeared, and ceased to write his friends. They learned long afterwards, through Madame de Chevreuse, who told it to two or three of her lovers, that he had decided to assume the habit in a religious house at Nancy.

Bazin became a lay brother.

Athos remained a musketeer under D'Artagnan's command till the year 1631, when, after a journey which he made to Touraine, he also quitted the service, under the pretext of having just inherited a small property in Roussillon.

Grimaud followed Athos.

D'Artagnan fought three times with Rochefort, and wounded him three times.

"I shall probably kill you the fourth," said he to him, holding out his hand to assist him to rise.

"Then it is better for you and for me that we stop here," answered the wounded man. "Zounds! I am much more your friend than you think; for after our very first encounter, I could, by saying a word to the cardinal, have had your head cut off!"

This time they heartily shook hands, and without retaining any malice.

Planchet obtained from Rochefort the rank of sergeant in the guards.

M. Bonacieux lived on very quietly, perfectly ignorant of what had become of his wife, and caring very little about the matter. One day he had the imprudence to recall himself to the cardinal's memory. The cardinal sent him word that he would see to it that he should never want for anything in future.

In fact, the next day M. Bonacieux left his house at seven o'clock in the evening to go to the Louvre, and he was never seen again in the Rue des Fossoyeurs. The opinion of those who seemed to be best informed was that he was fed and lodged in some royal castle, at the expense of his generous Eminence.

Contents